Isolde Ohlbaum

*About the Author*

BATYA GUR (1947–2005) lived in Jerusalem, where she was a literary critic for *Haaretz*, Israel's most prestigious paper. She earned her master's in Hebrew literature at the Hebrew University of Jerusalem, and she also taught literature for nearly twenty years. Her five other Michael Ohayon mysteries include *Murder Duet*, *The Saturday Morning Murder*, *Literary Murder*, *Murder on a Kibbutz*, and *Bethlehem Road Murder.*

# MURDER IN JERUSALEM

## ALSO BY BATYA GUR

*Bethlehem Road Murder*

*Murder on a Kibbutz: A Communal Murder*

*The Saturday Morning Murder: A Psychoanalytic Case*

*Literary Murder: A Critical Case*

*Murder Duet: A Musical Case*

A MICHAEL OHAYON MYSTERY

# MURDER IN JERUSALEM

BATYA GUR

TRANSLATED BY EVAN FALLENBERG

HARPER

NEW YORK • LONDON • TORONTO • SYDNEY

HARPER

This book is a work of fiction. The characters, incidents, and dialogue are drawn from the author's imagination and are not to be construed as real. Any resemblance to actual events or persons, living or dead, is entirely coincidental.

A hardcover edition of this book was published in 2006 by HarperCollins Publishers.



HarperCollins books may be purchased for educational, business, or sales promotional use. For information please write: Special Markets Department, HarperCollins Publishers, 10 East 53rd Street, New York, NY 10022.

FIRST HARPER PAPERBACK PUBLISHED 2007.

*Designed by Nancy B. Field*

The Library of Congress has catalogued the hardcover edition as follows:

Gur, Batya.

[Retsah, metsalmim. English]

Murder in Jerusalem: a Michael Ohayon mystery/Batya Gur; translated by Evan Fallenberg.

p. cm.

ISBN-13: 978-0-06-085293-1
ISBN-10: 0-06-085293-3

1. Ohayon, Michael (Fictitious character)—Fiction. I. Fallenberg, Evan. II. Title.

PJ5054.G637R513 2006

892.4'36—dc22 2005052833

ISBN: 978-0-06-085294-8 (pbk.)
ISBN-10: 0-06-085294-1 (pbk.)

07 08 09 10 11 ❖/RRD 10 9 8 7 6 5 4 3 2 1

## ACKNOWLEDGMENTS

*The impetus for this book was the screenplay of a miniseries I wrote in collaboration with director Ram Loevy, which was screened on Israel's Channel Two. Assaf Tzipor participated in the writing and editing of the screenplay.*

*I wish to express my deepest gratitude to Ram Loevy, who came up with the idea of writing a screenplay about Israeli television and whose perseverance enabled me to complete the job. Collaborating with him and with Assaf Tzipor over a period of nearly four years was both instructive and pleasurable.*

*Batya Gur*

# MURDER IN JERUSALEM

# CHAPTER ONE

Michael Ohayon laid *A Suitable Boy,* the heavy volume in which he had been immersed for weeks, especially the past two, during his vacation, at the foot of his bed. How was it possible to write a novel like this and at the same time live one's life? How suddenly familiar and true were the claims voiced by many women in his life, claims he had heard often enough from his only son as well, about the manner in which he lost himself in his work, how there was no approaching him while he was on a case. To create and write about some reality or to investigate it seemed suddenly to him like the very same effort, the very same anxiety.

A sudden noise cut his thoughts short. He hurried to the hallway, and from there to the bathroom. He had left the cabinet door under the sink open so that the dampness there would not grow moldy. The bucket he had placed under the sink had overturned, as if a cat had passed by. But no cat had passed by. The windows were shut and the blinds were closed and rain was pounding and a puddle of dirty water was gathering by the front door. There was no explanation for the overturned bucket. "The butterfly effect," Tzilla would say had she witnessed the scene, which would be certain to irritate Balilty: "Effects again?" he would exclaim. "Butterflies again? Aren't you fed up with all that yet? What's the matter, aren't there any other explanations in the world? Let's see you, for once, just say 'I don't know'!" Michael returned to his bedroom and glanced at the full packet of cigarettes lying next to the reading lamp on the small night table. He had not smoked the whole day. The first week of his vacation he had spent counting and rationing. Each day he had smoked two fewer cigarettes than the day before. Later, when he understood that he would need twenty days in order to quit smoking entirely while he had at his disposal only one last week to make his abstinence a fait accompli, he had stopped smoking all at once. Five days had passed since his last cigarette. Perhaps that was why he was unable to fall asleep. And now the overturned bucket had jolted him into wakefulness. He would return to his book, that would be best. One thing he could say about this book for sure was that its wonderful collection of characters and historical events managed, occasionally, to divert his attention from smoking.

At the very moment he managed to settle into just the right position and had nearly immersed himself in the book again, the telephone rang.

Every work of art must be the result of overcoming obstacles; the more meaningful its execution is, the harder the obstacles seem to be, as if the creator has been put to the test against the very right that was granted him—or that he took for himself—to fulfill his own dream. Sometimes it even seems possible to think of obstacles and difficulties as the motivating force behind such creativity; in defiance, spiteful, as it were, but without which . . . Benny Meyuhas shook himself free of these musings, looking first at the monitor and then at Schreiber, the only cameraman he was willing to work with on this film. Schreiber's smooth, large, white face was shining when he lifted his head from the camera lens. Benny Meyuhas touched his shoulders and moved him gently aside in order to get a peek through the lens, and then he too saw the figure standing at the edge of the roof, near the railing, holding the hem of her white gown in her hand, her drawn and pale face turned to the dark sky. He lifted his head and pointed at the moon.

Rain had fallen all week, especially at night, and even though the weather forecasters had noted repeatedly that these rains were beneficial, welcome, appearing now in mid-December as the harbinger of a wonderful winter, Benny Meyuhas was beside himself; it seemed to him that the head of the Production Department himself had ordered this rain in order to prevent him from the night filming of *Iddo and Eynam,* or, as he put it, "to finish up already with that thing that's eaten up our entire budget for Israeli drama." Just when Benny had lost all hope of completing these last scenes, which were being filmed in secret, if not absolutely underground due to the threat—which no crew member had actually mentioned but everyone knew—that Matty Cohen, head of production, could at any moment appear on the set and put a stop to the whole project, the rain suddenly let up and the moon appeared, as if it had consented to perform its role and cast light on the path of Gemullah the somnambulist, the heroine of Agnon's story, as she sleepwalked at the edge of the roof and sang songs from her childhood.

As a matter of fact, just then on that very night as the rain stopped and the moon appeared, Matty Cohen was on his way to the set, and at ten minutes to midnight was standing on the second-story catwalk in the narrow, open hallway above the storerooms, very near the doorway that led to the roof. The people on the roof, however, did not know this; no one had seen him pass by. As large and heavy as he was, his footsteps were always light and quick; he mounted the narrow metal steps quietly and passed by scenery and pillars illuminated by dim light from naked bulbs that created a mix of darkness and shadows. Matty Cohen stopped there, on the catwalk, and peered below to the long, narrow, darkened hallway on whose walls leaned pieces of scenery, their shadows climbing to the corners of the ceiling. Someone unfamiliar with the place—a child, a stranger, even a new employee—would think this was the kingdom of the dead and might panic; even he himself trembled for a moment when suddenly he heard voices—strangled, whispering, but clearly voices. Looking down, he could see the silhouettes of two people, could hear their whispered murmuring, the voice of a woman, quite familiar though he could not identify it, protesting: "No, no, no, no." He could not tell who they were exactly, apparently a man and woman, and in any event he did not give them his full attention at that moment. Perhaps they were a couple: love-thieves, yet another underground romance. From above he saw how they were standing so close to one another, the hands of the one, apparently the man, around the neck of the other, smaller person, apparently the woman, but he did not stop to take a good look at them; he merely leaned his head over the catwalk, peered at them, and continued on his way until, just before reaching the white metal door that opened to the roof, the cell phone in his pocket vibrated. If it were not for that call, Benny Meyuhas's production, the last bit of shooting on the roof, would have come to an end right then. But Matty Cohen could not leave Malka alone while Matan was suffering an asthma attack. He whispered the instructions to her, told her to call an ambulance, and hurried back the way he had come. He ran, so as to get there as quickly as possible; the third asthma attack that month, and the boy was only four years old. What could he have done? Stopped to check if the couple were still down there? Later he would chide himself, when he heard what had happened. But how could he have known? He had had an emergency on his hands.

None of the crew members on the roof heard Matty Cohen's footsteps, neither when he stopped by the white metal door nor when he turned around and retraced his steps.

"Nice," Schreiber the cameraman whispered into Benny Meyuhas's ear. "The frame looks good, don't you think?"

Benny Meyuhas nodded, snapped his fingers before calling, "Action!" and moved aside for a moment to watch Sarah saunter, eyes half shut, the hem of her white gown gathered in her small hand, her steps measured and her mouth slightly ajar, singing the heart-wrenching song of Gemullah the somnambulist, its otherworldly purity glowing even in the middle of the noisy, dirty reality of shooting a film. Although there was no one on the roof apart from a skeleton crew—Schreiber, Noam the soundman, Benny himself, and Hagar, his right-hand woman—and no sound obscured Sarah's singing, he cupped his hand to his mouth and in a loud voice called, "Cut!" Schreiber stepped back and regarded him with an overt look of exasperation, while Hagar, who was standing at the corner of the railing, approached.

"Why? Why was it necessary to cut it here?" she demanded, a note of bitterness in her voice. "It was really perfect, so . . . so beautiful!"

"Yes, it was beautiful," Benny Meyuhas said, rubbing his eyes, "but not close enough to the edge. Not frightening enough."

"Seventeen takes," Schreiber muttered. "Seventeen takes since eleven o'clock and now it's one in the morning, past one in the morning, and we're still not close enough to the edge for him."

Hagar gave him a furious look. "You? What do you care?" she chided him. "After midnight you get paid triple wages. So what are you complaining about?"

"Tell me, are you the only one who has a say around here?" Schreiber sneered. "Have you got special rights because you've been around so long? Was I talking about money? I have every right to say I think his demands are over the top. I was looking at the frame, wasn't I?"

Benny Meyuhas, lost in his own thoughts, was as usual deaf to the noise around him. He looked at the monitor and reiterated: "She isn't close enough to the edge. It's not frightening enough. I want her at the edge, I want it scary, so you think she's going to fall, I want a few breath-stopping seconds before you see she's okay. Sarah," he called to the crouching young woman hugging her gaunt body with thin arms that poked out from the wide sleeves of her gown. "I want you to come right up to the edge."

"But I could fall that way," Sarah said, standing. She looked around until her eyes met Hagar's, who was approaching her. "I could . . ." she muttered, "it's . . ."

"Don't worry, you won't fall," Benny Meyuhas told her. "After all, in the rehearsal, you remember? We saw that you won't . . . Hagar," he called to his producer, "take her to the edge and stand there with her." Hagar zipped up her windbreaker, wrapped her arms around the girl's trembling shoulders, and led her back to the improvised railing, a stone balustrade they had had designed especially for the edge of the roof.

Benny Meyuhas looked up in search of the moon and noticed the antennas protruding from the String Building—a funny nickname for the long, rectangular edifice that had once been a string factory. In the meantime all kinds of temporary staircases and wobbly wooden galleries had been tacked on to it; the building sported secret entrances from the parking lot used only by the lucky few who knew of them, and rooms and large halls and even underground passageways that perhaps led to the main building, whose original name only a handful of people remembered: the Diamond Building. Leaning on the red-painted metal railing and looking outward from the roof, it was impossible to imagine what treasures and expanses the String Building held: not only Tirzah's office and the scenery storerooms that occupied most of its space, but also a carpentry shop and wardrobe storerooms and lighting and sound systems and even the magnificent Nakdi Studio, used for filming comedies and the big variety shows. And the small storerooms under the stairs—which only the most veteran employees knew about—where a remarkable number of things were hidden, and the hallways in which the largest scenery stood, among them scenes from the hometown of Agnon's heroine Gemullah (designed by Tirzah), including a village and hills and flocks of sheep that looked like the real thing . . . and clouds and a sun and even the moon, round and yellowy; Tirzah had drawn them all. And the room that Max Levin discovered in the dig he initiated there, a sealed ground-floor room, hidden behind a wall, that contained an entire world: ten years earlier, when there had been a power failure and Max Levin had tapped on the wall, the sound he heard was hollow, so he tore a hole in the wall, peered inside, stood there, amazed—that was how Tirzah loved to tell the story each time she repeated it—and he walked away without a word and returned with a shovel-tractor that excavated the space, and that was how the huge hall where they filmed the big Friday-night variety programs came into existence. Later it turned out that this hall had been an ancient and empty well that had served a spacious German home long since razed. They filmed there, and thanks to Max Levin they also strung pipes along the roof and invested in an air-conditioning system that Max controls himself to this very day. Even a new, state-of-the-art editing machine—cutting-edge, Max promised when he submitted the price quote to the Accounting Department and watched the horrified face of Levy from Accounting—was stored there, in the room next to the carpentry shop. There, in the large halls used for painting scenery, the huge pillars that Tirzah built were stored, a few leaning over the door to the lighting room. It was Tirzah who had suggested using the scenery storeroom and the metal staircase to film the first meeting between Ginat and Gamzu, the heroes of Agnon's story, as a means of skimping on a set location. In this huge area, which was entirely the realm of Tirzah and Max Levin, head of Props, Benny Meyuhas's heart raced anew every time he entered. He wished he could use the whole space, every inch of it. There was even a den of sorts where they rested during breaks, with a huge poster of Kim Basinger hanging over the sofa on which the king of the stagehands lay most hours of the day. The long row of rooms on the interior side was known as the "transit camp," for its resemblance to the shanties erected for new immigrants in the early years of the state, and in one room—the coolest—they kept the sandwiches and beer. Benny had been working at Israel Television for thirty years and there were still secret places in the building he knew nothing about, but, as Schreiber said with a grin, as if joking, what is a television director anyway? The lowest rung on the totem pole. It was of no consequence to Benny Meyuhas, especially now that they had finally let him do what he really wanted. In any case, Max and Tirzah were the only two who knew every corner.

Tirzah. She was giving him hell—a full week she had refused to utter a single word to him about anything, good or bad. Two people living in the same house for eight years already, because they love one another, bound together by love and nothing else, nothing formal or external, no children, no property, no certificates signed by rabbis—and now she refused to exchange a single word with him. Every time he tried to explain, she . . . but she had in fact finished the scenery, even the huge marble pillar—smooth and perfect, as if it had come from an open-air castle, just waiting to be filmed—which Tirzah polished and placed next to the scenery flats. Stunning. Who would believe that someone could deface it with red graffiti: THIS IS AN ASHKENAZI WHOREHOUSE? Some people don't even care about defacing beauty. On the contrary: to deface beauty is exactly what they want. It would even seem that the instinct to mutilate is awakened in people—even intelligent, cultured people—precisely in the face of great beauty. That was, after all, the theme of Agnon's *Iddo and Eynam*. There, too, beauty was destroyed, as if destruction could decipher its secret.

Benny Meyuhas looked to the corner of the roof. Max Levin was the one who had suggested filming Gemullah's promenade on top of the scenery building. The moon lit up the cactus in the rusty bucket they had moved to the side so that it would not appear in the frame, along with the paint-spotted rooftop they had covered in sand. From a corner of the roof, the scent of smoke wafted upward from a grill. The first time Benny Meyuhas had come up to the roof with him and had stared in wonder at the charred grill and the remains of charcoal and the pile of thin bones that cats were gnawing nearby, Max Levin had been embarrassed, as if he were sorry he had brought him to the inner sanctum of his realm. "One of the crew members," Max explained apologetically in his strong Hungarian accent, "he has a hobby, he keeps a chicken coop next to the compressor, so at night and sometimes in the early morning the guys, you know, while they're waiting, they fry a few eggs from the coop, and sometimes they roast a chicken, not a whole one from the coop, just wings, or a steak on occasion."

"You people have a whole life up here, don't you?" Hagar had said with a grin. She was standing at the corner of the roof, checking the paint spots. "Turns out that here at Israel Television," she had said to the sky, "the head of Props is lord of the manor." Max Levin had grimaced, his face a study in denial and opposition that worried Benny Meyuhas. Benny always tried to remain nonconfrontational with them all: "Maintaining good relations is half the job," he would say to Hagar and anyone who would listen to him at the start of every production. "We'll have to cover this with something, maybe sand," Hagar had said as she wrote herself a note on the second page of her legal pad. "You want this place?" she had asked after Benny stood surveying the roof for several minutes. "Over there by the edge," she had added, "they have a basketball court, too. They've got it great up here, and we had no idea!" Benny had nodded his head, yes, he wanted the place. And to his great good fortune—he didn't even know why—Max Levin was being cooperative.

"Cut!" Benny Meyuhas was now calling, looking again at the film and then at the door to the roof. "Hasn't he come back yet?" he murmured as if to himself.

"Who?" asked Schreiber.

"Avi," Hagar answered from the corner of the roof. "Benny's waiting for Avi, he went to bring the sun gun."

"But we have enough moonlight," Schreiber protested.

"A while back, when he went, we didn't," Hagar said, glancing at her cell phone. "He'll be back soon," she said, consoling Benny, "and Max will probably be along soon with the horse."

But she was wrong. For more than ten minutes Avi, the lighting technician, had been standing in front of the guard booth at the entrance to the elongated building, a sun gun in his hand, trying to convince the guard to let him in. "Identification," the new guard repeated in his odd accent. "No ID, no enter." Nothing helped. There was no point in phoning Hagar on the roof to come down and save him, since they were in the middle of shooting and she would never answer.

Avi looked around, one-thirty in the morning, not a soul about. Only a persistent new guard, Russian perhaps, or maybe an Argentinian, who chased after him, fought him in his feeble attempt to get past him, unwilling to believe a word he said. Suddenly, at last, a car screeched to a halt and Max Levin stepped out. Short and chubby, he left the car door open as he approached the guard booth, his glasses hanging from a metal chain around his neck, his head inclined to the side. "Max!" Avi cried with joy. "Tell him, tell him I'm with you people on the production."

"He won't let you in, why should you come in? Don't let him in," Max instructed the guard. He walked in and waited until Avi's face had completely fallen, and only then returned, smiling, and said something in Hungarian to the guard, who pushed his long, straggly hair back from his eyes, answered Max, and let Avi pass.

"Iggen miggen?" Avi said as they passed inside the building, mocking the Hungarian he had just heard. He lit the way with the sun gun.

"If I were you I wouldn't spit into the well you are drinking from," Max said. "Especially if Benny is waiting for that sun gun of yours. If I were you I wouldn't be making jokes at all."

"Tell me something," Avi said. "Tell me what all this is about. Fetching this and fetching that at one in the morning. You'd think he was the king of England, with all due respect . . . and what about you? What are you doing here at this hour?"

"A blue horse," Max answered. "I have to bring him a blue horse. Come here, shine that light into the storeroom, there's not enough light in there," Max said as he stuffed his rotund body inside the enclosed space under the metal staircase.

"I don't understand anything anymore, nothing at all," Avi the lighting technician said, as if to himself. "Where you got a plug here? Think you can find it in the dark?" As he spoke he felt along the wall, unraveling the cord. He stuck the plug into a socket he had located and aimed the sun gun toward the inside of the storeroom, turned it on, and pointed it at the black shadows cast on the low walls by blurred objects. "I don't understand how they keep shooting when there's no budget, and how he can send us to bring things when Matty Cohen's on his way here."

"What are you talking about, on his way here?" Max asked, alarmed, as he extricated a large blue wooden horse from the storeroom. "Now?! You think Matty Cohen would show up here at this hour?"

"You talk as if you don't know what Matty Cohen's capable of," Avi said, lowering the sun gun to his side. "What's with the horse, anyway?" He did not wait for Max to respond. "I heard in the canteen. Someone leaked to Matty Cohen, whispered the big secret to him about them filming at night, and he wants to catch 'em red-handed. Maybe it's already too late, maybe there's nobody to bring your horse and my sun gun to, because maybe Matty Cohen already shut the whole thing down and everyone took off. That's what I heard in the canteen."

Max looked at Avi; there was a half-smile on the lighting technician's face. "What are you so happy about?" Max scolded him. "This is Israel Television's most important production, and to you it's a laughing matter."

"What's the big deal? What's so important about it, huh?" Avi protested. "Everyone's tiptoeing around here, going on and on about Agnon. I mean, it's just Agnon! Tell me, who's gonna watch it, anyway? The ratings'll be zero."

"You've been working on it for six months, and you don't even know what it's about? Shame on you."

"What is there to know, huh? It's just about some broad from India."

"Not from India," Max explained. "I don't read Hebrew all that well and Agnon is difficult language, and what's more, everyone says this story, *Iddo and Eynam*, is impossible to understand anyway, but she isn't Indian, that much I'm sure of. She's from an oriental Jewish tribe."

"Like Ethiopian?" Avi reasoned.

"Something like that, I guess, some ancient Jewish tribe," Max said. "She's a somnambulist, which means she walks around at night singing her songs. Her father marries her off to some intellectual, a researcher, who brings her to Jerusalem, and in Jerusalem she wanders the rooftops and sings, that's all I know."

"My sister's daughter . . . ," Avi began, pulling the electrical cord from the wall and stepping to the side to make room for Max to pass.

"Shine the light over here," Max urged him. "What's wrong, you afraid of using up the battery?"

Avi shone the light down the hallway ahead of them as he continued talking. "My sister's daughter had moonsickness, the sleepwalking disease," he announced to Max's back as he walked quickly behind him, trying to keep up. "She'd wander around at night, and once I woke up and found her standing next to my bed. God, was that scary! I was still a kid myself, I didn't know what moonsickness was, but I sure knew what it was to be scared!"

Now he was shining the light on the scenery flats and the pillars. "Hey, come here, there's someone . . . ," Avi whispered. "Look, over in the corner next to the pillar, someone's there."

Max, too, saw the white boot, and then the whole leg in dark pants. Only when they drew near and stood next to the pillar did he bend down for a closer look. Avi shone the light on the face, and a muffled scream escaped his mouth. In a swift movement he turned his head and the sun gun wobbled in his hand, shining in the far corners, on the ceiling, and then it fell to the floor, landing next to the wall and shining on a dark puddle.

"It's Tirzah. Tirzah," Max Levin whispered. "What's wrong, Tirzah?" he asked hoarsely, crouching to touch her arm. "It's Tirzah," he said, stunned. He raised his head and looked to his hand. "There's blood, a lot of blood. Her face . . . look at her face . . ."

Avi did not respond.

"Listen," Max called out, choking on his words, "I think something fell on her . . . the pillar . . . call an ambulance, she doesn't have a pulse, call an ambulance, quick."

Avi did not respond. He coughed and coughed, then Max heard him retching. There was blood all around them. Again Max heard Avi vomiting, and with a very cold hand he felt for the cell phone clipped to his belt, and dialed.

At that very moment it started raining harder, a heavy downpour that pounded at the windows of the building. But neither the rain nor the pellets of hail that were beating the thin walls made a difference to anyone, not even to Shimshon Zadik—head of Israel Television—who arrived after the police, nodding at Max Levin, who was waiting for him at the entrance as if he had not noticed the rain at all. Dripping water, Zadik stood for a moment in front of the entrance to the String Building and looked suspiciously into the brightly lit hallway. "There was a terrible accident on the way here, just outside of Mevasseret Zion," he said. "You can't imagine. . . . There's still a two-hour backup, I made a detour. . . . It was terrible . . . two kids . . . destroyed the car, totaled it, they had to cut the car open with a saw to pull them out, I saw the whole thing with my own eyes . . ." His face, wet with rain, glowed in the blue light from atop the police van, while the headlights of the ambulance lit up the puddles on the asphalt parking lot. Water flowed from his leather jacket and from his close-cropped hair and from the collar of his shirt, and every step he took down the long hallway lit by spotlights belonging to the team from forensics left a wet footprint in its wake. ("Hold on, hold on a minute," the guard shouted as he ran after Zadik. "I need your ID!" he had yelled when Zadik first stepped out of the car until Max Levin, who was smoking a cigarette at the entrance to the building, grabbed hold of his arm and said kindly, "Quiet now, it's all right. That man is the head of Israel Television.")

Water pooled under Zadik as he stood near the body, turning his face away as he murmured, "Tirzah, God, Tirzah!" A police officer whispered something in his ear, and Zadik glanced at the huge pillar lying near the body, and at its bloodstained capital. He bent down and tapped on the pillar. "I don't believe it!" he shouted. "This is real marble, where would she have gotten real marble? What is this, Hollywood?" he asked, choking. Zadik rose to his feet and looked around him. "This is terrible, terrible," he muttered. "What was she doing here in the middle of the night?"

He shifted his gaze from Avi the lighting technician, who was crouched in the corner, to Max, standing next to him. Then he looked at the crew, who had descended from the roof, his gaze resting finally on Sarah's face, which was pressed into Hagar's shoulder. Zadik noticed her arms trembling in the sleeves of the white gown, and her thin legs, her bare feet. "What's going on here?" he asked hoarsely. "What are all of you doing here at such . . ."

Max Levin moved closer and whispered something in his ear; Zadik gave him a look of sheer astonishment. "I don't understand," he said in a parched voice. "You're still filming that? Didn't Matty put a stop to it? Where's Benny? Where is he?" His voice rose with the last words he spoke.

Max indicated with a nod of his head that Benny was up on the roof. "They're trying to keep him away as long as possible, detain him upstairs for a while," he told Zadik, "until . . . I thought maybe they would cover her up or something. . . . He's going to take this very hard."

Zadik noticed the doctor standing next to the body; the doctor returned his gaze and approached, his hand extended in greeting. "I'm Dr. Elyashiv. As I've already told these people," he said, indicating the police captain and the members of the forensics team crouching by the body, "this pillar crushed the victim. She was standing here," he explained, pointing to the wood-frame flats, "and it somehow moved, apparently, and toppled onto her. Her skull is cracked, that much I'm sure of. The pillar could have caused the fracture if she was standing there, and—"

"It's too early to tell," said a man from forensics as he rose to his feet.

"What's too early to tell?" Zadik demanded to know. "Too early to tell how . . . ?"

Zadik fell silent because just then Benny Meyuhas ran in, pushing through the small crowd and, ignoring the people from forensics, bent his knees and fell on top of Tirzah's body—fell or collapsed, they would argue about it later in the newsroom when they were describing the scene, and someone said it was a shame that Schreiber had not been filming at that moment, but was instead standing in the back, his arms stretched wide as if apologizing for failing to prevent it. Benny Meyuhas lay on top of Tirzah's body, ignoring the protests of the investigators and the chalk outline on the floor and all the careful work of gathering proof and evidence, shouting again and again, "It's my fault. . . . it's because of me . . . because of me . . . I . . ." Hagar bent down and tried to pull him up. He forcefully shook himself free of her grasp. A bright light blazed, the flash of a police camera.

"Is this the husband? Is he her husband?" a uniformed policeman asked Zadik as a few men pulled Benny Meyuhas off Tirzah's body.

"Yes, her partner," Zadik answered. "They've been together for a number of years. Very much in love. You . . . do I know you?"

"Bachar, Chief Inspector Bachar." In a whisper he added, "I want everyone out of here, they're keeping us from getting our work done."

"I told them," Zadik lamented, "I kept telling them all the time that there would be some sort of disaster here. But I didn't believe . . . how did it happen?"

The police officer pointed to the white pillar, which at that moment was being moved to the side with great effort.

"That crushed her? How? What, she didn't move aside when it fell? And how is it that she's buried under those scenery flats? They're only made of plywood, how—"

The police officer reiterated, "Just as my men told you, it's too early to know. We'll only be able to determine that when . . . ," but Zadik was not listening. Instead, he raised his head and said, "We need to tell Rubin. Has anybody tried to contact Rubin yet?"

No one answered.

"Call Rubin," Zadik ordered, and Max Levin looked around the room until he caught Hagar's gaze and she nodded, stepped aside, and dialed. "No answer," she said a minute later. "His cell phone isn't in service at the moment."

"Maybe he's in the building," Max said. "Try the editing rooms."

"Where *are* the editing rooms?" asked the uniformed police officer.

"Over at the main building," Max explained.

"Never mind," Zadik said. "Let him have a few more hours in peace. There's certainly no rush now."

• • •

Indeed, Arye Rubin was in an editing room on the third floor of the main building, and he had company. Natasha was standing next to him, plucking split ends from her fair, disheveled hair, peering at the monitor and occasionally out the window. A short while earlier, when the ambulance and the police van had arrived, she had approached the window and looked out.

"Rubin, come look, something's happened. There are lots of sirens, it's two a.m., what can it be . . . maybe a suicide bomber?"

"Forget about it," Rubin told her with an air of distraction, his eyes on the monitor. "Whatever it is, if it's important then we'll hear about it." He stopped the videotape and turned to look at her, pensive.

Natasha had surprised him, flinging open the door to the room at one in the morning, short of breath. She had tossed her shabby canvas bag and her waterlogged army jacket onto the blue wall-to-wall carpeting without considering the wet spot that was forming there, and slammed the door behind her. Her words had come in a torrent. Although Arye Rubin had tried to stop her—"I've got to finish something here," he had said, giving her only part of his attention—Natasha had jabbered on breathlessly: "Two whole weeks . . . days and nights . . . every free minute . . . I can't stop now . . ." Then she had taken hold of his sleeve. "Rubin," she had said to him without looking at what he was working on—in fact he had been totally immersed in his work but nonetheless stopped the monitor—"Rubin, you've got to see this, Rubin. Believe me, you're going to die when you see this." Then she emptied the contents of her canvas bag onto the carpet, read the labels on three videotapes, selected one, and inserted it in the monitor.

Rubin regarded her, skeptical. He was in the middle of work on a piece about an interrogatee beaten while in the custody of Israeli intelligence operatives. Several days earlier he had explained to Hefetz, the newsroom chief, that he was less interested in the interrogators than in the behavior of doctors in Israeli hospitals who covered up for them, and that for the first time he had succeeded in breaking through the doctors' silence. He had been lucky, he told Hefetz, had stumbled onto one doctor, a member of B'tzelem, the human rights organization, who could no longer stomach what he was forced to deal with. From the moment that doctor had opened up to him, a whole chain of events was set in motion. Even the director of the hospital had been unable to stop Arye Rubin as he shadowed Dr. Landau, the physician attending to the interrogatee, refusing to leave Dr. Landau alone until he filmed him tossing Rubin out of his office. This had already been a breakthrough of sorts.

"Natasha," Rubin said wearily, "it's almost two o'clock and this has to be ready first thing in the morning. Why can't this," he asked, indicating the videotape, "wait until morning? What's so urgent?"

"You'll see in a minute," Natasha promised him, and without wasting a second, she bent over the monitor, pressed a button, ejected the video Rubin had been working on, and inserted her own. Before he could even protest she had already pressed PLAY, then she stopped to say, victoriously, "There you are. Feast your eyes."

Against his will, Arye Rubin looked at the screen. He intended to protest, but the black-hooded figure captured his attention. "What is this?" he asked her without removing his gaze from the screen.

"Not *what* is this," Natasha corrected him, pointing at the screen with her small, thin finger, the nail gnawed to nothing, "but *who* is this. Why don't you ask who it is? Because you know very well who it is, you recognize him, don't you?"

"Yes, I do," Rubin said with a sigh. "I recognize him. Chief rabbi, head of the movement. Where is this? Is it the airport? Was this filmed at the airport?"

"Yes," Natasha said, straightening up. "At the airport, on his way overseas, dressed as a Greek Orthodox priest. It looks like his clothes were taken from Wardrobe or something. . . . Admit it, Rubin, this is really something."

"Okay," Rubin said, "I'll admit, it's really something. But what is it exactly?"

Natasha announced gaily that she had been trailing Rabbi Elharizi for quite some time. "I figured out that once a week he meets with people, in some, like, restaurant in the French Hill neighborhood of Jerusalem—"

"Why 'like'?" he asked irritably. "'Like' he meets with people or 'like' a restaurant?"

"There's this place in French Hill, I'm not going to tell you where, that's like, well, it's not exactly a restaurant, it's sort of a coffee shop, and that's where he meets once a week with these people. I don't know who they are. But he goes in and comes out of there with this sort of black briefcase, like . . . here, have a look," Natasha said as she rewound the video, stopping at a frame in which Rabbi Elharizi could be seen holding a small, thick black suitcase. "Like that," she said, "no, not like that, *that's* exactly the one. And look: the suitcase is attached to his wrist with a metal chain, did you see that?"

Rubin nodded; he had seen it. "So they meet in this restaurant, and—?"

"That's just it," Natasha said, "I don't know exactly what. But a lot of money passes hands there. I peeked inside once. Money, bills, dollars, everything. And I also know that Rabbi Elharizi has been traveling regularly to Canada, he's been there three times in three months and he always takes the suitcase with him. So what do we learn from that? Somebody's giving him money, which he then moves to Canada!"

"So?" Rubin said, looking at Natasha expectantly.

"What do you mean, so?" Natasha said, annoyed. "Like you really think that's normal. What's so normal about getting money and transferring it to Canada?"

"Maybe he came into an inheritance. Or sold his house."

"No way!" Natasha shouted. "I know exactly where he lives, he hasn't sold his house and he hasn't come into any inheritance. And anyway, look," she said as she fast-forwarded the tape and stopped at a frame showing Rabbi Elharizi in priestly garb again. "He's moving money to Canada for something big—big and illegal—look at this getup, that means something, doesn't it? I'm telling you, it's something big and illegal. That much I'm sure of."

"How can you be sure?"

"Rubin," Natasha said with a laugh, "you yourself taught me: I do not divulge my sources, I've got my source and I'm sure not giving it out. But I need you to help me. I need you to persuade him to give me a crew, I want to get to the bottom of this thing."

"Persuade who? Hefetz?" Rubin asked, surprised. "You want *me* to persuade Hefetz? Who could possibly persuade him better than you? You certainly don't need any help when it comes to Hefetz. You know that *nobody* has more influence over him than you do."

"Listen, Rubin," Natasha said, her lips trembling as if she were about to burst into tears, "you're wrong. And as one who . . . never mind, you're totally wrong. That's insulting. I don't have any influence over him, you're talking stereotypically."

"Ah," Rubin said with a wan smile. "Stereotypically? I get it . . ."

"Don't patronize me, Rubin," Natasha said, pulling on the sleeves of the oversized sweater she was wearing. "You're thinking in terms of stereotypes, like in American movies or something, but it doesn't work that way in real life. On the contrary . . ."

"Enlighten me," Rubin said, folding his arms across his chest and pushing his chair back. "Explain how it works in real life."

"All right. I know you have experience, I know that you yourself have already . . . never mind," she said, slapping her thigh as if to close the subject. "I didn't say that . . . never mind, Hefetz won't ever help me, he won't help me—"

"Natasha," Rubin said, making an effort to sound fatherly and patient, "how can I possibly bypass the news chief to help you? Explain that to me. Especially when you and he—"

"On the contrary," Natasha implored him. "It's exactly the opposite of what you think: if a man like Hefetz sleeps with a woman, he doesn't think she's worth much anymore. He knows how to talk nice, I guess, but you'll never catch him taking me seriously, treating me like my work has any value. I think that . . . in general, if a person of his rank screws around with a nobody, a new reporter, do you really think he's going to promote her because of that?!"

Rubin grimaced. "I don't like . . . why are you talking like that? Why do you talk about yourself with such disdain? This isn't a matter of getting it on the sly, it's totally clear that you two have had something serious going for quite a while."

"It's not important what we have going," Natasha said, cutting him off. "It doesn't matter what Hefetz says, he can talk about love from morning to night. I'm telling you, if a married guy messes around with a girl half his age it's called screwing, that's all it is, and I don't have any intention . . . in your case maybe it . . . but in any case, it's over."

"Aha. Over. Now it's all clear to me," Rubin said, raising his eyes to the ceiling.

"What's clear to you?" Natasha demanded to know, and with a trembling finger she pressed the button that slowly ejected the videotape. "Because it's clear to me . . . that you don't want . . ."

"Oh, come on, Natasha, don't be so touchy, at least spare me that," Rubin said, grabbing tightly the bony hand that held the tape.

"So do you admit it's explosive?"

"Explosive?" He pursed his lips as though tasting the word. "All right, I'll give you that. Or at least it's the start of something explosive, if we must use such words. But an explosion is also destructive, they may not even let you screen it, especially if that's all you've got—"

"I got two more," Natasha said, bending down to her canvas bag.

"You *have* two more," Rubin said, correcting her. He gazed toward the window pensively. "Since when?"

Natasha stood next to him, gazing out the window. "Look," she said, alarmed, "what is all this? All those flashing lights, police vans, maybe . . . something must have happened, something awful. Look," she said, moving aside.

Rubin looked. "I really don't know," he said. "It's hard to see from here. Shall we go down and check it out?"

"Maybe we can just call and ask. Here you go," she said, holding out the videotapes. "I *have* two tapes that I am now giving you, I know how much you like it when I speak properly. What do you mean, 'since when'?"

"Since when is it over between you and Hefetz?" he asked, ignoring the tapes in her outstretched hand.

"Since today, since now, a half-hour ago," she answered as she inserted the video into the monitor and rewound it. "Anyway, his wife is coming back tomorrow. During the two weeks she was gone I understood . . . okay, never mind. I'm already twenty-five, I can't waste my whole life on . . ."

In her worn jeans, her thighs seemed gaunter than ever, the look on her face vacant.

"You've got something there," Rubin said. "I'm in favor of family, kids."

Natasha chuckled. "Sure you are," she said with a smile. "That's why you've got a family and children." As soon as she said it, she shut up and looked at him with misgivings. She had overstepped the boundary.

Rubin did not respond.

Natasha was dismayed. She knew that since the breakup of his marriage to Tirzah eight years earlier, there had been no other woman in his life. Everyone noticed that he was careful not to get mixed up in any kind of binding relationship with a woman. Rubin, who had been known at Israel Television throughout his marriage to Tirzah as a real Don Juan, as someone who always maintained two or three relationships with women "of every age and every color," as Niva, the newsroom secretary, put it, had been uncharacteristically discreet in the past few years. No one knew to whom he was giving "limited, no-illusion pleasure," as Daphna from the film archives quoted him as describing it. With all the women he had had affairs with, according to rumors, Rubin maintained good, cordial—even friendly—relations. With everyone, that is, except perhaps Niva; Natasha had twice glimpsed Niva trying to speak with Rubin, who would brush her off. Everyone—in the canteen and the newsroom and the hallways—everyone talked about the child, how he resembled Rubin. Rubin thought no one knew about the boy, and Natasha had no intention at all of being the one to tell him what people said behind his back. Only a few days earlier Niva had said something about a gift for the kid's seventh birthday. Natasha wondered whether Tirzah knew about the boy. People said Rubin refused to see him. They said Niva had tricked him, set a trap, that she had thought if she had a baby, Rubin would agree to live with her. But the opposite had happened, sometimes that is how things play out. Natasha was dismayed: maybe now that she had reminded Rubin that he himself had no family or children, she had ruined everything.

"You look awful, Natasha," Rubin said, and in his voice she was surprised to discern not anger, but compassion. "Have you eaten anything today? You look anorexic, no, no, no, don't light a cigarette here, the windows are closed because of all this rain and my throat is already killing me. Come tell me what you think is really going on with Rabbi Elharizi, what you think he's plotting to do with all that money and that getup and Canada. Let's try to guess what could be going on there and why, and then together we'll figure out what to do about it."

# CHAPTER TWO

Here's the lineup. In spite of everything, we managed to get it done on time," Niva said as she placed a sheet of paper with the list of news items for the evening program on the table in front of Zadik. "Just look at them," she added incredulously, handing an identical sheet to Erez, the news editor, who was sitting next to Zadik, and placing another in front of the empty seat next to him. "Unbelievable. I can't get over the fact that everyone's already here. I've never seen this place so full this early in the morning."

Zadik sat at the head of the long conference table. Pale light penetrated the room through the large window spotted with dried raindrops, throwing light on his short gray hair and the last traces of night in his red eyes and in the dark circles under them, which gave his full, round face the look of an exhausted playboy. He looked at the serious expressions of all those present, then glanced up at the clock hanging on the wall opposite, behind the two monitors broadcasting Channel One and Channel Two, respectively. He intended to reply to Niva—the veteran secretary of the News Department, known for her sharp tongue—with something witty, but his own secretary, Aviva, beat him to it. As usual, she was sitting behind him in a comfortable chair as though not even listening, scrutinizing the dark line she had drawn around her full lips, then placing the lipstick and the small, round mirror inside her makeup kit and the makeup kit inside her purse. She zipped up her purse with a flourish, placed it under her seat, and said, "It's just too bad that somebody had to die around here for people to show up for the morning meeting on time." She stretched one long leg to the side and added, "And it's already eight-twenty, even today we're running late," then examined her calf and the narrow ankle below it.

Zadik pulled the perforated edges from the paper, went over the lines of the chart and the air times for each item with the pen he had just banged on the table to call the meeting to order, and added two exclamation points after the words "gaining momentum," which appeared next to the headline STRIKE TODAY. From the corner of his eye he glimpsed Niva's pink scalp peeking through her short and wispy red hair. She had arrived at work a few days earlier with this new red haircut in place of the disheveled gray curls she had had previously. She leaned toward Aviva, touching her shiny red shoe. "New?" she asked.

"Can you believe it, one hundred and twenty shekels, Italian leather, and look how nicely it shows up my leg," Aviva said, smiling, as she meticulously straightened the sleeves of her thin blue sweater, folded her arms, and stretched her body so as to show off her breasts. For a brief moment Zadik regarded these two women, so different from one another; he had often thought about Niva as a woman who had "let herself go," an expression he had learned from Rubin that meant she did not make an effort to cultivate her femininity. It was Rubin who had explained to him once, on a trip abroad, that women who stop dyeing their hair or watching their figures, the ones who hide their bodies in flannel shirts and thick wool socks, can claim a thousand times that they are in favor of the "natural look" and that they are tired of looking like Barbie dolls and that they are fighting to free women from all the bullshit that men have conditioned them to, but the truth is that these are women in despair of ever attracting men again. And worse: these are women who have given up on the need to appear as if they believe there is still a chance that someone could love them, given up even on the need to *pretend* that they hope they will find some such man. It stood to reason that Niva would be jealous of Aviva, or mock her, because in appearance Aviva was her total opposite, a gorgeous blonde who, according to Zadik's calculations, had to be at least forty years old but did not look a day over thirty-five. Her fluttering eyelids, her long, long lashes, her laughter that rang out everywhere, the full-lipped smile she had for every male, the way she touched one long red fingernail to the edge of her lips in a way that promised . . . had he not known her as long as he had, he might have . . . but it was better not to think of such things, they would only bring trouble. Instead, it would be a good idea to get the lineup started. Every morning he had to remind them how important it was for them to be present and focused at the morning meeting, and how important it was to begin the critical summary of the previous evening's program on time and to move on quickly to that day's first lineup, which was bound to change twenty times. But nothing helped. For three years he had had to clap his hands and yell and shout, and suddenly disaster had struck, and at least this: they had all assembled around the table—or nearly all of them. "It's too bad that it takes a disaster," he said, removing his glasses, "for everyone to be here at eight-twenty in the morning." Again he banged his pen on the table. "People, people," he called. "Quiet, please!"

"What's all your shouting about?" Niva quipped as she placed a mug of coffee next to the page in front of him. "It's as quiet as a cemetery in here." She was immediately sorry and threw him a look that begged forgiveness. "Excuse me," she said, lowering her gaze.

Aviva waved her hands in the air, and she too shouted, "Quiet!" then moved her chair to the side so that Hefetz, director of the News Department, could squeeze by to get to his seat between Erez, the news editor, and Zadik. Zadik cleared his throat, and just then, with all eyes upon him, the room filled with the noise of a drill and the pounding of a jackhammer, the kind used to break walls down. Through the glass partition he could see the profile of a maintenance man in the foreign correspondents' office next door, a large drill in one hand, his mouth covered against the dust.

"I don't believe it," Zadik muttered. "Now? Right now? This is absurd, like . . . like some Marx Brothers movie."

"Stop right now!" Niva shouted. "Keep quiet a minute!" she exclaimed as she ran to the window and pounded it with her fists. The maintenance man stopped working and the drill fell silent. The jackhammer pounded twice more, and there was the sound of a wall crumbling before it, too, ceased.

"People," Zadik said in a low, hoarse voice as he scribbled lines on the page in front of him, "first and foremost I want to say a few words about this tragedy that has befallen us. A tragedy," he said with a sigh. As he raised his head he caught the eye of Danny Benizri, the correspondent for labor and social affairs, who was sitting at the far end of the table, near the corner, his chin in his hand. "A tragedy, there is simply no other word to describe it. We have lost our Tirzah. Anyone who worked with her knows what a tragedy this is. That woman . . . what can I say? If you say 'Tirzah Rubin,' you've said it all. Isn't that true?"

The telephone rang stubbornly and incessantly; Niva pounced on the receiver, speaking in a loud whisper: "What do you mean, 'it needed a double cutting'?" Zadik took in Danny Benizri's long, dark, narrow face as he straightened up, rubbed the thin pink scar that ran from his right eyebrow toward his ear, and nodded in confirmation.

"One could even say there was a certain symbolic meaning in the way Tirzah . . . ," Zadik said, now refusing to allow the telephone or Niva or anything else to prevent him from saying what he had prepared and practiced since six o'clock that morning, ". . . by a scenery flat, near the scenery room. A terrible accident, but . . ." Just then he noticed the murmuring around him, sentence fragments ringing in his ears: "Did it happen quickly?" Miri, the language editor, asked Aviva. Karen the anchorwoman butted in. "Yes. She didn't suffer."

Zadik raised a finger to each temple and pressed hard. He had not slept all night. Only at four a.m., after he had sat with a police officer and answered all his questions, had he informed Rubin. After that he sat with Rubin for an hour or longer while Rubin, pale and trembling, shook his head, buried his face in his hands for a long moment, straightened up, wiped his forehead, and said angrily, "How could you have let Benny see her like that? Why didn't you call me? I was in the editing room, you didn't even try to find me. Who was with him? I've got to get over to Benny's, I've got to see him."

Zadik could not for the life of him understand how someone like Arye Rubin could mourn a woman who had left him years earlier, or how he had remained best friends with Benny Meyuhas, the man she had left him for. No one even understood why Tirzah had left Rubin. It was clear how much he loved her, even if she'd been no raving beauty, even if he'd had dalliances with other women. Rumor had it that women were crazy about Rubin. He, Zadik, himself had seen Rubin in action more than once, most notably on a business trip they had made together to England ten years earlier; he would never forget the way the young assistant to the director of the BBC archives had looked at him. She was a platinum bombshell, like Jayne Mansfield—who remembers Jayne Mansfield today?—with the body of a starlet. Rubin and the girl had disappeared that same evening for twenty-four hours. To this very day, if he needed something from the BBC, he asked Rubin to use his connections there. He'd heard that the young lady had been appointed to an important position there and that she had had two husbands since then, but for Rubin she was willing to toss everything aside and meet him at any opportunity, even once during a stopover Rubin made on the way to the United States. Rubin had never told him all this, but someone had seen him; maybe it was Matty Cohen himself, he couldn't be sure. But with Tirzah it was something altogether different; everyone knew it was she who had left Rubin, and not vice versa, though no one knew why. If it was because of other women, well, Rubin had always had someone on the side, so that was nothing new. Maybe, in fact, Tirzah hadn't actually known about the other women and had suddenly heard about them from someone for the first time. Maybe someone had informed her.

Zadik stole a glance at Niva and caught her profile, noticed how she had aged in the last year: the sagging double chin, the wobbly flesh of her neck, everything betrayed her age, no matter that she had cut her hair as short as a boy's and dyed the stubble bright red, as if she had suddenly been frightened by her own longtime self-neglect and had decided to make one last feeble effort. But nothing would help—not even a diet. He would love to ask her how she felt now that Tirzah was gone, how she *really* felt, but he would not dare. What was there to ask? The path to Rubin was obviously clear now, maybe Niva would get him to commit to her and the kid and all that. It was strange to think that Tirzah had gone to live with Benny Meyuhas; he had never been able to understand that. On the other hand, all those years everyone had known that Benny Meyuhas was in love with Tirzah, that because of her he had never married. But in comparison with Rubin, Benny was, well . . . he looked like he could be Tirzah's father, with his small, pinched face; really, you couldn't compare the two men at all, even though they were the same age. He, Zadik, had had a lot of time to think it over—after all, he had not slept all night, and there were all those questions the police officer, Eli Bachar, had asked him. He had supposedly come to question him about what had happened, to discuss the accident and shoddy work procedures, but after he had spoken with someone over the phone—Zadik did not hear the conversation, he merely saw Eli Bachar move aside and lower his voice to a whisper—after that, Bachar was asking for a list of the engineers, contractors, technicians, and God knows who else to determine whether this was a case of criminal negligence; that was what he had called it. At first it had seemed as if the whole affair would end with a coroner's examination, and then all of a sudden the guy was asking questions about Tirzah and her personal life, as if there was some connection. How ironic that in this case, Tirzah had been the most negligent party. Zadik should have explained to Police Inspector Eli Bachar how she had always insisted—this time more than ever—whenever it was one of her husband's films and the scenery was particularly expensive, that the scenery should stay where it was, and how in this case she hadn't even agreed to store the scenery in the carpentry workshop until the shooting was wrapped up. Ultimately, even though he was not directly responsible, even Benny Meyuhas could be charged with negligence, as well as Hagar, his assistant and the film's producer. That police inspector had asked to summon them too, even after Zadik repeated himself several times about Tirzah's work procedures and how she herself had instructed the carpentry shop workers where to place the scenery, including the marble pillar. Marble! He goes nuts every time he thinks about that marble pillar. What do these people think, that he has piles of money to dish out? All those claims from Benny Meyuhas that an actor performs differently if he's leaning on a marble column and not a piece of plywood—what bullshit! If it weren't for those crazy ideas of his, no pillar would have crushed Tirzah's skull in. He himself was telling them all the time that this insane wastefulness was the mother of all sins. And if he's already thinking about money, where the hell is Matty Cohen, the guy who had promised to shut down that production? In another forty-five minutes a meeting of department heads was scheduled to take place in his office, and Matty Cohen was expected to attend. But nobody had seen him since yesterday. That stupid production had to be shut down, it had already cost them more than two million—the whole budget for drama—but now they would say it wasn't the appropriate time, that it wasn't fitting to stop Benny Meyuhas just when he'd lost his life partner. Zadik himself couldn't care less whether Tirzah was his legally wedded wife, he was open-minded in these matters, didn't have any prejudices, and anyway, Benny Meyuhas presented her as his wife, so to him, she was his wife. If only someone could explain to him how those two, Rubin and Benny Meyuhas, had remained friends.

With women it could never happen, Zadik had told Hefetz that morning before the news meeting when they were discussing the police investigation. Women would hate each other for the rest of their lives. Forever. Only with men could a friendship like that endure. "But even me, as a man, I'm not sure I could handle it," he had admitted to Hefetz. "I don't know how I'd manage to remain close friends with a man living with the woman who was once my wife. Even worse, I don't know what I'd do if I still loved her."

"Close friends? They're more than close friends," Hefetz had said. "They're like . . . they're like brothers, like brothers, they've been together since childhood, it's like they're family. Don't you think they're like family? They were like family! I myself have heard Rubin call Benny 'practically my own flesh and blood.' So what would you do in his place? Give up on your own brother? What would you do? They were like family, don't you think they were like family?"

"That's why it's even harder to comprehend," Zadik had said. "I wouldn't be able to handle it."

"Nobody ever knows what he can handle and what he can't," Hefetz had exclaimed fervently. "What person knows what he's capable of? Does anyone know what he's capable of? No, nobody knows, how could they? As for me . . ." He fell silent suddenly. Zadik followed his gaze and caught sight of Natasha at the newsroom door, her hair disheveled, wearing her usual getup: army jacket, jeans, and a ratty red scarf. She stood scanning the room as though looking for someone until she fixed her large sky blue eyes on him, on Zadik. For a moment she gazed at them both, then turned around and walked back down the hall. Hefetz's face clouded over.

Zadik could not for the life of him understand these entanglements that people got themselves into. Okay, he himself had not been completely . . . but with a twenty-five-year-old girl?! Only one year older than Hefetz's own daughter? These people had no limits, and at work, no less! To get mixed up with a girl you worked with, that's something he himself would *never* have done. Anyway, not here, maybe overseas, where nobody could . . .

The drill started pounding again, and a cloud of dust rolled out from the open door of the adjacent room straight into the newsroom.

"Tell them to lay off," Zadik instructed Aviva.

"How can I?" she answered with a shrug. "I've been waiting a month for them to come. You wanted renovations, you said the foreign correspondents' room needed renovating. That's what you said, didn't you? I've been waiting a month for these guys, so today's the day they start work. I'm not going to tell them to lay off now. If you want to, tell them yourself. Call Maintenance."

"Stop!" Zadik shouted. "Take a break, go drink some coffee, come back in an hour!" The two workers stood at the doorway of the foreign correspondents' room, staring at him. Zadik tried to soften his tone. "Haven't you heard what happened?" he asked. The worker holding the drill stared at him in silence. "Didn't you hear that one of our senior employees was killed last night?" The second worker shook his head and whispered something to the first. They emerged from the correspondents' room and stood at the doorway of the newsroom stealing furtive glances at the people seated around the conference table. Aviva hurried over to them.

"Come back in an hour or two," she told them. She turned to Zadik, casting him a look of reproach. "It took me *ages* to get these guys here, *ages* for them to find the time to do the job, and then you go and toss them out."

"We've got to get the lineup started, there are all kinds of problems and changes with tonight's topics," Hefetz said, to which Zadik nodded. Erez made a show of rattling the page in front of him.

"Just another word or two," Zadik told him, clearing his throat again. "There's more I need to tell them." Erez sighed, and Hefetz covered his sheet of paper with his two large hands.

"We all know," Zadik began, his voice choked with emotion, "we all know how devoted Tirzah was to her work, how much she gave of herself. Anyone who worked with her knows that she was on the job day and night. Now it turns out that she literally gave her life . . . how shall I say, her life was an offering on the altar of her work. I don't need to tell you all," he said, glancing at the ginger curls of David Shalit, the correspondent for police affairs, who was sitting not far away from him and jotting something down in his PalmPilot, "that Tirzah was a true artisan, a perfectionist and a person of real integrity. I don't need to tell you those things about her—she and I spent thirty years together in this building, we were around when there was nothing here, she and I and Rubin and Benny Meyuhas. You too, Hefetz, we've been together right from the start. And I never heard a bad word about anybody from her. You know, Tirzah . . . Tirzah, was, she was . . ." He fell silent and looked around; it had never been so quiet in the newsroom, it had never happened that he could complete an entire sentence without someone interjecting a wisecrack. "But in the meantime," he said slowly, emphasizing each word, "we can't let everything come to a halt. With news, there's no time for mourning, we don't have the luxury of mourning, especially as Israel's official television station." His eyes blurred with tears as he glanced around the table at all the assembled, their faces cast downward. "There's no stopping the news," he said with determination, then he fell silent and bent his head forward into the palms of his hands.

"There's no choice," Hefetz chimed in in his deep bass. He ran a hand over his clean-shaven pate, then stroked his whiskers. "Do we have a choice? No, we don't have a choice. Will someone else do the job for us? No. Nobody's gonna do it for us. That's what I'm trying to explain: there's no choice." How long, Zadik asked himself absentmindedly, how long would he have to put up with watching this Hefetz angle uninhibitedly, shamelessly, to replace him? After all, any idiot could see how Hefetz parroted him, repeated everything that came out of his mouth like a broken record, seven times at least until you wanted to throw up. . . . Suddenly Hefetz stiffened, his eyes on the door of the newsroom. Zadik followed his glance: Arye Rubin stood in the doorway, Natasha at his side, clinging to his jacket. That Natasha is too thin, Zadik thought, she's an unholy mess, and that wool scarf she never goes anywhere without, wound around her neck, her chin buried inside it, gives her the look of a waif. But those blue eyes . . . She seems glued to Rubin. Doesn't make sense that Rubin's got something for her. First of all, she's Hefetz's girl, and Rubin wouldn't . . . he would never . . . Rubin's got style, he would never let himself get caught up in . . . It seemed to Zadik that the silence was deepening, and everyone was looking dumbly at Rubin until Niva rushed up to him and laid her hands on his arms, peering into his face as though they were the only two people in the newsroom. She stood there as if she were acting in some American movie, talking in hushed tones that everyone could hear. "What a terrible tragedy, we've been worried about you, Arye. Are you all right, Arye?" Rubin nodded his head and otherwise ignored her, gently removing her hands from his arms. He looked at Zadik, walked quickly to him, leaned over, and whispered in his ear: "I've got to speak with you, Zadik, as soon as possible."

"Not now," said Zadik, startled. "After the morning meeting I have a meeting with the department heads. Only after that, after ten—"

"No way," Rubin whispered. "Right away, as soon as the lineup is ready. It's urgent."

"Okay, okay," Zadik said, acquiescing. "But for now, take a seat."

Hefetz quickly scooted his chair aside, closer to Erez, and Rubin took a seat at the corner of the conference table. Aviva, who was standing behind him, placed a soft hand on his shoulder, pressing gently, while David Shalit caught his glance, shrugging his shoulders in a gesture of helplessness. It really was an insufferable situation; no one knew what to say or what to think. Arye Rubin lifted the page and glanced at it. Hefetz was watching Natasha as she cast Rubin a questioning look, then threw her canvas bag on the corner sofa next to the water dispenser.

"There's no choice," Hefetz said again, wrenching his gaze from Natasha, who was leaning on the wall next to the sofa and playing with the fringes of her red wool scarf. "As they say, we don't have the luxury of mourning. Do we have that luxury? No, we don't. We've got to discuss the lineup."

"So what have we got today?" Zadik asked with a sigh. "The way it looks to me is that today the strike is entering a new phase, the taxi drivers and the whole health system out on an open-ended strike. Soon they're going to take to the streets. So, what have you people got?"

"Ben Gurion Airport, trash collection," Erez said. "We'll start with a piece on the trash in Tel Aviv, we've got pictures for the opening credits, and lots of stories from the airport."

"Yesterday I said—about the airport—bring in an interesting angle, something new: foreign workers, Arabs," Hefetz complained. "I said get some foreign workers, didn't I? I did, that's what I said. And it's not a bad idea to get on the phone with some folks stuck overseas, is it? No, not a bad idea at all."

"Overseas? Why overseas? We've got a general strike right here, lots of stuff going down," David Shalit interrupted. As always when he was talking about something that mattered to him, his forehead turned red and he blushed to the tip of his pointed chin, concealing the freckles that dotted his cheeks. "The overseas operator is connecting people stuck overseas free of charge. In Tel Aviv . . ."

"Yesterday I heard that soldiers have been fighting over seats on buses," Niva added from the far end of the conference table, where she was engaged in disentangling the phone cord from the receiver of the hotline.

"Guys," Erez said, raising his voice as he tinkered with the metal frame of his glasses, "we've got the Mossad affair, Zohar's handling it, he's got some great stuff."

"Where *is* Zohar? Isn't he in Turkey covering the exercises the IDF is doing with the Turkish army?"

"Tell me something," Miri the language editor interjected, removing her reading glasses. "Don't you think it's high time we do something about those daily ads that keep appearing in *Haaretz,* the ones that read LIAR? Don't you think people are interested in knowing who's behind them, and who's the liar? After all, they cost a fortune." She stared expectantly at Hefetz.

"No," Hefetz said to Erez, "Zohar is back in the country, but he phoned to say he'd be late. He doesn't even know about Tirzah yet, about what happened. Something's going on, I don't even know where. He went out with a crew . . . he'll be calling soon."

"Everyone knows who those ads are about," Aviva said, her lower lip protruding. "Who doesn't know that the liar is Bibi Netanyahu?"

"Are you certain about that?" Miri asked as she raised her thick-lensed glasses to her eyes and leaned forward to read from the lineup. "Sometimes what seems totally obvious—"

"A *thousand* percent certain," Aviva answered assuredly. "There's not a soul who doesn't know that."

"And then there's Bezalel," said Erez, continuing, "who lands two hours from now with the prime minister. There's an unscheduled meeting about the new round of talks with the Palestinians, and then this evening a specially convened assembly of the Labor Party—"

"Oh, give me a break," said Niva mockingly as she reconnected the phone cord to the hotline.

"You'll be surprised to hear this," Hefetz said, "but there is still such a thing as the Labor Party." To Erez he added, "Am I right? Isn't there still a Labor Party? Yes there is, there is still a Labor Party. You people want to bury the Labor Party? What is this? Is the Labor Party your mother, that you can bury her? No, it is not your mother. You haven't even mentioned a word about Golda in your lineup. It's the anniversary of her death, and yesterday I said that I want photos from the ceremony. If there aren't any photos, then at least I want her mentioned."

"And what's this item about Bassiouny?" Zadik queried them. "All that's written here is 'The Egyptian Ambassador and the Scandal.' Have we got anything new? Or do we have to wait another hour or two for Bezalel to come back from Washington with the prime minister?"

"Listen," Niva called out, waving the telephone receiver, "we haven't got the studio in Tel Aviv. You hear me?" She looked to Hefetz, who nodded. "So what are we gonna do?" From experience she knew not to expect an answer, and she followed Hefetz's gaze as it shifted cautiously from David Shalit to the far corner of the room, near the water dispenser, where Natasha was sitting. "You wanted to interview Amir Peretz live from Tel Aviv about the strike," Niva reminded them. When no one responded, she waved the room away in a gesture of desperation and caught sight of her fingernails, now painted neon green. After years of ignoring her fingernails she had decided to paint them—bright green, no less! What can you make of human beings,

Zadik said to himself with a start; that bright green is out of place after what happened last night. Niva raised her foot, which was ensconced in a thick wool sock, from the heavy wooden clog she was wearing and brought it to rest on the chair next to her.

"Listen up a minute," David Shalit said as he reached into his black turtleneck to scratch an insect bite protruding from his skinny neck. "About Bassiouny, I heard an item about him on the radio, and they mentioned the name of the doctor that woman took to court, but not *her* name. She's allowed to sue for a million shekels and drag everyone through the mud—Bassiouny and that doctor who examined her—but then only *she* gets to come out smelling like a rose? I say let's not release the name of the doctor."

"Why? What for? What's it to you?" Hefetz asked. "What do you care about the doctor? Do you care about that doctor? He ever do anything for you? You ever get anything from him? You never got anything from him. You don't owe him a thing."

"What's it to me? What do you mean, 'What's it to me'? What's going on here?" David Shalit asked, enraged. "Here's this woman who claims she's in distress—a victim, she says—and drags everybody through the mud, and only she comes out clean? Let's either violate the gag order on revealing her identity or drop the doctor's name. Otherwise, all the men get screwed."

"Wait a minute, wait a minute, I want to get something straight here," Zadik said, bending forward and looking straight at David Shalit, who had thrust his fingers into his reddish curls, pulling them down over his forehead. The young reporter tugged at his turtleneck again, scratching at the itchy spot and making it bulge even larger. He leaned back in his chair as Zadik said, "What exactly are we talking about here?"

"She's suing them both, Bassiouny and the doctor," David Shalit said, banging the table. "Both of them! There's no gag order on *their* names, she's free to ruin them. But as for her, not a spot of dirt on her! Imagine tomorrow some chick popping up and claiming that I . . . that you . . ."

"First of all, it was the judge who gave the order. Are you responsible for that? No, you are not responsible. Did you give the order? No, you did not give the order. The judge did," Hefetz said, stealing a glance at Natasha.

"So, he gave the order!" David Shalit was shouting now, his face redder than ever. "For once let's just blow it off. I'm sick of all these girls who fuck like rabbits and shout, 'Rape, rape!' These days any chick can say she was raped and ruin some guy's life even though she was the one who—"

"There's nothing we can do about it," Zadik said, cutting him off. "When the story was first broadcast, Bassiouny's name and the doctor's were revealed. As I've already mentioned, we're Israel's official television station, we're the last ones who can violate—"

"Right, but the court says there's no factual basis for the case, so now she claims they've slandered her and she's taken them to court—"

Tzippi, one of the assistant producers, opened the door from the reporters' room next door to ask which translator was due in. "The Turkish defense minister still needs to be translated," she informed them.

David Shalit stood up and moved to a chair against the wall, next to the junior secretary who was taking the minutes. "Stay right here, we're not finished yet," Hefetz ordered. He wiped his large face with his hand. "It's so damn hot in here. Will someone turn the heating down?"

"You want me to call Maintenance?" Niva asked in mock innocence as she removed her foot from the chair and returned it to her clog. "Suddenly you've forgotten that we have no control over the heating?"

"I can hear just fine from over here," David Shalit said, "and as for speaking, there's no point in me saying anything. Nobody's listening anyway, and I'm not the one who makes the decisions around here."

"What's this about 'military documents' written here?" Zadik queried. "What's the story about military documents?"

Hefetz leaned forward and massaged the back of his neck. "I told you about this," he said, fatigued. "I told you: they found some top-secret military documents in the garbage. We've shot it, but there's still no text. Look, I've given it eight seconds, two words per second."

The door to the reporters' room opened again and Tzippi plodded toward Hefetz, buttoning with difficulty the plaid flannel shirt that barely covered her burgeoning belly. "You could die from the heat in here," she complained. "This temperature is definitely not for pregnant women." She repeated her need of a translation from Turkish of the report sent in by the military correspondent.

The telephone rang again. "Hefetz," Niva called, "Bezalel's on the line. What do you want to ask him? Hefetz, I'm talking to you, what did you want to ask him? Hefetz, are you listening? I'm talking to you, am I not? Answer me already!" Her tone was that of a petulant child, her thin lips set in a crooked slant of dissatisfaction.

"Just a minute," Hefetz shouted. "I need to make a calculation here, don't I? What's he got for us? Ask him if he's got anything new before we finish the lineup. When we've heard from him we can put out an updated lineup, ask him exactly . . . here, let me talk to him."

All at once the sights and sounds grew indistinct to Zadik. As if under water, he could hear people talking around him, as if through a sheet of glass he could see the news director pull Karen aside, he could hear the assistant producer phoning Turkey from the foreign correspondents' room and Erez verifying the details of a survey done on the *Popolitika* talk show and Karen asking, "What's this about Clinton? Why is 'Clinton' written here?" And Erez, answering her before turning away: "No clue."

"People," Zadik said authoritatively, because this is what they were waiting for, for him to say something—anything—authoritative. "Let's keep on track, stick to our timetable, there's no going overtime because *Popolitika* is going to be longer than usual today."

"So is the lineup okay? You haven't said," Erez complained.

"Other than the piece about Moshe Leon, your stories are garbage," Zadik answered.

"Those are heartrending human stories!" Erez cried out, agitated.

"Heartrending? They're garbage, a big heap of—"

Suddenly, both television monitors began broadcasting from the wall opposite the conference table. "Turn down the volume," Zadik instructed Aviva. "We should only have the pictures, why is there sound? They should be silent now."

"Why is it always me?" Aviva grumbled. "I don't even have the remote, Erez took it, he wanted to see something on Channel Two. Turn down the volume on the monitors," she said, looking at Erez.

A voice shouted in from the graphics room. "What time are we lighting the first Hanukkah candle this evening, before or after the broadcast?"

"Are you kidding? Before, of course it's before, every year it's before," Niva shouted back as she retrieved a sheet of paper from the computer printer. "Here's the updated lineup," she announced, pulling the perforated edges off the page.

Danny Benizri stood up and stretched, and Zadik caught sight of his profile, his flat stomach. That's the way he had looked when he was Benizri's age: twenty years earlier when he tucked his shirt into his trousers, nothing showed, certainly not this mountain of a belly under his shirt and jacket that precedes him wherever he goes.

Danny Benizri straightened the hem of his black knit sweater. "What about the people laid off at the Hulit factory? Why did you make that item number twenty-seven?" he asked bitterly. "I'm talking to you, Erez, don't pretend you don't hear me." Benizri shot Erez an angry look, which Erez returned with a shrug of his narrow shoulders and a nod of his head toward Hefetz. Benizri, the correspondent for labor and social affairs, glanced at Hefetz. "Tell me, Hefetz, did you notice that?" he demanded to know.

"That," said Erez, "is out of the lineup completely today. No layoffs at Hulit, we've already got enough stuff on the strike."

"And what about the murder in Petah Tikva?" David Shalit asked. "Last night I brought you eyewitness reports from the neighbors and all that, it's not anywhere in the lineup."

"The murder in Petah Tikva is out," Erez answered indifferently as he fiddled with the zipper on his blue sweater.

"Out?" David Shalit was astounded. "How can you pull a story like that? A guy knifes someone just because he complained about the noise from his car horn? Does that seem like a normal everyday occurrence to you? As far as I'm concerned, that should be our top story!"

"Can't do anything about it," Erez said nonchalantly. "We're going with Moshe Leon instead. Hey, did someone turn off the heating? It's freezing in here."

"Niva!" shouted Zivia, one of the assistant producers. "We don't have a studio in Tel Aviv. Did you hear me?"

David Shalit called out to Erez, "You want the text for your lead? You're going to have to write it yourself."

"Oh come on, give it to me now and I'll write it down," Erez said.

"I don't want to now," said David Shalit defiantly. As he turned his head he blinked his small blue eyes—which appeared even smaller behind the thick lenses of his eyeglasses—and caught the glance of Eliahu Lutafi, the correspondent for environmental affairs. Lutafi had been around for years, and his hesitant speech gave him an air of helplessness, which invariably brought out a certain malaise in Zadik, a feeling of guilt for not having promoted him all these years. "Did you want something from me, Eliahu?" David Shalit asked.

"No, nothing. I mean, that is, if . . . if you're not giving him the lead just now, if you're free for a minute, I'd like you to see the report I've prepared on rubbish on the Tel Aviv shoreline," Eliahu Lutafi requested. "I could use some feedback."

Niva picked up the receiver. "It's Liat on the line, she's having trouble with the satellite, I can't—"

"'A stinking mess like this is inhuman,'" Erez read aloud. "It's from the text of the report on garbage," he explained to Zadik.

Zadik pored over the new page that Niva had handed him. "Miri," he called out without looking up, "have you gone over this yet? There're no markings to indicate you've been over this."

The language editor rose heavily from her place and went over to Zadik.

"This text," Zadik said, incredulous, "is even more subversive than last night's. You people can't talk that way about the Likud World Congress." But Miri did not hear the end of Zadik's sentence, because at that very moment the telephone next to which she was standing rang and Benizri, who was positioned next to another phone and rolling his eyes to the ceiling in dramatic desperation, was talking into the mouthpiece as if to a deaf person or an idiot. "I won't wink at you, I'll simply adjust my tie—" But the rest of *his* sentence was obscured by Niva, who was shouting, "Hey, wait a minute, what's going on here? Look!" Something in her tone caused everyone to fall silent and look toward the monitors on the wall. Doors to the adjacent rooms opened, and Tzippi, Zivia, and Liat, the assistant producers, stood watching, along with Irit, an intern with the foreign correspondents.

Tamari, the graphic artist, was standing in the doorway to the graphics room. "On Channel Two they're saying there are some terrorists in the tunnels on the Jerusalem–Etzion Bloc road," she said.

"I heard they've taken a hostage," said Ye'elah, the cultural affairs reporter who had just rushed in, breathless, to the newsroom.

Everyone in the room was staring at the monitors: not their own Channel One, which was showing a studio with an interviewer and two guests—an older man and a young woman—but rather the competition, Channel Two, which was showing a reporter in a military parka with a microphone, interviewing a policeman.

Hefetz slapped his thighs in anger. "Channel Two beat us to it again," he complained aloud.

No one moved to turn up the volume. At the bottom of the screen there was a caption: SUPERINTENDENT MOLCHO. "Where is this? What's going on?" Niva asked, agitated.

"Can't you see? Look, it's the Jerusalem–Etzion Bloc road," David Shalit said impatiently.

"So, what's happening there?" Aviva asked. The caption now read, ENTRANCE TO THE TUNNEL ON THE JERUSALEM–ETZION BLOC BYPASS ROAD.

For a moment there was utter silence in the room. The loud ringing of a telephone was the only thing to break it.

"The telephone's ringing, are you people deaf?" Niva asked. "It's the hotline, someone's got to answer it. Is someone picking up? Aviva, answer it, it's the hotline!" When the telephone next to her began ringing too, she picked it up without taking her eyes from the television screen. "I don't understand," she was saying into the mouthpiece. "Talk clearly. Are they from Hamas or what?" Just then the opening notes of Mozart's Symphony No. 40 rang out noisily from a mobile phone, sending Niva scrambling for her large black leather bag. After fishing through it madly, she managed to extricate a silver cellular telephone, took a look at its display panel, pursed her lips, and said, "Yes, Mother, what is it?"

Zadik stood in front of the wall monitor, watching the interviewer and his two guests, whose lips were moving soundlessly.

"What are you doing at the supermarket on Agron Street?" Niva shouted into her phone. "Oh, Mother, we agreed that you wouldn't leave the house until I get there!"

"Hello?" Aviva said into the receiver of the hotline. "Hello? Yes, he's right here, just a minute. It's for you," she said, handing the phone to Zadik.

Zadik listened for a moment, raised his head and announced, "Quiet, everyone, you can calm down; it's not terrorists."

Only then did someone raise the volume on the monitor so that it was possible to hear the military correspondent from Channel Two summarizing the turn of events: "And so," he said, facing the camera, clearly emotional, "we now have official confirmation. This is not a terrorist attack. To sum up events, we know that at six-forty-five this morning a tunnel on the Jerusalem–Etzion Bloc bypass road was blockaded by four trucks parked inside the tunnel. It appears that the car of the minister for labor and social affairs is trapped—"

"Turn down the volume!" Zadik shouted. "I don't understand why Zohar isn't on the air! How is it that their military correspondent is there but ours isn't?"

"As of now you no longer need a military correspondent there," Aviva said spitefully, as she removed her makeup kit from her purse. "Didn't you hear him? It's not a military maneuver, it's just some strikers, and they've kidnapped what's-her-name, Madame Minister Ben-Zvi."

"Yeah," said Hefetz, "but we didn't know that until now. Zohar was on his way there, now I get where he was headed so fast before. He should be right there with their correspondent. Never mind. Benizri, get down to the studio, we'll interrupt programming. Go on, get down there!"

"Here, here he is!" Aviva announced, and everyone looked to the Channel One monitor, where they could see Zohar, microphone in hand, a thick gray wool scarf wrapped around his neck. He was speaking into the camera, but there was no sound. A second later the image disappeared, and in its place a caption: TECHNICAL DIFFICULTIES, PLEASE STAY TUNED.

"Naturally," Tzippi scoffed from the doorway. "Were we really expecting a problem-free broadcast? We'd all go into shock!"

"Just tell me how we expect to make the ratings with shoddy work like this?" David Shalit grumbled.

"What I can't understand," Hefetz said despairingly in a hoarse voice, without taking his eyes from the monitor, "is why it always happens at moments like these. Sometimes I swear it feels . . . it feels like it's on purpose . . ."

"I totally don't get why a military correspondent is there," said Danny Benizri to Hefetz. "You heard them: if it's really a bunch of unemployed workers, then I'm the one that should be there, don't you think?"

"Listen, buddy," Hefetz said, cutting him off, "where's your jacket? Get yourself down to the studio right now, we're breaking in to the program. You read me?"

"Me?" Benizri protested. "There's no reason for me to be in the studio. I told you, I should be—"

"You will do what you're told to do!" Hefetz bellowed. "And one more thing: Niva, are you listening? Get me the documentary about the Hulit workers, the one Benizri showed on Rubin's program about a year ago. Get it fast."

Niva punched in the numbers on the internal phone. "The line at the archives is busy," she said quietly, and Zadik could have sworn he heard a note of satisfaction in her voice. "It could take hours," she said, her eyes fixed on the screens. Once again Zohar was on the screen, standing in front of the tunnel, a microphone in his hand, behind him pillars of smoke billowing forth. The picture disappeared again, and again the screen read TECHNICAL DIFFICULTIES, PLEASE STAY TUNED. The picture on the second monitor showed the correspondent in a military parka. "It's Sivan Gibron, the Channel Two military correspondent, their news department's latest acquisition," Hefetz declared as he tugged on his nose with fervor. "What a lucky break this guy gets on his first day on the job," he complained. Just then Zohar returned to the screen, along with his voice. The room fell silent as everyone listened to Zohar announce, his voice choked with emotion, that it had been "planned like a military operation: four trucks manned by workers from the Hulit factory trapped the car of the minister for labor and social affairs. It was the minister's driver who alerted the police . . ."

"We've never had anything like this before," Hefetz said as he slapped Zadik on the shoulder. Hefetz's gesture could have been interpreted as an expression of nervousness or anxiety, but the yellowish sparkle in his brown eyes indicated a totally different kind of excitement, an eagerness that was not entirely foreign to Zadik himself, but which had no place that morning, after the tragedy, and Zadik was about to remind Hefetz of the fact that just hours earlier they had lost Tirzah, but just then he saw, in the doorway of the newsroom, not far from where Natasha stood leaning on the door frame as though she had no interest whatsoever in what was happening in the tunnel on the Jerusalem–Etzion Bloc bypass road, Inspector Eli Bachar, who was looking at him and gesturing to him. Zadik skirted his way around the reporters and assistant producers, two maintenance workers standing in the doorway of the foreign correspondents' room, the language editor, the graphic artist, and everyone else who had heard that something big was taking place and had rushed in for an update, until he was facing Eli Bachar, and, with an odd sort of schadenfreude owed to the circumstances that were preventing him from giving Bachar his full attention, Zadik said, "So, you see how it is. . . ."

The inspector nodded. "I heard on the way over. What a catastrophe."

"You'll have to give us a few minutes," Zadik said. "I haven't had a chance to prepare people yet." He raised his eyes to the monitor and saw, on the screen, a policeman standing next to Zohar, listening to him. "One of your men. You know him?" Zadik asked. Eli Bachar blinked—he had long, dark eyelashes like a woman's, and narrow green eyes and a high forehead, only his chin was too small for such a face—and answered reticently, "Yes, that's Superintendent Shlomo Molcho, a decent guy." Zohar's voice was filling the newsroom now that someone had turned the volume up full blast.

"If that's so," Zohar intoned nasally from the entrance to the tunnel, "then the police have reason to believe that the unemployed workers are in possession of explosives, and there's no telling how far they'll take this. In the meantime," he said into the microphone, "there are still no negotiations between the unemployed workers and the police. We have been asked to inform the public that the Jerusalem–Etzion Bloc bypass road is closed to traffic and that drivers are requested to travel by alternate routes and to refrain from approaching this area."

"Benizri," Hefetz shouted at the glass partition, "what are you still doing here? Didn't I tell you to get down to the recording studio and get on the air? Nehemia is already down there, and Niva went to the archives to fetch that documentary you made about the Hulit workers last year. Why are you still here? Didn't I tell you to get down there? Did I or didn't I? Everyone heard: I did!"

Danny Benizri, who was standing inside the graphic artists' room, did not respond immediately. Zadik could see him leaning over the computer screen and explaining something to Tamari. He hurried into the room and saw the sketch she had already prepared, the roads and the tunnel with two trucks at one end and two at the other. So there actually were a few departments here where things worked properly, Zadik wished to tell someone when he had returned to his place, but when he looked up from the computer screen, his eyes met those of Arye Rubin, who was standing next to him expectantly.

"I only need two minutes," Arye Rubin told him. "Maybe three." Zadik shrugged his shoulders and spread his arms in a gesture of helplessness.

At the doorway to the room, Inspector Eli Bachar stepped backward to make way for Benizri, who was on his way out at a run, en route to the recording studio on the ground floor.

"Just two minutes," Rubin pleaded with Zadik. Zadik caught sight of Natasha watching them from the corner of the conference room.

"Hang on, Rubin, just hang on," Zadik said, pointing at the monitor. Once again the picture faded and Zohar disappeared; in his place the screen showed policemen running in every direction. "I don't get this at all," Zadik said, annoyed. "Where are they running now, what are these guys filming? Look where the Channel Two cameraman is positioned and where—"

"Zadik, calm down." Hefetz had popped up suddenly at his side and was watching both the monitor and Inspector Eli Bachar, who was leaning against the wall next to the bulletin board. Thanks to his white shirt and his short gray jacket, probably no one else there knew what he was doing in the newsroom.

"For your information," Hefetz told Zadik, "Zohar was tuned in to the police broadcasts the whole time. He's always first on-site, no other reporter was there when he arrived, but what do we get for all his efforts? Do we get anything for all his efforts? No, we don't. Who's running things around here? Us? No. Not us. Who? The technicians! So don't tell me afterward that it's a disgrace that Channel Two gets there before us, because they don't have a technicians' union!"

Zadik hoped that because of the ensuing tumult—the noise of two monitors running at once, the constant ringing of telephones, the incessant chatter—no one had heard Hefetz, but just then an unfamiliar burly man in blue coveralls poked his head in from the foreign correspondents' room and said, "How 'bout not blaming the technicians for everything that goes wrong?"

At the same time, David Shalit approached Eli Bachar, tapped him on the arm, and in an intimate, almost mocking tone said, "Inspector Eli Bachar, sir, to what do we owe this pleasure?" Eli Bachar smiled awkwardly, narrowed his eyes, and in lieu of an answer, shrugged his shoulders and nodded toward Zadik.

"What? Our big boss called you?" David Shalit asked doubtfully. "And why would that be? What have the police got to do here? And if we're talking police, where's *your* boss, Ohayon? I've heard he's on vacation. So does that mean you're his replacement?"

"Maybe they're here to look for the person who's been leaking information to us about the police," Aviva teased. She had come up behind Rubin and looked as if she were waiting in line to talk to Zadik. "You know how it is with the police, they only show up when you don't need them anymore."

"If I were you," Eli Bachar told her, "I wouldn't be quite so jovial the morning after a colleague of mine was killed. I wouldn't be up to such joking."

Hefetz turned to Zadik. "Did you invite him here?" he asked accusingly. "What are the police doing here now?"

"Ladies and gentlemen, your attention please," Zadik called out from the doorway of the newsroom, and—miraculously—the room fell silent. "This gentleman standing next to me is Inspector Eli Bachar of the Jerusalem District Police, who is here regarding Tirzah. The police are investigating possible negligence, and . . . to make a long story short, he'll be talking with people here—he'll decide who—and I would ask each and every one of you to cooperate with Inspector Bachar and any other representative of the police, because we would like this investigation to end quickly."

Natasha stood behind Rubin, pulling his sleeve; Rubin touched her arm with a calming hand. "Zadik . . . ," he said.

"Just a minute, Rubin, just wait a minute. Can't you see that I'm . . ." Natasha took a step backward.

"I don't understand this," Hefetz said irritably. "What exactly have they got to investigate here? Have they got something to investigate here? Did someone do something wrong here? She was crushed under the scenery flats and a marble pillar, wasn't she?"

"What's wrong with you, Hefetz?" Niva whispered. "Suddenly you've forgotten the rules about death under unnatural circumstances?"

"Hey, what's going on?" said the maintenance man, walking out of the foreign correspondents' room with a large plastic bucket and a putty knife splattered with white stains. He ran straight into Elmaliah the cameraman, who had entered the newsroom carrying an oversized sandwich.

"Watch where you're going!" Elmaliah scolded the maintenance man. "You almost knocked the sandwich right out of my hand." To Hefetz he said, "Don't you know that when someone dies like that, not in his bed, not from some disease, not in the hospital with a doctor's certificate, the police have to investigate if it was an accident, and if so, to determine who was responsible?"

"Sometimes the engineer has to be charged with criminal negligence—if it's a case of faulty construction," David Shalit added, placing his empty Styrofoam cup on the edge of the table.

Eli Bachar whispered something to Zadik, and Zadik raised his head and asked, "Has anyone seen Max?"

"Max Levin?" Aviva asked, surprised. "What's he got to do with . . . ah . . ." Realization dawned on her. "Because he was the one who found her . . . but he must be in the String Building, in his office."

"That's just it," Zadik explained, "he's not there. Find him for me, Aviva, we need him urgently. Avi Lachman, too, the lighting technician who was with Max when . . ." To the inspector he added, "Go with Aviva, she'll get you anyone you need, and you'll have more peace and quiet in my office, which you can use in the meantime . . ."

Aviva flashed Eli a pleasant smile and wound a platinum curl around her finger. The inspector followed obediently.

"Niva," Hefetz called. "Did you bring the VTR from the film library to the studio?"

"Yeah, yeah," she grumbled, out of breath. "I run down there like a madwoman, get to the archives, and find that Hezi . . . I'll kill him if he does that one more time . . . next time I'm not going down to the archives for you people under any circumstances, he is so disgusting. . . ."

"Why, what did he do?" David Shalit asked with a look of innocence.

"Here, they've cut into the program," Zadik said with an air of satisfaction at the sight of Nehemia the interviewer, Danny Benizri, and the director general of the Finance Ministry on the Channel One monitor. "Good job, Hefetz, you got the director of the Finance Ministry," he said, adding, "and damn fast, too."

"What do you think?" Hefetz said, making light of Zadik's praise. "They've kidnapped the labor minister, this is no game, they're gonna blow themselves up and the minister, too. So what could the director of the Finance Ministry tell me, he doesn't have time to come down to the studio? Oh, look at this guy, Sivan . . . what's his name?"

They were watching the Channel Two monitor again, the volume turned all the way down. The military correspondent stood wrapped in his parka, shivering from the cold, wiping raindrops from his brow, the microphone pressed close to his mouth, and his lips moving without a sound.

Hefetz turned up the volume on the Channel One monitor. "Sir," Danny Benizri said, addressing the Finance Ministry's director general, who sat tight-lipped as he pressed a pale blue ironed handkerchief to his shiny bald pate, "there's nothing to get angry about. I simply wish to understand what was done with the money that the government promised to give as aid to the Hulit factory last July, during the previous crisis . . ."

"First of all," the director general said, cutting Danny Benizri off as he tugged the sleeves of his blue tweed jacket over his shirt cuffs and moved his chair to the side, "I wish categorically to denounce an act that is, in my opinion, not only extremely grave, but a very, very, *very* dangerous precedent."

Danny Benizri's dark eyes were shining. He turned to the interviewer, who held up his hand to request that he wait to speak, but Danny Benizri refused to wait. He, too, cut off his interlocutor. "That's not what I asked you," he cried out.

"I want to make something perfectly clear," the director general said. "Violence such as this has no place—"

"There hasn't been any violence yet," Danny Benizri corrected him, fingering the top button on the sky-blue shirt he had slipped into just before going on the air.

"Benizri is totally out of line," Niva said in the newsroom. "What do you call *that*?" she said pointing at the Channel Two monitor, which was showing smoke billowing from the tunnel. "What's that, if not violence?"

She pinned her eyes on Arye Rubin, who was standing next to Zadik, watching the monitor. Finally he nodded in agreement.

"Hefetz," Niva said, "Tell Dalit to get Nehemia to shut Benizri up. He can't say that's not violence."

Hefetz snapped his fingers at Tzippi, the assistant producer. "Come here," he said. "Go downstairs and check what's with that VTR Niva brought from the archives, see if they've even gotten it ready. Ask Dalit." He resumed watching the monitor.

On the screen appeared the three participants in this spontaneous interview: the director general of the Finance Ministry; Danny Benizri, the correspondent for labor and social affairs; and the host, Nehemia, a veteran newsman famous for his evenhandedness, his formal manners, and the special brand of boredom he cast over his viewers. It appeared as though Nehemia had lost control for a moment; Danny Benizri was staring the director general down with sparks in his eyes.

"Ex*cuse* me," the latter was saying as he fingered the edges of his tie, "I am very sorry, but—"

Judging by the actions of the host—Nehemia was touching his earlobe, behind which was located a transmitter that was providing him with instructions from the control room—it appeared that he was indeed being told to rein in the correspondent. "Danny," he said, "Danny. Please, I must to ask you to . . . just—"

But Danny Benizri ignored Nehemia completely. He leaned toward the director general and asked, quietly, "Tell me, please, sir, what alternatives do they have?"

The thick, pale eyebrows of the director general rose halfway up his forehead, giving his round face a look of shock and wonder. "Mr. Benizri," he said, straining to maintain his composure, "are you aware of what you are implying, that it is indeed an acceptable way to get what they want? We're talking here about people who earned large sums of money from shift work, and some of them live in luxurious villas—"

"Gentlemen!" the host cried, though neither man paid him any attention.

"What?!" Benizri said, shocked. "What are you saying? Maybe they're actually millionaires!"

Nehemia touched his earlobe again, and his brows furrowed until a deep crease formed between them. "Uh . . . Danny, please," he said, waving his hand at the control room on the other side of a glass partition that could not be seen on-screen. He cast a pleading look toward the director and the producer and the rest of the staff sitting in the control room, but they could do nothing to rescue him. It was an unplanned live broadcast, and he had been unable to take charge of his guests, who were arguing as if completely oblivious to his existence.

"I can only discuss the facts," said the director general as he pored over the pages spread out on the table in front of him.

Nehemia leaned over the pages, inspecting them like someone who had been taught it was forbidden for a participant—and certainly the host himself—to appear as though he were not actively engaged in what was taking place. But there was something pathetic about the way he feigned interest in the pages on the table when in the background Benizri could be heard demanding to know, "What luxurious villas?"

The director general laid his hand on the pages. "There are workers who earned more than 30,000 shekels a month during the weeks they worked shifts—"

"You are purposely misleading the public!" Danny Benizri shouted, and cast a look of reproach at Nehemia. "He is misleading the public, not a single one of them is rich," he said emphatically, "and not a single one of them earns the kind of money he's talking about. There was only one such worker, his name was Baruch Hasson, and even in his case it was just one month, three and a half years ago, when there was a big order from Greece—"

A sudden commotion broke out in the control room, and the producer waved her arms and called on Nehemia to take charge of the discussion. Nehemia cleared his throat, shifted in his chair, touched his ear as a way of drawing strength and authority from the transmitter and from the producer's voice, and interrupted the director general. "These difficult events remind us of the tragic case of Hannah Cohen," he said, turning to Danny Benizri. "In your opinion, can matters deteriorate as dramatically in this case as they did then?"

Benizri, too, glanced sideways toward the glass partition. "If you ask me," he answered slowly, emphasizing every word, "mismanagement by the police could once again bring about tragic—"

The Finance Ministry's director general shifted in his seat and waved his hands. "Ex*cuse* me, I am terribly sorry," he insisted, "but when a small group of individuals decides to take the law into its own hands, the police have no choice but to—"

"They don't have any choice either!" Danny Benizri shouted.

In the newsroom, all eyes were on the monitor. "Whoa, has Benizri totally flipped out?" Elmaliah the cameraman asked, his mouth full. He laid the rest of his sandwich on the edge of the table and said, "What's he arguing like that for?"

A look of absolute loathing on the face of the director general shone through the television monitor. "Excuse me," he sputtered angrily at Benizri, "with all due respect, you are the correspondent for labor and social affairs, are you not? Not a spokesman for the workers. It seems to me you are meant to remain neutral, don't you think?"

Danny Benizri started to say something but Nehemia, after touching the transmitter once again, laid his hand on the reporter's arm.

"Just a moment, sir," he said to the director general, and to Danny he said, "Danny, please, I'm asking you . . . let's watch for one moment a documentary film you made about Hulit one year ago, for Arye Rubin's program *The Justice of the Sting* . . ."

But the director general refused to remain silent. He pointed an accusing finger at Danny Benizri and exclaimed, "This is outrageous, sir, simply outrageous the way you are speaking to me here!"

Salvation came from the control room, where the director cut into the discussion to run the film showing events that had taken place at the Hulit bottle factory one year earlier. Before Nehemia had a chance to say a word or announce the transition, on the screen there appeared a woman on a roof, shouting. Only someone who had been completely attuned to the program would have known that this was not taking place live.

Utter silence fell on the newsroom, until Hefetz went to the telephone, dialed, and said into the mouthpiece, "Pass me to Dalit." A moment later his shouts could be heard everywhere: "Why are there no captions? People will think this is happening now! I want him to announce again that this is footage from the archives! Take care of it, you hear me?" He turned to Niva, his face red with anger, and shouted at her. "See? You wanted a woman to be news editor?! Screwup after screwup! Am I the one screwing up here? No! Did you see who's screwing up? Did you or did you not?!"

But Niva remained unflappable. She smiled slightly and said, "Oh, yeah? And a man would have pulled it off better?"

In the meantime, Hannah Cohen could be seen and heard on the factory roof; at the bottom of the screen ran the caption, FROM OUR ARCHIVES, an overlay to an earlier caption: HANNAH COHEN, HULIT BOTTLE FACTORY, SOUTHERN ISRAEL. "Every morning for six months I've been coming to his office like a dog, I say, 'Pay us our wages, this isn't charity, it's for the work we've done,' and he, he says, 'Come back tomorrow, come back tomorrow.' Well, that's it, there are no more tomorrows! They sit in their villas, they drive Volvos, and we don't have food for our kids. No more tomorrows—what am I supposed to give my kids to eat?" People could be seen at the foot of the building, gazing up at the roof. Next, the screen showed policemen knocking at the door to the roof and threatening to break it down if the protesters tried to block it with their bodies, until finally the policemen did break the door down and the protesters were pushed backward. Some were shouting, "Don't you dare come closer," and others were hollering, "We'll burn down the factory," and in the ensuing tumult Hannah Cohen could be seen being shoved backward with the rest of the protesters, trying to maintain her balance as two policemen pressed toward her; in the next frame she was shown falling from the roof.

"Sir, would you like to comment on what we have just seen here?" Nehemia asked the Finance Ministry's director general, whose eyes were downcast.

There was silence in the newsroom for a moment until Elmaliah the cameraman, who was standing next to the water dispenser pouring sugar into a Styrofoam cup of coffee, said, "What are they showing this stuff now for? Always trying to stir up a scandal!"

"What do you want?" Niva said. "I think it's actually good that they're showing it!" She glanced at the large clock on the wall, stuck her hand into her black leather bag, and thrashed around inside it, without looking, until she succeeded in fishing out her mobile phone. "Mother," she chided after a quick automatic dial, "why didn't you call me? When did you get home?"

"As if it's going to have some effect on someone," Tzippi said from her post in the doorway. "No one gives a damn."

"So don't go out anymore," Niva chastised her mother loudly, "do you hear me? Mother, I am asking you: do not leave the house." She returned her phone to her bag, sighed, looked around to see whether there had been witnesses to this conversation, shook her head, and raised her eyes to the monitor.

"Hey, hey, look what's happening there!" Erez shouted, pointing at the Channel Two monitor. A policeman standing at the entrance to the tunnel was shouting into a megaphone. "Shimshi, I'm coming in alone, just me. Look at me." In the background stood an older, bearded man peering from behind the trucks parked near the tunnel entrance. The Channel Two correspondent was broadcasting in a whisper, as if he were filling a few dead moments in a soccer game, since the strikers had just explained that they had nothing more to lose and if the police entered they would blow themselves up along with the labor minister, her driver, and her car. "To quote him precisely," the correspondent reported, "strike leader Moshe Shimshi told police that if they enter the tunnel, 'the only thing they'll find is dead bodies,' and, uh, just a minute," he said, his voice rising. "It appears there are new developments." Suddenly the studio interview on Channel One was interrupted, and Zohar appeared on the screen, shivering in a military parka, a scarf wrapped around his neck. He was standing at the entrance to the tunnel, pillars of black smoke in the background, and speaking into the microphone. "As you can see, the strikers are burning tires at the opening of the tunnel. They are demanding to meet with Danny Benizri, the Channel One correspondent, whom they wish to make their representative during negotiations. They are burning tires and threatening to blow themselves up. The life of the minister for labor and social affairs is still endangered."

"What was that? What was that? What did he say?" Hefetz shouted, astonished. "What is it they want?"

"Exactly what you heard: they want Danny Benizri to represent them in negotiations with the government," Erez said.

"I'm going down to the recording studio," Hefetz said as he dashed out of the newsroom. Zadik opened his mouth to say something, but in the end merely followed suit after Hefetz.

Hefetz stood behind the control panel, looking into the studio through the large glass partition, Zadik at his side. Both saw the look of astonishment on Nehemia's face as the three men watched and listened to Zohar. "Did you hear what he said?" Nehemia called out to the partition. At the same instant Danny Benizri rose to his feet, quickly disconnected the microphone from his shirt collar, and stood at the doorway of the studio.

"Danny," Nehemia said, alarmed, "where are you going?" Benizri did not respond as he removed his jacket from a hanger at the door to the studio. "Danny," Nehemia called out to him, "you can't just pick up and leave in the middle of a broadcast!" On-screen the policeman with the megaphone was calling Shimshi. "Don't break contact with us. If we bring Benizri, will you let him come in?"

Danny Benizri left the studio and passed through to the control room.

"Where exactly do you think you're going?" Hefetz asked him, but—unbeknownst to Hefetz—Zadik had already confirmed it with a nod of his head and Dalit, the editor, had left her chair and was running after him with a monitor and lighting. "You're not going anywhere!" Hefetz bellowed, but Danny Benizri was already on his way out. Just then the phone rang with a request that Zadik return to his office, since the department heads were already waiting to begin their meeting with him.

At the entrance to his office, Rubin was waiting for him, an accusatory look on his face; Natasha stood behind him in the hallway as if she were his shadow. "No way," Zadik said, "I don't have time now. You saw what's going on," he said, scolding Rubin. "Matty," he called to Matty Cohen, who had just entered the secretary's office.

Matty Cohen cast a look of misery at Aviva. "I didn't hear about Tirzah until now, when I came into the building and saw the death notices. I didn't know anything about it. Zadik, I've got to have a word with you—"

"Take a number," Zadik said with a sigh. "I don't know what's with all you people today. We've got a meeting."

"Zadik," Matty Cohen said, breathing heavily and wiping the sweat from his ruddy jowls with his hand, "I've got to talk to you for a minute." He looked around suspiciously, grabbed Zadik by the arm, and whispered, "Or with someone from the Police Department, it's about something . . . I . . . last night . . ." Zadik, too, looked around, taking in the department heads standing in the doorway; the head of Maintenance was already in the office making himself a cup of coffee, while Max Levin and Inspector Eli Bachar were on their way to a side office that Aviva had requisitioned for them.

"Okay," Zadik said to Matty Cohen. "But just for one short minute, and then we've got to get this meeting started. Come, step outside."

They stood in the hallway. Matty Cohen peered toward the stairway and to the far end of the hallway, as if to verify that no one could hear them. "Listen," he said, a note of urgency in his voice. "Last night I came to the String Building, I was on my way up to the roof to put a stop to the filming, Benny Meyuhas's project, but in the end I didn't get there because my kid, the little one, you know, I've told you, he's got spastic bronchitis, my wife didn't know what to do and I had to get him to the emergency room. That's why I didn't hear anything about Tirzah until I came in this morning and saw the death notices."

Zadik looked at him, impatient. "But what's this got to do with Tirzah? And what have you got to tell the police?"

"That's just it, I . . ." Matty Cohen hesitated, passing his hand over his huge belly. For a moment they could hear only the voices that burst forth from the television screens in every room, sentence fragments from which they could discern certain words, like "Hulit factory"; Zadik caught wind of Danny Benizri's name alongside Matty Cohen's noisy, quickened breaths. Cohen whispered, "I think I saw Tirzah there, next to the scenery flats. I was walking up above, you know, on the catwalk toward the roof, I was holding on to the railing, and I looked down, . . . I saw her with someone, I'm almost certain it was Tirzah, not completely sure but almost, and there was someone there with her, a man or a woman, I only heard Tirzah saying, 'No, no, no.'"

"What time was this?" Zadik asked.

"I can tell you exactly, since I told you that because of my kid . . . my wife called just then . . . a minute later she phoned, and that was at ten minutes to twelve. She'd said right from the start that I was crazy for going out in such bad weather in the middle of the night to catch them filming, as if . . ."

Zadik suddenly felt weak, and leaned against the wall. In a shaky voice he said, "Ten minutes to twelve? Are you sure?"

"Absolutely. I told you, my wife phoned just then."

"But they say that she apparently died at around twelve," Zadik said, thinking aloud. "You understand, that means that . . . it's as though . . . but you're not certain it was Tirzah you saw?"

"No, not completely," Matty Cohen admitted. "Fairly certain, but I don't know who . . ."

"So let's forget about it for a little while," Zadik advised. "Later, after the meeting, we'll talk about it, maybe we need to . . . but then the police will be all over the place here and . . . let's wait a bit . . ."

"Zadik," Aviva called out to the hallway, clearly displeased, from her desk just outside his office. "Everyone's waiting in there. What should I tell them?"

# CHAPTER THREE

"If you don't pull your head out of your own heap of garbage, you'll never know what's happening on your own street—even if you are a smart guy like Shimshi," Rachel Shimshi announced. "When he's stuck in his own shit he can't see nothing." She tightened her grip on Esty's arm and pulled her down next to her at the edge of the sofa. Of the five women gathered in front of the television in her living room silently watching black clouds of smoke encircle Danny Benizri as he stood at the entrance to the tunnel, Rachel was most worried about Esty—not only because she was pregnant after a string of troubles that had made them think she would never be able to give birth, but because of the promise she had made to Adele. During Adele's last days, when she was barely able to utter a word, Rachel had promised to watch over her daughter.

Esty shook off Rachel Shimshi's grip, stood up from the sofa, and, pointing at the television, shouted, "Let go of me! Do you see what's going on here?"

"No one here's blind, we all see what's going on," Rachel Shimshi said, her eyes on the black smoke pouring from the tunnel that had completely engulfed Danny Benizri. Years earlier, Danny Benizri had visited their home, had eaten with them, and because of that Shimshi thought he was on their side and had specially requested his presence, alone. When Rachel had awoken at two a.m. and found Shimshi dressing in the dark like a thief, she had tried to stop him. She told him there was no point to it. She still couldn't calm down when she thought about how he had tried to get out of the house without her noticing, how he had taken his clothes into the kitchen and dressed there; he had even placed his shoes in the hall, thinking he would manage to leave without waking her. Shimshi didn't want trouble. But a woman, even if she's only given birth to one baby, is never able to get a decent night's sleep again. And if you've raised six children, well, forget it, one ear is always open, listening for their cries. Ever since they were born, she's heard every little noise. Noise? Even when there's no noise at all, it's enough that somebody just shifts in his bed. On tiptoe, barefoot, Shimshi went to the kitchen. He didn't even drink coffee or turn on the light. How many times had she told him there was no point to waging war, that the owners of the factory would win out, as always: the rich get richer from every little thing, it's only the poor that get screwed. How many times had she told him that it was a waste of time, that they'd already lost everything anyway, that they were better off getting their severance pay and taking their chances. But Shimshi, he couldn't give in, especially not him: he was the local union leader; he had to set a good example. But why did he have to take Avram with him, with Esty here, pregnant, after so many troubles? And not just Avram: he'd taken four trucks from the factory.

Ever since Shimshi had left home that night—with the expression he'd had on his face when she caught him, she would have thought he was headed for some other woman if she didn't know him so well—she'd had this movie in her head, something starring Clint Eastwood she'd seen a while back. She couldn't remember the name of the film, but these scenes kept playing again and again where this guy does things his own way, even if it means he'll die for it, die fighting the scoundrels. That's what they certainly were, scoundrels, she knew it for sure, all those politicians in the government, and that labor minister—it's clear the woman would never lift a finger to help anybody. Rachel had told Shimshi "over my dead body" and had tried lying in front of the door, and if he'd tried to fight with her, she would have managed to stop him for sure with her fingernails. But Shimshi was no fool. He knew her too well. He refused to fight; instead, he got down on his knees next to the door and said, in his quietest voice, "Rachel, do me a favor, I don't have a choice. If I don't do this I won't even have my honor left. Try to understand, this is bigger than everything, bigger than paying the electricity bill." She could not stop him. He did not want to tell her what exactly they were planning; she thought they were going to shut themselves up inside the factory. But now, what she was watching on television, well, she'd had no idea they were talking about dynamite and blowing up the tunnel and kidnapping the minister. Not a clue. Nothing, either, about wanting Danny Benizri there. But Shimshi had looked at her in that particular way he had, and she no longer had the heart to give him more trouble than he already had—and anyway, she understood it wouldn't do her any good.

It was high time to empty the ashtrays and make some more tea. Rachel Shimshi narrowed her eyes to slits: the television people were stalling for time, while here, all the girls were waiting for her, like she was their leader or something. As if it wasn't enough already that her husband headed the union. Fanny, tugging at the ends of her yellow hair and patting her baby's back even though he had already quieted down, smoked cigarette after cigarette. Esty, too, with that big belly; even after she'd finally gotten pregnant she didn't stop smoking. And Rosie, with her legs swollen from diabetes. If you looked at them, all you would see was—there was no denying it—a sorry bunch of women. And the children, what would be with them? Better not to say a word about what she thought about that, what would happen to their children. She already knew what would become of their men, whether Danny Benizri managed to help them or not: they would wind up in jail, every last one of them. Her Shimshi and Fanny's Gerard and Simi's Meir and Esty's Avram. To leave behind a woman in her first pregnancy after all those troubles and run off in the middle of the night with a bunch of old men who have nothing to lose; that's what she herself said to Shimshi when she caught him trying to slip out of the house at two in the morning without her noticing, thinking she's some old lady who doesn't hear well anymore. You're an old man, she'd told him, you don't have the strength for these kinds of wars anymore. That's exactly why, he'd answered: because I'm old I have nothing to lose. It wasn't that she didn't understand him: and how she understood him. But when a guy like him, with his intelligence, someone who cared about his kids and grandkids, about little Dudy just one month away from his bar mitzvah; how could he have planned all that—fire and smoke, kidnapping the labor minister—without breathing a word of it to her? Only someone bent on self-destruction would kidnap the minister of labor and social affairs and set an ultimatum for blowing himself and everything else up. Here in her living room the girls are shouting. What are they shouting about? she wonders. Only God can help them now, only He knows what will happen.

In the backseat of the mobile communications van speeding toward the Jerusalem–Etzion Bloc bypass road, Danny Benizri changed out of his blue shirt and into a black turtleneck he had in his bag, calculating that he had twenty minutes until he would be on the air again, twenty minutes until they would reach the tunnel. In those twenty minutes he would have to have a word with Tikvah, and calm his mother down. He knew he could not appear too elegant or self-satisfied; that would come off very badly on-screen if he were reporting from the field or even inside the tunnel, with all those explosives and everything. He was glad he had his khaki windbreaker along; it looked good, as though in the hustle-bustle of an emergency he had not had time to get it all together. Before he had even finished shoving his arm into his sleeve, his cell phone rang and he knew exactly what to expect. "What is it, Tikvah? What's wrong?" he asked, feigning ignorance, because perhaps she had not heard the news yet and did not know what was happening. For a long moment he listened to the cries of Danny-I'm-so-frightened she managed to slip in between sobs, and then said, "Tikvah, calm down. First of all, calm down. Pretty soon the baby will start crying too. Oh, there, she's started up, see what you've done? There's nothing to be frightened about, you know Shimshi and his whole family, they won't do a thing to me. Not to me or anybody else."

For a moment she stopped wailing, but she reminded him what Shimshi had said on television, how he had threatened to blow himself up with everyone.

"So he said he was going to blow himself up," Danny said dismissively. "So what if that's what he said. Haven't you learned anything yet? It's all for the purpose of attracting attention. Tell my mother, tell her . . . calm her down, tell her everything's just . . . tell her not to . . . not to call me now." Quickly, before she had time to start crying again, he asked about the vaccinations and the visit to the Mother & Child Clinic and the droplets of salt water that Tikvah had tried to drip into the baby's nose on the recommendation of the pediatrician Tikvah adored and he could not stand. After that he looked at the rain-washed streets out the window of the van as it raced through the city. Who could have guessed that the morning would pass thus, beginning with talk about Tirzah's death and ending with a mad dash to the bypass-road tunnel. Then again, the day was not over yet, nothing was over yet: at the entrance to the tunnel, not far from the parked police vans, black smoke was billowing from within, where Moshe Shimshi, in a gray woolen cap and blue dungarees, was waiting for him.

Zohar, the military correspondent, moved aside, his mouth askew. "The asshole won't let me in," he whispered to Danny Benizri. "He knows I'm from Israel Television, but he won't let me in. They're waiting for you—and only you—like you're the messiah."

Danny Benizri spread his arms in a gesture of humility as if to say he had not brought about any of this, then eyed Zohar with suspicion, slapping him on the back. "Good job, Zohar, you did really nice work here," he said. It is easy to stir up envy in someone you work with without ever doing anything to provoke it, without even noticing it at all, and then one day you find yourself with another enemy, just because once someone asked only for you. What could he do about it? After all, he had not intended to take anything away from anyone. It was not his responsibility. On the other hand, to lose an opportunity like this would be simply inhuman. "Listen," he said, clearing his throat, "I don't . . . ," but Zohar had already turned away and was gathering his belongings.

"Go on already, get in there," Zohar said as he climbed into the van. "I'm leaving this guy here for you," he added with a grin as he put his hand on the shoulder of Ijo the cameraman. "You owe me one: they caught us with our pants down, no soundman, nothing. Ijo is your whole crew."

"Will they let him in with me?" Danny Benizri called to a policeman armed with a megaphone who was standing near Moshe Shimshi.

The policeman shrugged, turned to Shimshi, and pointed to Ijo. "Are you willing to let the cameraman in, too?" he asked.

"Just Benizri," Shimshi answered, his eyes downcast. "Only him and nobody else."

"If you need me, I'll be waiting right here," Ijo said, handing Benizri the video camera and the monitor he had taken from the van. Danny Benizri approached Shimshi cautiously, fearful of his reaction to the camera or the monitor. But Shimshi took a long, silent look at him and said, finally, "You see? You didn't come visit us at home, so we're meeting here."

Benizri forced a smile. He knew there was nothing to fear, he had known Shimshi for years, way back from the time he was a junior television researcher and Shimshi was already active in the Histadrut, the General Federation of Labor. It seemed funny to be wary of Shimshi at all, but still he felt a certain panic awaken in him. Maybe it was Shimshi's quick, noisy breaths, or Shimshi himself, who looked like he was stuck inside some sort of nightmare. It is a known fact that fear can turn a harmless creature into something quite dangerous when it is pushed into a corner.

"Listen," Shimshi said as he pulled him into the tunnel. "We have a problem here."

Benizri's palms grew moist, the handle of the monitor sticky in his hands. Shimshi ran ahead into the tunnel, and he followed suit, the monitor and the video camera slowing him down. From a distance he could see the two trucks that were blocking everything behind them. A group of men in blue dungarees and wool caps stepped aside to make way for him to pass by. A gray Volvo was parked on the far side of the trucks, and already from a distance he recognized Azriel, chauffeur to Timnah Ben-Zvi, the minister of labor and social affairs, who stood with his elbows on the roof of the car, his head between his hands. Shimshi came to a sudden halt at the car. Azriel straightened up, ignoring Shimshi, fixing his large bright eyes on Danny Benizri and rubbing his heavy chin with a trembling hand.

"Where's the minister?" Benizri asked.

Azriel indicated the back seat of the Volvo with his head. "She's not in good shape," he whispered. "I don't know what to do."

Shimshi cleared his throat. "That's it, what I was telling you," he explained to Benizri. "We have a problem, she doesn't . . . how should I say, she doesn't feel so well. Better we should finish this business quick." He removed his wool cap and thrust his fingers into the thinning gray hair plastered to his scalp.

"What's wrong with her?" Benizri asked, alarmed. He breathed deeply and coughed as a cloud of black smoke filled the tunnel.

"She didn't feel well," Shimshi said as Benizri laid the monitor at Azriel's feet and rushed to look inside the car.

The minister of labor and social affairs lay crumpled on the backseat of the car. Someone had placed her purse under her head. Her eyes were closed. Benizri squeezed inside the car. "Is she conscious?" he asked.

"She passed out!" Shimshi called.

"My ass, she passed out!" shouted one of the two workers standing nearest the car. "She's just pretending. It's all a big act."

Benizri pressed her wrist; her pulse was faint and irregular. He looked at her ashen face and listened to her labored breathing, then took a look around the car and proceeded to lift her into a sitting position. He removed her black wool jacket and unbuttoned her light blue blouse.

"Hey there!" Azriel called to him, alarmed. "What are you doing to her?"

"Don't worry, I was a combat medic in the army," Danny Benizri said. In one swift movement he lifted her into his arms and unfastened the hooks of her bra, raising the cups off her chest and exposing her small, white breasts. He was surprised at their erect firmness, and the fact that he was even noticing them suddenly embarrassed him, so that he looked around to see whether anyone else was watching. He slapped her cheeks lightly; she nearly slipped out of his arms, but he held on tightly, and with his foot pushed open the door of the Volvo so that it would not close. "Shimshi," he shouted, "Shimshi, it's dangerous what you guys are doing."

"Not at all," called back the younger of the two men standing near Shimshi lighting a cigarette. "It's all a big act. She learned it watching soap operas."

"Shimshi," Benizri warned, "I'm telling you, I was a medic in the army, I've seen things. This is dangerous. You can't know if she has some kind of medical problem, you can't take that chance. She could have asthma or an allergy or even diabetes—"

"Asthma. She has asthma attacks," Azriel said, raising himself to his full height. "I told them, but they won't listen."

Danny Benizri covered her with her wool jacket, climbed out of the car, and stood close to Shimshi. "Listen to what I'm telling you," he whispered. "This could end badly, it could . . . she could suffocate, and then you guys are totally screwed. Believe me, I know what I'm talking about. Get her out of here, fast. If something happens to her, the police will come in here full force, explosives or not, and they'll be pulling bodies out of here. I'm telling you, it'll be a disaster."

Mauling his wool cap between his fingers, Shimshi glanced toward his cohorts as they walked toward the trucks.

"Let her leave now," Danny Benizri said. "Get her out of here before you have a disaster on your hands, and I . . . Get her out of here and keep me here in her place. I'll be your hostage."

"I'm not in this alone," Shimshi whispered, folding his cap. "I can't make a decision like that on my own, I need to consult with my men."

"So consult with them. Quickly," Benizri said, glancing at the monitor. He saw the director general of the Finance Ministry blinking at the social worker brought into the studio in place of him.

Shimshi stepped aside and gathered the men around him. Danny Benizri climbed back into the car and placed the minister's head in his lap.

"Got any water?" he asked Azriel, who quickly opened the front door of the car and handed him a small bottle of mineral water.

"I always . . . I keep a bottle on hand in case of . . ." Azriel stammered.

"Do you know if she has an inhaler?" Benizri asked. At the same time he pulled the purse from under her head and opened it. "Does she have Ventolin or something?"

"Hey, what's with you?" Azriel asked, stunned. "What are you doing, taking her purse . . . that's the minister's private stuff, you can't . . ."

Danny Benizri searched through the purse, found an inhaler, opened the minister's mouth, blocked her nose, and pressed on the inhaler.

Azriel stood next to the car, and from where Benizri was sitting, he could see only his hands, the knuckles of which Azriel was busy cracking. "God help us," Benizri could hear him mumbling.

Shimshi sidled up to the car, shaking his head. "She stays put," he said. "We're only willing to let her leave after we've reached a deal."

"Shimshi," Danny Benizri pleaded, "did you explain to them how you guys are complicating matters? This is serious, there'll be dead bodies here, I'm telling you."

"Nothing I can do about that," Shimshi said quietly. "She stays put until we have a deal. If she leaves, nobody will talk to us. They won't give us the time of day."

"How can there be a deal?" Danny Benizri asked, his eyes on the monitor. "How can you possibly reach a deal under these circumstances?"

"You're going to get it for us," Shimshi said. "That's why you're here. We'll explain what we want, and you'll get it for us. It's all up to you now."

Eli Bachar stood in the small anteroom leading to the director's office and watched the people gathering there in front of the television monitor. Aviva's desk, with its telephones and computer, stood under the window, between the entrance to Zadik's office and the door to the left, which led to the room known as the "little office." The little office contained a desk, a few chairs, an armchair covered in orange plastic, a large, empty hot-water urn, several coffee mugs, and a container of artificial sweetener. The room had the look of a place meant for the director's more intimate meetings, or gatherings of senior staff members. From the way the mugs were arranged and from the layer of dust that had collected there, it was clear that no one had used it in a while. Zadik opened the door for him and instructed Aviva to summon Max Levin, head of the Props Department, along with Avi the lighting technician. Both were now standing in front of the monitor in the secretary's office, while Eli Bachar himself stood in the doorway, watching what was transpiring there.

It was possible to learn exactly how matters were handled and settled right there in the hallway in front of the office of the secretary to the director of Israel Television. With great interest Eli Bachar watched Arye Rubin, the man responsible for exposing the bribery scandal that had rocked the Israel Police and brought about the dismissals of several high-ranking police officers and the commander of the Northern District, turning Rubin into the most resented man among all the district commanders. The scandal had also undermined relations between the director of Israel Television and the local district commander, and—there, Arye Rubin had just slipped quietly into Zadik's office and shut the door behind him. Too bad: it was precisely that conversation which Eli Bachar would like to have heard. Four other people were already crammed into the crowded anteroom, but the secretary would not let them enter until the door opened and Zadik called them. That young woman with the wool scarf was leaning in the doorway biting her fingernails.

Eli Bachar had seen her earlier, standing in the hallway; now she was glancing in turn at her watch and the door to Zadik's office as though her life depended on what came out of there. She's not beautiful, this young woman, there is something hungry about her drawn face—that's what Michael Ohayon would say if he were describing her; it was he who had taught Eli Bachar how to look at people. He could not predict what Michael would say about Aviva, the bombshell secretary, who was constantly playing with her blond curls and who had not taken her eyes off him, even when she was whispering on the telephone, which never stopped ringing. He had trouble discerning the true nature of the way she stared at him; ostensibly she was watching him with suspicion—testing him, as it were—but there was something else, a certain sparkle, that made it seem she was making eyes at him.

They were all watching the small television screen mounted on the wall, and from every office you could hear the voices of Danny Benizri from inside the tunnel and the director general of the Finance Ministry, who was now sitting in the recording studio with Nehemia, the host, and with a very fat woman who clearly had once been attractive; at the bottom of the screen a caption flashed: SARIT HERMONI, SOCIAL WORKER. The broadcast flipped back and forth between the two locations, and everyone watched in silence; only Aviva continued whispering into the phone so as not to disturb the people gathered around her. Everyone was behaving as if they were in a command room at the outbreak of a war, in spite of the fact that nothing was happening there, where they were, but rather on the screen. Matty Cohen was sitting next to Aviva's desk; Zadik had suggested that Eli Bachar speak with Matty after their meeting, since he had been there the night before and there was a chance Matty had even seen Tirzah. ("Too bad we weren't talking about the messiah," Aviva had exclaimed in her nasally voice when Matty walked in. "We were looking for you before. Where have you been?" Matty Cohen had drawn near and said, "I was in the emergency room at Hadassah Hospital with my kid, that's where." He had fallen heavily into a chair and added, "I am dying for a cup of coffee, I didn't sleep a wink all night, haven't even changed clothes. I've been wearing this suit since yesterday. Look," he said, pointing at a spot on the end of his tie. "Well," Aviva had replied, "you can at least take off your tie. What are you so dressed up for? Got some reception, a meeting with the minister?" "I told you," he retorted, "it's from yesterday, and yesterday there was a meeting of the board of directors with the minister. I couldn't . . .") And now he was watching the monitor, his hands folded across his enormous belly. Eli watched him with interest, trying to figure out how people could let themselves go to the extent that their breathing sounded as if they were choking on their own corpulent flesh. This Matty Cohen did not even look very old, not much beyond forty.

"Give us a few minutes while we figure out what's going on there," Zadik had told him when he had left him in the little office. But Eli Bachar was no clueless little schoolboy: he refused to sit alone in a closed room. That was why he was now standing in the doorway, listening to Matty Cohen say, "They've gone completely insane," without taking his eyes off the screen. "Who's ever heard of such a thing?"

"They're not insane at all," retorted Niva, the newsroom secretary, who was leaning on Aviva's desk perched like a stork, one foot in a wool sock removed from its heavy clog and resting on her other calf. "They're not insane, because you really can't get anywhere without resorting to violence."

"But they won't gain anything!" Hefetz, the newsroom chief, shouted at her. Earlier, Eli had watched him trying to speak with the girl standing in the doorway, biting her fingernails while staring intently at the door to Zadik's office. She appeared to be the only one there uninterested in what was happening in the tunnel, her only interest being Zadik's door, as if she were awaiting some redemption from there. "What will they gain? Will they gain anything this way? No, they won't gain anything!"

The telephone rang, but Aviva did not answer. Her eyes did not move from the screen; she was transfixed.

"Listen." Matty Cohen was speaking to him suddenly in a quiet voice. "I want to tell you something, when this," he said, indicating the monitor, "is over. Zadik told me you're, well, looking into what happened last night, and I—" He looked around suspiciously, then waved his hand as if sorry he had said anything at all. "Later, I'll tell you later, when this is over," he repeated, wiping his shiny forehead and loosening his tie.

There are rare moments when the news media bring about true, immediate, and visible changes in reality itself. Such was the moment when Danny Benizri metamorphosed from a reporting correspondent or even a negotiator between warring camps into an active factor in attaining an agreement between the workers and the Finance Ministry. Thus, as Eli stood watching the monitor, he saw how, all at once, the broadcast moved from the television studio to the tunnel, where Danny Benizri was acting as spokesman to the workers. "You're standing there," he would tell Ohayon later, "and suddenly you see how the director general of the Finance Ministry has been pushed into a corner on live television! I couldn't believe my eyes! He had no way of getting himself out of it! All at once you see Shimshi dictating to Benizri, and on a split screen, what can I tell you? I felt like, I just couldn't believe my eyes! I'm telling you, we were all standing there watching, everybody who was in that room, and not one of us was breathing!"

Not only in Aviva's office, but in the halls and the canteen and the control rooms and the foyer; everywhere in the building and, it would appear, everywhere in the country, people had stopped to watch and listen. Shimshi, his voice hoarse with smoke, dictated the text of the agreement that the director general would sign, which Danny Benizri repeated word by word. Utter silence reigned in Aviva's office when the monitors broadcast Danny Benizri, seen standing next to the labor minister's car, saying, "Nehemia, perhaps the director general will take a pad of paper and write . . ."

"Danny," the studio host said, cutting him off, since just then the camera had returned to the studio, and the director general of the Finance Ministry was whispering something to Nehemia, who nodded and said to the camera, "Can you hear us?" while the director general hastened to say, "This is no way to handle matters."

One of the people present in Aviva's office could have been expected to interject a sarcastic comment in response to the words of the Finance Ministry's director general, but they all remained silent, as Danny Benizri returned to the screen from inside the tunnel.

"You have no choice, sir," Danny Benizri said, hunched over with cold. He gestured to the gray Volvo. "Mrs. Ben-Zvi has got to be taken out of here quickly, her condition is . . ." As he spoke, the camera returned once again to the studio, where someone had entered and was, at that very moment, placing a pen and paper in front of the director general.

"I don't believe it," Matty Cohen whispered without removing his eyes from the monitor. He wiped his face again.

The monitor was showing the tunnel again, Benizri and Shimshi standing next to the trucks. Shimshi's face could be seen clearly as he issued a warning: "He'd better be writing this down, 'cause I'm not gonna repeat myself." Shimshi turned to the men behind him and shouted, "Quiet, keep it down!" To Benizri he said, "Go on, get started. Tell him to get started."

In spite of all the preparations, the people crammed into Aviva's office were stunned to listen to the television correspondent reciting in rhythm, as if dictating. "The director general of the Finance Ministry promises to . . ." Benizri turned to Shimshi for confirmation.

"*Personally* promises," Shimshi added.

"Personally promises," Danny Benizri repeated, his pale face filling the screen for a moment before the camera returned to the television studio and the shocked face of the Finance Ministry's director general.

"Will you look at that," Niva mumbled, still leaning on Aviva's desk, "the DG is actually writing."

Benizri and Shimshi returned to the screen. Danny Benizri was dictating straight to the camera: ". . . and will carry out in full within twenty-four hours all agreements regarding salary and severance pay signed by the director general himself seven months ago but never implemented."

Behind him, Shimshi's voice could be heard. "I want to see the agreement in writing."

"How are they going to show it to him?" Aviva asked, startled, her eyes on the monitor.

Benizri said to the camera, "Show us the studio."

As he stroked his neck, Eli Bachar could hear Matty Cohen's noisy breathing. "What a production," Matty Cohen said as the screen split into two again: the right side showed the studio, the camera focused on the director general as he leaned over the paper in front of him and signed; the left side of the screen showed the group of workers huddled around Danny Benizri, looking into the monitor in front of him.

"Okay, Danny," Nehemia said from the studio, holding up the paper to the camera. "The director general has signed, now it's time for your side to act."

On the left side of the screen Shimshi's hand could be seen fluttering over the paper, hesitating, then finally signing. One of the men had leaned over, and Shimshi was using his back as a desk. Then Benizri took the paper from his hands and held it up to the camera.

Everyone in the secretary's office applauded and cheered, except for Aviva, who hurried to dig about in her large purse as though she had been waiting for the moment she would be free to do so. Just then the door to Zadik's office opened, and Zadik stood there, radiant, and called to everyone standing nearby: "Don't say we always screw up. Did you see who saved the day?"

Hefetz, who was standing quite close, said with a big mirthless grin, his eyes blinking behind the thick lenses of his glasses, "Good work, everybody, great job. A big day for the News Department."

"I don't know what you're all so excited for," Aviva grumbled as she pushed her purse aside in anger. "Nothing good will come of it, you'll see. Remember what I said. Remember, Niva. Are you listening?"

"Why do you always have to be such a killjoy?" Niva said, offended. She returned her foot to her clog. "You always have to put a damper on everyone's happiness, as if—"

"It's not my fault," Aviva said irritably. "That's life."

Arye Rubin emerged from Zadik's office and approached the young woman in the doorway. Eli Bachar could only hear him say, "It'll be fine," saw Rubin place his hand on her shoulder, watched her face brighten. He also noticed Hefetz watching them. For an instant it seemed to him, to Eli Bachar, that Hefetz's dark face paled when the young woman embraced Rubin.

"Who's she?" Eli Bachar asked Aviva quietly.

Aviva looked at Eli and then at the young woman and answered distractedly, "Who? Natasha? That's Natasha." She clapped her hands like a nursery school teacher and called aloud: "Hefetz, Matty, Yaacobi—all the department heads—you can go into Zadik's office, the meeting is beginning. You're already way behind schedule."

Hefetz stopped for a moment to watch the monitor as Benizri gazed at the minister's Volvo being escorted by a police car, its siren wailing. Hefetz shook his head, muttered, "*Nu, nu,* if you think this is all behind us you've got another thing coming," and entered Zadik's office. Inside the office he could be heard saying, "Don't say I didn't tell you so. Did I or did I not tell you: nothing good will come of this. Can something good come of this? No. Nothing good at all will come of this."

"You, too," Aviva said, pointing Rubin and Matty Cohen to Zadik's open door. "Max will be in in a moment, after the policeman is finished with him." Eli Bachar stood in his place, watching them enter Zadik's office. At the entrance to the office Rubin stopped Matty Cohen and asked him quietly—Eli Bachar strained to hear the question—"Is it true you were there last night?" He saw Matty Cohen nod, his face averted to avoid meeting Rubin's gaze, but his eyes met Eli's instead, and he lowered them quickly to the brown wall-to-wall carpet.

"You wanted to put a stop to the production?" Rubin asked him, his tone threatening. "You wanted to stop work on *Iddo and Eynam*?" Matty Cohen breathed deeply and spread his hands wide, as if to say he had no choice.

"Now?! At this stage, after the whole thing has almost been completed?"

Matty Cohen merely shrugged his shoulders and made a face as if to say there was nothing he could do about it.

"We'll talk about this after the meeting," Rubin told him.

"After the meeting I have to speak with the police," Matty Cohen answered, glancing to the side at Eli Bachar.

"Why do you have to speak to the police?"

Matty Cohen shrugged and looked around. "That's what they want. Because . . . ," he said, shifting his weight from foot to foot, "because of Tirzah."

"So after that," Rubin said.

"Where is everybody, what's with you people?" Zadik shouted in the direction of the door to his office. "Why aren't you coming in? We're waiting for you two."

Matty Cohen cast Zadik a questioning look. "Should I talk to him now or not?" he asked, indicating Eli Bachar.

"Now," Eli Bachar said from the doorway of the little office. "Come speak with me first." He made way for Matty Cohen to pass by.

"Hang on a minute," Matty Cohen said. "I've got to have a cup of coffee from Zadik's room. I didn't sleep all night. I'll just bring myself a cup of coffee."

At first the two men sat without speaking. Each time the monitor in Aviva's room fell silent, or between rings of the telephone, Matty Cohen could be heard gulping down his coffee noisily or breathing heavily. His flushed and swollen face and his belabored, grating breaths roused Eli Cohen's suspicions: the man looked as though he might choke to death at any minute. Michael Ohayon had taught him to be quiet and wait, but time was pressing and Matty Cohen was not suspected of any wrongdoing and quite shortly he would have to speak with Max Levin and with the lighting technician; after all, this was only a work-related accident, so there was no point in creating a ruckus. (That's what Ohayon had said at night when he had phoned him: "There's no point in my coming. This is an accident, it's standard; what's the matter with you? Are you crumbling under the pressure?" And Eli, in a flash of inspiration, had said, "It's just that I miss you so much, I have no life without you," to which Ohayon had responded with a laugh: "You've got just a few more hours to endure. It's after one a.m. now, just hold yourself together for another seven or eight hours.") "I understand you were in the vicinity last night," Eli Bachar said at last, noting wistfully that Matty Cohen had at that very same moment opened his mouth to speak, then closed it, like some fish in distress.

"Vicinity?" he asked. "What . . . oh, you mean the place where Tirzah . . . ?"

Eli Bachar nodded. "Were you there at night before she was killed? Did you see her there?"

Matty Cohen explained that just before midnight he had taken the catwalk over the scenery storerooms and that Tirzah had been standing below him, next to the scenery flats.

"Did she see you?" Eli Bachar asked.

"I don't know, I don't think so," Matty Cohen said thoughtfully. "I was on my way to the roof, where they were filming Benny Meyuhas's film. I didn't want to dawdle. And she . . . she wasn't alone down there."

"She wasn't alone?" Eli Bachar swallowed his astonishment and repeated his question to gain time. That, too, he had learned from Ohayon years earlier: exaggerated expressions of surprise will cause the person under investigation to guard his tongue; he will no longer be spontaneous, and you will no longer hear what you could have heard from him. "That is to say, she was with someone?"

"Yes. But I don't know who that was, because it was pretty dark down there and she was hidden by the scenery flats. I could barely make her out, just her boots and her voice."

"Did she say anything in particular?" Eli asked.

"Not exactly, she just said, like, what I think she said was, 'No, no,' or something like that."

"Who was she talking to?" Eli Bachar asked without disguising his agitation. His pulse was racing with this sudden change of circumstance. "Who was with her?"

"That's just it," Matty Cohen said as he pulled down the sleeves of his blue suit jacket and inspected a gold button. "I don't know."

"Male or female?" Eli Bachar asked pleasantly, as if there were no urgency in the response.

Matty Cohen frowned in bewilderment. "I can't for the life of me say, it was dark and the other person wasn't talking."

"What exactly did you see?" Eli Bachar asked. "Describe it for me as if . . . as if I were a news reporter asking you exactly what you had seen."

"It was like this," he answered. "Someone phoned to say that Benny Meyuhas was filming at night—"

"Who?" Eli Bachar asked. "Who called to tell you that?" He scribbled something on the pad of legal paper perched on his knees.

"What does it matter who? Someone phoned," Matty Cohen answered irritably. "It had been decided that he would have to stop filming because the entire budget had been used up. I came there to catch them red-handed and put a stop to the production. I knew they were on the roof of the String Building."

Eli Bachar's hand stopped moving across the page. "What? What's that?"

"The String Building," Matty Cohen answered impatiently. "The other building, where they build the scenery, where . . . *nu,* String, haven't you been over to the other building? Weren't you there, where they found Tirzah?"

"Yeah, I was. Is that the String Building?"

"That's what it's called, because once it was a string factory," Matty Cohen explained. "I don't know if you noticed or not, but there is this small flight of stairs that goes up to the second floor, a sort of half-story up, and there's this narrow open hallway, a catwalk with a railing that's above the carpentry workshop and the rooms where they build the scenery. Anyway, you can walk down that catwalk and see what's going on below, no problem. So I was holding on to the railing and walking fast. I was really tired and in a pretty bad mood because I knew that . . . well, it's not very nice to have to put a stop to filming in the middle, especially not with someone like Benny Meyuhas, who . . ." Matty Cohen fell silent, lifted himself from the chair with difficulty, removed a crumpled checkered handkerchief from his trousers, and wiped his face. "Are you hot too, or is it only me? The heat is killing me here," he complained.

"No, I'm not too hot, but maybe it's the central heating that's bothering you," Eli Bachar answered. He touched the radiator, and a layer of peeling yellowed oil paint stuck to his finger. "Actually, it's stone cold," he said with surprise. "The heating isn't even on."

"Cutbacks," Matty Cohen said with satisfaction. "We only begin heating from four or five in the afternoon, depending on the temperature outside. Where were we?" he asked, glancing at his watch impatiently.

"It wasn't very nice for you to put a stop to Benny Meyuhas's production," Eli Bachar reminded him. "You were walking along the catwalk, and you looked down below you."

"Yes, but I didn't stop or anything, because I was on my way to tell Benny . . ." He sighed. "In the end, I never told him."

"Why not?"

"Because I never made it there. My wife phoned on my way to the roof, I had to take my kid to the emergency room. He was having an attack, he's got spastic bronchitis. I couldn't . . . you can't wait with these things, it was really urgent. When he gets these attacks, he chokes. Once he'd turned blue by the time we got him to the hospital. I had the car. My wife doesn't drive, so there was no choice, and she, she's pregnant, and we've already lost . . . never mind." He grimaced as if disgusted with his own complaining, with the details, with his own loquacity. "I had to get home urgently."

"Did you return the same way you came?" Eli Bachar asked.

"Sure, there's no other way. Well, there is, from the back, a shorter way, out to the parking lot, and another from the main building. But my car was in the small parking lot—"

"Which means you went back along that catwalk?"

"Yeah, that's what I said," Matty Cohen said with annoyance.

"So she was still there?"

"Who? Tirzah?"

"Tirzah and the person who was with her."

"I didn't notice," Matty Cohen said, as though astonished by the absurdity of the situation. "I didn't look down, I was anxious about . . ."

"You were in a hurry," Eli Bachar said as a way of helping out.

"Exactly, I was in a hurry because of my kid, because my wife said he was already . . . that's it, I was in a hurry, and I can't tell you if she was still there or not. I don't know where they found her, because only this morning I saw that . . ." He spread his arms in a gesture of helplessness.

"She was found next to the scenery, by the pillar, a white marble pillar."

"I think I remember something like that," Matty Cohen said. "With a capital at the top? I saw it sometime."

"That capital crushed her face and her skull," Eli Bachar stated. He kept his eyes on Matty Cohen, who paled.

"You don't say," Matty Cohen mumbled as he licked his lips, which were suddenly parched. "Is there . . . is there any water around here?" he asked as he rose from his chair and made his way unsteadily to the urn. He peered inside, poured himself a tepid glass of water in a Styrofoam cup, and drank it down in one gulp.

"I'm very sorry," he said as he sat back down. "I didn't look down on my way back out, I don't know if she was still there, but when I was on my way to the roof she was standing with someone and talking, I mean . . ." He fell silent. Eli Bachar, who had noted the hesitation in his voice, folded his arms and waited. He hoped that through patience he would hear the end of Matty Cohen's sentence, since people cannot—as Ohayon had taught him—stand silences. But Matty Cohen did not continue speaking. His puffy face was contorted with some effort, the nature of which Eli Bachar was hard pressed to identify, and his eyes were half shut as though he were trying to decipher the details in a picture he was carrying around inside himself.

"They weren't just shooting the breeze," Eli Bachar guessed.

Matty Cohen shot him a startled look. "What do you mean, 'They weren't just shooting the breeze'?" Eli Bachar thought he heard a note of insult or desperation in Matty Cohen's voice. "I can't tell you what . . . because I really don't know who she was talking to. I don't have a clue."

"Not even whether it was a man or a woman?" Eli Bachar persisted.

"Not even. Nothing. It was pretty dark in there, I don't even . . . If Tirzah hadn't spoken, I wouldn't have known it was her. Even now I'm not completely sure."

"It's actually very important for you to be sure it was Tirzah, very important to remember exactly what she said. You have no idea just how important it is."

Matty Cohen regarded him with a look of confusion. After a while his face brightened, as though finally comprehending something. "Is it because of the insurance?"

"Yes," Eli Bachar said, since he had no intention of sharing any of his thoughts at this stage. "Because of the terms and conditions. It's a completely different story if this is an accident."

"But I'm telling you everything I know," Matty Cohen said pleadingly. "I'm really trying, but what am I supposed to do? On the way to the roof I was thinking about Benny Meyuhas and on the way back not even about that and the whole matter—I mean, we're only talking about a couple of minutes here, for crying out loud, from when I nearly reached the roof to when I turned around after her phone call."

"The people filming up on the roof didn't hear the phone ringing?"

"Which? What? My cell phone? Like, who?"

"The people on the roof," Eli Bachar said in a new attempt, "or even Tirzah. If she was down below, wouldn't she have heard the ring? Wouldn't she have reacted, noticed that you were there. Called to you, or to someone?"

"No," Matty Cohen said and shook his head strenuously as if to emphasize his own words. "I didn't want anyone to know that I was . . . that . . . nobody knew that I would be turning up in the middle of filming. I set my cell phone on vibrate so no one would hear. It was in my pocket. I was standing right next to the door to the roof, I could see it was my wife phoning, and all I said was, 'What?' when I answered. She spoke and then I said, quietly, 'I'm on my way.' Nobody could have heard that, certainly not on the roof, it's completely open up there and there's no way, but not down below, either, nobody could . . ."

"So then you immediately started running back in the same direction?"

"I told you, I was afraid my kid—"

"No one knew you were there?" Eli Bachar asked again.

"No, it was a secret, you know, I wanted . . . I needed to catch them in the act, because there had already been a decision to stop filming."

"How can that be?" Eli Bachar asked, surprised. "Israel Television decides to stop a production, and people keep working on it anyway? How is that technically possible?"

"First of all," Matty Cohen said as he lowered his head and scrutinized his fingers, "such a decision is made without fanfare, we didn't want to . . . nobody knew about it yet, only Benny Meyuhas himself and his producer, Hagar, and maybe I said something to Max Levin, I don't remember exactly. We didn't want a big ruckus on our hands, but I'm pretty sure Hagar told someone else. She's so committed to Benny Meyuhas that . . . for many years she—"

"Now I get it," Eli Bachar mumbled. He removed a crumpled piece of paper from his shirt pocket, unfolded it, and read in silence the names written there. "That's why you're not on this list."

"What list?" Matty Cohen asked, dismayed.

"The list of who was in the building last night, when the accident occurred. You're not listed because nobody knew . . . but Zadik knew, he's the one who told me."

"Zadik knew," Matty Cohen agreed. "Of course he knew, he's the one . . . I mean, I didn't make the decision to stop filming on my own. But he didn't know that it was last night that I was planning to show up. Nobody knew that."

"What about the guard? The person in charge of security? He didn't see you enter?"

Matty Cohen poured water into the foam cup, shook his head, and took a long sip. "No, he didn't see me. He couldn't have seen me, because I came in the back way, from the parking area in the back."

Eli Cohen threw him a puzzled look. "What parking area in the back?"

"There's a small parking lot behind the String Building. All the old-timers here know about it, there's an entrance from there up a flight of stairs and straight into the building. The door is locked, but there are people with keys. Senior staff. That enables us to park behind the building and enter without anyone—"

"What does that mean, 'senior staff'? Who does that include?"

"Well, department heads have a key, but lots of other people, too: carpentry shop workers, people in the Scenery Department, people involved in the big shows produced in the String Building. I suppose the people who produce *Popolitika,* you know, there's this big studio downstairs for the Friday-evening programs, that sort of thing. So the people working on those shows, the regulars, they have keys. It's hard to say anymore who does and who doesn't."

"What I would like to ask of you," Eli Bachar said, stealing a glance at his watch, "is that after your meeting you'll come down to police headquarters at the Russian Compound. I have an idea—"

"That's impossible," Matty Cohen said, visibly dissatisfied. "I've got to speak with Rubin after the meeting to see what's going to be happening with this *Iddo and Eynam,* and then this afternoon . . . I can't *not* be at the funeral, it's bad enough I didn't know . . ."

"You'll be back in time for the funeral," Eli Bachar promised. "I personally will bring you back in time."

"But what . . . why do you need to—"

"First of all I need a signed statement from you," Eli Bachar said. "And second, there's . . . I had this idea about memory. You'll see. Trust me."

"But first I've got to get to this meeting," Matty Cohen said reproachfully. "I've got a few matters that can't be postponed."

"I'll be waiting for you here," Eli Bachar promised, "either in this room or in Aviva's office."

"You want me to send Max Levin in?" Matty Cohen offered.

"That's all right, I'll call him," Eli Bachar said, accompanying him to the door. From there he watched Matty Cohen enter Zadik's office, saw Aviva talking on the phone. She swiveled her chair toward the window and lowered her voice.

When the door to Zadik's office closed, Eli Bachar motioned to Max Levin to step into the little office.

"I'm a wreck," Max Levin said as he sat in one of the two upholstered chairs near the wall. "There's no blood left in my veins, only coffee. I'm simply a wreck, a total wreck." He looked at Eli Bachar, fatigued. "I already told them everything last night. I don't have anything more to add." Eli Bachar took in the small, wrinkled face while Max Levin rubbed his red eyes. "Thirty years, right from the beginning I'm here. All those years you work close to someone, your lives are all tangled up with each other, and suddenly, in a single moment—"

"I just want to go over what you told us yesterday, and your signed statement," Eli Bachar explained. He read aloud the details of the moment Max Levin had discovered Tirzah's body under the marble pillar, how he had happened to be there because he had been looking for a blue horse for Benny Meyuhas's production, how the guard wouldn't let in Avi, the lighting technician who had been sent to fetch the sun gun, how he, Max Levin, had gotten him in. "Is that just the way it was?" he asked in the end, and Max Levin nodded and added,

"Her whole face was crushed . . . blood . . . it was . . ." And he fell silent.

"So, you don't have a key to the back entrance of the String Building?" Eli Bachar asked matter-of-factly.

"You'll find this funny," Max Levin said with a sigh. "I'm the person who came up with that back entrance, and I always use it because most of my work takes place at the String Building, that's where my office is. But I had left the keys in the pocket of my jacket, and when I came at night I was wearing a windbreaker . . . because Benny Meyuhas called me—"

"Tell me, is it always like that?" Eli Bachar asked. "Do you always work so late into the night?"

"Benny Meyuhas called me, it was urgent. And because . . ." He stopped talking a moment, then muttered, "I've been working with Benny Meyuhas more than, well, nearly thirty years, so he gets special treatment from me. He can ask me for something in the middle of the night, and he only calls me if it's really urgent," Max Levin explained, stroking his wrinkled, grizzled cheeks and clicking his large, white teeth, which were too perfect to be real.

"What was so urgent here?" Eli Bachar asked. "There were so many of you here—actors, a lighting technician, Tirzah, you—why at night?"

"These were night scenes, I explained that yesterday," Max Levin said. "From *Iddo and Eynam,* a project that Benny Meyuhas has been working on for years. The screenplay was written years ago, and filming started three months ago, and now . . . it's almost finished."

"But why at night?" Eli Bachar persisted. "It's December, dark already around five p.m., why is it necessary to film in the middle of the night?"

"No, you don't understand," Max Levin said, propping up his head by putting his elbows on the dusty glass desktop. "They needed the moon. They were filming Gemullah, the heroine of the story. She walks on roofs at night, she suffers from moonsickness. That's the way it is in the story by Agnon," he explained. It seemed to Eli Bachar that he heard a note of pride in the last sentence, as though Max Levin knew that he, Eli Bachar, was not familiar with the story by Agnon, which was in fact true but which he had no intention of revealing.

"I understand," Eli Bachar said with assurance, "that Matty Cohen was there last night. What was he doing there?"

"I only heard this morning that he was there," Max Levin said carefully, stealing a cautious look at Eli Bachar. "He's the head of the Production Department, in charge of the money. Didn't you ask him that? He was just sitting with you, wasn't he? Last night he didn't come to . . . but what's that got to do with anything?"

"It's just that I understood he was coming to put a stop to the production," Eli Bachar explained. "So did he?"

"Nobody saw him there. If he was there, he left before—" Max Levin's voice was full of scorn. "Nobody is going to shut this production down in the middle, even if it's over budget. It's not . . . it's a project that too many people . . . have taken too seriously—"

"So how is it that if so many people are involved in it," Eli Bachar asked, "and so much money, and people are putting in time in the middle of the night—how is such negligence possible?"

Max Levin explained at length the way Tirzah worked and ran her operations, how she never permitted a soul to touch the things she made, even he, Max Levin, who had worked with her for thirty years: "And believe me, she knew I am a very responsible person, she knew very well, but still she did not allow me." He clasped his knotty fingers and gazed intently at the blackened edges of his large fingernails. "Nobody was allowed to touch her stuff," Max Levin said, "nobody was responsible for it but her, and that's just . . . I don't want to use the word 'fault,' but it's only her fault. She would have told you that herself." He continued to talk, about Tirzah's perfectionism, about the way she insisted on getting every detail right, about long hours they had worked together, he as the head of Props and she as head of Scenery, and about how—in spite of her pedantry—everyone loved her, how they went out of their way to help her. "Everyone: the workers, the seamstresses, everyone." Especially on this project, *Iddo and Eynam,* not so much out of respect for Benny Meyuhas—"Not that he isn't respected, he's very respected, he's still an important director even if they haven't been letting him take on projects he wants for years. But he's a person who keeps his distance, who doesn't really relate to people personally"—but rather for her, since Benny was her husband.

"Well, *as if* her husband," he corrected himself. "They lived like husband and wife for seven or eight years, ever since she split up with Rubin. But Rubin is Benny Meyuhas's friend, too, until this very day, even though his wife . . ." He wiped his eyes and paused for a long moment.

"Never mind all these details," he summed up, "it's a terrible tragedy. But nobody but Tirzah is to blame. That is to say, not exactly to blame, but she's responsible . . . I mean . . ." He stopped speaking and cast a look of sheer misery at Eli Bachar. "Any way you try to say it, it sounds awful," he said. "But that's the truth. I'll tell you that, and anyone else will, too. Avi the lighting technician, everyone."

"You know," Eli Bachar said after a moment, in a wistful tone he was adopting in order to provoke Max Levin, "the folks from forensics measured the angle of the pillar and calculated the way it falls and all that, and they believe it couldn't have fallen by itself, such a marble pillar could not have just fallen on her skull and crushed it. She would have moved aside."

Max Levin pressed his hands to his face and rubbed again like someone who had just awakened. From behind the hands covering his face he said, "Believe me, I myself don't understand it. Maybe she was tired . . . when you're tired you move more slowly, you don't pay attention, maybe—"

"You don't think it's possible that someone pushed the pillar on top of her?"

Max Levin lowered his hands, straightened in his chair—even so he looked short, an impression reinforced by his thin body—and looked at Eli Bachar in astonishment. "Impossible. No way someone would . . . What? Accidentally?"

Eli Bachar remained silent.

"No, no. That's impossible," Max Levin said, renouncing the very idea. "Not even worth discussing." He stared at Eli Bachar and made him feel a certain discomfort in spite of his years of experience. He had asked this question in a mechanical manner, almost without intending to, and had not expected so vigorous a response, that Max Levin would be so personally offended. He wondered about his accent—it did not seem exactly Russian, he could not place it—which thickened when he raised his voice and repeated, "Impossible! No way, you should not even be talking that way. Who would ever want—what is this here, Hollywood? No way that Tirzah—do you know how much people loved her here? Thirty years she's been here, and she doesn't have a single enemy. Believe me, she wasn't an easy person to work with, she drove us all crazy, but you know what? She was fair, so very fair, you just don't find people like that anymore. And how much, how much she cared about people, and helped them. Ask the seamstresses, and even the painters, the carpenters—no question. Ask Avi the lighting technician, he'll tell you the same thing."

Eli Bachar nodded and rose from his seat. "Yes, Avi's waiting outside, I'll talk to him in a minute. But . . . where is he now, Benny Meyuhas?"

Max Levin shrugged. "I imagine at home, he's probably . . . I would bet he's not alone, Hagar must be with him. That's his assistant, his producer, they've been together for years. And friends must be with him at home, but ask Aviva, she'll find out for you. He stood up in a rush and moved to the door, opened it, and called, "Aviva, can you help the policeman here find Benny?"

"Of course," Aviva said. "Come here, Eli. Your name's Eli, right? Let's try and find him at home. Arye Rubin told me before that he's at home. Come, sit here." She removed several files from the seat next to her desk and patted it for him to sit there. Eli Bachar looked at her and sat down obediently.

# CHAPTER FOUR

You see this guy?" Intelligence Officer Danny Balilty asked Matty Cohen as he placed his hand on the shoulder of the tall, thin man who had risen from his seat when he entered the room. The man had come around the desk, stopped in front of Matty Cohen, and shaken Balilty's proffered hand with cool politeness while Balilty hoisted the belt on his trousers over his bulging belly with his other hand. Next to one another the pair looked like Laurel and Hardy. "Take a good look at him," Balilty continued with obvious pride, as though discussing a close relation he had raised himself. "You're looking at a real artist, and don't forget it. Ilan here is a painter, not just some technician. He's doing us a big favor here, isn't that so, Ilan?"

After nearly an hour sitting across from Ilan Katz, Matty Cohen was wringing his hands and rocking from side to side in the chair, which was too small for his huge frame. He had to give an answer—any answer—not only to satisfy this Ilan Katz, who had sympathetically entreated him to tell him anything that came to mind about the moment he had spotted Tirzah with another person as he made his way above them across the catwalk, but also because he was so very tired and his feet hurt and his left shoulder was bothering him and maybe his arm, too; all he really wanted was for them to leave him alone so he could go home and sleep.

"I'm not really even certain it was Tirzah," Matty had declared with hesitation at the outset of their conversation. "There was very little light, that area is always dark," he had said in a pleading voice, but this Ilan Katz, who sat beside him, was staring at him through narrowed lids as though he had heard nothing Matty Cohen had been saying and had no intention of letting him off the hook. His eyes, inside their web of tiny wrinkles, radiated patience and trust and expectation; he merely sat there and without averting his gaze said, for the thousandth time, "Anything. It doesn't matter what, any little thing you can recall, a spot on the wall, a crack in the tiles, anything."

And because of his persistence, just to get him off his back, Matty Cohen added, "I think he was taller." He took a sip of water. "The person whose back was to me, he was taller than she was."

"Aha!" Ilan Katz exulted. "You see? I knew you'd remember!" He tossed aside the vague drawing he had made, quickly scribbling instead on a new blank white sheet of paper two figures, the profiles of a woman and a slightly taller man. "You see? Every single word teaches us something," he summed up with satisfaction, squinting at his work. "You said 'he,' so it's clear it was a man you saw, and you said 'back,' which means he was facing the woman and maybe he attacked her, even if you yourself don't know it. Let's give him a few more characteristics according to what you remember. We always remember more than what we think we do," he added in a paternal tone.

The events of that morning after a sleepless night, his son's ceaseless cough and red face burning with fever, Malka's hysteria—what kind of mother was she, always at wit's end?—the news about Tirzah, all these people that would not stop questioning him and pleading with him and demanding things from him and putting pressure on him, the talking, the threats—all these had unnerved him. Even Hagar, who had caught him on his cell phone on the way back from the hospital and warned him not to try and put a stop to Benny's production, had left a bad taste in his mouth. True, he had told her he was not a person to be threatened, had added that there was no reversing the decision; but still the conversation with her had been highly distressing and weighed heavily on him. "You are completely heartless," she had told him. Why heartless? Are responsibility and heartlessness one and the same? Let someone try and tell him that being responsible meant being mean. All in all he merely had a sense of responsibility. What was she talking about, what had he wanted? After all, this wasn't exactly his father's money; he was just doing his job properly. But he hated to be the guy who cut off the money supply, the guy everyone loves to hate. People at work thought he was the bad guy simply because he was the one who doled out the money. No one knew he was really a good person, someone who hated strife and contention. He should have left this job ages ago; he belonged elsewhere, in a different job. He should have been an accountant or at least a tax consultant. He had started studying accounting, and if it had not been for Tamar, he would have finished his studies by now and would have had his own firm, the works. But she had run off with their daughter after two years of marriage and for the past eight years had been bleeding him dry. He had been willing to let her go—"Just leave the kid here and get out"—but she would have none of it, had gone instead to a lawyer who had milked him for everything he was worth. He had given her half the apartment, half their savings, alimony, and in addition to everything she had turned the child against him. And now this morning, first Tirzah Rubin, then that officer from Investigations, Eli Bachar, then the trip to police headquarters; he had never set foot in there before, except for one time when he had come to give testimony on behalf of a neighbor who had been attacked. What reason would he have for being at police headquarters? He had never broken the law. And here he was like some criminal, entering from the back gate, from the parking lot. From there Eli Bachar had led him through the building where everyone could see him—in fact he thought he had caught a glimpse of Epstein from Maintenance—through a long hallway, motioning him to follow him up to the third floor. Eli Bachar had run ahead; Matty Cohen was breathless trying to keep up, he was nearly choking by the time he reached the end of the hallway, and just at the end, when it seemed that there was no more hallway left to pass through, Eli Bachar had opened a white door and suddenly another hallway appeared, a completely new wing, the smell of fresh paint and wood pungent, the rooms empty. In the last room sat this intelligence officer, Balilty, with bags under his beady eyes. Both men had sat facing him, and once again he had had to drink coffee even though he was forbidden to do so; he felt the blood humming behind his ears, the throbbing in his head. How the men had pestered him! Was Tirzah well liked, did she have enemies, what was her relationship with Benny Meyuhas like, did one of the Scenery Department workers hold a grudge against her, was Arye Rubin a real Don Juan, could there be women who . . . they even mentioned Niva and the boy. As for him, he had always hated gossip and slander. How many times had he told them that Tirzah was a fine person, pedantic but fair, and that she had had no enemies, and that anyway, it had been an accident. After that they were all over him, asking him over and over again why he had gone there at night. And he had tried to explain about their work procedures, why it had been necessary for him to go there in the middle of the night to put a stop to the filming. "You don't understand," he had said. "We have a certain budget for original drama, and he used it all up. Now he's filming additional scenes, patching up scenes, and these additions alone are costing fifty thousand dollars."

"I don't understand what these additions are," Eli Bachar said. "Does it mean he's shooting the same scenes over again, or new ones?"

"Both, really, along with changes in the screenplay that require reshooting the scene."

"I've heard he's a perfectionist, Benny Meyuhas. Is that right?" Eli Bachar asked him.

"And how," Matty Cohen said, then immediately felt he had said too much. The way Benny Meyuhas worked was nobody's business outside of Israel Television.

"How much have you people invested in this production?" Balilty asked. "What's the budget for a film like this?"

Matty Cohen hated answering that kind of question and especially disliked discussing the budget with people who had no need to know. "I don't recall exactly," he said at last. "A drama like this costs a lot to produce, believe me. But this isn't connected to Tirzah's accident . . ." He could feel his shirt growing damp with sweat. It was cold, and rain was falling outside, but inside this room it was too hot, he felt he was suffocating even though he had removed his necktie, folded it neatly, and stuck it inside his jacket pocket. He felt as though he were being choked, as if something had tightly encircled his neck. He did not say a word about how Benny Meyuhas had been shunted aside over the years, how he was only given the unimportant directing jobs: children's programming and shows about religion, that sort of thing. He said nothing about the charitable foundation that had suddenly popped up from overseas, some anonymous benefactor with a fund for adapting the masterpieces of Hebrew literature to the screen. Were it not for that fund, Benny Meyuhas would never have been given the go-ahead to start with Agnon. But nothing was good enough for Meyuhas. He had used up all the foundation money as well as the entire budget for original drama.

Balilty was persistent. "How much is 'a lot'? How much are we talking, a million? Two?" His eyes were twinkling, and it was clear he would never give up.

"I don't exactly recall," Matty Cohen answered. No one would force him to give out such information to no end. He was not the type to air dirty laundry in public.

Balilty would not let it go. "I'm asking ballpark, I'm not looking to quote you."

It was clear this would never end. He had to tell him something. "Around two million."

"Dollars or shekels?"

"Dollars, dollars, with productions we talk in dollars, but we write the budget in shekels."

Balilty whistled.

"That's not a large budget for a film," Matty Cohen said defensively. "Overseas that's small change, but here in Israel . . ."

But Balilty looked at Eli Bachar and said quietly, as though Matty Cohen could not hear, "Look what kind of money we're talking about here. Did you hear that? This is no laughing matter: with sums like that, anything's possible."

"That's not money that someone receives," Matty Cohen explained. "That's money for the film's budget; no one gets his hands on it. Everyone's on salary."

Balilty did not respond, merely scribbled something on the paper he was holding, folded it, and said, "I'm asking you again: you don't remember anything about what you saw down below? Who was with Tirzah? Anyway, correct me if I'm wrong, but wouldn't you agree that at that hour not just anybody could be standing there?"

Matty Cohen explained once again that when he had seen her, he was in a hurry, that he had been on his way out to the roof, and then afterwards, making his way back across the catwalk, he had peered down but could not stop to look because he was rushing home to take his son to the emergency room. All to no avail; nothing helped his cause.

"Don't worry about it," Balilty had said as he rose from his chair, "we'll help you remember. Come with me, I'm taking you to someone who knows how to make you remember. We've got this guy, it's like he fishes out your memories, he's an expert in pulling them out from way down deep."

Now this tall, thin man sitting across from him, whose angular knees were almost touching his own, was fingering his blond, wispy beard and tugging on his pointy nose. "Now just tell me, without giving it any thought: you must have seen his head. Was he wearing a hat? A skullcap?"

"I don't think so," Matty Cohen said as he wiped his face. A wave of cold passed through him, then the shivers, like symptoms of a high fever. His shirt was now completely wet with sweat, but he was cold, and slightly nauseous. His left shoulder was in pain and he had chest pains and he could feel the food rising in his stomach. But what had he eaten? A few cold bourekas and all that coffee. Still, he felt as if he had eaten something rotten.

"So he wasn't wearing a hat. Was he bald, or did he have a head of hair?" Ilan Katz touched his own high forehead, readjusted his skullcap, tugged at his nose again. He reminded Matty Cohen of a picture of Pinocchio in a book he had had as a child.

"No, he wasn't bald," Matty Cohen said, feeling as though any minute he would vomit on the white paper attached to the clipboard perched on the jutting knees of the man sitting across from him.

"How about a skullcap?" Ilan Katz asked while penciling in hair on the taller of the two figures he had drawn. "Straight hair? Curly? Don't think, just say whatever comes to mind. Quickly."

"No skullcap," Matty Cohen told him, mopping his sweaty face again. "Can we take a break? I'm not feeling so well."

"We're almost finished, we're making great progress," Ilan Katz assured him. The contours of Katz's arm, which was moving rapidly across the page, dimmed, and suddenly Matty Cohen could see several arms in a blur moving up and down, and heard the voice, filled with excitement, as if from a great distance and behind a glass partition asking, "Curly hair or straight?"

"Straight, I think," Matty Cohen said, forcing himself to sit up straight, grasping the sides of the wooden chair for support and breathing deeply, as if a deep breath might drive away the pain he was feeling in his chest. This was a pain he had come to recognize, not just from several years ago but from these past nights, a paralyzing pain, as if someone had clamped an enormous vise on the left side of his chest and was crushing and bending him; a pain that took his breath away, but which he hoped would pass quickly by itself, without anyone knowing what was happening to him.

"Good job, Matty. You're doing great. Here we go, straight hair. What do you think? Dark or light?"

Matty Cohen did not respond. Because of the pain he was unable to speak, but the artist was oblivious. "Did you notice his legs? His shoes? Let's try the legs. Were they long? Thin? What kind of shoes was he wearing?" Ilan Katz was ecstatic, completely unaware of the man's labored breathing. Matty Cohen had placed his right hand on his chest.

Ilan Katz drummed his fingers, the pencil tightly pressed to the page in front of him. Suddenly he jumped up from his chair with a start, knocking it backward, and stood in front of Matty Cohen. "You've got to tell me quickly, we've got to strike while the iron's hot, it only gets tougher over time. Memory doesn't get better, only worse. Believe me, every hour we remember less." He waved one long, slender, yellowed finger in front of Matty Cohen's nose. "Something about his clothes. Was he wearing a coat? A suit jacket? A sweater? What?"

Matty could hear his own voice; it too sounded as though it were coming from far away. The words were flowing out of him: "No, no coat, I don't . . . don't . . ." Suddenly everything was spinning around him and the pain in his arm grew stronger and the one in his chest, too. Not a stabbing pain, but a prolonged one, as though someone were trampling him with a large foot . . . worse . . . as if . . . he were being smashed, something was smashing his chest, something huge, something of enormous strength—another minute, and he'd be hearing the snap of his own bones. He could hear mumbled voices, people were touching him, opening the buttons on his shirt. He was cold, cold and in pain. It became impossible to breathe anymore. Suddenly everything was a fog.

"Well, well, well, this is truly a surprise," Zadik said without a hint of joy at the sight of Chief Superintendent Michael Ohayon in his doorway. "I never expected to see *you* here." He rose from his chair, hastening to the door to greet him and blocking the way into his room. He cast an expectant look at Eli Bachar, but Eli Bachar, who had no intention of explaining why he had brought his commander along with him, returned his gaze with a blank look.

"I knew the police would get in here to ask questions," Zadik sputtered, passing his hand over his stubbled gray chin. "But I never thought they'd sent their big star over."

Michael Ohayon spread his arms as if to say, Look what's been happening around here, what do you expect? "We're here in the matter of the . . . accident involving Tirzah Rubin," he said, casting a sidelong glance at Zadik's clouded face. "And about another matter—"

"What matter?" Zadik asked. "Something that justifies your presence at Israel Television?"

Michael paused. They had not notified Zadik of Matty Cohen's heart attack, and at the emergency meeting convened by the district commander and the commissioner of police—after they had summoned an ambulance and after it appeared that Matty Cohen's heartbeat had stabilized, though he was still unconscious—Emmanuel Shorer had warned Balilty and Ilan Katz about what might be in store for them with regard to the family; he even mentioned the possibility of a lawsuit, and asked how it was that they had not discerned Matty Cohen's condition. "Believe me, sir," Balilty said, his hand on his heart, "there were no signs whatsoever. He was breathing with difficulty, but with the kind of weight that guy had on him . . ." Michael was well aware that Matty Cohen had complained about feeling unwell, but he remained silent. Eventually the commissioner of police cut the meeting short, reminding them all that this was not the time for investigating the matter, expressing hope that Matty Cohen would return to normal, and promising that they would engage in a proper discussion "when things settled down a bit." He departed, leaving a whiff of threat behind him, which Emmanuel Shorer reinforced when he turned to Michael and instructed him to inform Zadik—with sensitivity and gentleness—what had happened to Matty Cohen "before we conduct our own internal inquiry into the matter."

Eli Bachar, who was standing behind Michael, watched how Aviva moistened her lips until they were glossy, and left her pink tongue fluttering at their edges without once taking her large eyes, outlined in blue eye shadow, off Michael. Here again was proof of what Michael had always told him: No matter what situation people find themselves in, their true personality will always burst through and overcome the circumstances. Aviva would barely admit that she was searching for love, and would never acknowledge that she was looking for a husband. Some people think those are one and the same, but Eli Bachar knew better. There was no fooling *him*, he knew how to recognize the difference: a woman looking for love was less active about it than Aviva. Until Michael had shown up, she had been considering Eli Bachar for the role, but now he had suddenly been cast aside. If he looked at Michael through Aviva's eyes, as if seeing him for the first time, like we look afresh sometimes at people close to us, people we've stopped really noticing, then he saw how impressive his height was, saw his youthful profile, how his short graying hair gave him a look of restrained austerity, how the dark eyes under the heavy brows gave him an air of mystery. Eli Bachar stole a glance at the arc of his aquiline nose—Eli's wife Tzilla, who worked with them on one of the Special Investigations teams and did not care if she was a secretary or a coordinator as long as Michael was in charge, would call his nose "manly"—at his pronounced cheekbones, and at his slightly crooked chin. Tzilla had once remarked that "if it had had a cleft in it, he'd be a darker version of Kirk Douglas," and Eli had never forgotten this remark, which even now, for a split second when he recalled his wife's voice as she said it, awakened in him a spark of jealousy that he hastened to extinguish. He was incapable of jealousy toward Michael, the godfather of his children, after so many years in close proximity. After all, he, too, loved Michael, not only Tzilla. But there was no doubt about it, the man was what, forty-six, forty-seven? but he seemed ageless, and with just one look at him you knew he was a free agent, not tied down to anyone, that there was no woman in his life. You could tell by . . . well, Eli did not know just how. Maybe it was his gaze—lonely, severe—the way sometimes he would stare at a point just over the shoulder of the person he was talking to, the gaze that was now causing Aviva to take stock of herself in the compact mirror she kept in her drawer. Or maybe it was because of his smile, even though he wasn't smiling just then, that special attention he gave to women, the way you could tell he wasn't afraid of them. Eli noticed, too, the look Michael gave Aviva when he entered her office; he saw Michael's eyes narrow for just an instant and knew that he was aware she was checking him out. Eli knew, too, that Michael had not remained indifferent to it.

"Why don't we step inside your office?" Michael suggested to Zadik in a soothing tone. "I understand that you haven't been having an easy time around here. We're going to have to—" He caught sight of Aviva, her chin propped in her hand, her large, moist green eyes fixed unabashedly on him. She made no attempt to hide the fact that she was listening to their conversation.

"All right," Zadik said with a sigh, and with heavy footsteps he turned around and walked to his large desk, behind which he sat down. "I'm still in shock," he said as Michael and Eli Bachar seated themselves across from him. "I'm talking to you as if everything's just fine, but don't think it is. I'm still in shock. Anyway, what exactly is there to investigate here? This wasn't some murder, it was an accident. And I've been thinking: the entire police force is dealing with the strikers today . . . never mind, I'm getting off the track . . . what . . . what *are* you doing here?"

Michael nodded toward Eli Bachar. "I've been called in to help."

"Just like that government minister, who shall remain nameless: when your friends call, you come," Zadik muttered. "Not that I'm not glad to see you," he hastened to add wryly, "but believe me, we're talking about a woman who . . . a person that worked with me like this," he said, holding up two crossed fingers. "I still can't, I still can't . . . don't you have anything better to do today?"

"The striking workers from the Hulit factory have already been arrested," Eli Bachar said. "They're all taken care of." In a slightly bitter tone, he added, "Believe me, they'll get what's coming to them. But the truly guilty parties won't be punished at all."

"That's the way it is in this country," Zadik agreed under his breath. He pressed the telephone intercom. "What would you like to drink?" he asked them.

"Coffee," Eli Bachar answered. He turned to Michael with a questioning look on his face. Michael shrugged in halfhearted agreement.

"Cream? Sugar?"

"Whatever," Eli Bachar responded.

They waited for Zadik to instruct Aviva to bring them coffee.

Eli Bachar glanced at Michael, who nodded. "We would . . . we'd like to request that the funeral be postponed."

"Postponed?" Zadik said, stunned. "Tirzah's funeral? How can we postpone it? The announcements have been printed, we've notified the whole world, how can we postpone it? And why? Why? And until when?"

"Look," Eli Bachar said, "there's . . . the pathologist found several things that—"

"What is this?" Zadik asked, perplexed. "What did he find? Where?"

Michael chose his words carefully. "There were findings that raise questions," he explained.

"What kind of findings?" Zadik asked.

"For example, there were bruises on her neck."

"On Tirzah's neck?" Zadik asked.

"Yes," Michael said. "The kind of bruises you get when someone places two hands around your neck and presses hard. Both hands, both sides."

Zadik opened his mouth, then closed it right away. He opened and closed it once again. In the ensuing silence one could hear his heavy breathing and voices on the other side of the door.

"What does that mean?" Zadik asked in a whisper.

"It means," Michael explained slowly, his eyes fixed on Zadik, "that perhaps what Matty Cohen saw on his way to the roof changes the picture entirely. Only an autopsy will give us the exact time of death, and that's something we absolutely need to know. I mean, as exact as possible, you know, a lead."

"But . . . but he didn't see anything that . . . he didn't tell me . . . he isn't even certain it was Tirzah, he said it was dark there . . . he didn't—"

Eli Bachar interrupted Zadik. "Sometimes people see more than what they think they've seen."

Zadik intended to say something, but at just that moment Aviva pushed open the door to his office with her shoulder and entered, carrying a tray. "I didn't want to let Amsalem from the canteen disturb you in the middle," she explained as she laid the tray on Zadik's desk. "I figured you needed your privacy, or . . ." She smiled sweetly at Michael, placing a glass mug in front of him. "Turkish coffee?" she asked as if she knew the answer already. "Sugar? Sweetener? Cream?" She was standing quite close to him, her arm nearly touching his shoulder; even Eli caught the scent of her lemony perfume, light and surprising, could see the pores on her cheeks, the fine blond hairs above her upper lip. "Zadik, I forgot to tell you," she said as she straightened up, "someone called from Sha'arei Zedek Hospital looking for you, wouldn't say what it's about. I asked them to call again in an hour. Do you know what it's about?" Zadik shook his head.

"Two sugars, please," Michael said, then took two sugar packets from the tray, slit them open, and emptied them into his mug.

"Some people don't have to worry about their weight," she said as she placed a mug in front of Zadik. In the tone of a nanny intimately familiar with the idiosyncrasies of her charge, she told him, "I've already added one sweetener to yours, and I brought you all some hot bourekas." Aviva placed a mug in front of Eli Bachar as well.

"Good job," Zadik murmured. "I wonder why Sha'arei Zedek Hospital is looking for me. That bothers me. . . . Try to find out what they want."

"Okay, I'll look into it. Look at these bourekas, they're filled with spinach, the good kind," Aviva said, obviously proud. "They're straight from the oven, exactly the way you like them, Zadik, because you've got a long day ahead of you. Just so you know."

"What? What are you talking about?" he asked, straightening up.

"Danny Benizri is waiting for you, and Arye Rubin is outside with Natasha, he's got some urgent matter he needs to discuss with you. He says you promised, and he's very tense. She is too, but especially him.

He needs to see you quickly because he's on his way to Benny Meyuhas's house, because this policeman," she said, indicating Eli Bachar—suddenly she no longer knew his name—"this policeman wants to talk with Benny Meyuhas, and Rubin has to accompany him. Did I get that right?" she asked Eli Bachar, who nodded.

"Can't you see that I'm . . . they're going to have to wait until I finish with the police, at the very least," Zadik said. "And Rubin, well, I've already spoken to him once, I thought . . ." He batted his hand in the air as if to wave away the issue. "Tell him that when I finish with them—"

"I'm leaving the tray here, we'll take it back later," Aviva said. She nodded at Eli Bachar and smiled at Michael. On her way out of the office she stopped, looked at Zadik, and said, "People are talking." Zadik looked at her expectantly. "They're saying . . . they're saying it wasn't an accident . . . Tirzah . . ."

"That'll be all for now, Aviva, thank you," Zadik said, cutting her off. She threw him a hurt look and left the room.

"Where were we?" Zadik asked seconds after the door had closed.

"We were talking about what Matty Cohen did or did not see," Eli Bachar said.

"That's just it," Zadik interjected. "He didn't see anything, and there wasn't anything *to* see, nobody—"

"Zadik," Michael said, "we need the family's permission to perform an autopsy. That's what we're here for."

Zadik pushed aside the plate of bourekas and gathered up the sesame seeds that had scattered across his desktop. He did not speak.

Eli Bachar leaned forward to explain. "The pathologist said—"

"I get it, I get it," Zadik said irritably. "Tirzah's family is Benny Meyuhas, you'll have to get permission from him. But in any case, Matty Cohen said that he even—"

"We thought we might have ways of helping him remember," Eli Bachar said. Michael threw him a look of warning, which made him hasten to add, "I'm not talking about something bad, God forbid. It's just that sometimes people don't know what it is they're seeing, or they don't remember until someone helps them."

"What are you planning to do, hypnotize him?" Zadik asked mockingly.

"The truth is," Michael said slowly as he leaned forward, "we know that the phone call from Sha'arei Zedek Hospital has to do with Matty. We had planned to—"

"What? Why, what's happened to Matty?" Zadik asked, distraught.

"He didn't feel so good while he was telling us what had happened, and we called an ambulance for him," Eli Bachar explained.

"It's your fault!" Zadik raised himself in his chair and slid his mug of coffee aside. "You made him totally crazy, what with the night he spent in the emergency room and everything that's happened with Tirzah! He needed to—why did you guys mess around with his head, that's what I want to know. Did you frighten the guy?"

"Don't be ridiculous, Zadik," Michael said sharply. "Why would we frighten him? We weren't even putting pressure on him. We have this memory expert, and he had been working with him for a while when Matty recalled a few details of what he'd seen with Tirzah at night—"

Zadik prodded his face like a man who had gone numb and was trying to revive himself. "No way that . . . and what . . . ? Listen, I've got to get over to the hospital. Matty is . . . we're close, I had a hand in his divorce, and in . . . I . . ." He fell silent, kneading his left arm with his hand.

"There's no reason to go rushing over there at the moment," Eli Bachar said. "He's in intensive care. They haven't stabilized him yet, but they're saying he'll be all right. Still, it'll be a while before they let anyone in to see him."

"I can't . . . ," Zadik began to say as he stood up, pushing his leather armchair back. "I can't just sit here while—have you notified his wife?"

Eli nodded. "We did. She's there with him."

"What about the kid?" Zadik asked, dismayed.

"He's fine," Eli Bachar assured him. "Her mother is with the boy at Hadassah. Everything's taken care of."

"I can't—" Zadik said as he lifted the receiver.

"Just a minute, Zadik," Michael said, placing a restraining hand on his arm. "I want us to get back to the previous matter. Let's verify a few things. All that I'm asking is for cooperation on your part and for you to postpone the funeral. Not by days, just by a couple of hours."

"I don't know what you're talking about," Zadik said, returning to his seat. "Tirzah's death was an accident!" He wiped his brow. "I don't want you coming in here investigating things if there's no good reason. It seems to me you're just taking advantage of an opportunity. I know you people—how long have you and I known each other?" He squinted at Michael, touching the tip of his ear, then prodding a small scar by his right eyebrow. "After all, we practically grew up together, didn't we? I remember you before you were even shaving. You were two years behind me at school, you were in the same class as my cousin Uzi, his house was your second home. I remember—so do me a favor, don't try pulling the wool over *my* eyes. I don't want this place to be crawling with police trying to dig things up for no good reason."

"What kind of things, Zadik?" Michael asked calmly. "What kind of things have we got to look for around here?"

"Ohayon," Zadik said, a hint of warning in his voice. "I'm asking you, without . . . in short, you know very well what I'm talking about."

Michael remained silent.

"I'm talking about the leak. You people will take advantage of the situation to go looking for the person who leaked to us, I know it for certain, and there's no reason for me to help you find the person who leaked to Arye Rubin. It's the job of the media to expose such things. You had a high-ranking officer who was embezzling. It's our job. . . . Arye Rubin is a first-rate journalist: you're not going to shut off his sources."

"I have no connection with that, and I don't even know exactly what you're talking about," Michael said, clearly indifferent. "There was an obvious instance of unnatural death here, but what is not yet obvious is whether we're talking about an accident or not. I would think you'd have an interest in knowing exactly what happened, that you wouldn't evade—but perhaps you don't. Do you or don't you?"

Zadik made a show of crossing his arms over his chest. "You should be ashamed of yourself. What's this business about 'I don't even know exactly what you're talking about'? What kind of bullshit is that?" he said, raising his voice. "Are you trying to make me look like a fool? What do you mean, you 'don't know'? You don't know that we shook down the entire police force with the Fueler case? That thanks to us you cleaned out your stables? You don't know that your own commissioner of police will not rest until he finds out who informed us about the district commander's bribe-taking?" His voice grew louder and louder, until he was shouting. "If that's the way you're going to speak with me," he roared, pounding his fist on the desk, "then don't bother coming back until you've got a search warrant. Understand? Have you got a search warrant or not?"

Michael shook his head. "Zadik, calm down. I thought that with our kind of relationship we wouldn't need a search warrant," he said pleasantly. "Take it easy, I'm not concerned with those affairs just now. I'm here because of Tirzah Rubin, and because of things that became clear from what Matty Cohen was telling us, and, like I said, because you should have a clear interest in all this. Unless, of course, you have an interest in keeping matters *un*clear."

"What's that supposed to mean? What are you hinting at? You think I've got something to hide?"

Michael said nothing.

"Are you crazy?" Zadik shouted. "What have I got to hide here? I showed your people last night exactly where—and you!" he said, pointing at Eli Bachar. "Didn't I give you help with everything you required? Didn't I tell people to—"

"Yes, yes, people cooperated," Eli Bachar said, trying to calm Zadik down. "But try and understand: Matty Cohen saw something. There's no denying it."

"What? What did he see?"

"Enough for us to request an autopsy," Eli Bachar answered.

Zadik glanced at the telephone on his desk, pursed his lips, and returned his attention to the policemen in front of him, remaining silent.

"Listen, Zadik," Michael said. "The police need to get in here, that's clear. Do the math yourself: do you prefer me or someone else? I'm not saying they'll let you choose anyone you want. But now I'm going to pose the question in a, well, if you'll forgive me, didactic manner. Are you certain you want to push me out of here?"

Zadik did not speak.

"Okay," Michael said. "So let's just say you and I understand one another. If that's the case, I'd like to verify a few facts."

"What facts? Everything is perfectly clear," Zadik grumbled.

"Not perfectly, no," Michael insisted. "That matter of the back door to the String Building: the guard didn't even see Matty Cohen enter the building because he came in the back way."

"Of course he came in through the back," Zadik said, brushing off the question. "He was on his way to Benny Meyuhas up on the roof of the String Building, he'd parked his car in the lot out back, why would he need to pass by the guard on his way in?"

"But anyone can come in through the back door," Eli Bachar claimed.

"No, not just anyone," Zadik said, rubbing his cheek. "Only people with keys: veteran department heads and all kinds of . . . just the people who actually work in that building."

"We'll need a list of everyone with a key," Eli Bachar noted. "Everyone who could get in to the building without the guard seeing him."

"Aviva will get it for you, and there's somebody over in the String Building, Max Levin, who knows—but what do you think, that somebody pushed the pillar on top of Tirzah?"

"When we were reconstructing events with Matty Cohen, it turned out that some argument might have been taking place there," Michael said carefully. "We would like to speak with her husband, too, with Benny Meyuhas. But we'll do that when we talk to him about performing an autopsy."

Zadik regarded him with interest. "Okay, I'm willing to help you, on one condition."

"I'm listening," Michael said. "I'm not big on conditions, but I'm willing to listen."

"That if you don't find anything, you'll get off our backs about the informant. I'm not willing to hear another word about it."

"And what about vice versa?"

"What vice versa?"

"If we do find something."

"If you do find something?"

"Yes," Michael said, folding his arms. "If we find something unnatural, then what? Will you give us the name of your informant?"

"No way!" Zadik shouted. "I'm not giving you anything, just help, no arguments."

"It was a joke," Eli Bachar explained.

"It wasn't funny," Zadik said. "Nothing is funny right now. You people can talk with Benny Meyuhas, but I doubt you'll learn anything new from him. There's no way he'll be cooperative now, I've heard he's completely catatonic. He's been lying on his bed, not talking to a soul."

"Who is close to him?" Michael asked. "Are you?"

"I . . ." Zadik hesitated. "He's an introvert, no, I . . . but there's Hagar, his producer, she's over there with that actress, the Indian woman. She hasn't left his side."

"I understand that Rubin is close to him," Eli Bachar said. "That's what I've been told."

"Rubin, yes, he's close to him," Zadik said, glancing at the door. "If Benny will talk to anyone at all, it would be Rubin."

"So we were thinking maybe we should take Rubin with us," Eli Bachar said.

"He's here, outside my office," Zadik mumbled, and pressed the intercom.

"What?" Aviva answered, her voice loud and metallic.

"Ask Rubin to step into my office for a minute," Zadik instructed her.

A moment later the door opened and Rubin stood in the doorway, the edges of Natasha's red scarf clearly visible behind him.

"Wait outside for a minute, Natasha," Zadik told her. "Come on in alone for a minute, Arye. Come, meet . . . Chief Superintendent?"—Michael nodded—"Chief Superintendent Michael Ohayon."

"I've heard of you," Rubin said, proffering his hand.

Michael shook his hand and said self-consciously, "I'm an old fan of your program. Inspector Eli Bachar, too. In fact, all of us."

"Really?" Arye Rubin asked without a smile. He pulled at the cuffs of his wool sports jacket. Eli Bachar glanced at his long, narrow face, at the two deep creases in his cheeks, at his narrow brown eyes, at the focused, burning gaze that radiated from them. Rubin shook Eli's hand as well and then turned to Zadik with a questioning look. "Natasha's been waiting—" He glanced toward the door.

"I know, I know, she'll have to keep waiting," he said impatiently. "I've got to tell her something, anything. First, to put her out of her misery," he said, passing his hand over his cropped gray hair. "And second, Zadik, she's onto something pretty big."

It was hard for Eli Bachar to hide his excitement. He wondered whether Michael remembered that Arye Rubin was Tzilla's hero. He had to admit that up close, live, Rubin was even more impressive than on the television screen. The man didn't seem to have an inflated ego, he seemed like he was just some regular guy. He really did inspire esteem.

Esteem and modesty, humility and quiet admiration: these feelings accompanied Eli Bachar on his way to the car and after he had seated himself inside it. The radio was on, and the chirping noises from the transmitter did not drown out a live radio report about the laid-off workers, who were at that moment alighting from the police van in handcuffs, their wives waiting in ambush at police headquarters. The reporter mentioned Danny Benizri, too, "the hero of the day," he called him. "He's with us right now. Hello, Danny Benizri."

"Hello, Gidi."

"Danny Benizri, what now? Where will you go from here?" he asked theatrically. But Eli Bachar did not hear what the television correspondent answered, since at that moment Michael was telling Rubin how important he thought his weekly program, *The Justice of the Sting,* was. Then he said, "I've been curious for a long time about the name *The Justice of the Sting.* Where does it come from?"

"It's the title of a poem I loved," Rubin said.

"Which?" Michael asked.

"It's by Dan Pagis, and it's about wasps. But the wasps are really only a parable," Arye Rubin muttered, looking out the window. "Never mind how it's connected, but it does connect to the program."

"It's a program with balls," Eli Bachar dared to say from the back seat. Even as they reached Benny Meyuhas's house and Rubin was saying in his deep, unique voice, "Maybe I should go in alone first and then you can come in in another minute, what do you think?" Eli was thinking how he would tell Tzilla about meeting him. He wanted to remember every detail.

"Sounds like a good idea, you're his good friend," Michael said. "That's what I understand, right? Zadik told us you're very close."

"From the age of ten, from grade school," Rubin said. "We did everything together. Benny is . . . like my own flesh and blood." He got out of the car. "I'll call you in a few minutes," he promised.

# CHAPTER FIVE

After about a quarter of an hour waiting, Eli Bachar lifted the brass knocker under the ceramic nameplate decorated with birds and flowers, in the middle of which was written RUBIN-MEYUHAS, and knocked on the wooden door. A gaunt young woman whose long black hair enveloped half her pale face opened the door. For a moment she stood there, silent, blinking her eyes and rubbing one black-stockinged foot against the other. She glanced over her shoulder seeking confirmation, and when this did not come she shrugged as if to say, "I've done all I could," and, eyes lowered, whispered, "you can come in, it's very cold outside." She stepped aside to let them pass.

"We've been waiting out in the rain for nearly half an hour," Eli Bachar said by way of reproach when they were inside the apartment. "Rubin said he would call us after a few minutes, but it's already been more than twenty."

"I'm just . . . ," the young woman began, clearly embarrassed, "this isn't my house, I can't—"

"Who are you?" Eli Bachar asked sharply.

"I . . . my name's Sarah," she said, rubbing her hands together. "I . . . I'm an actress, I'm in Benny's film. I play Gemullah, but my real name's Sarah."

Pale light that filtered into the foyer through a large arched window lit up the dark wall painted in deep blue, as well as the model house built of wood that stood on a sheet of plywood with a small sign affixed to it: THE HOUSE OF GREIFENBACH. Michael looked at the wooden house, at the windows and grilles and doorways and hallways that connected one wing to another, at the lighted rooms between the wings, at the darkened rooms. Painted sheets of plywood covered the open spaces on the upper level of the house, creating surfaces—roofs of different heights that were, at certain spots, bordered by dark railings. Between one railing and the next or one wing and the next there were ramps without railings. On a bookstand next to the model house a video monitor stood lit, the screen filled with blue light and no picture.

"What is this?" Eli Bachar whispered to Michael, "a doll house? I didn't know they had any little kids. Look, it's got real working lights and everything."

"This," Michael said, "is a maquette, a model of the house in *Iddo and Eynam*. That's the way it looks, or is supposed to look, in the film they're shooting."

"How do you know that?" Eli Bachar asked, his expression one of annoyance and awe all at once.

"I remember it from my studies. In my first year at university I took Introduction to Agnon, I've told you this, don't you remember? It was an elective course. I studied this story, *Iddo and Eynam*." He looked at Eli's face and hastened to add, "To this very day I don't understand it. It's a beautiful story, but dense, unclear. A very strange story full of symbols. I remember the lecturer explaining them, and even then I didn't completely understand, or really, I didn't *want* to understand what the man thought Agnon was saying. But I remember the name of the house," he said, pointing at the sign. "Greifenbach. And there's this young woman who walks around at night on the roofs and sings the hymns of Iddo and Eynam." He did not mention Dr. Gamzu and Dr. Ginat, the book collector and the folklore researcher, whom he remembered well, or the description of Gemullah's meeting with Ginat. More than anything he recalled the frightening ending; he could still hear the echo of the professor's murky voice calling out with great emotion: "What is it that caused Ginat to sabotage his own handiwork, destroying in a short period of time things that he had toiled over for a great many years?" Occasionally over the years that question would return to him, bubbling up when he witnessed, with his own eyes, the destruction that human beings were capable of bringing about in a single action against what was most dear to them.

From the kitchen a woman in her forties dressed in shabby jeans suddenly appeared. It was clear from the disheveled locks of silver hair, the terribly lined face, and the narrow gray eyes that regarded the visitors with suspicion that she was the exact opposite of the other, younger woman. "It's because of me, it's my fault," she told them, unabashed. "Arye Rubin asked me to call you, but I wanted to wait until—" she gestured with her head toward the closed door at the end of the wide hallway. "Benny isn't up to—I thought it could wait," she concluded.

"Are you a family member? His sister or something?" Eli Bachar asked.

"My name's Hagar," she said as she shook out her hair and placed a hand on her neck.

"Hagar what?" Eli Bachar persisted, while Michael looked around and noticed, close by, a row of framed photographs, all of them black and white, hanging on the wall opposite the front door. One in particular stood out, a large photograph of three young men dressed in hiking boots and kaffiyehs and khaki shorts and shirts, their sleeves rolled sloppily up their tanned arms. Between them stood a girl, thin and tan, in dark shorts and a white shirt, who was fingering the fringes of a white kaffiyeh wrapped around her neck. Her long, fair hair was blowing in the breeze, one lock of it touching the tallest of the three boys, whose arm was resting on the girl's shoulders. Michael narrowed his eyes; he could only recognize the tallest, whose forelock cast a shadow over his brow and his broad smile. As for the other two and the girl, he had never seen them before. The photograph gave him a pang; something about it made him think of a time that would never return, and that what had been lost was not only the look of youthful exuberance shining from their faces in black and white on a background of white sand. Even today Arye Rubin was a handsome man, but his face did not retain the slightest hint of that joie de vivre so evident in the photograph taken more than thirty years earlier. They looked the part of a joyous band of kids on the annual trip of a youth movement. He himself had photos like these, with larger and smaller groups of friends, from annual treks and journeys in the Negev and the Galilee. They seemed to be his age, or at least of the same generation. And the girl: how much charm there was in her thin silhouette, in her long leg extended forward! Her upper lip was stretched over prominent front teeth, and the little guy with freckles to the right had curly hair and a broken front tooth.

"You're Benny Meyuhas's producer," Eli Bachar said in a tone that indicated he knew everything there was to know about Benny Meyuhas.

"His producer, assistant, and close friend, too. I'm everything wrapped up in one," she said dryly, as if clarifying that she was the one who wore the pants in the family.

Michael turned to her. "Who are the people in this picture? This is Arye Rubin, isn't it?" he asked, pointing to the tallest of the three boys.

"Yes, that's Rubin on the right. The girl standing next to him is Tirzah, and this," she said, coming close to the photo and touching the face of the short guy with the freckles, "is Benny. They were together in the army. This photo was taken during a trek in the Negev after they finished high school, before their enlistment. And here they are in the army," she said, pointing to a different photograph in which the three young men appeared in uniform and dusty paratroopers' boots, berets tucked into their shoulder straps, their arms slung around one another's necks. Rubin was standing in the middle. To his right was Benny Meyuhas, and to his left the third youth from the Negev trek.

"And who is this?" Michael asked, returning to the previous photograph. The young man he was pointing to was thin and dark and smiling from ear to ear, his arms spread wide in a clownish gesture of someone wishing to embrace it all.

"I don't really know him," she said reticently. "I've never met him. His name is Sroul, they were a group, a clique, together all the time. They were like the Three Musketeers, never separated. They grew up in Haifa, went through the new immigrant camps and Reali High School, and joined the paratroopers. Everyone knew them."

"Where is he now?" Michael asked. "Where's Sroul?"

"In the United States. He left right after the Yom Kippur War. He was seriously wounded—burned—so they sent him there, at first for plastic surgery and treatments, and then he just stayed on. I've heard that he's become quite ultra-Orthodox, a genuine religious fanatic."

"And they've stayed in touch all through the years?" Michael inquired. Hagar intended to answer him, but just then the door at the end of the hallway opened and suddenly the gray floors lit up, and only then did he notice that they were painted green and gold, the wooden doors in turquoise. Rubin stood in the doorway. "You can come in," he said to Michael, and then to Hagar added, "Could you make him a cup of tea? He's getting dehydrated. Put three teaspoons of sugar in to give him some energy."

"Since yesterday he hasn't touched a thing, only a few drops of water," Hagar complained. "Has he stopped the business with the wall? I can't stand it, I was afraid he would split his head open."

"He's stopped," Rubin said. "Now he's quiet."

Rubin returned to the room and left the door open. Michael followed him inside. The bedroom was spacious, high-ceilinged. A double bed stood next to the wall, and atop the disheveled sheets sat a thin man, his head leaning against the wall. He did not direct his gaze at Michael, who was standing in the doorway, nor did he relate to Rubin, who was sitting at the edge of the bed. Michael took in his small, wrinkled face and his bleary blue eyes, which were fixed on the opposite wall. Not only was there no trace of that chubby, freckled youth of the photograph in this man, but it was completely incomprehensible that he and Rubin could be the same age. Behind the bed stood two arched windows, and beyond them, past the raised blinds, were two large planters filled with pansies. It had stopped raining. Michael pulled up a chair from the corner of the room and sat not far from the bed. Eli Bachar stood hesitantly in the doorway. Muffled voices could be heard from another room, then someone apparently opened a door and the voices grew louder and clearer. Only then did Michael realize they were coming from a television or radio. Distractedly he heard the beginning of a news broadcast: "The hospital spokesman has informed us that the condition of the minister of labor and social affairs is stable and that she is expected to be released within the next few days."

Michael introduced himself to Benny Meyuhas, who blinked, stared, and grimaced, his lips parched and cracked. "Arye tells me," he murmured quietly, "that you want to postpone the funeral, that you want to perform an autopsy. . . . I don't . . . it's not my decision, we were not officially married. Arye Rubin will have to give his consent. Officially, he's still her husband."

"We'll get to that," Michael said as he threw Eli Bachar a questioning look. Eli shrugged his shoulders to say that he had no idea whose consent was needed. "But you have no objection as such, do you?" Michael asked.

"What does it matter?" Benny Meyuhas responded finally with a frown. "Tirzah is no longer with us. She has left us."

"You'll have to clarify whose signature is necessary," Michael said quietly to Eli Bachar.

Eli Bachar nodded. "I'll take care of it," he said on his way out of the room. To Rubin he said, "Why don't you step out with me, we'll leave them alone."

Rubin straightened in his chair. "Why should I step out?" he asked, astonished. "I'm here to be with Benny."

Benny Meyuhas pounded the wall with his fist. His knuckles were ruddy and raw. "He doesn't need to go anywhere," he said in a parched voice. "I keep no secrets from him."

Eli Bachar walked out of the room quickly, in the direction of the foyer. Michael shut the door. The only sound in the room was Benny Meyuhas's noisy breathing. He sounded as though he might choke.

"I also wanted to ask you," Michael said, "if you knew that Tirzah was there, in the middle of the night. We're trying to understand what she was doing there so late. Did you know she was there?"

Benny Meyuhas shook his head and passed his hands over his cheeks and his thinning hair. "I didn't know," he said at last.

"How could that be?" Michael said. "You were filming on the roof of that same building. How was it that you didn't know?"

"She didn't tell me," he said dismissively and turned his head toward the wall.

Michael asked whether he had any idea why she would have been there so late at night.

Benny Meyuhas had no explanation. She had not told him that she would be at work, and he did not know of any unfinished scenery that demanded her presence.

Michael asked whether it was possible she had made an appointment with someone in her office.

"Anything is possible, how can I know?"

"No, I'm asking whether it was normal, whether there were precedents for such a thing," Michael explained.

Benny Meyuhas grimaced as if to deny the possibility. She was always meeting with people in the office or the canteen, but never in the middle of the night.

"I'm trying to understand," Michael said slowly, emphasizing each word. "What did you mean when you shouted, 'It's my fault, it's because of me'? What did you mean when you saw Tirzah—when she was no longer alive?"

The look Benny Meyuhas gave him was one of confusion.

"You do remember that you said those things."

"I remember," Benny said, perplexed. He pursed his lips into an expression of loathing. "But what is there to explain?"

"Perhaps you meant that because of you she was at work at that hour?"

"No, not that."

"What then? Did you do something that caused her death?"

Benny Meyuhas flashed him a furious look. "The marble," he said at last, smothering his face in his hands. "They say it was the marble pillar that crushed her."

"Don't think about that, Benny, you don't need to be thinking about that," Arye Rubin interjected, a look of worry on his face. He leaned on the bed, hooking his arm around Benny Meyuhas's shoulder. "It's not because of you. Nobody could tell Tirzah what to do. You could have told her a thousand times to move the pillar and she wouldn't have, she wouldn't have given a damn about your opinion or anyone else's."

"Did she generally tell you where she was going?" Michael said, feeling his way.

"Sometimes, not always. It depended," Benny answered reluctantly.

"On what? On where she was going? On the time of day? What?"

Benny Meyuhas did not look at him. He was staring at his fingers, which were pleating the edges of a page of the *Haaretz* newspaper lying on the bed next to him. Between the small advertisement at the corner of the page in which LIAR was printed in bold black letters, just as it had been every day for the past two months, and an item about the Jerusalem hairstylist and his girlfriend the model who had been found shot to death, there was a small notice about the head of the Scenery Department at Israel Television, who had been killed in an accident.

Benny Meyuhas remained silent.

"How is it that she didn't say anything to you? You were both in the same place, you worked together. You yourself were there, up on the roof."

Benny Meyuhas frowned. "Yes, I was."

"From what time? Approximately."

"A little after six, after it got dark. We were waiting for the moon; we were hoping it would poke through the clouds."

"Who knew that you were up there?" Michael asked.

Benny Meyuhas shrugged. "I don't know, I don't have a clue," he said without looking up. "Whoever needed to know."

"Were you aware that Matty Cohen was on his way?" Michael asked, aware that Rubin was tensing up.

"The tea will be here in a minute," Rubin said to Benny Meyuhas. "It's hard for you to speak because your mouth is so dry." Rubin cast a glance at Michael that contained a measure of warning, but Michael ignored it.

"Matty Cohen was on his way to the roof," Michael said to Benny Meyuhas, "to put a stop to your production. Did you know that?"

Benny looked up from his fingers. "No," he said in his parched voice, "no, I didn't. There were rumors. . . . I had heard they weren't going to let me complete the missing bits, Zadik had already hinted . . . but I didn't know that he was—" A note of astonishment had crept into his voice. "But he didn't come, I didn't see him."

"He was on his way, and he saw Tirzah at around midnight, before—" Michael waved his hand instead of completing his thought. "She was still alive at the time."

Benny Meyuhas regarded him; unlike his voice and the rest of his body, his round blue eyes were now filled with expression, his pain alive and writhing. They were bloodshot, the eyes of a man haunted.

"She was not standing there alone; she was with someone else," Michael said carefully. "Someone was arguing with her."

Benny Meyuhas did not speak.

"We thought that perhaps you might have some idea who she could have been speaking with in the middle of the night," Michael said.

"I don't," Benny Meyuhas said. "I didn't even know she was there. If I had known, I would have—" He fell silent and covered his face with his hands.

"What would you have done?" Michael hastened to ask. "What?"

"I would have spoken to her, I would have told her—never mind."

"Are you certain she did not tell you she would be at work?" Michael persisted.

Benny Meyuhas shook his head. "I did not know."

"I understand that there was some . . . disagreement . . . crisis . . . rift between you two?" Michael said, venturing a guess.

Benny Meyuhas's amazement was visible. "We—how did you know that?" A note of suspicion entered his voice. "Nobody knew," he said, wiping his face with his hands. In the ensuing silence, the only sound was his heavy breathing. Arye Rubin laid a hand on his shoulder.

"Generally speaking, did you two get along well?" Michael asked, studying Benny Meyuhas's face and ignoring Arye Rubin's look of reproach.

"We got along beautifully, beautifully," Benny Meyuhas said. "God . . . how . . ." and he pressed his hands to his face.

"You yourself were there," Michael said to Arye Rubin.

"When?" Rubin asked, surprised.

"Last night, when Tirzah . . . you were at the television station, weren't you?"

"Yes, I was, but in the editing rooms. They're in the main building, nowhere near. . . . I had no idea, I didn't see Tirzah, I was busy working," Rubin said.

"There's no connection between the two buildings, no passageway?" Michael asked.

"None," Rubin said emphatically. "There's practically no connection between floors of the same building. Anyway, there are always people around. Apart from the security guards, there are rooms manned twenty-four hours a day. The broadcast monitoring room, for example: you can check who was on duty monitoring local and foreign transmissions, the place is never unmanned."

Michael asked suddenly, "What was the disagreement about? Did something specific happen?"

Benny Meyuhas glanced at him, dismayed. "It's something personal, it's not relevant— something personal."

Michael looked at the newspaper. A headline at the side of the page caught his eye, the story of an explosive device planted at the door of a West Jerusalem apartment occupied by three female Arab university students. Apparently the bomb had been placed by some ultra-Orthodox fanatics, and the police sapper sent to defuse it had been slightly injured when he touched the bag. "You can never know," Michael said after a few long moments of silence, "if it's relevant or not. Sometimes something that seems relevant—"

"I don't want to talk about it," Benny Meyuhas sputtered.

"Was it a serious argument?" Michael said, groping. "Was it something important, something that might affect the future of your relationship? Was there some talk of a separation?"

Benny Meyuhas slumped until he was lying on top of the bed, pulled his knees to his chest, and burst into tears. Arye Rubin's face wore a look of astonishment; after a moment he leaned over and touched Benny's shoulder.

"Did you know about all this?" Michael asked Rubin, as though Benny Meyuhas were not in the room.

Rubin shook his head. "I had no idea."

Hagar pushed the door open with her shoulder, carrying a cup of tea on a saucer with a teaspoon clinking inside. Michael hastened to make way for her to pass and went to stand by the window, where he could observe her placing the cup and saucer on the nightstand next to the bed, and where he could watch her as she threw an inquisitive and accusatory look at Rubin. Rubin shrugged his shoulders as if to say, "I don't know." When she touched Benny Meyuhas's arm, he removed his hands from his face and glanced at her as though he were seeing her for the first time in his life.

Michael stood watching the window and the side of the bed near it and noticed a pair of black velvet embroidered boots shoved underneath, partially hidden by the bed. He wondered if they belonged to

Tirzah, but there was something coquettish and juvenile about them which did not quite jibe with the impression he was forming of her.

Michael was still pondering this when he heard Rubin say, "Drink up, Benny, otherwise we'll have to put you on an IV; you're dehydrating. You don't have to eat, but you've got to drink."

The sound of Benny's head butting the wall behind him sickened Michael. "She's left us, Arye," he wailed. "She didn't want to be with me anymore."

The door opened again. Eli Bachar stood for a moment watching the two men on the bed, then said to Michael, "They say that Arye Rubin has to sign. If he agrees."

Rubin regarded him, stunned, then nodded his consent. To Benny he said, "I'm going to give my consent to an autopsy, if that's okay with you. Do you agree?"

"I've got to get going," Eli Bachar said impatiently. "Someone will call you and bring the forms around, okay?" Without waiting for an answer he left the room.

"Benny," Rubin said hesitantly, "do you consent? Is it all right with you?"

"She's left us, Arye, she didn't want to live with me anymore. I don't have . . . I didn't have any reason to go on . . ."

"That's the way he's been the whole time," Hagar said from the corner of the room, her brows knitting to the point where the crease between them deepened even further. "That's the way he's been talking the whole time," she said, and left the room.

Michael followed her. She was standing in the foyer, next to the kitchen door, her arm on the door frame and her head resting on her arm.

"It's my impression that you're the person closest to him," he said, looking at her unabashedly. "Do you think you might know what was going on with them?"

She lifted her head and stepped away from the doorway. "With who?" she asked suspiciously.

"Benny and Tirzah."

"Going on? Who says anything was going on? When?"

"Rubin told me you'd know the details," Michael said, "about the rift between them lately. He said you would know, that you'd certainly felt it, even if Benny had never mentioned anything about it to you. He says you're the only person who always knows what's happening with Benny."

Her face softened. "Believe me, I have no idea. I was very close, I mean, pretty close, but . . . he never talked to me about Tirzah." She scratched at an invisible spot on the door frame with the tip of her fingernail. "I was close to him in matters of"—she gestured toward the maquette—"anything related to work. In those matters I'm an expert. But where his private life is concerned I'm not, not where his life with Tirzah was concerned."

"But you certainly must have felt something, perceived something. Sensitive people can recognize things in people they're close to even without talking about it explicitly, don't you think?"

She looked down the hallway as if to verify that no one was listening. "Where's Sarah?" she wondered aloud. "Her coat is here, so she hasn't left yet. Maybe she's in the other room watching television," she said, indicating the living room. "There was tension between them lately, something was weighing heavily on Benny, that much was clear to me. I know him like the palm of my hand; there's no question that something was going on. I didn't ask him because I didn't dare to, but it was clear to me also from the way Tirzah was behaving, even from the way she talked to me lately. But I don't have a clue what—" She glanced at her watch, startled. "Are you planning to be here for a while?" she asked quickly, and without waiting for an answer added, "because if you are, I'd like—look, I've got to get back to the station to talk to Zadik about continuing filming. We can't stop now, there's only a little more to wrap up, we've got to—I'm going to Zadik with Rubin. . . . Sarah," she said, turning to the young woman who had suddenly appeared from the next room. "Can you stay here a little longer? I don't want to leave Benny alone."

"No problem," Sarah said, rubbing her feet one against the other.

"Where are your shoes?" Hagar asked, surprised, and the young woman blanched.

"Over there," she said, pointing to the living room. "I took them off in there. I'm going to—it's cold in here, but there was mud on them . . ." She fell silent. But Hagar was already putting on her coat and made no response.

"Arye," she called toward the bedroom. "Arye, let's get moving." As she spoke, she moved toward the room.

"Where *are* your shoes?" Michael asked in a whisper, and Sarah blushed, indicating with her head the room she had just emerged from.

"Black boots? Embroidered?"

She cast him a suspicious look and nodded.

"Know where they are?"

She shrugged, her answer unclear.

"I actually know where they are," Michael said. "Shall I tell you?"

"That's not necessary," she whispered, her frightened eyes on the bedroom door. "I just don't want Hagar to know. If she did, she'd—" Sarah did not complete her thought.

"Yes, what would happen if she found out?"

"She would think that we . . . that I . . ." She spread her arms wide.

"That what? That you what?"

"That I, you know, like, like that I was with him," she said, averting her glance.

"And the truth is that—"

"Nothing. I mean, yes, I . . . he . . . he was crying so hard and asked me to . . . and Hagar wasn't here . . . so I, not that I, I just lay down next to him. He put his arms around me and cried and talked and I . . . what could I do? I let him talk."

"And what did he tell you?"

"Truth is, I didn't understand most of it," she admitted. "He said she didn't want him anymore, that she—Tirzah—had already gone away before this happened, that she'd left him. I don't understand why, but he said, 'She couldn't forgive me.' I don't know what it was she couldn't forgive him."

Rubin and Hagar emerged from the bedroom. "We're on our way to Zadik," Hagar said. "Are you going to be around here much longer?" she asked Michael.

"No, not much longer," Michael assured her. In fact, he had no idea how much longer he would stay.

"But you're staying," Hagar commanded Sarah.

"Sure," she responded, nodding vehemently. "For as long as necessary."

When the door had shut, Sarah regarded Michael with suspicion. "You won't say anything to her, will you?" she asked.

"Why are you afraid of her?" Michael asked. "Do you think she's jealous? That she'll be angry with you?"

"Of course!" she said with a look that made it clear she thought he was thickheaded. "Everyone knows. She . . . he . . . always, right from the beginning people told me."

"And Tirzah?"

"What about her? There was nothing going on between Benny and Hagar, they were just . . . they didn't sleep together, people just said she always wanted to. Tirzah didn't . . . well, I don't know."

"What's it like working with him?" Michael asked.

Her face lit up. "He's amazing, the best, everyone says so. He's a wonderful director, teaches you everything. But he demands a lot, all the time."

"Who built this model, this maquette? Tirzah?"

"Yes, it's the model of the house," she said, pursing her thick red lips, which gave her face a look of exaggerated earnestness. "The whole story takes place there. Do you know *Iddo and Eynam*?"

Michael mumbled something incomprehensible.

"I play the part of Gemullah," she said, and her eyes shone with visible pride. "That's why I had to understand the story really well. *Iddo and Eynam* is the story of ancient Jewish Hebrew roots," she declaimed. "Benny says it's about the missing link in the ancient history of the Hebrews and about the attempt by the Ashkenazi intellectuals, like, to castrate the Eastern Jews, to annihilate the missing link in the ancient history of the Hebrews. He talked to us about it before we started filming. I don't completely understand, but Hagar says it's about a woman, and the two men fighting for her, and in the end everyone dies because of the war between them."

"Everyone?"

"No, I mean, Gemullah dies and Ginat dies and Gamzu buries them, but it's like, spiritually and emotionally, he dies later, too."

"So it's safe to say you have enjoyed taking part in this film."

"It's been a real experience." She pushed her long, shiny hair behind one ear. "It's a big privilege," she added, regarding him with large, black, flashing eyes. "He chose me from all those . . . lots of them . . . there were lots of girls at the audition. Singers, too. I wish it wouldn't end, you have no idea how beautiful it is . . ."

He glanced at the cassette protruding from the video player and took a gamble. "I see you already have a videotape of it here," he said as he leaned over and pressed the play button.

"No, no!" she said, mortified. "Don't touch that, you're not allowed! It's only a working copy to help us correct our mistakes, to show us how we're acting. I don't—it's not edited, and Benny will be furious if someone not involved in the production sees it without—"

The sounds of a song in some strange language filled the room as they emerged from the mouth of Sarah-Gemullah walking along the rooftop railing, dressed in a flowing and lightweight white gown, her arms extended to the sides in sleeves as wide as wings, her black hair shiny and the moon dangling above her. Then the film cut short, and for a moment other images sped by until finally the film returned to the screen. Now a bearded man, tall and very dark, dressed in a heavy silver robe with a sort of breastplate, was carrying something in his arms; it took a few seconds for Michael to realize it was a slaughtered goat dripping blood. Gemullah in her white gown, head bent, stood next to a man in a light-colored suit and top hat before the bearded man. "Who is that?" Michael asked, pointing to the man thrusting his hands into the blood of the slaughtered goat.

"That's Dr. Gamzu," she whispered in response, as the man in the top hat smeared a streak of blood on Gemullah's forehead. "That's before their wedding ceremony. It's not in the story, it's an image that Benny added. You're not allowed, nobody's allowed yet—" The scene was accompanied by a high-pitched flute and the vague murmurings of the bearded man.

They did not notice Benny padding down the hall in bare feet and entering the foyer. Michael only caught sight of him when he was standing next to him. Without a word he pressed the button and stopped the player. For a moment the room was filled with the sounds of an orchestra and a group of children sitting around a Hanukkah menorah shouting the answer to a question asked by the host of the show, Adir Bareket, whom Michael recognized thanks to his son. Fourteen years earlier, when Yuval was ten, he had been addicted to the programs hosted by Adir Bareket and had begged his father to take him to participate in one of them, at least as a member of the studio audience. He had mentioned the prizes the kids could win and the exciting surprises and had even used the trick that almost always failed but which he tried again and again, claiming in a teary voice that everyone else had been allowed to go. But Michael, who generally liked to grant his son's wishes, had stubbornly refused and had not even pretended that there was some technical difficulty. Instead, he had repeatedly explained to his only son who, at that time, he saw only twice a week and every other weekend, what exactly it was he hated about that program: how a few children received prizes and gifts after degrading themselves to the satisfaction of the host and the jubilant cries of the children in the studio, how they exposed their hidden weaknesses or their ignorance or their excessive innocence to the whole world. Now he looked for a moment at Adir Bareket, who preceded the lighting of the first Hanukkah candle with greetings and an insipid joke, and noticed how his face had swollen with the years and his eyes had sunk into the folds of his copious flesh, even though his looks had apparently had no adverse effect on his success: he had become the superstar of a prime-time Friday-evening entertainment program for adults, a show devoted to exposing the intimate relations between couples, as copied from a popular American television program.

"They're putting a stop to my production," Benny Meyuhas said with more astonishment than bitterness. "We're only fifty thousand dollars short, and they won't let me film the final bits. So how much does a program like Bareket's cost? Live, with five cameras in the big studio in the String Building, with all the warm-up performances they do with the kids beforehand and the 'A Wish Comes True' segment. How expensive all that is, and how repulsive," he said derisively. "But that's what the riffraff wants, that's the way it is the world over. If it weren't for the special grant for Eastern Jewish culture, they never would have given me the chance—" He dismissed the rest of what he was going to say with a wave of his hand and fell silent.

"What I saw here was quite impressive," Michael said hesitantly. "I imagine that—how much money are we talking about here?"

"All in all another fifty thousand," Benny Meyuhas repeated, adding in a mechanical tone, "for a sum like that they want to put a stop to the largest production they've had in the last few years. Anyway, nothing matters now, nothing matters anymore."

The young woman began to protest but quickly shut her mouth and lowered her head in the manner of a person who knows her place. "In the end they'll provide the budget," she said to Michael in a feeble voice. "In the end—"

"Sarah told me," Michael said, turning to Benny Meyuhas, "that you explained your interpretation of the meaning of *Iddo and Eynam* to the participants before you started filming, but she couldn't quite repeat it. Perhaps you'd be willing to tell me what—"

"Now?" Benny Meyuhas asked, amazed. "Now I can't—anyway, why is it relevant?"

Michael looked at him expectantly and did not respond to the question.

"Look," Benny Meyuhas said, fixing his eyes on the wall behind the monitor as though reading a speech written there. "I do not believe that this story, *Iddo and Eynam,* is about ancient Jewish documents or the tribe of Gad, which supposedly never returned from Babylonian captivity. I believe that this is a story about Jews of Eastern origin in Israel, and what Zionism has done to them. The East is Gemullah singing her songs to the moon, and Zionism is that which treats her at best like some folkloric finding, and the West is what tries to identify the grammar—grammar, can you believe it?—in these songs, which were created by a man and his daughter. And you know what's so beautiful about all this?"

Michael shook his head and watched Benny Meyuhas expectantly.

"What's so beautiful with Agnon is that he really loves what you call 'communities of different cultures' and that he doesn't think they're perfect—"

"Who?" Michael asked. "Who doesn't he think is perfect?"

"Eastern Jews. He thinks that they, too, were in a process of degeneration, that they were sinking. This story is truly a tragedy, and it touches, if you'll excuse the word, on the *mystical* nature of our lives here. In my opinion this is the most beautiful and the saddest story about Zionism that exists, and I don't need to tell you that Agnon was larger than life, perhaps like Shakespeare, and for me—"

Michael wished to respond; what Benny said about Agnon's attitude toward Eastern Jews had touched him in a way he was not prepared for. It was so far from the gloomy impression that that professor of literature had made on him twenty years earlier. Benny's words, combined with the delicate images he had seen on the screen just minutes before, were so emotionally saturated, so pierced through with deep sorrow and, especially, with honesty, that he had not expected something like that at all, especially not from a production for television.

The chirp from his beeper caused Benny Meyuhas to stop talking and look around, alarmed. Michael waited a moment, but he understood that Benny Meyuhas would explain no more. He glanced at the display on his beeper and asked to use the telephone. Benny Meyuhas nodded his absentminded consent, pressed the remote control, and the screen went black. Michael could hear Eli Bachar's muffled voice along with the television, reporting the arrests of the laid-off workers from the Hulit factory and their anticipated trial. He listened to what Eli Bachar was telling him and said, "I'm on my way now. First I'll talk to Zadik."

"Has something happened?" the young woman asked.

"Yes," Michael said. He looked at Benny Meyuhas, who was shutting off the video player. "Matty Cohen died half an hour ago."

A tremor passed through her, and she covered her mouth with her hands as though suppressing a scream. Benny Meyuhas's face showed no signs that he had heard. Slowly he rose from where he had been bending over the screen and, without uttering a word, walked in the direction of the bedroom.

# CHAPTER SIX

Natasha had already been standing for nearly half an hour, again, in the corner next to the ladies' room at the end of the hallway on the second floor, where she could watch everyone who entered Aviva's office and could know who was inside with Zadik. Twice she had passed through the hallway as if by chance, and peeked in. Aviva was talking on the phone and did not notice her; Natasha returned to her post by the bathrooms, and every time someone approached, she rushed inside the ladies' room. It wasn't that she cared whether someone saw her there or not; it's that she didn't have the energy to talk to people and explain what she was doing there. In fact, she herself did not exactly know how to explain it; she only knew that at first she had been waiting for Rubin to arrive, and now, after he had arrived, she was waiting for him to leave Zadik's office, even though she knew quite well that he was not speaking with Zadik about her, since she had seen Hagar arrive with him and understood that the only thing they had on their minds was Benny Meyuhas and his film.

She could speak with Hefetz, light a fire under him as they say, but she did not have the courage to talk to him. How could she ask him to give her a crew after having said to him, "You disgust me"? It really did disgust her just thinking about Hefetz. She could not bear to hear one more time about his wife's flight, how she was supposed to have arrived in another two days but had come home early. She had not even heard him out, had walked away in the middle of his sentence. She was tired of being his plaything. And she was no idiot; she knew Hefetz well. If he knew what she was onto, he would take the whole thing away from her and give it to someone else. He would promise, as always, that she—and only she—would broadcast it, but in the end he would take away both the report and the credit: with Hefetz, there was no mixing love and business. He would even say he was motivated by concern for her welfare. And anyway, he would never dare to allow her, no one would now; hadn't Zadik himself told her, "Everything's on hold now, Natasha"? If the head of Israel Television had told her this, surely nobody else would take it lightly. A couple of policemen and one accident, and everyone was peeing in their pants. True, it wasn't just any old accident, it had been fatal. And she had better stop acting like she was indifferent, as if she didn't care about Tirzah. It wasn't that she didn't care, in fact she cared a lot, even though she had barely known her; you don't have to know somebody to feel bad for them. It was a shame about anybody who died before their time, and an even bigger shame about Rubin. She knew him well and liked him and knew how important Tirzah was to him. But there was no doubt that for her personally, Tirzah's death had ruined everything. It was clear that nobody would talk to her now; like Zadik said, as soon as the police got involved, he had to maintain a low profile. Everyone had to maintain a low profile. He wasn't willing to risk complications with anyone: "That's all I need right now," he had told her as he rooted between his teeth with a toothpick he had removed from his shirt pocket, "trouble with the ultra-Orthodox. As if I don't have enough grief as it is." She had tried to tell him again, had chased after him down the hall like some puppy, explaining, when Rubin was already at Benny Meyuhas's place with the police and everything, that if not today, then who knew when she'd have another opportunity to catch them red-handed, "in real time," she had said, using his own language. But he had said, without breaking his pace or even looking at her, "Listen, sweetheart, nothing can be done right now, this isn't the time."

From the end of the hallway she had first heard Rubin's voice and then seen him and Hagar entering Aviva's room, and after that they disappeared into Zadik's office. She strolled down the hallway two more times, peering in at Aviva. The first time Aviva had not even noticed her, but the second time she had said, "Hey, Natasha, come here a second." She had entered the office and stood next to Aviva's desk, straining to hear, without attracting Aviva's attention, what was happening in Zadik's office. But it was impossible to hear anything, not without putting your ear to the door, which she obviously couldn't do with Aviva there and people from the *On the Circuit* program entering and leaving the little office next to Aviva's and shouting like crazy about the lineup for that evening's show. Aviva said, "Do me a favor, Natasha, I can't take it anymore." She cast a furious glance in the direction of Zadik's office. "He won't let me budge, as far as he's concerned I could live here and everything. He forgets that human beings have needs occasionally. I swear, it'll only be a minute. Just one thing," she added, indicating the little office with her head. "Don't let anybody from the crew, from *On the Circuit,* make phone calls from here. They're not allowed to tie up the lines. These people are all I needed this morning," she mumbled, "but they're doing renovations downstairs, so I couldn't very well toss them out. Where else could they hold their staff meeting?"

As if on cue, Yankeleh Golan, chief producer of *On the Circuit,* let out a roar; there was no mistaking his deep bass: "A whole week of work, and that's all you people have to show for it?! I am *not* opening with the chairman of the Israel Aircraft Industries' workers' union; that's not an item! It's practically noon and you don't have anything better than *that*?!" Aviva dashed out of the office, the phones on her desk ringing, but Natasha did not answer them. She stood between Aviva's desk and the door to Zadik's office. Ringing telephones and loud voices were issuing from the little office, along with a woman complaining: "Don't smoke here, Assaf, do me a favor. You can't manage for ten minutes without a cigarette?" The door to the little office flew open and Assaf Cooper marched out to the hallway, failing to notice her. He stood outside, close by the door, his back to her, speaking into a cellular phone he had lodged between his shoulder and his ear. "I don't want a lot of screaming, I want it to be painful and sensitive . . . you're representing a murderer . . . talk to me about it . . ." He was speaking very loudly, lighting a cigarette with one hand and pulling his belt tight with the other. She glanced at the skullcap threatening to drop from his head. "If any dilemmas arise . . ." he was saying into his phone. "What, no dilemmas? How do you explain that? What did you say? It's all a matter of money? That doesn't sound too good, just money . . ."

Natasha crept toward Zadik's office, her back to the window and her eyes on the doorway, making sure no one would catch her with her ear to the door. That was how she managed to hear Rubin say, "Zadik, come on, just watch one little bit—just one little bit of the rough cut, do me a favor, that's all I'm asking. Look, just look, it's a series about the splendor of Eastern Jewry. Think about how 'in' that is these days." She could also hear how Hagar was butting in, cutting into Rubin's words as if she was his equal; in that artificially sweet voice of hers, like a kindergarten teacher, she said, "Zadik, it's Agnon! Nobel Prize, Zadik, during your tenure, the credit will go to you, and Benny will dedicate it to Tirzah's memory." It was hard to comprehend how people dared to be so transparent. How could Hagar speak to Zadik as if he was some kind of idiot? What did she think, that Zadik didn't understand why she was saying those things?

Zadik was saying something, but Natasha could not understand exactly what, and then she couldn't hear anything at all. Then suddenly there came the sound of a woman singing in a clear, truly pure voice that gave her the shivers. Whenever she heard Mercedes Sosa sing, she got hot and cold and trembled all over. Now, too, such a tremor passed through her. But this wasn't Mercedes Sosa, this was a different, unfamiliar language and a strange melody, sad as a lamentation. Natasha backed away from the door and sat down at Aviva's desk, which was quite lucky since at that very moment, as she sat down and answered the telephone, Niva appeared in the doorway. She was waving a sheet of paper in her hands, and without looking into the office said, "Aviva, there's a fax here that Zadik has got to see." Only then did she look inside. "Oh, Natasha," she said with an air of disappointment. "Where's Aviva?" Without waiting for an answer, she said, "Gone to the bathroom? Tell her I'm looking for her," and she turned to go, then turned back again and added, "I totally forgot, Hefetz has been looking for you, a few times this morning already. Why aren't you answering your beeper?" Before Natasha had a chance to answer, Niva had rushed on, her clogs banging heavily down the hall. Her voice rang out: "Benizri, Benizri, where are you off to? Danny Benizri, you're not leaving here without a word with Hefetz. He's waiting for you!"

Natasha didn't expect life to be easy; she was willing to work hard and engage in first-rate journalism. Like Danny Benizri. It was great, what he'd done, going straight into that tunnel with the laid-off strikers, fearless. That's how reporting should be done. But they'd let him do it, he hadn't had to convince anyone to let him. She wasn't afraid either, she was willing to risk a lot to do the job right. A real lot. Like what, she didn't know how dangerous it was dealing with those ultra-Orthodox, especially the ones with the black skullcaps? Boy, did she! But she had no intention of sitting quietly and waiting for the powers-that-be to find it in the goodness of their hearts to let her pursue it. There was no way a young woman like herself wasn't going to find a way on this, her only real opportunity. After all, she knew how to handle situations far more hopeless than this one. Hadn't she managed to catch a flight to Israel—the only woman on board, no seats available—in the middle of the Gulf War, just as SCUD missiles were falling? Hadn't she started working as a reporter when there had been no job opening? True, they hadn't even given her a job as a researcher—only freelance: hourly wages, no benefits—but not just anyone could have gotten to where she has. And it wasn't because of Hefetz, it was on her own. If anyone at all had helped her, it was Schreiber. Hefetz had only entered the picture later, and he hadn't done her any good, he'd only screwed things up with his jealousy. Like, what was there to be jealous about her? She wanted to know what it was she had going for her; if she knew, then maybe she, too, would believe she was lucky. There was nothing to envy: quick sex in his office late at night, telephone calls all the time from his wife, who is always looking for him. Had he ever taken her anywhere? Given her anything? Nada, he hadn't even helped pay her rent, hadn't even taken her out for a good meal for fear they'd be seen together. No perfume, no flowers, nothing on her birthday. She didn't mean to say he was a miser, because she'd seen how sometimes he paid for a meal out of his own pocket—not with her, with other people—but with her only one thing was for sure: he hadn't spent a shekel on her. And now, wasn't she the one who'd succeeded in getting the secret address of the apartment where Rabbi Elharizi met with that lawyer who everybody says is super-close to the prime minister? And wasn't she the one who had filmed him dressed as a Greek Orthodox priest at the airport? No one could tell her she didn't have first-rate journalistic instincts. She only needed the right opportunity, then everything would fall into place. And this was just that once-in-a-lifetime opportunity, she knew it. The frightened voice of that woman who had phoned her and assured her of the address and the appointed hour. That woman—when this was all over, Natasha would track her down and thank her properly. She'd even send her flowers. Well, it wasn't clear how she'd find her; on the phone she'd refused to explain how she'd reached Natasha, how she'd gotten hold of her mobile phone number, why Natasha in particular. But Natasha was not worried; she knew that at the end of the day, whatever information needed to surface would surface. If they would only put her on the air today, at least with that business about the allocations being paid to yeshivas for students who were actually dead. She needed to make her report before the Knesset finance committee had its meeting and it was too late. This was something she had heard about by chance, not from that woman, but from a guy who had once been religious and had left the fold. She didn't know why he'd come to her with the story; he had simply told her the facts, hadn't told her why she was the one. "Nathan told me to contact you," he had explained. She didn't know anyone by that name, but she hadn't let on because this could be the opportunity she'd been waiting for. She would go on air with this business about the allocations, and then everyone would let her move ahead with the big stuff. If she didn't get it on air today, they'd be able to continue collecting money on dead people. Everyone knew it was true; she was in possession of documentation, death certificates, the names of people who were supposedly living but were really dead. So who was going to tell her to go on television with it that night? And who was going to give her a crew, a soundman and a lighting technician and a cameraman, to film her at night? No one. She was certain of it.

"Thanks, hon," Aviva said. Natasha left the office and returned to her corner at the end of the hallway, next to the bathrooms. Now she could hear Zadik's voice, so she peeked. He had left his office without Rubin or Hagar and was standing in the hallway calling to passersby, then opened the door to the little office and said, "Come here, Nahum, Schreiber, Assaf, come, come see what a work of beauty we've created here, the splendor of the Orient, roots, we've got a rough cut of a new dramatic series here . . . Agnon, gentlemen, Agnon—" and everyone filed in. Hefetz entered—he did not notice her—and someone else, Max Levin, that nice man from Props, and Avi the lighting technician, too. They were probably there about the stolen spotlights. She had heard in the newsroom that along with the business with Tirzah, they were investigating the thefts.

Schreiber ducked out for a minute, on his way to the bathroom. That gave her an idea.

"Schreiber," she whispered to him, "come here a minute."

He stopped next to the door to the men's room and gazed at her with surprise. "Come where?"

She pointed to the door of the ladies' room behind her.

"Are you crazy, Natasha? I can't go into the ladies' room. You want to get me in trouble? They'll say it was sexual harassment." He passed a large hand over his shaven head, and the gold ring on his pinky finger sparkled.

"Schreiber," she said in the small voice that always worked with him, "do me a favor."

He looked up and down the hall and opened the door to the office of the director of the Drama Department, which was right next to the ladies' room. No one was there, and Schreiber was allowed everywhere because he was a cameraman. What could they do to him, fire him? He explained this to her as she looked around suspiciously before they entered the room. Now they were both inside. He tilted his head to the side and regarded her carefully, as if he could look into her head and see exactly what she was thinking.

"What's going on with you, Natasha?" he asked, his voice filled with something . . . full of goodness, it almost made her cry . . . in fact, it made her feel how alone she was, like that time he had questioned her and held her while she cried and then he had taken her, without anyone knowing about it, to that doctor on Palmach Street and had gotten rid of the problem, just like he had promised. He'd even paid, and never once brought it up to her.

"Schreiber," she whispered to him, "you've got to help me with this business with Rabbi Elharizi."

"What business are you talking about?" he asked her with studied patience, prodding the back of his head. She knew that even mentioning the name of the rabbi made his blood boil, so she quickly recounted what she had found out. "Come on, I'll show you the video, I haven't shown it to anybody, only Rubin, and he went nuts. But now, because of Tirzah and Benny Meyuhas and all that, he doesn't have time to—"

Schreiber looked at her as though she had fallen from the moon. "Natasha," he said in a hoarse voice as he lit a cigarette without taking his eyes off her, "don't even dare talking about it. Do you know what they'll do to you if they hear about it? And don't you dare ask anyone to help you, either. Do you want me to get suspended? Do you think this is a game? They told you not now. So that's it, not now. They told you the police are running around here, and it's not the time to be dealing with these religious fanatics. Don't you understand that this isn't the time for that?"

And even after she repeated her explanation and pulled him over to the monitor in the room and stuck the cassette inside and showed him Rabbi Elharizi dressed as a Greek Orthodox priest, and even though Schreiber whistled and laughed and shut the machine off, he sounded no less resolved and said, "No, no way. I don't take risks like those."

"What risks?" she said. "It's like the only thing we need to do is stand behind the door when the money is changing hands and watch. That's all. After that we film them, and I bring the lists. You don't need to come to Givat Shaul with me where the fanatics have their yeshivas and you don't have to come to the Interior Ministry for proof that those guys are dead, 'cause I already have all that stuff, that's all ready for my report this evening. I'm going on the air this evening with the names of the fictitious yeshiva students. You only need to bring a camera and come with me to see that apartment in Ramot. What's the big deal with that?"

"Natasha, you need a crew and a mobile unit, you need a soundman and a lighting technician, the works—"

"Schreiber," she said, cutting him off, "get me a mobile unit without a crew and bring—you be the crew. The dead-live yeshiva students I'm taking care of myself, don't forget—"

"I don't get it," Schreiber said as he opened the door and looked down the hall. "Wait, wait, now I understand: there are two different things here, you're talking about two different issues, aren't you?"

"If you ask me, they're connected," she replied. "First there are the fictitious names that I need to . . . it's . . . I told you, I did it all on my own with a video camera. But that's peanuts compared with—"

Drops of sweat glistened on Schreiber's bald head as he cut her off with a warning: "Natasha, you can't go against the wishes of the workers' union. If somebody gets wind of the fact that you've filmed it yourself without a proper crew, well, you have no idea what grief you'll be bringing on yourself. I'm forbidden from going out without a soundman or a lighting technician, absolutely forbidden. They'll shut the whole place down. Does Hefetz know you're doing this on your own?"

She shook her head, a bashful smile on her face.

"So what *does* he think?" Schreiber asked her, a look of suspicion on his face. "What did you tell him? Did you tell him I'm involved, did you, Natasha?! You're going to drive me crazy, Natasha." Now she thought he was mad at her for real.

"I had no choice, Schreiber, they won't let me . . . if I told him, he'd send someone else, he'd say I didn't own the story."

"Natasha, it's without authorization!"

"Rubin promised he would work things out with Hefetz, that there'll be after-the-fact permission," she mumbled, "and that he would cover for you if we get in trouble on the other issue. Look, he promised. He's seen the material."

"Tell me what exactly you think we would see there."

She told him about the restaurant and the meeting with the piles of money and maps and suitcases. His eyes grew wider with fear as he listened.

"Natasha," he said, his voice choked with emotion, "you're playing with fire. You have no idea who you're dealing with here. Don't forget, Natasha, where I come from. I know them, they won't let you get away in peace. They'll take revenge on you, I know them better than anyone else around here, I was one of them." He tugged at the ring in his left earlobe. "They'll kill you, arrange an accident for you, they'll put a curse on you without batting an eye if you're onto them, and it's all true. It would be the end of you."

"That's what journalism is all about, Schreiber," she said pleadingly. "Think about it seriously."

"I don't like journalism, I like shooting dramas, didn't you know that?" he said, teasing her. "I like filming *Iddo and Eynam* for Benny Meyuhas. I don't have any time for you." He was smiling, drumming a finger on his nose.

She grabbed his shirt. "Schreiber, please, I'm begging you."

"Natasha, I can't," he protested. From the hallway they could hear people running and shouting. "Now what's happened?" Schreiber wondered as he fished a cigarette from the front pocket on his safari vest and rubbed his double chin. His small mouth disappeared into his wide face as he listened to the noises from the hall. "God only knows what's happened, maybe a terrorist attack or something. I can't just toss everything aside and stand here chatting with you. You understand, don't you, Natasha?"

"Schreiber," she said as she removed her red scarf and mindlessly slipped off her black coat and her sweater and her black undershirt, too, so that she was blocking the door with her body, her small nipples erect. "Listen, Schreiber—you want to fuck me?"

He gave her a look of terror, and for a moment she was frightened, as though he might slap her across the face. But then something familiar flickered in the hazel-colored part of his slightly crossed right eye, and a tremor passed through his thin lips and he began to smile, and then laugh a stifled laugh. She would have been offended if she had not known him so well.

"What's with you, Natasha?" he said, coughing. "Put your clothes back on right away, the sweater—what's with you? Like you're willing to do *anything* for—" The noises in the hallway were growing louder. "Something's happened," he said as he pulled the sweater over her head and pushed her arms into the sleeves as though she were a little girl. "Natasha, let's get out of here."

"First of all, promise," she demanded. "Promise you'll help me."

Schreiber rolled his eyes to the ceiling. "If you weren't such a . . . if you weren't so . . . so . . . like, alone in the world," he said, shaking his head reproachfully, "if I didn't know you well enough to know you'll do it anyway, I would tell you to go to Hefetz. But you won't go to Hefetz, will you?"

"There's no reason to," she fumed. "But if you come with me—look, I'll . . . I'll pay you."

"Like with money?" Schreiber laughed even harder this time, shaking his head. He wiped his mouth on the sleeve of his checkered flannel shirt, straightened his safari vest, zipped closed one of the pockets. "How exactly are you going to pay me? You're going to give me the savings you don't have? You're going to start working as a cleaning lady? Hit the streets? Okay, I'll give you an answer in a little while, all right?"

She would not be placated. Holding his arm, she asked, "When? When will you give me an answer? When it's too late?"

Schreiber removed her fingers from his arm. "What time is it now, eleven-fifteen? I'll have an answer for you by two o'clock, okay?" He was holding her hand in his own and caressing it with the other. "But don't go and do anything until I get back to you. Don't go anywhere, don't talk to anyone. Nothing. You got that?"

Natasha nodded, following his movements as he stuck the cigarette back into his vest pocket, opened the door, and peered into the hall. "Go on," he told her, "you first and then me, so that nobody catches us coming out of a closed room together and think . . . I don't have the strength to fight with Hefetz over his girl."

"I'm not his girl," she whispered angrily as she left the room and fell straight into Hefetz's arms. His face was grave, and she could not see his eyes behind the dark lenses of his eyeglasses.

"I've been looking for you all morning," he intoned. "Where have you been hiding?" Without waiting for an answer, he asked, "Did you hear about Matty Cohen?"

She shook her head.

"He died," Hefetz said, removing his glasses and rubbing his bloodshot right eye. She did not care that once again his eye was infected, she wished it would spread to his left eye, too. "A half hour ago, just like that. What do you say about that?"

What *could* she say? She very nearly shrugged her shoulders. She had barely known Matty Cohen, who was she anyway? The guy was too important for someone like her. Nevertheless, she forced her face into a serious expression as Hefetz continued speaking.

"A guy wakes up in the morning healthy, well, not completely healthy, but pretty healthy, maybe a little overweight, but not obese, really, and a few hours later he's dead."

Natasha nodded. "What did he die of?"

"His heart, a heart attack while under investigation at police headquarters in the Russian Compound. They were talking to him about Tirzah. He didn't sleep all last night, and then the interrogation this morning . . . too much effort and excitement, the doctors say." His gaze drifted to the stairway and the two people coming up the stairs. "Here they are again, they're back," he said, frowning.

"Who?" Natasha asked under her breath.

"Can't you see them? The police. Those are the guys who were here earlier. They're back."

The only thing she could think about was how she had no chance whatsoever anymore; who would give her the time of day now? Now they might not even let her on the air with the item about the yeshiva students. She watched the two men, noticed they were the same two she had seen in the newsroom that morning. The taller one—the one with the dark eyes and eyebrows—was nodding to Hefetz and seemed to be watching her with special interest; his gaze made her wish to behave herself so that he would look at her and think she was all right. The other one was saying something to Aviva, and everyone was walking out of Zadik's office now. Rubin was explaining something to Hagar. When she touched his arm, Rubin said, once again, "Not now, Natasha. A little later."

"A weekly meeting?" Michael verified. "Same day each week in your office?"

"If I'm in the country," Zadik confirmed.

"And everyone drinks coffee?" Michael asked.

"Whoever wants to," Zadik answered. "Look, you see we've got everything we need right here: a kettle, and over in the corner there's herb tea and regular tea and decaf coffee and instant coffee and Turkish coffee. And sugar and artificial sweetener and milk. Styrofoam cups for those who don't mind them. I for one can't stand them, so we've got mugs, too—you can see for yourself. Once upon a time we had filter coffee too, and hot chocolate. But we've cut back."

"Did Matty Cohen always drink coffee?"

"Turkish coffee, two packets of sweetener and half a teaspoon of sugar, no milk. Two cups. What's this thing you've got about Matty's coffee? I don't get it, do you think—?"

Michael ignored the note of complaint that echoed in Zadik's question. "Everyone knows how everyone else takes his coffee?"

"More or less," Zadik said. "Some people remember, some don't. I always know exactly who drinks what and how they take it. Hefetz, too. I think Amsalem from the canteen remembers, but he used to own a coffee shop so it's natural. . . . Everyone else, what can I tell you? I've never noticed."

"Do people usually make their own coffee?"

Zadik flashed Michael a look of astonishment. "What are all these questions about? What are you thinking? That the coffee was spoiled? Or poisoned? I'm telling you, that guy was a walking time bomb, a dead man walking, with all that weight and all that coffee."

"So what usually happened?" Michael persisted. "Did one person prepare the drinks for everyone? Or what?"

"Sometimes, and sometimes not. Sometimes we have bourekas or cookies," Zadik said irritably. "Sometimes someone asks who wants what, sometimes they make it for themselves. Come on, already, who pays attention to things like that anyway?"

"I know that people don't pay attention, it's true. When everything's fine, people don't pay attention. But in this case I'm asking that you try to remember."

"Remember what? Who made Matty Cohen's coffee for him? That's what you want me to remember?"

Michael nodded.

"I did, okay? Are you satisfied? Don't look at me like that, I'm telling you: I made his coffee myself. What's wrong with that?"

"You made it, and you gave it to him? With your own hands?" Michael asked.

"Exactly," Zadik said. "What's wrong with that? You think that because I'm the big boss, I can't make coffee for my friends? I haven't got a fat head. I haven't forgotten where I come from."

"With your own hands?" Michael repeated.

"What, what about my own hands?" Zadik bellowed. "I put it on the table in front of his seat. Anything wrong with that?"

"We need to check that coffee," Michael informed him. "It's standard procedure, just like an autopsy."

"What? What?" Zadik said. "What autopsy? Who requested an autopsy?"

"Hmmm, just so," Michael said, clearing his throat. "We did. We spoke with Matty Cohen's wife. At first glance it looks like a heart attack, but his doctor gave him a checkup just two or three weeks ago, and everything was fine. His wife says he felt really good these past few days, he'd even started a diet. This was quite unexpected."

Zadik thought for a moment. "There's no need for an autopsy. I'm telling you, it was a heart attack. I'd bet a month's salary on it."

"Maybe," Michael said. "It's certainly possible, it stands to reason. But just to be absolutely certain—"

The door flew open, and Aviva stood there, staring at Zadik. "Excuse me," she said, tossing off a small smile in Michael's direction, "I didn't want to disturb you, but first of all, Benizri is here—you asked him to see you the minute he arrived. I'm a wreck, Zadik, a total wreck. Everyone here—he's been waiting fifteen minutes already. And second, there's some guy on the phone, he won't give me his name, but he says—"

"Can't you see what's happening here? Right now I can't—do me a favor Aviva, take care of—"

"So what should I tell him?" Aviva demanded. "He's been waiting on the phone. Benizri's waiting, too."

"We're almost through here—tell Benizri to wait. The guy on the phone, too, tell him to wait. What's it about, anyway? Why—" He looked at Michael and Eli Bachar. "All right, I've told you everything I know, and you can take anything you need with you. If there's going to be an autopsy, well—never mind, I'll go pay her a visit later anyway."

"Who? Who are you going to visit?" Aviva asked from the doorway. "And what about all these people—"

"Malka, Matty's wife. What, you think I shouldn't visit her?" Zadik leaned on the table and shoved his chair out from under him. Danny Benizri appeared in the doorway.

"Come on in, Danny," Zadik called to him. "Did you hear about Matty Cohen? Did you hear what happened to him?"

Danny Benizri nodded, his expression grave. "Yes, I heard, that's really awful."

Zadik sighed. "I don't know how we'll manage with all this. . . . But you, you did a great job, excellent work. Come here, let me give you a hug. Did you guys see him?" Zadik asked Michael and Eli Bachar, who had already risen from their chairs and were on their way to the door. "Did you see how he handled the situation, how he saved the whole operation? Afterward, people come to complain. If we hadn't been there, who knows what might have happened."

"About Matty Cohen," Benizri asked, "was it his heart?"

Zadik confirmed the news by spreading his arms wide to his side.

"I don't know what to say," Benizri said.

Zadik's face grew serious. "There's nothing *to* say." He bent his head forward and back, rolled his eyes, and added, on a philosophical bent, "What can you possibly say? A man's days are like chaff in the wind, that's all there is to say. That, and don't smoke. Quit smoking. How did things end out there? I understand they hauled them off."

"The minister was moved to Hadassah Hospital at Ein Kerem. Shimshi and the others were taken into custody and driven off in a police van."

"Well, that was to be expected," Zadik said. "Here, have a cigar." He handed a large box of cigars to Danny Benizri, who selected one and eyed it with suspicion. "Cigars are not for observing," Zadik informed him. "They don't *do* anything: smell it at least." He waited for Benizri to stick it between his teeth and lit a match from one of the packets in a large glass bowl sitting at the edge of his desk. "Want one, too?" he asked Michael, who was standing by the door waiting for Zadik to open it.

"No, thanks," Michael answered. "Each man to his own poison."

Zadik grimaced, took hold of the doorknob, and waited for them to pass through.

"Can I call you after two this afternoon?" Michael asked. Zadik nodded, closing the door after them.

Outside the office Michael could hear Zadik muttering, "It's incomprehensible: a guy just falls down dead . . ."

Arye Rubin was standing in the secretary's office by the door to the little office next door, whispering to Natasha; Eli Bachar observed them while Michael took the package from Aviva's desk. "It's lucky they left the cups here. We're always getting annoyed when they don't come to clear up, but this time it's just lucky that everything remained here. You can never know what's best." Aviva sighed. "I wrapped them up in a manila envelope and then in a plastic bag. I didn't touch anything. First in a manila envelope and then in a plastic bag, just like the movies. And I didn't touch a thing, only the plastic. Was that okay?" she asked, batting her eyelashes.

"Excellent," Michael said.

"I just don't understand why you need it," Aviva said, turning her head to the side and fluffing out her curls. "And I wanted to know if you need anything else. Zadik told me to give you anything you need—people's phone numbers, addresses—" Her voice was soft and playful, and Eli Bachar noticed the curiosity that appeared on Arye Rubin's face as he shifted his gaze to Michael Ohayon, as if suddenly something had caught his interest.

"Chief Superintendent Michael Ohayon," Rubin said, "I didn't tell you this before, but I'm an old fan of yours. Ask her," he said, nodding toward Aviva. "I've told her so many times." Aviva nodded vigorously.

"Really?" Michael asked, embarrassed. "I don't know that we . . . I thought . . ."

"What are you so surprised about?" Rubin asked. "I spent the civilian service portion of my army duty on Kibbutz M.," he said, mentioning the murder that had taken place there. "While a lot of water has passed under the bridge since then, and you could say that today the kibbutz as an institution is anachronistic, back then it was the first time the police had investigated a kibbutz murder, the first time in fact that they had entered the gates. I could tell you about two or three other cases that didn't make it to the police, that were solved locally. Natasha, come meet Chief Superintendent Michael Ohayon. It won't be the last time." Michael shook her dry, bony hand and introduced Eli Bachar as well.

"Can we go in?" Rubin asked Aviva. "I'm sure Benizri won't mind if we're there, and it'll speed things up a bit, don't you think? What do you say, Aviva? We made an appointment for ten o'clock, and in the meantime people are dropping like flies around here."

Aviva shrugged. "I don't know what's so urgent, Rubin," she said, tossing a cool look at Natasha. "People are dying, and you people are wrapped up in your own affairs. Anyway, go ahead and try."

Rubin put his hand on the doorknob, but Zadik beat him to it and pulled open the door from inside. He was standing there, one hand on the shoulder of the correspondent for labor and social affairs, his puffy face unusually ashen. "Rubin," he said gravely, "we have another funeral, have you heard?" Rubin nodded. "What a tragedy," Zadik said, mopping his brow. "But what do you say about this guy, huh, our own Benizri?" he asked, trying to sound festive. "In the midst of all these tragedies, what do you say about him?"

"Well done," Rubin said absently. "Mind you, you'll have to follow up on those workers," he told Benizri. "Reporting during a crisis, at the height of the drama, is no big deal; the real work will be afterward. But you showed a lot of courage out there."

"Not courage," Benizri said modestly. "That's the job, I learned it from you. Absolutely from you. What you said about follow-up, well, I just came from police headquarters. Shimshi's wife and the other wives are already there, what a mob scene! I promised them I'd speak with the minister about dropping the charges, otherwise they'll be up on criminal charges."

"Don't waste your time," Rubin said. "They'll be up on criminal charges no matter what, it's not in her hands. Kidnapping and intent to kill? It's already been handed to the State Prosecutor's Office, you've got nothing—"

"I promised," Benizri said, "I have no choice."

"Where's the minister hospitalized? Hadassah? Matty Cohen's wife Malka is there, too, with their son," Zadik said. "I'll go over there with you. Wait for me a minute, will you, I just have to finish up with—" The telephone on Aviva's desk rang just as Zadik pointed to Rubin and Natasha and moved aside to let them pass into his office.

"What? Who?" Aviva was asking into the phone. "I can barely hear you. Who is this?"

She listened for a moment in silence, a disconcerted look on her face. "Zadik," she called out, "Zadik, hang on a minute, it's—"

"Don't bother me now, Aviva," Zadik said, his hand on the doorknob.

"Take care of it yourself. Make decisions, for once be a self-starter, okay?" Without looking at her, he entered his office and closed the door.

Aviva looked at the telephone and said into the mouthpiece, "Hello? Hello?" But the line had gone dead. She laid the receiver gently in its cradle, sat down, and looked around her. "I haven't eaten a crumb today, haven't gotten a single thing into my mouth yet," she said aloud to the silent room, which was momentarily empty. Listlessly, she removed a plastic container from her large purse, placed it in front of herself on the desk, opened it, and peered inside as if she did not know what was there. After a moment she sighed, pulled out one carrot stick and then another along with two thin stalks of celery, gave them a piteous look, stared straight ahead, and began, slowly, to chew.

# CHAPTER SEVEN

No one seemed to notice the mobile unit as it made its way to the Ramot neighborhood of Jerusalem. Schreiber examined the signature he had scribbled on a request form—for equipment, a cameraman, a soundman, and a lighting technician for an interview by Arye Rubin with Dr. Landau, the physician on whom Rubin was focusing his report about doctors who cooperated with and abetted the Shin Bet—then shoved it into the glove compartment. The interview had actually taken place—there was documentation to prove it—but Schreiber had stolen time from a second interview, with the hospital spokesman. When the spokesman had caught sight of Arye Rubin and the camera behind him at the entrance to his office, he had listened to a single question before slamming the door shut. That was why there was extra time, unaccounted for, that enabled Schreiber to commandeer the mobile unit.

"Over there," Natasha told him excitedly. "It's the second building over, see it? The one with the stone fence and the sign about charitable contributions." The whole way there a lump of apprehension had clogged her throat. What if Schreiber suddenly had a change of heart? What if they paged him? True, he had shut off his cell phone, but they could reach him on the beeper. Schreiber, for his part, had tried to calm her fears, had told her he had left explicit instructions that he was going to sleep and would be turning his beeper off, but not for a single minute did her misgivings let up, misgivings that he would have had enough, that he would suddenly say, That's it, I'm sick of this, and take off, dropping her at her house and disappearing. After all, what did he have to gain from all this? Just thinking about the possibility gave her a sour feeling of anxiety in her stomach. How was it that nobody believed she could bring in something important, that her work was truly serious? How was it that only by asking favors could she . . . why did they think she had nothing worthwhile to say?

To stop herself thinking so much, she glanced at her watch. She had another two hours until she had to report to police headquarters in the Russian Compound. The green-eyed cop had told her it was an interrogation, but the other one, the tall guy with the dark, narrow face and the thick eyebrows, the one who always had an unlit cigarette in his hand and who hid it behind his back each time someone tried to light it—"Not now," he would tell them pleasantly, "I'm trying to cut back"—that one had apologized, changing "interrogation" to "a chat." And when Natasha had asked him whether it was absolutely necessary for her to come in, he had smiled at her as though she were a little girl and told her she had watched too many police shows on television. Of course she did not *have* to, he had said, emphasizing his words and causing her to feel slightly embarrassed, but why wouldn't she be willing to help them shed light on the circumstances of Tirzah's death? He was certain that she would be eager to help in the matter of Matty Cohen's death as well. He had inclined his head to one side, studied her with interest, and reminded her that they had summoned everyone who had been in the String Building or the main building, and that everyone had agreed willingly. Why would she be unwilling to come, he had asked, staring into her eyes with that look she had already noticed earlier, a dark, sad, look, very wise but sad. It was the downward slope of his eyelids that made him look sad, she realized now as she caught sight of Schreiber glancing in the side-view mirror. When you looked into the guy's eyes, you could see he was intelligent, and powerful too—maybe it wasn't power, but strength. He had looked into her eyes as though he was learning her, like she'd seen once in a science fiction movie where this character is just walking along looking at people when all of a sudden everyone's inner thoughts flash really, really fast in front of his eyes. She didn't understand what he wanted her for anyway, why he had asked to speak with her and what he hoped to get out of her. Maybe it was all because of Hefetz, who had given her an imploring look from the corner of the room when she was talking to the two police officers. Everyone noticed how he stared at her. On the other hand, Hefetz always stared at her like that, or at least had been for the past two days, since she'd told him it was over between them. For her, the breakup with Hefetz had been easy, she really was sick and tired of the whole complicated affair, sick of his shiftiness and his fear of his wife. "It's about time," Schreiber had said when he'd started the van and asked what was happening with Hefetz and she had replied, frigidly, "Who's Hefetz?" Schreiber had laughed. "Thank God," he said. "It's about time you started acting like a human being and thinking that you're worth something, that you deserve better." To the policeman she had explained that she would be busy the entire morning and that she would only be available later in the day. Gnawing on the toothpick that had replaced the unlit cigarette he had thrown into the trash, the policeman had said, "All right, later," and had added that when she came to headquarters she should ask to speak with Michael Ohayon. For some reason her eyes had fixed on his neck; it was long and narrow, a blue vein winding its way above the clavicle, and it seemed to her that she could see the vein throbbing; she had noticed his hands, too, the fingers tapered, dark and graceful, exactly the way she liked them: they gave her gooseflesh, those fingers. She had to shake herself free of them and turn her face away. What would have happened had he known what she was thinking? But just at that moment he had not been looking at her, focusing instead on the toothpick he had just removed from between his lips; "I can't manage with substitutes," she'd heard him say to the other policeman, the one with the green eyes, who had slapped him on the arm and said, "You made an agreement? So stick to it. You wanted Yuval to stop smoking, right? Well, you've got to sacrifice something. You're the one who's always telling me that being a parent means having to make sacrifices, that parenting *is* sacrifice." And from this exchange she had understood that he was married and father to at least one kid, who was already old enough to smoke. Married. Everyone was married. All the good ones, anyway. Even the not-so-good ones. How was it that men, even if they were ugly or stupid, always had someone? They were never alone. Plenty of times she'd seen them with beautiful, intelligent women, women with everything going for them, even if they themselves weren't worth shit. What about her? How was it that she . . . Schreiber was interested, she knew he was interested; a few days earlier Aviva had whispered to her, over the sink in the second-floor bathroom, "Hey, Natasha, haven't you noticed that Schreiber is crazy about you?" She had looked at her and chuckled. But Schreiber hadn't said anything to her, in fact he was really shy. He tried to come off austere, abrasive . . . maybe it was because of Hefetz. Maybe because of Hefetz he didn't dare to approach her in that way. But he'd known her first, before Hefetz. And if Hefetz needed something from her, never mind what, she planned to take advantage of it—she didn't know how exactly, but . . .

Schreiber parked the van at the corner, at a spot from which they could see the four-story building, whose barred, curtainless windows overlooked the street. All the buildings on the street were semi-detached and built of Jerusalem stone gone gray and dingy; all were four stories high with one arched window on each floor. No shrub or flower added even a spot of color to the uninterrupted stone landscape, the black shadows cast by the window grilles and the fences, or the wet pavement on the street.

"They don't even have any trees around here," she said to Schreiber.

"Naturally. Everybody knows the ultra-Orthodox don't like greenery, that nobody plants anything in their neighborhoods," he muttered, as if he knew what she was thinking. He pulled the curtain on the rear window so that it parted slightly. The moment he looked up to the third-floor window the blinds snapped shut, as though someone had caught him spying.

"Check this out," he said as he backed away from the parted curtains, wiping his bare and shaven head, which was already glistening with moisture. "I just get near them, and I break out in a sweat." Fishing around in his shirt pocket, he added, "It's Hanukkah, mid-December, freezing cold, and I'm sweating."

"Take a picture of the entrance," Natasha requested. "Do me a favor, film it quickly."

"Okay, okay," he assured her, rooting about in the pockets of his safari vest.

"What are you looking for *now*?" she asked him impatiently. "What's so urgent in those pockets?"

"Found it," Schreiber said as he pulled a small, light blue tin from one of the side pockets of his vest. "*That's* what's so urgent—"

"Not now," she pleaded. "Later, when we're finished. Come on, Schreiber."

He sighed and returned the tin to his pocket. "How do you expect me to pass the time, and in this neighborhood no less? You know what it does to me to be here!" he scolded.

His father had died a few years earlier, and he had thought he would have an easier time of it then, that he would no longer have to masquerade as a religious man. ("I had no doubts at all," Schreiber would tell people who asked what kind of doubts about religion he had had that had caused him to stop wearing a skullcap and become secular. "No doubts whatsoever, I simply became a heretic.") Still, he wore the skullcap on visits to his aging mother in Bnei Brak; even his oldest brother, who lived with his family in their parents' house, had no idea.

"Schreiber," Natasha said, gazing into his hazel eyes, "I am so . . . I owe you so much, not just for this but—"

"Oh, come off it, Natasha," he said, embarrassed.

He had never been capable of accepting her gratitude, even when he had picked her up from the doctor's office on Palmach Street and brought her to his place in Gan Rehavia. She recalled the odor of mold and dampness in his basement apartment, only half a barred window rising up above street level, the neon light that stayed lit in one room all the time, the underpants and socks left hanging to dry on the building's hot-water pipes, which ran through his flat.

He said, "If only you would tell me who it was that gave you this information—"

"I've already told you you're not going to get it out of me, so don't ask me a lot of questions," she warned him. "I don't reveal my sources."

Schreiber inclined his head to the side and regarded her with amusement. "Don't I have rights as a partner?" he teased her. While speaking, he moved to the backseat of the van and positioned the camera lens in the parted curtain. Then he returned to the front seat and removed the tin again, this time extracting from it a pinch of reddish grass and a piece of rolling paper.

"Now?" Natasha protested. "Right now? Do you really have to?"

"What are you so worried about?" he asked dismissively. "Do you really think anyone's going to show up? You've been had! Nobody's around, nobody's on his way here, all the blinds are shut, nothing. What do you expect me to do with myself? I'm not even allowed to listen to the radio, for crying out loud." He leaned forward and wet the paper with saliva.

"Of course things are dead right now," she argued, "because everyone's at school or at work, but—"

"At their yeshivas," he said irritably, correcting her. "They're all in yeshiva while their wives are working. You don't know what you're talking about, you don't have a clue how they live. Not a clue," he said, and went to lie down on the backseat.

"My sources told me," she began, with elaborate seriousness, imagining the woman she had spoken with by phone, who had a hoarse, unaccented voice; a child had been crying in the background. For some reason she was sorry her informant hadn't been a man. In her mind's eye she replaced her with a man with a French accent. Truth be told, she would have preferred it be a man, they were more reliable: it's like they acted on some principle, not because of some personal vendetta. That's just the way it was. She pictured a bearded man in a dark suit and hat, his head turned to the side whenever he spoke with her, because suddenly they were no longer conversing by phone—as had happened with the hoarse-voiced woman who had called her "my dear"—but rather in the hallway of the television station, on the stairs leading to the canteen. "My sources told me," she said, imagining now the Frenchman, "specifically, that we're talking early afternoon. They said not in the evening, because then everyone's around—"

"Ah, your sources," Schreiber said, exaggerating each word. He yawned. "What more can I say? There's nothing I can say where sources are concerned." He lit the thin cigarette, took a deep drag from it, coughed, and offered it to Natasha.

"Leave me alone," she said angrily. "Just leave me alone."

"Natasha," he pleaded, "I'm so damned tired from last night, and you know how it is, I don't feel so great when I get near them. I just, it's something physical, medical, I don't know, they . . . I just don't feel well," he tried explaining, waving the smoke away with his hand.

"Anyway, this joint is really weak. But without a little help, I wouldn't be able—"

"Shhh. Shut up!" she hissed urgently under her breath, alarmed. "Look over there and start filming. Fast, from the end of the street—"

Schreiber sat up and looked through the part in the curtains.

"You see," Natasha said. "Take a look and stop telling me I'm making things up."

The windows of the large black car were also covered by curtains. They could just barely make out the thickly bearded man in the black cap driving the car. No one sat in the passenger's seat, but when the car came to a stop, two men emerged from the backseat. They looked around and hurried into the building.

"Schreiber," Natasha shouted, her voice choked with emotion. "Film them walking into the building. Did you, did you get them?"

"Yeah, yeah," Schreiber said, hoping to calm her down. "What are you so nervous about? I shot the whole thing, but how's this footage going to help you? So what if two people came to Rabbi Elharizi's apartment? Who cares?"

"What are you talking about, 'two people'?" she whispered. "Those weren't just any two people. Didn't you recognize them? Don't you know who they are?"

"Sure I do." Schreiber sighed. "So you'll tell people that Rabbi Yitzhak Bashi and Rabbi Elyashiv Benami, Elharizi's two close advisers, came to visit. So what? Of course his two close advisers would come to his home, that's the most natural thing in the world, isn't it?"

"They're not just his close advisers," Natasha pressed him. "One, Yitzhak Bashi, is known to be the treasurer of the movement, he's always in the news. The other, Benami, handles their international relations, no?"

"All right," Schreiber said as he peered into the lens. "So you've got a meeting here, a gathering, a conference of the heads of this religious movement of Eastern Jews. So what? What's so significant about that? They're allowed to meet, aren't they? What have you proven? I filmed them. . . . What are you so worked up about?" As if to prove she was right, three bearded men in dark clothing appeared and unloaded two black leather suitcases and a heavy trunk from the large sedan.

Suddenly the skies cleared and a ray of sunlight, reflecting from a puddle in the street near the car, shone on a single gold lock that secured the trunk.

"Schreiber," Natasha whispered, "Look! The trunk . . . suitcases . . . don't stop shooting—"

"I heard you, I'm not deaf, I heard you," Schreiber said impatiently. "But who's going to care about a bunch of suitcases? What do you think they put in them? I'm telling you, it's got to be holy documents or books written by their rabbis or the latest volume by Rabbi Elharizi. What do you think's in there, gold? Maybe a stash of guns? Hey, how about a dead body? You've been watching too many movies."

"What I wouldn't give . . . ," Natasha said as her eyes followed the three men as they entered the stairwell of the building. Suddenly she grew tense again. "Schreiber," she said anxiously, "you've got to go see, you've got to get in there, go knock on the door as if—"

"Natasha," Schreiber said, shutting her up, his voice a warning. "That's enough. "I'm not going in *anywhere.*"

Still, she heard in his voice the slightest crack, something that enabled her to lay her hand on his arm and plead. "Schreiber, *please,* Schreiber, we've come this far. Don't you think it would be a shame—"

He did not need that much convincing.

"Just don't try telling me how to go about this, okay?" he said as she adjusted the skullcap on his head and straightened the ritual fringes he had brought along and was now wearing. "All you have to take care of now is the camera and the microphone." He patted the front of his black coat. "I've known these guys since before you were born," he said in a rush on his way out of the van, shooting glances up and down the street.

While Schreiber was making his way up three flights of stairs to Rabbi Elharizi's apartment, Danny Benizri stood facing the information desk at Hadassah Hospital. "She's probably in the respiratory intensive care unit," he told the receptionist in his final attempt at convincing her to reveal to which ward the minister had been admitted, and he scolded himself for being so stupid as to ask for the minister of labor and social affairs, and not simply Timnah Ben-Zvi, as though he were a childhood friend or member of the family; otherwise, the receptionist may not even have noticed. Then again, it was likely she would have noticed no matter what he had done. "Why won't you tell me?" he asked malevolently, hoping to trip her up. "For security reasons?"

"Sir," she said, without looking up, "you'll have to talk to the hospital spokesman. I'm not giving you any information."

Benizri was just turning to leave when a doctor passing by caught sight of him and smiled. "You're on television, aren't you?" he asked. "The news. Education reporter, right? No! Of course, the tunnel, the laid-off workers. Great job, we watched you—"

Benizri approached the doctor, smiled pleasantly, and nonchalantly told him he was hoping to find the minister of labor and social affairs.

"Come with me, I'll lead you there!" the doctor said exuberantly. "How do you like that? You're looking for her, and here she is, right in my ward. Would you call that coincidence or fate?"

Benizri followed obediently. The doctor told him to wait in the outer hallway for a few minutes before entering the ward itself, which he did. Once inside, he encountered no one. A prime minister's been murdered in this country, he thought, and yet a government minister gets no protection. With no protection, kidnapping them or trapping them in a tunnel or sneaking into the hospital and snapping their pictures is no trouble at all. But he did not have a camera. Light blue curtains covered the windows of the three private rooms along the hallway. The minister was in the last of them, at the end of the hall, which was where the doctor had entered and from where he was due to emerge. Benizri progressed to the end of the hall; the curtain did not entirely cover the window, so that he could glimpse the minister as she sat on her bed. Her back was exposed, white, and the doctor was leaning over her, his eyes fixed on a point far in the distance as he listened through his stethoscope. When he finished, she straightened up, asked him something, her face fearful, anxious; she listened to his response, then smiled. She had a wonderful smile, childish and innocent, her arms folded over the small, pert breasts he had already seen once; it took his breath away for a moment. Thinking about the color of her hidden nipples caused a slight current to pass through him, exciting him suddenly: the peeping sleuth always on the make for information.

There was something about the narrow back of this woman—a woman thought to be so aggressive and influential, and whom he himself had mocked more than once in his own reports—that stirred his heart. Now she seemed even more vulnerable, aroused his sympathy even more than in the tunnel. The doctor helped her find the sleeve of her robe; Benizri stepped back, thinking to return to the outer hallway, but suddenly he changed his mind and approached the doorway to her room. The doctor was saying, "I'll prepare your discharge letter," without lifting his eyes from the chart on which he was writing something. "It'll just take a few minutes, and then you're free to go."

"Today? Already?" Danny Benizri could hear the shock and dismay in her voice.

"I thought you'd be glad," the doctor said, surprised at her reaction. He tucked his stethoscope into the wide pocket of his green smock, which set off his reddish hair and his pale, freckled cheeks. "The professor said, when he made his rounds . . . I thought . . . we can't hear anything wrong with your breathing, there's no reason to keep you here. We simply recommend a few days of rest at home." He closed the file with a tap of his hand. "Why?" he asked, flirtatiously. "Would you prefer to stay a little while longer with us?"

"No," the minister answered. "It's just that I thought, well, I sent my driver home, I gave him off until tomorrow, and my parliamentary assistant isn't available, and my husband . . . oh never mind, I'll manage."

Just then Benizri entered the room with bold steps, confidently, and with false exuberance said, "Perhaps I can be of service?"

"I totally forgot," the doctor said, "I brought you a visitor," and he rushed off.

"You," Timnah Ben-Zvi said, her face clouding. "Who let a reporter in here?" But the doctor was already out of the room and did not hear her protest.

"He knows what's been going on," Danny Benizri said. "He thought you would be glad—"

As if she had suddenly remembered who he was and what he had done for her, her face softened. "Actually, I haven't yet had the opportunity . . . I haven't thanked you properly," she said, averting her eyes as if embarrassed. Her face was small, guileless; a pair of thick-lensed glasses sat atop an overturned leather notebook on her bed near a large oblong box of chocolates, two cardboard cartons, and a few newspaper clippings. "Please," she said, offering him the box of chocolates, "help yourself."

"That's not why I'm here," Danny Benizri muttered, his eyes on the chair sitting in the corner, under the window. "May I?" he asked. He had not gotten where he had in life by being overly sensitive or hesitant. Without waiting for an answer, he dragged the chair close to her bed, ignoring the frightened way she moved her legs as if to edge away from him. Something about the anxious look she had cast his way, her pouting lips that gave her a pampered look, made him want to touch her. He could have brushed her hand as one would a friend's, or placed it warmly, intimately, on her knee, on her shoulder, on her arm, but instead he trusted his intuition and laid it on the edge of the bed. "Please," he said obsequiously, "I'm at your service. I understand you have no way of getting home, so here I am."

"No, that's not necessary," she said, taken aback. "I'll have them call me a cab."

"A government minister does not ride in taxicabs," Benizri said aggressively, never lifting his eyes from her face. "Hasn't enough happened to you already?"

"I can't accept a ride from you," she said. He watched as her fingers toyed nervously with the edge of the sheet. There was no evidence at all of the power people associated with her; he himself had always thought of her as the essence of aggression, precisely because, he claimed, she was a woman and felt the need to prove herself. It was strange to think that this woman in the pale blue flannel robe with a white flower embroidered on the collar, the woman who was now holding her robe closed with one hand and sweeping up her unruly curls with the other, was the same woman who aroused such animosity in the Hulit factory workers; even at police headquarters that morning one of Shimshi's friends had spat when someone mentioned her name, and she had, on more than one occasion, raised his own ire by what he perceived as her indifference, her arrogance, her smugness. He was tempted to tell her that in person she seemed completely different, but instead he asked why she could not accept a ride from him.

"You've already—"

"I understand there's no one available to take you home," he said, touching his knee to hers.

"No, not at the moment. My husband is only due back in the country tomorrow."

"How can that be?" Benizri asked with calculated sanctimoniousness. "You're in the hospital, and he's . . . abroad? Didn't someone let him know?"

She winced with displeasure. "He's a businessman, he's got business overseas, things that were set up way in advance. He left the day before yesterday, before this . . ."

Benizri wanted to ask about children, or how it was that no friends were at her bedside, but something held him back. "Why won't you take a ride with me?" he asked, cocking his head. "That way, you'll be safe: if you get kidnapped, I'll already be there."

She smiled wanly, but he took it as acquiescence.

"I'll wait outside until you're dressed, okay?"

She gave a vague nod, and Benizri went out into the hallway. This time he did not dare stand near the curtain at the window to her room. Fifteen minutes later, as he stood waiting, a nurse appeared walking briskly and carrying a bag. She entered the minister's room while Benizri positioned himself close enough to hear her explaining about the inhaler and what the minister should do in case of emergency, if she should have trouble breathing. He was anxious for the nurse to depart.

"May I?" he asked, nearly running into her.

The nurse glanced at him, a look of recognition in her eyes. "Aren't you—"

"Yes, I am," he confirmed quickly. "May I come in?"

"She's ready to check out," the nurse said, a wrinkle of surprise forming between her brows. "Is she expecting you?"

Benizri nodded and knocked on the door, heard the feeble affirmation, and entered.

Everything went smoothly until they got stuck in a traffic jam on the road leading up from Ein Kerem. A long row of cars stretched out in front of them, and the road was blocked by a police van, an ambulance, and curious onlookers who had stopped at the bend in the narrow road to peer at the overturned truck, which looked like the carcass of a large animal, and the car that lay crushed next to it. Benizri shut the engine off, and the minister sighed. He paid only partial attention to the comment she was making about the number of traffic casualties in the state of Israel and the aggressiveness of Israeli drivers, their vulgarity, their impatience, their lack of manners, and all the rest. Until then they had spoken with pleasant reserve. He still had not dared to raise the matter he had come to discuss with her. Now he pointed at the road ahead, noting that it was not fit for car travel, could in no way support all the traffic. "The problem is not the personality of the drivers," he said, igniting the engine, "it's that the government does not take care of infrastructure, the state of the roads, which is something you know about only too well from your cabinet meetings: no Israeli government is prepared to invest in programs that will only come to fruition after its term. No government is going to improve roads that the next government will reap the praises for. That's the guiding principle of Israeli politics: politicians take care of their own egos, they take care to get reelected, but they won't go out of their way to bring about real change because then their successors will get the credit." The minister's lips curled in displeasure as Benizri spoke. When he paused, he noticed that she was about to say something but had decided against it. "What?" he asked defiantly. "Isn't everything I just said true?"

"Of course not," she answered angrily. "What do you think? That I don't care what happens in this country?" Now she was enraged. "Do I look like someone who spends all her time looking out for the hypocritical interests of politicians? Do you think I'm a cynic?"

Benizri licked his lips and looked sideways at her profile, noting the beautiful line of her lips and the light blush that had risen in her cheeks, breaching her pallor. "No," he answered slyly, weighing his next move. "No, you don't seem like a cynic to me. On the contrary, you come across as a person of principle. Someone whose humanity is accessible," he added, falling silent for a moment, hoping his words would sink in, go to work on her. Watching her hands lying idly in her lap he said, "That's why I want to speak to you about Shimshi and his friends."

"What is there to say?" she sputtered, her hands now clasped. "Those hooligans are going to sit in jail."

"They're not hooligans," Benizri said, turning the wheel to allow an ambulance to pass on its way to the emergency room. The police van moved off to the side of the road, and the cars in front of them and facing them began to move. "They're just a bunch of desperate men, and you know that."

"What?!" she exclaimed, alert. "Desperate? Very nice! Then every desperate person should kidnap a government minister and threaten his life, and people will say he's just an unfortunate guy!"

"Listen, Timnah," he said, daring to use her first name. "Do you mind if I call you Timnah?" Without waiting for a response he hastened to add, "When everything's said and done, you and I . . . we have . . . I thought that because of what happened to us, together, I could approach you and tell you . . . ask you . . . ask you to withdraw your charges against them, because I know you're not one of those people who . . . Look, in the end it all worked out, and you're not a vengeful person, so I was thinking . . . I'm asking—"

The snort that escaped her lips contained surprise and anger and astonishment. Then she fell silent, the windshield wipers squeaking on the glass due to the light rain, and they made their way slowly along the narrow, pitted road, the car lurching forward, then speeding as traffic cleared and the minister, frightened, wrapped her hand around her neck, her thin gold wedding band glittering. After a while, she said dryly, "You are absolutely nuts," adding in an even voice that there was no way of withdrawing the charges. "It's in the hands of the prosecutor's office now, not mine," she concluded. "Kidnapping and the intent to kill are criminal offenses, there is no arguing that." She added that even if the matter were hers to decide (which it was not), she would not retract her claim against the Hulit workers because that would encourage the anarchy already rampant everywhere, where might makes right; it was inconceivable that if people wanted to achieve something, they had to resort to physical strength.

As they passed the enormous monster-sculpture in a playground on the road leading to Kiryat Yovel, Benizri said, "You haven't considered the fact that they've been trying to reach you for a while, but each time you gave them the bureaucratic runaround. These guys are desperate, and . . ."

She sat up straight in her seat, folded her arms dramatically, and looked at him at length before asking coolly what special interest he had in this affair, aside from his interest as a journalist, which, in her opinion, he had long since exceeded. Perhaps, she suggested, he had a relative among the workers.

He wove carefully between the potholes, making slow progress.

"Well, what's your connection to those workers?" she demanded.

Danny Benizri turned his head so that she would not see how worked up he was. He had no intention of telling her about his relationship with Shimshi. "It's complicated," he said reticently, his tone indifferent. "You wouldn't understand. You're incapable of understanding such things," he told her, "because it's not part of your world. You're from a totally different place."

"Why don't you try me?" she taunted him.

Stopped at a traffic light just before the bridge over Golomb Street, he told her about his father, about the stroke he had suffered when the bakery he had worked at for thirty years was shut down, about the years during which he could neither speak nor walk. About the similarity between his father and Shimshi he said nothing. He looked into her face and saw that she had understood.

"But your father did not kidnap anyone or threaten to blow anyone up," she reminded him.

"I told you you wouldn't understand," he answered quickly—now they were stuck in a new traffic jam, on Herzog Street, just before the turnoff to Tchernikovsky—"I shouldn't have said anything. After all, you know quite well," he said in a burst of emotion, "that the deprived actually never get anything except through violence. What revolution ever succeeded without it?"

"Danny Benizri," the minister said with fatigue, wiping her brow, "do me a favor and don't give me any history lessons just now. And turn here, please," she said, gesturing to the parking lot of the two-story buildings at the end of Palmach Street. "Here, the second building."

Danny Benizri parked the car. "Wait," he said, looking around after he had shut off the engine. "Watch out for the puddles and let me take your bag," he said, and ignoring her protests, he followed her to the door, waiting for her to remove her key from her purse and slowly open the door. He entered the living room behind her, watched her draw the curtains. His cell phone rang just as her home phone did. He glanced at the display on his phone as she slowly raised the receiver. "Yes," he heard her say, looking directly at him, "I'm completely alone." He shut his own phone off. "My parliamentary assistant," she mouthed to him. He moved behind her, quite close, while she explained to her assistant that she needed to rest, that no one knew she was back at home, that she did not wish to be disturbed. He watched as she lay the receiver next to the telephone, turning around with the thought that he was at the other side of the room, near the door, surprised to find him right behind her. As he folded his arms around her he noticed a deep crease near her left eyebrow, and it dawned on him that she was at least ten years older than he and that this was the first time in his life he had touched an older woman in this way. But something about her narrow back dulled this realization, as did the taste of her full, dry lips.

Panic and anger flashed through her at the liberties that Benizri, this journalist, was taking with her, and a dull alarm of suspicion and danger rang in her mind, but the wave of heat rising from them both was stronger than the two of them and born of great loneliness and prolonged torment that she suddenly, at that very minute, had had her fill of. This journalist, who had stated so openly what he wanted and needed, had said something to her that she had not heard in years, which made her think that he was her friend, as illogical and unexpected as that was.

By the time they awakened, he had already missed by two hours his appointed "chat" ("I'm only requesting that you come in," Michael Ohayon had said to him; "this isn't an interrogation, and you will not be read your rights"). There were five messages on his cell phone, three from Tikvah, who had been searching for him with desperation in her voice. In the third message she told him she simply did not know what to do with the baby, who had been crying since the morning; he imagined Tikvah's gaunt, forlorn face, could picture her wandering helplessly with the baby carriage. In this cold weather she had taken the baby out in her stroller to bring Gilad home from nursery school; now Tikvah would be shut up in the house with the two of them because of the rain, and suddenly he remembered the promise he had made to Gilad. He had never lost his head like this before; he had no explanation for it, and he searched for one in Timnah Ben-Zvi's face. She was leaning on pillows propped behind her, her eyes half closed. She opened them and returned his gaze.

"Are you sorry or something?" she asked him quietly.

"Sorry? No, no way. I just . . ." He fell silent and began dressing.

"I . . . don't think that I . . . do you usually . . . ?" she stammered.

"Oh sure," he said sarcastically, "every day, what do you think?" Then, as her face darkened, he said, "Hey, I was only kidding. I'm not the philandering type."

"Nor am I. I mean, I've never—"

"You've never had an affair?" he asked. She shook her head.

"So maybe *I* should be the one asking if *you're* sorry," he asked with a slightly curious lilt to his voice, trying to conceal his own self-doubt.

"No, I'm not at all sorry," she answered, crossing her arms. "I'm just . . . how can I say this . . . I'm just a bit . . . in shock at my own behavior."

"In shock. She's in shock," he repeated as if trying out the words. "I've heard," he said hesitantly with a smile, "that women make fun of men who ask if it was good for them, but I'd like to know . . . maybe you'll tell me why you're in shock—"

"If anyone were to catch sight of us right now," said the minister of labor and social affairs as she plumped up the large pillow behind her head, her eyes on him as he dressed, "we'd become the lead item on this evening's news, ahead of the strikers, ahead of everything."

"Not on television," Danny Benizri said as he shoved his arms into the sleeves of his sweater.

"Well, not yet, but soon that kind of thing will be on television, too, some sensationalist program on Channel Two or—"

"Not at Israel Television," he assured her, pulling on his shoes. "Not at Israel's official station," he announced cheerfully before bending down to where she lay propped up against the headboard of the large double bed. She began to smile, but stopped when he placed his lips on her face, on her mouth. "That's why I'm still at Israel Television," he said as he straightened up and glanced at himself in the large mirror facing the bed. "*Our* priorities are still intact," he said, and flashed her a genuinely serious smile.

In his office at police headquarters, Michael sat listening to Natasha's explanations. She asked if they could cut the interview short, if she could go. "I know I was late and everything, but I've got to be at work in another half an hour, and it's rush hour," she said, explaining that she still needed to put the finishing touches on her report for the evening news. She did not answer his question about the topic of her report, and after he queried her again, she said, "Journalistic immunity. I'm permitted not to answer—you said this wasn't an interrogation." He let her get away with it. She also refused to explain why she had arrived late, but her eyes were sparkling and she would not let go of the canvas bag in her lap. "You'll know soon enough," she said, trying to suppress the note of victory in her voice. "Really soon, I promise you," she added, gazing at him with such childish exuberance that he longed to pat her gaunt cheeks. There was something about her that reminded him of an alley cat, the kind you could not tame or tether, the kind that would do anything for a fish head, or less. "I heard about that," she said, lowering her eyes when Michael mentioned Matty Cohen's death. "But I don't have . . . I didn't have anything to do with Matty Cohen, I'm not . . . I'm not important enough."

"You will be, one day." He was surprised to hear himself answer like that; it was, he thought, due to the keen and open desire he could see in her slender fingers, which never stopped moving, and her long, narrow lips, which were incessantly contorting, and the way she kept stealing glances at her watch. She answered the questions that had nothing to do with her news report willingly and even enthusiastically, describing her meeting with Rubin in the editing room: "He was working on a report of his own, and I blew in like the wind, but he's so . . . so professional, so understanding, that he dropped everything and gave me . . ." When he asked her what time it was when she came to Rubin's office, she frowned as if to say she had no idea, but after a moment she remembered and said, "It was after one a.m. because—before that—I passed through the newsroom on the way up to Rubin's office and I saw—no, someone told me—" At this point he stopped her to ask about Hefetz. She neither blushed nor paled, but she held on to her chair, stretching her arms and raising her shoulders until they reached her ears. She bowed her head so that her face was covered by a fan of her long, straight, fair hair. "Look," she said in a quiet, muffled voice, "I don't know what you've been told, but whatever it was, it's no longer relevant."

"But you saw Hefetz in the newsroom, before you went up to Rubin's office, didn't you?"

"Yes," she said. "He caught me as I was running upstairs to Rubin, but I didn't tell him anything about—" She touched her canvas bag, and he understood that she had not spoken to Hefetz about what she was working on. She explained that as she had only been at Israel Television for less than a year and a half, she had hardly known Tirzah Rubin at all. "I started as a teleprompter, you know, the person who gives the cues. I've only been in the News Department for a few months, I barely knew her. I knew who she was, but she didn't know who I was." Almost in passing he asked about Hefetz's relationship with Tirzah Rubin, and she gave him a look of surprise. "Hefetz? What about him? There was nothing special between them," she rebuffed him. "He was in news, she was in something else altogether. They only ever met occasionally in the canteen. Nothing special." And as with all the others he had spoken to, she denied categorically that Tirzah Rubin's death could be anything but accidental. To the question about who, in her opinion, Tirzah could have been meeting with there at midnight, and confronting, she shrugged her shoulders and asked if he was sure it had been a prearranged meeting. She reminded him that Tirzah had been very popular, that she had never heard about her having any enemies. "But I'm not sure, I really didn't know her—only Rubin, and he has always helped me, no strings attached." She looked into his eyes with a gaze that made him ponder—it contained a plea, excitement, who knew what else—and then she lowered her gaze as if she were embarrassed. For a few moments he found it difficult to concentrate; he wished he had a cigarette. He chewed his toothpick, but did not derive even a flicker of satisfaction from it.

• • •

During their staff meeting the team commented on Michael's restlessness. Tzilla noted graciously that it must be a difficult period for a person who had smoked for so many years and given it up all at once; this roused Balilty, who inclined his head, gazed seriously at her and said, "Now his true personality will come out. You all thought he was a calm person? Nice, gentle? *Tranquil*? It was all thanks to the cigarettes, you can see for yourselves."

Tzilla scolded him. "Why are you—it's really hard to quit smoking—we have to help him."

"That's the way of the world," Balilty said serenely. "There are gentle people and caring people who help and support others, and there are the people who don't—I, for example, did not need to take a vacation in order to give up smoking. I just woke up one morning and said, That's enough. I went to that guy I told you about, the one out in Beit Shemesh, I paid whatever I paid him, I was there maybe seven minutes, he did this laying on of his hands, and that was that, I quit. How many times have I told him to go there?" he asked, indicating Michael with his head. "But him? He can do it on his own: so be my guest! Did he listen to me? You know what he said about it, don't you, Tzilla? 'You went to one of those guys who says, Special for you today, only six hundred shekels? *I* don't believe in witch doctors.' So, please, be my guest: witness the results."

Michael squelched a smile. From the beginning of their relationship it had been Intelligence Officer Balilty's custom to give him useful advice in every aspect of life: how to court women ("Look at her once like you're crazy about her and then the next time like you couldn't care less"); how to invest in the stock market ("Some people go to investment brokers, but I've studied up on it, and I can tell you just where to invest right now"); how to look for a new apartment ("Why do you live like a bag lady, all these years in such a dive? There're a few new developments going up near our place, one right across the street"); how to gain extra days off ("How often do you get sick? Call in with a bad back, a slipped disk, just say the word and I'll set you up with a doctor that'll provide you with a note"); how to talk to his ex-wife ("Why do you always keep quiet? She's the one who took you for everything you had, no?"); and how to manage his son's life ("Give him direction, give him advice so that he thinks he's come up with it himself, that's what young people like"). And afterward, if Michael did not take his advice, he would be deeply offended.

"How could I have gone to him? For what? Anyway, it only helps people who believe in it," Michael said in self-defense.

"So you prefer wasting two weeks of vacation on it?" Balilty grumbled. "You don't travel abroad, you don't go out, you sit at home reading books and thinking thoughts and you quit smoking. You probably took Valium, too, didn't you?"

"All right, cut it out already," Eli Bachar said, intervening. "We've seen how well you do on your diets. Where are all the diet witch doctors? And didn't you take a vacation to go to a fat farm? Just cut it out already. Can't you see you're getting on his nerves?"

Michael forced a smile, a smile that was meant to conceal the restlessness and malaise he was feeling in general, and especially his impatience with Balilty's comments. He knew he would end up exposing his true feelings if Balilty did not shut up.

The report on Matty Cohen's autopsy had been placed in front of each of the team members.

"Digoxin is the stuff they give to regulate the heart rate, isn't it?" Tzilla asked.

"Of course. It's already written here," Lillian said, "right at the beginning." She pointed to the first page of the autopsy report. "It says he had four times the proper amount of digoxin in his blood."

Tzilla raised her eyes from the page and glared silently at her. Michael thought he noticed a quiver of annoyance in her pursed lips, but he could not be certain, not yet.

"For a new team member she's pretty involved," Balilty had said earlier, when they were standing in the hallway and he was watching Lillian from behind as she entered the meeting room. "You'd think she'd learn a little, get organized, get to know the territory. Ha! I wish I had her confidence. An hour ago she came up to me and told me that she has 'a few suggestions' to add to the file on this case. At first I was like—speechless—a person's brand-new on the job, and she's already got suggestions! What do you make of that?"

Michael had hemmed and hawed but as usual Balilty had not waited for a response. Instead he had said under his breath, "I told her that it's not even clear if we've got a case here, this is only an initial briefing. So she says, 'Whatever,' but you could see she was offended. Oh well, I guess that's the way it is with Russian women. She's Russian, isn't she? How exactly did we get stuck with her here anyway?"

"She's been in Israel for more than twenty years, since the age of five, and went through the school system here, so I don't think you can exactly call her a Russian," Michael had said quietly. "She came to us from Narcotics with excellent references."

Balilty whistled under his breath. "Forget references, check out her ass," he said quietly. "Tell me, have you ever seen an ass like that in your life? It's like—there's nothing like it. I'd love to give an ass like that a try once, wouldn't you?"

Under Balilty's watchful gaze, Michael glanced with embarrassment at her rear end. Indeed, it was full and round beyond proportion to her narrow back and her slim hips.

"That's not a woman with an ass," Balilty concluded, "that's an ass with a woman. And her legs are too skinny. But she's got a nice face, don't you think?" Michael smiled against his will and sighed. It was clear that from here on in he would be hearing about her face, her rear, her chutzpah. He had accepted her onto the team because of a request made by Yaffa from forensics, who was doing a favor for a neighbor. Yaffa had told Michael how great a neighbor she was, how she was always ready to lend a hand ("If I'm stuck, like without sugar or something, she's always got some, and she never turns down any request. So now that her daughter's in trouble, how could I not return the favor?"); and how the daughter, who was very talented, had gotten into a romantic entanglement with someone at work ("This guy comes along and says that he's separated, that he's in the process of getting a divorce; they're *always* in the process, that divorce is *always* just about to come through, but then they tuck their tails between their legs and run for home, "for the kids' sake"—yeah, right—and then you're stuck alone. Why? Don't you deserve better? Aren't you a human being?"); and how she wanted to get away from him ("She's eating her heart out over this guy, and how's she supposed to get him out of her head when she sees him every day at work?"). "So what do you think of her?"

Balilty had said with an expectant look, which had caused Michael to pause, intending to say something noncommittal. But just then Tzilla had called them into the meeting room.

"Has the final report on Tirzah Rubin come in yet?" Michael asked.

"Yeah, it's here," Tzilla said. "But in my opinion we don't have a case. What do you think?"

"I don't either," Michael said absentmindedly, looking at the cigarette Lillian was holding. "Aside from a couple of things Benny Meyuhas said, which I'm not sure—"

"You can't smoke in here," Tzilla said sharply to Lillian. "There is no smoking during meetings."

"Oh, I had no idea," Lillian said with dismay as she tossed her cigarette into a half-empty bottle of mineral water.

"Since when?" Michael asked, astonished. "We've always smoked during meetings, and—"

"First of all," Tzilla said without looking at him, "the boss has quit smoking—and anyway, it's a windowless room, the heating's on, it . . . it makes me feel ill."

"All right," Lillian said, crossing her legs and shifting uncomfortably in her chair. "I had no idea. I'm sorry."

Michael looked at Tzilla in wonder. All these years she had never complained: windowless rooms and stuffy cars and everywhere, she had never been with him without his smoking, and she had never once commented on it or asked him to stop. Sometimes she would sigh and give him a sorrowful look when he lit up, and only once she had said to him, "You know, one day some doctor is going to tell you you have to quit, and you will, so why wait until then?" He glanced around and saw that Eli Bachar had lowered his gaze at his wife's outburst and said, "Enough, Tzilla, let it go." Suddenly Michael perceived that something was going on between the members of his investigations team. After all, it was clear that the cigarette had not brought on this outburst; anything, if necessary, could serve as the excuse.

"You've spoken with Danny Benizri," Michael said to Eli Bachar. "What have we learned from him?"

"Nothing significant," he responded uncomfortably. "First he showed up two hours late, even more than that, saying he'd been with the Hulit factory workers, that he'd escorted them or something like that. Then later he wasn't sure, he didn't know anything about Benny Meyuhas or Tirzah Rubin, didn't know anything about anyone. Only Rubin, who was his guru. And Hefetz, who he doesn't get along with. That sort of thing. That was all."

"Right," Balilty said mockingly, "like all the rest of them. Nobody knows anything. On principle they won't help us. I've heard there's like this tradition, all over the world, that police and journalists don't get along—"

"Bullshit," Lillian said, cutting him off. "I've sat with that correspondent for police affairs, the redhead, Shalit, and he's always been very cooperative. He's never quoted something I asked him not to. All these reporters have given us their full cooperation—"

"Only if it's vice versa," Tzilla noted. "Only if they need you. But if you need them? I mean, I just saw in the paper that the Union of Television Workers, about 350 people, is striking against the Tel Aviv police force for assaulting them, for denying them access to crime sites—"

"First of all, those people are not employed by the Israel Broadcasting Authority; they're government employees," Balilty explained. "And anyway, there are things we know on our own," he mumbled, peering at the coffee grinds at the bottom of his mug as he rotated it in his hands. All the others were drinking from Styrofoam cups, but Balilty claimed they ruined the taste of the coffee, so he had brought his own mug from home, which was kept in Michael's desk drawer. Everyone was expecting him to continue speaking, but he fell silent.

Michael chewed the end of his pencil and waited.

"So," Eli Bachar asked Balilty, "what are you waiting for? For us to get down on our knees and beg?"

"There are all kinds of issues," Balilty answered mysteriously. "Where there are people there are problems, tensions, interests. All kinds of things."

"How about something in the matter of Tirzah Rubin?" Michael asked finally.

"Yeah, her too," Balilty confirmed as he examined the bottom button on his shirt, which looked as if it were about to pop off. He straightened the sleeves of his blue sweater, which everyone knew had been knitted by his wife in only two weeks ("And I didn't even know about it"), and wrapped them around his large belly, and only then he started speaking about Tirzah Rubin, who was Arye Rubin's wife and then had gone to live with his very best friend, Benny Meyuhas ("Instead of the opposite, the opposite happened. Did you get that? Instead of going from the boring one to the interesting one, she went from the interesting one to the boring one, from the classy one—Rubin is one classy guy—to Benny Meyuhas, who looks like her grandfather"), who she'd been with for seven, eight years. "She left Rubin because of all his skirt-chasing," he explained, examining his fingertips, "but I don't know whether she knew about the son he had with Niva Pinhas. Have you people met her?"

"Yeah, yeah," Eli Bachar said with a sigh. "There was no avoiding it, was there? She's not exactly the shy and fearful type."

"She screams all the time, there really are women like that," Balilty explained, as if he was particularly knowledgeable in this area. "Secretaries in the media are known to be especially tough—all of them, even the junior ones—so imagine one in the newsroom. . . . I always say, you want to get to the director general, make sure you get on the good side of his secretary. . . . Never mind, where were we? Oh, yeah, whether Tirzah Rubin knew about the kid. I don't know, but I do know that Rubin took great pains to keep any information about him from reaching her, even after she'd left him. He'd be about six, maybe a little older, and he doesn't have a clue who his father is," he said in wonder, explaining that Tirzah could not carry full-term. "She had four miscarriages, lots of fertility treatments, poor thing, you should see her file at Hadassah Hospital. They couldn't help her."

"That means," Lillian chimed in, stroking her pointed chin and prodding the dark mole at the base of her neck, "that now the kid can be told. Like, now Rubin has nothing to hide?"

"Yes," Balilty affirmed, "that's exactly what it means. What do we learn from this?"

"That Niva Pinhas gains something from Tirzah's death?" Lillian ventured.

Michael nodded. "But Niva Pinhas was in the newsroom when Tirzah was killed. She never left there. In fact, she just happened to be filling in for someone else that evening, we checked."

"There were a lot of people in the building. They were there, and people saw them there," Eli Bachar said. "Hefetz was around, and Rubin, and the skinny young woman with the blue eyes—"

"Natasha," Tzilla said.

Balilty added, "Meyuhas and Rubin had a very strange relationship—sort of like brothers, unconditional love and all that, but there couldn't be two more different people—"

"They served together in the army," Michael explained. "First in the youth movement and later as paratroopers. I understand they spent the Yom Kippur War in the Sinai Desert, nearly their entire platoon was wiped out—only six of them survived, of whom three are alive today: Rubin, Benny Meyuhas, and a friend of theirs who lives in Los Angeles."

"Aha!" Balilty shouted. "Now I get it." He stood up from his chair and went to look out the window, at the front courtyard and the main gate to the Russian Compound. "Hey, check this out," he said, as if to himself. "The wives of the guys laid off by the Hulit factory are still out there. What are they hanging out around here for?"

Michael drummed his fingers on the edge of the table. *"Nu,"* he said at last, but Balilty continued to stare out the window and did not speak up.

"What? What is it you 'get' already?" Eli Bachar shouted.

"What? What's the matter?" Balilty said innocently. "It's nothing important, it's just that in Rubin's office there's this corkboard with all kinds of large photographs. Not pictures from his news reports and not babes—not like Zadik's office either, with pictures of VIPs—you know, Zadik with Clinton or Defense Minister Yitzhak Mordechai or lots of other people—no, there's none of that with Rubin. He's got this big photo of an Arab kid with these bulging eyes, like he's starving or something, and a photo of himself with Tirzah, at the Sea of Galilee, I think, and then there are these, like, historical photos, Japanese POW camps in World War Two, and American POWs, I guess in Vietnam, they're sitting on the ground with their hands in the air—"

"What's that got to do with anything?" Lillian asked, looking suspiciously in Tzilla's direction, who was acting as though she had not heard the conversation.

"A lot," Balilty said, strumming his lower lip with a fat finger. "Rubin and Meyuhas and those other guys were probably POWs or something. If you're with somebody under enemy fire or in a war, well, that's a bond for life, even stronger than brothers. They were together in the Yom Kippur War? There was some story about the paratroopers in the Sinai, we should look into it, but—"

"Let's get back to the medical report for a minute," Michael said; Balilty's incessant chattering was getting to be more than he could bear. "First of all, there are these marks, the bruises on Tirzah's neck, as though someone had a firm grip on her. But the pathologist can't determine exactly when. It could be from her argument with Benny Meyuhas, which was a few days before that. The pathologist says that couldn't be, but still—"

"What?" Tzilla said, taken aback, "you want to tell me that Benny Meyuhas is a wife-beater?"

"What are you so surprised about?" Lillian exclaimed. "Don't tell me you think that just because someone's a celebrity he must be a decent human being."

"Not just any celebrity," Tzilla said, standing her ground. "He's the most respected director in television, the most—how shall I say it, someone that everyone knows is reputable—and now with that film of his, the story by Agnon. And the man looks, well, he certainly doesn't look like a wife-beater."

"What exactly, in your opinion, does a wife-beater look like?" Lillian asked with forced calm. "Do you think he has some sort of crazed look about him or something? I—in Narcotics, where I used to work, there were lots of . . . one thing I learned was that if someone wants to hide it, he hides it; it's not like a common criminal, where you can see it written all over him. With a white-collar guy there's no external sign that gives him away, especially if he's a drug addict."

It seemed that Tzilla was about to say something, but Michael cut her off. "In any case," he concluded, "you can see in the report in front of you what the pathologist has to say. He writes 'inconclusive' at the bottom of the first page."

"One thing's for sure: there's something very strange about this accident," Tzilla muttered. "How can a pillar fall on you, and you don't move aside? And what about how Eli heard him saying, 'It's because of me'? They must have had some serious argument."

"But," Lillian reminded them all, "in the affidavit it says that Benny Meyuhas was on the roof the whole time. He never left."

"That's not exactly true," Michael said. "There was a break. Two in fact, one for food and one for cigarettes or something. The first was at ten o'clock and the other was"—he paused to thumb through his papers—"at eleven-thirty, when they sent for the sun gun. But who knows? He's the director. He couldn't very well disappear without someone seeing him."

"Sure, and people could have gone to the bathroom, too," Balilty noted. "Maybe they did, and maybe they didn't. But if you ask me, we don't have a case here. Nobody has a motive, and someone from the outside, well, there was a guard on duty and it doesn't make sense that—even if someone had the key to the back entrance, we don't know of anyone who—like who? Who?"

"We don't know yet," Michael emphasized. "In fact, we don't know anything yet. The question is whether to start poking around or not. The decision is based more on intuition than on some particular finding."

"What about the digoxin they found in Matty Cohen's body?" Lillian piped in. "If we add Tirzah's accident to the surplus of digoxin in Matty Cohen's blood—"

Balilty cut her off. "Even though it fits in with the general picture, the guy was taking digoxin for five years, he was a bona fide heart patient. It appears he accidentally took too much of the stuff. We don't have a case, it's just that . . ."

While he was speaking, Tzilla passed around additional copies of the medical documents to her husband, who gave them a quick look and handed them to Lillian.

Michael waited until Lillian had passed them on to Balilty and said, "In any case, two dead bodies in under twenty-four hours, each an accident, and with some connection between the two of them—I think it's a bit . . . how shall I say it—"

"Okay," Balilty protested. "There is such a thing as coincidence, don't you think?" He smiled. "Well, then again, not where you're concerned, there's no such term as 'coincidence' in the Ohayon dictionary, is there? But there you have it," he said, a note of victory in his voice, "you always disagree with me, but this time it turns out you're wrong."

"I haven't said anything yet," Michael reminded him. "But, yes, this time, too, I have this—never mind, we'll give it another day or two, we'll put it on the back burner, but we'll keep our feelers out. I have to go back there in any event to talk to Hefetz, since he can't make it over here. They've got something big on tonight's program, and you," he said, pointing to Eli Bachar, "you're going back to Benny Meyuhas's place like we talked about?"

Eli Bachar glanced at Tzilla, and for a moment it seemed to Michael that he saw a flicker of fear in his eyes; Tzilla lowered her gaze and shrugged. "It won't take very long," Eli said. He looked at Michael and smiled. "Today's our anniversary," he said quietly. "We thought we would . . ."

Michael looked at them both. "That's right," he said, remembering. "The first night of Hanukkah. How many years has it been? Fourteen? You celebrate according to the Hebrew date?"

"Fifteen years. How could *you* not remember?" Tzilla said, scolding him. "You orchestrated the whole thing."

"Well," Balilty said mockingly, "in fact he was only the go-between, that's all, I remember how Eli—"

Michael gave him a look: all they needed now was for Balilty to start telling about how Eli Bachar had had this "fear of commitment," and how he had given Tzilla such grief until Michael had finally intervened, speaking with him and arranging matters. Balilty lowered his gaze, grinning, but stopped talking. Michael summed up: they would meet again the following morning.

On his way out of the room Eli Bachar said suddenly, "I can't believe what an idiot I am! I don't understand how I didn't think of this earlier: Benizri told me he was with the Hulit workers, but I saw with my own eyes, when I got here I saw the wives, they were standing outside waiting for the men to be transferred from here to—and Shimshi's wife said to me, 'Benizri is our only hope, we're waiting for him to come.' So how . . . where was he?"

Balilty stopped. He was fingering a cigar he had pulled from the pocket of his tweed jacket. "Don't worry." He chuckled. "It's nothing urgent. And anyway those things always come out sooner or later."

# CHAPTER EIGHT

For a long moment Michael stood in the doorway of the large room, quite close to the two death notices—one announcing the death of Tirzah Rubin, the other that of Matty Cohen—and took note of the goings-on. It was impossible to recognize the place from that same morning: now, people were rushing helter-skelter, completely absorbed in preparing for the broadcast, so that anything other than the news—even the deaths of Tirzah Rubin and Matty Cohen—was shoved aside. People stood around the conference table, reading the sheets of paper that had been placed on it, talking among themselves, and shouting to others in the inner rooms. Telephones rang from every corner, muffling the sound of the computer printers busy spewing out pages: one mobile phone burst forth with *Carmen,* while another one, quite near by, rang to the theme for *Mission: Impossible* again and again until Dror Levin, the correspondent for political parties, picked up the phone and shouted, "Hello! Hello!" a look of exasperation on his face. Through the glass partition Michael could see Danny Benizri standing behind the graphic artist in her room, pointing out something to her on the screen, and in the next room he caught sight of a translator named Rivi as she spoke with a young woman in jeans and a red sweater who was gesticulating and pointing to another cubicle, where a correspondent for foreign affairs was hunched over the keyboard in front of him, typing and speaking into a telephone at the same time. If you could not hear the voices, the people in the newsroom appeared as absorbed in their activities as children at play. "Tell me, does that look like enough makeup for you to go on-screen?" he heard someone ask Karen, the anchorwoman, who was sitting on a corner sofa near the door reading from the same lined printout that had been placed in front of every seat around the conference table, until they were removed by Niva, the newsroom secretary, as she shuffled around the table handing out updated copies, her clogs registering a noisy complaint at having been commandeered into action once again. Suddenly, the voice of a child saying the blessing over the first candle of Hanukkah drowned out all the other noise in the room. Michael raised his eyes to the monitor and saw a dark-skinned, curly-headed child, his hand trembling with excitement as he stood before the glowing menorah. "What's going on here? Who made it so loud? Turn down the volume on Channel Two!" Niva shouted, adding under her breath to David Shalit, the police affairs correspondent: "See that? Channel Two uses an Ethiopian kid, and in another five minutes we'll be putting a new immigrant from Russia up there. How do you like that? We know how to play the game, too!" David Shalit did not even look up at the monitor, he merely shrugged and pointed to the page he was holding, as if to say there was no need for another one.

"Can't you see that it says six-forty-nine p.m. on this one?" she asked, indignant. "If you haven't noticed, this is the *latest* lineup; the last one was over an hour ago. Look here, see for yourself how much it's changed." She scanned the room and called out to Karen. "Have you been to makeup? Where's Natasha? I don't understand why she isn't here!"

"Here I am, I am *too* here, what do you want?" Natasha responded from a corner of the room and approached the table.

"What's that you're wearing?" Niva scolded her. "It's not at all my job to be worrying about such things." She tugged the sleeve of a wrinkled woman whose pale hair was gathered into a sloppy bun. "Ganit," she said, "you're a producer, so why don't you produce already? What's with Natasha's blouse?" Niva sighed loudly, spreading her arms and raising her eyes to the ceiling. "Why should I have to worry about this? Natasha, get down to Wardrobe, do you hear me?"

"Did you edit the cabinet meeting yet?" Erez asked the political correspondent, Yiftah Keinan, who nodded.

"It's almost ready," he said.

"Well, you're going to have to do it again, with Bibi and David Levy this time," Erez said.

"What are you shouting for?" Yiftah Keinan protested as he tucked the shirttails sticking out from under his light blue vest into his trousers. "I only need twenty seconds for the VTR."

"Yiftah," Erez said impatiently, "are you prepared to tell me whether to begin with David Levy or with Bibi?"

"I told you already, start with David Levy," he said as he went over the new lineup. "Just tell me if the VTR covers everything."

"Yes, yes, it does," Erez grumbled. "How many times do I have to repeat myself?"

Once again, Niva raised her eyes to the ceiling. "Why are you people shouting? Why can't people talk pleasantly to one another for once?"

Hefetz sat at the head of the table, and Michael stood behind him, peering over his shoulder at the lineup, while Erez, at the other end of the table, waved the new page at the language editor, who was quickly and carefully applying lipstick in the corner of the room. "Miri," he called, "have you gone over this?"

"What am I, God?" she asked bitterly. "When exactly would I have had time to go over it?" Miri snapped her lipstick closed and approached the conference table.

Hefetz was talking on the phone and scanning the pages in his hand. "So you want to tell me that having one driver under the age of twenty-four is going to push my policy up by two thousand shekels?" he grumbled into the receiver. "Don't try and sell me that bullcrap, I'm no sucker and I'm not paying that kind of premium on my car. What? No, they won't pay for it from work, of course not." He raised his head for a moment, and when he noticed Michael, he glanced at the large wall clock, nodded to him to indicate he was aware of his presence, and covered the receiver with his large hand. "You're going to have to wait," he told him, "I just can't meet with you right now—you see what's going on. That's the way it is, you can't make any plans with someone responsible for the news. I can't stop everything. You're welcome to wait here, you can sit in that armchair at the side, you won't be in the way. Or you can go out and walk around, whatever you like. Take a seat down in the canteen, we've got a big mess with the satellite. Let's wait until she's on the air," he said, indicating Natasha. "We've got something pretty big going down, you can stay here if you're interested. Whatever you want," he concluded, returning to his phone call.

Erez moved his chair aside, making room for Michael to sit behind him, and said to Hefetz, "It would be nice if we knew what this 'pretty big thing going down' was. When exactly are you planning to tell us? What am I supposed to write on the lineup? How can I edit the news without knowing what—forty minutes to air time, and look what's written here: ITEM X TWO MINUTES FIVE SECONDS NATASHA. So how do you expect me to give this a title?"

Michael sat down to observe them until Hefetz was free, since you could always learn something about people if you watched them in secret while they were occupied with their own affairs and paying no attention to you. But Zadik, who had entered the room, waved to Hefetz and, just to be sure, hurried over to him. "Where do we stand?" he asked as he leaned over the table to have a look at the papers. "What do I see here? You took Yaacov Neeman off the lineup?"

"There's no room, and I can't go overtime tonight," Hefetz said, rising from his chair and pushing it backward. He glared at Zadik. "Can I go overtime tonight or not? No, I can't. You told me not to go overtime, so—"

"Okay, okay," Zadik said, disconcerted, and stepped away from Hefetz. "I'm not getting involved," he said, trying to placate him. "I was just asking. Asking is still allowed, isn't it?"

But Hefetz ignored him, shouting, "Karen, go to Miri and see about the corrections. Miri, get a move on it, this isn't a doctoral dissertation. You've still got to approve these corrections, and even then—"

Mozart's Symphony No. 40 was playing again from inside the large black bag at Michael's feet, and in an instant Niva was at his side, fishing through it. By the time she had managed to locate her cell phone, it had stopped ringing. "Oh, not again!" she grumbled as she hit the memory button. She bent down next to her bag, very close to Michael, and he heard her heavy breathing as she said, "Mother? What? What?" And then, after a minute, "Now?! We're on the air in less than an hour, and I don't have time to . . . never mind, in the upper right-hand cabinet . . . no, not there, on the top shelf . . . listen to what I'm telling you, why aren't you listening? Did you find it? Okay, so take it now . . . no, not later, God, I'm hanging up—" She turned off the phone and tossed it into her bag, shoved the bag under Hefetz's chair, and hurried to the computer printer, which was just then producing a new printout, and another, and another.

"Erez. Erez!" David Shalit shouted to the news editor, "come here, we've got to make a change in the Jerusalem murder, there's a gag order on showing photos of the barber and his girlfriend." He shut his cell phone with a snap and said to Erez, who had joined him, "It's the hottest story today, he wasn't just any old barber, he cut the hair of the prime minister's wife. There may be fallout from this, and I have material filmed by a local television station and also—"

"The prime minister's wife?" Niva asked, butting in. "Didn't Bibi say the guy had 'served' as his own barber?"

"His precise words were, 'served in our home,'" David Shalit corrected her. "With a guy like Bibi and all his regal pomposity, even barbers 'serve.' Erez, did you hear what I said? About this item, we've got to—"

"All right," Erez answered calmly, "I heard you, don't get all worked up. First of all, I'm not sure that's really the hottest item we've got today, and second, you're going to have to be patient: I've already contacted our Tel Aviv office about this and told a lawyer for the Israel Broadcasting Authority to be prepared, there's still a chance we'll run the photos, but we have to wait and see what the judge on duty says. Now just give me a few minutes to write the titles, I've got to concentrate." He sat at the corner of the table and hung his head over several empty pages before speaking up again. "If you ask me, this is the last time we'll hear about the laid-off strikers, tomorrow they'll already be yesterday's cold noodles."

"Don't be so sure," Danny Benizri said defensively. "It's not over yet."

"Hey," the correspondent for political parties shouted from his place at the table, "what's happening with the story about the violence at the Kahane memorial service?" He had shifted the knitted skullcap from the crown of his head and was scrutinizing a small comb he had pulled from the back pocket of his trousers. "I can't find it on the lineup. Our lives are out of control, and nobody gives a—"

"Look again," Hefetz bellowed. "Have you people forgotten how to read? Look at item number thirteen, see where it's written, NO-CONFIDENCE / POLITICS? Is it written there? Yes? Very good. That item includes the threats to television crews, there's a shot of policemen on horseback hiding behind a tree. We talked about it this morning. Weren't you listening?"

"Wait a minute," Zohar, the military correspondent, interjected angrily. "How is it that the story about Yitzhak Mordechai meeting with army officers about the new round of talks with the Palestinians has been dropped?" He blew his pointed nose noisily. "I spent hours on that, and—" He rapped a sheaf of papers on the table and looked around, but no one was listening to him. "I can't even get an answer," he said bitterly. "If you'd only give it even thirty seconds . . . I've been out freezing my ass in that tunnel since before dawn and then caught in a downpour down south running after . . . and nobody even—"

"What about the mining disaster in Russia?" Tzippi called on her way in from the next room, her hand resting on her oversize belly. "Is that still pertinent?" When no one responded, she turned to Niva. "What should I do about the Russian mines?" she asked.

"Keep it, maybe we'll use it on the late-night broadcast," Niva answered distractedly as she leafed through the pages emerging from the printer.

"And what about the Nazi gold?" Tzippi asked as she approached Hefetz. From up close the brown pregnancy splotches on her forehead were noticeable. "When did you plan that for?"

"Save the Russian mines for the week-in-review show, it'll still be pertinent by Friday," Erez promised her. "As for the Nazi gold, we need a filmed announcement but no sound. Leave it in."

"What do you mean, leave the Russian mines for Friday?" Tzippi complained. "If I'm still at work on Friday, you people are going to have to deliver this baby right here!"

"So leave it with Rafael," Hefetz instructed her. "He's handling all the international news anyway, he's taking over for you, isn't he?"

"Rafael!" Tzippi shouted as she heaved herself with a loud sigh into a chair at the side of the room. "We need you in here—"

Michael glanced at the bespectacled young man with the intelligent expression, who looked to be about the age of his own son. Hefetz slapped him on the back and said, "Listen, Rafael, we've got two American stories I'd like you to do voiceovers for. One's about that shooting in a high school, a couple of teenagers who shot everybody up. Where was that again?"

"Colorado," Rafael answered in a pleasant voice as he scrunched up his face, his eyebrows touching. "A place called Littleton, near Denver. The school is called Columbine."

"Yeah, that's it," Hefetz said, as if he were really in the know about all the details. "And there's another story about a new virus called Monkey Fox that's threatening to wipe us all out. Have you heard anything about that?"

Rafael nodded. "There are some pretty good pictures of the fire in Australia, too."

"Don't need 'em," Hefetz said. "Australia doesn't interest us today." Turning to Erez, he said, "I understand there's no financial report today, so how about having Rafael do a voiceover about the school in Colorado."

"Tell me more about this virus," Erez said to Rafael.

"It comes from monkeys," he said, adjusting his glasses. "Something that passes from monkeys to people, some disease."

"How does it get transmitted?"

"Sexually," Rafael answered.

"That's by sex, too!?" Hefetz exclaimed, glancing at Niva, who was holding two telephone receivers, one on each ear. "In the end we'll all wind up in a monastery."

"You haven't told me yet if you want the school shooting and the mining disaster," Tzippi reminded him as she rubbed her swollen belly.

"Problem is, they'll come one right after the other," Erez said, thinking aloud.

"Virus?" Hefetz interjected. "You want the virus after that? What about the item about Scientology? Are you going to put that in? Anything about cults is very interesting, or else I can go with the Nazi gold, Scientology, and the Colorado school shooting."

Erez did not respond. Instead, he turned to Karen. "Come sit next to me, and we'll get started," he said, and the anchorwoman did as she was told. To Rafael he said, "Get upstairs and start editing."

"Niva," Hefetz called out, "get me Rubin on the line. I need to know what's with his story about the doctors who cover up for Israeli intelligence operatives. Is it ready for today, or are we postponing it to tomorrow?"

"It's not even for the news, it's for his own program. Next week, I think," Niva said, thrusting her hand into her thin red hair. "Anyway, I can't get through to him, I've been trying. He's at Benny Meyuhas's house, and he's not answering calls."

"So," Zadik said, addressing Michael, "I see you've become a permanent fixture in the News Department. You think that Israel Television is only the news? Come, let's get out of here, nobody here has time for you now, they're running full steam ahead. I'll take you down to the canteen, that's where everything important takes place anyway. Maybe they'll even have a leftover Hanukkah doughnut for us. I love doughnuts. Not the American kind, but the Hanukkah kind, like my grandmother used to make."

The two death notices were posted throughout the building, on walls and doors and everywhere, and still it seemed as though life was carrying on at its usual mad pace. The sound of the blessing over the first Hanukkah candle and the holiday song "Rock of Ages" as sung by a children's choir could be heard blaring from several monitors along the way. The canteen itself was so overrun with people that the children's choir was nearly drowned out, and on top of all that, Dror Levin, the correspondent for political parties, who had come running in and pushed Michael and Zadik aside as they stood at the counter, could be heard shouting at the top of his lungs at a young man in a gray suit ("That's the lawyer who was appointed assistant legal counsel last month," Zadik explained): "Who do you think you are? How dare you throw that bullshit at me!" Dror Levin said, indicating the open booklet that the lawyer was holding. "What are you reading to me from that for? You're brand-new here: you think *you've* got something to teach *me* about the Nakdi document?" In a calm and level voice the lawyer said, "Everything I said is written right here," indicating the booklet, "and I quote: 'An issue in which a correspondent or cameraman has a personal involvement and the results of which report he/she has prepared may have a direct effect on his/her private interests, his/her involvement disqualifies him/her from covering the topic.'" He raised his eyes from the booklet. "That's all I said, so if you have no personal involvement, then there's no problem. I don't understand why you're so upset," he concluded as he stuck the light blue booklet into a file he was carrying and made as if to leave. Then he added, "If Member of Knesset Yossi Beilin invites you to his son's bar mitzvah party . . . ," and he spread his hands in lieu of finishing his sentence.

The correspondent said, "Well, since I am certainly guilty of this corrupt act, I guess I'll just have to—" and turned away from the lawyer, hastening to sit at one of three tables pushed together, around which sat a large crowd. "That's the team from the week-in-review program," Zadik said with a sort of odd pride, "our flagship, personal stories and everything. Arye Rubin can usually be found here, but not today—and there's Shoshi, the editor. See her? As tiny as she is, that's what a terror she is." Michael looked at the diminutive woman, whose helmet of gray hair topped a surprisingly young face.

When they reached the table, she turned to Zadik and said, "We're talking ethics here. The question is, if the mayor invites all of us in this forum on a tour of Jerusalem, is there anyone who objects?"

A bearded correspondent said in a deep voice, "I do. We're crossing boundaries: on occasion I interview the mayor in our studios."

"I don't see any conflict of interest here," Shoshi declared. "Have a seat, Zadik. In that context, but not really in that context, I wanted to request that we be trained in this new audience measurement system, the People Meter. That'll be the ratings we live by—"

"Not now," said the deep-voiced correspondent as he stroked his beard. "I wanted to say that I think we should make a tour of some of the development towns in the south, places that we—"

"Do you people know Ohayon?" Zadik interjected as he fell into a chair. "Chief Superintendent Ohayon?" They regarded him, and someone made room for him to sit down. "As long as you're all here, I can talk to you about what's bothering me, which I keep repeating like a parrot: that we're using material that is not ours. Last Wednesday we broadcast four shots from a film by Naomi Aluf. The material was not ours, and we have to request permission to use it, otherwise we'll have to pay hundreds of dollars."

"I suppose the director did it because he didn't know about the copyright issue," the bearded correspondent said. "I'm going to get some sweetener, but I just wanted to say I saw it, and it looked like part of a journalistic report, not some documentary film from someone outside Israel Television."

"Who says you people have got it right?" the political correspondent said as he pulled up a chair and sat between Zadik and Michael. "Maybe they didn't use shots from that film. It looks to me like they didn't use any footage from the film; those were just similar shots lifted from the *Mabat* program."

Zadik leaned his head back and said, with fatigue, "It's been proven."

"Where?" said the bearded correspondent.

"In the archives. We've already discussed this issue, when you people used material from the last Academy Awards ceremony."

A parade of children entered the canteen dressed in various Jewish costumes—Yemenites, the ultra-Orthodox, a Jewish peasant in a *sarafan*—followed by Adir Bareket, who called loudly after them, "Children! One doughnut, a quick drink, make a tinkle, and in three minutes we're going back. Got that?"

"Yes!" the children shouted in obedient chorus. Zadik winced. To the people gathered around the tables he said, "I don't get it. What are all of you doing here? Is this an official meeting? Here? Now?"

"Well, we couldn't have our regular meeting, since we lost part of the workday because of Tirzah's funeral," Shoshi explained. "And of course I went to pay my respects at Benny Meyuhas's. Don't forget, we go back a long way together, in fact, he's the one who brought me in to work here. So we postponed our meeting until now, and we haven't even gotten to reviewing the previous program yet."

Michael moved his greasy doughnut aside and drank the coffee, which made him nauseous. All around the table people were smoking, in spite of the NO SMOKING signs posted around the canteen (though no one called these to the attention of anyone else), and he felt the clouds of smoke and breathed them in deeply, lustily. How long would he be bothered by this feeling of missing something? And why was he sitting there, waiting for Hefetz, to speak with him again about these two deaths, which, just because they had taken place there . . .

"Why did Channel Two come out with the story about Iraq before us?" Zadik complained.

"Zadik, we've discussed this a thousand times," Shoshi said. "First of all, a story like Iraq has no place in a news magazine like the week-in-review program. People don't want another news show, they want a magazine, personal stories— What was the story with Iraq anyway? They uncovered an undercover operative of ours?"

"Furthermore," the deep-voiced correspondent said, "Channel Two doesn't employ union technicians, they work according to clear, fixed contracts through tenders that leave the power and authority with the technicians themselves."

"Poor Matty Cohen," Shoshi said with a sigh. "Who would believe—"

"Quiet, quiet a minute," Zadik said. "Turn up the volume."

Michael looked up at the monitor, which featured Karen the anchorwoman. "People tried to put a stop to our next report in a variety of ways," she was saying. "The reason? This has been discussed for years, but only now, for the first time, are there facts, names, and numbers. A Channel One scoop: how the national budget funds yeshivas. Here's Natasha Goralnik with the report."

Natasha's face—serious, yet jubilant, not a trace of the abandoned waif—filled the screen. "Israeli yeshivas," she began, "receive funding according to the number of students enrolled. But what happens when the budget does not provide enough money? Well, it turns out all that is necessary is to bring more names—even those of the dead. Thirty-seven," she said, then excused herself, coughing, "thirty-seven names you see on the screen." A list of names appeared, with a pointer. "Here, for example," Natasha said, "David Aharon, identity card number 073523471, who supposedly lives at 33A Kanfei Nesharim Street and studies at Ori Zion yeshiva, in fact passed away five years ago, but for the past five years—five years!—he has been considered a yeshiva student, in whose name the yeshiva receives monthly financial funding. So it is for Hai Even-Shushan and Menasheh Ben-Yosef, whose identity card numbers you see on the screen now." Natasha's voice rose dramatically. "The Ori Zion yeshiva receives monthly payments in the names of thirty-seven people who are in fact certifiably dead." The complete list appeared on the screen.

"Good job," Zadik said, glowing. "Good job. That girl is top-notch, I'm even considering promoting her," he said, as if sharing a secret. "We have—never mind, have you met her?" he asked Michael. "What did you think of her?" Michael nodded his head but remained silent. "Come on, let's go down to the newsroom. I'll treat you to something special: a visit to the studio." Michael followed him, and soon they stopped at the narrow entrance to the studio; he preferred not to push his way between the rows of people sitting in front of the control panels and the producer's desk, so he huddled in a corner next to a side room and watched the guest interviewees who had been invited to appear on this live broadcast as they sat obediently in a row of chairs glued to the wall and waited their turn to enter the recording studio. Among them sat the minister of labor and social affairs, apparently in regards to the striking workers. Natasha, all smiles, stepped out of the studio, and everyone in the vicinity clapped her on the shoulder; even the people at the control table turned their heads to smile at her. No one was prepared for what was about to happen, it all appeared to have gone so well, and then the telephone rang, and rang again and again, and Ganit the producer answered. In the general confusion no one heard what she was saying, but then a moment later she called over anxiously to Zadik. "It's a good thing you're here," she said. "I don't know—someone on the line says . . . shit, here, just take the phone." Just then Hefetz burst into the studio, a sheet of paper in his hands. "A fax came in," he said to the people gathered there, "and we've got big trouble." Natasha was still glowing. "So, Hefetz, what do you say?" she said, baiting him, and he handed her the paper.

After poking his head into the room to glance at the unmistakable look of pride on Natasha's face, Michael stood thinking quietly at the entrance to the room as he observed the tumult, which had nothing to do with him and was not connected to his investigation. "What?!" he heard Zadik shout. "What does this mean, 'living'? Who's living? All right, I'll go up to the entrance. Where is he? By the security officer?"

"That was Niva," he said, troubled, to Ganit, who ran upstairs after him. Hefetz was on her tail like a cartoon character, Michael thought as he, too, raced along with them, mostly due to his instincts, but also because he had been waiting to talk to Hefetz. Had he not been waiting for Hefetz, he would have missed the whole matter.

By the security officer's station, at the entrance, stood three ultra-Orthodox men. "I didn't let them in because—" the security officer started to say, but Hefetz ignored him and stood examining the identity card that one of the young men, his dark jacket draped over his shoulders, had handed him. The man was smiling into his beard, and in a voice filled with wrath asked, "Do I look dead to you?" The other two stood behind him.

"What is this?" Hefetz shouted as he looked at the identity card. Perturbed, he lifted his eyes and looked at the ultra-Orthodox man, then read aloud: "'David Aharon, 33A Kanfei Nesharim Street, identity card number 073523471.' You're alive?"

The man spread his hands as if to say, Yes, it's a fact, to which Hefetz responded, "I am sorry, sir, we will correct this mistake."

Natasha raced upstairs from the recording studio, and Schreiber was already there next to the security officer, waving his hands trying to grab her attention, but she went to stand in front of Hefetz, who was holding the faxes Niva had brought him. Niva herself was standing by the stairs, pale, wiping her brow. "We've never had anything like this before," she said, horrified, though it was not clear to whom she was speaking. Still, there was a hint of satisfaction in her voice when she added, to Schreiber, "I told you people, she's young and inexperienced," to which he replied, the loathing on his face clear, "You viper," and he moved to Natasha, who was examining the identity card that Hefetz was showing her and the face of the bearded man in front of her. He said, "I'm David Aharon, I'm David Aharon, you heretic!" "Natasha, Natasha," Michael heard Schreiber whispering to her. "This will blow over, Natasha." "Forget it, Schreiber," she said, her mouth dry. "Nothing doing. Can't you see I'm screwed?!" She took to the stairs leading to the newsroom and ran into Rubin, who was racing down them. "Natasha," he cried, "where are you going?" "To clear out my stuff," she answered, her voice lifeless. "You'll do no such thing," Rubin said as he grabbed her arm. "Hefetz," he said. "Hefetz, did you hear her? Zadik, please—"

But Zadik did not even glance at him; he was bent over the telephone on the security officer's station, saying, "Yes, sir," and "I am sorry, sir," and "Yes, rabbi."

"Leave Zadik out of this, Rubin," Hefetz said. "Can't you see he's busy trying to mop this mess up?"

"She was set up, Hefetz," Rubin cried. "What are you shouting at her for? Can't you see she was set up? You yourself sent her to cover this story.

"Zadik," Rubin said, "tell him." He turned to Natasha, pulling her back toward the entrance. "Why aren't you saying anything?" And to Hefetz: "Why don't you tell him they set her up because of the other matter? Why aren't you telling him about it? After all," he said, turning to Zadik, "it's precisely so that you'll read her the riot act and you won't agree to air the other matter. Why don't you get it, it's the other matter that's got them scared. That's why they set her up, to get her into trouble."

"No way," Hefetz said. "That's why we're journalists. That's what journalism is all about. News journalists can't be set up. It only happens if they run ahead too fast without thinking, without checking and rechecking and rechecking again."

"I was with her there myself," Schreiber interjected, "I stood there knocking on doors. We talked to the neighbors. This guy doesn't live there, this could be a fake ID—"

"Schreiber, Schreiber, forget about it," Natasha said, her voice fatigued. "I am finished here, I'm washed up, no two ways about it. Just leave me alone," she said as she turned and made her way slowly up the stairs.

"Wait here for me until the end of the broadcast," Hefetz instructed Michael, and raced after her, calling, "Natasha, Natasha." She did not turn her head. Schreiber followed her as well, and Michael hesitated a moment: since when did he take orders to wait? He glanced at the double glass doors at the entrance to the building, where a large group of ultra-Orthodox men had gathered and were shouting. Suddenly a tall, lean, middle-aged man in a large, torn overcoat burst in, wisps of his thinning gray hair sticking out from under the large embroidered skullcap that covered his head. His arms were flailing, his hands in tattered wool gloves, and he shoved the security officer with his outstretched arms as if pleading. He shouted, "Where's Arye Rubin? Arye Rubin is expecting me!"

The security officer wobbled for a moment, trying to grab on to the man's arm. He said, "Hang on, sir, you can't—" But the man shook him off in one swift motion.

"Who is this?" the security officer shouted to two of his colleagues, who had dashed in behind the counter in an attempt at taking hold of the interloper, but he shook them off as well, with great strength, as he wept: "Let me see Arye Rubin. He . . . he . . . he's expecting me, he made an appointment with me!" Rubin approached the man, stood in front of him, and said, "I'm Arye Rubin. Here, I'm right here."

In an instant the man relaxed, as though his strength had seeped out; he seemed ready to crumple into a heap. The security officer grabbed hold of his arms and pulled him backward.

"Let him go, Alon, can't you see who—" Rubin said, holding the man's shoulder.

The security officer looked hesitantly at Rubin but did not release the man.

"I've come to talk with Arye Rubin, he knows me, he knows—he'll tell me—" The man's voice trembled with a thick Russian accent.

"Let him go, Alon," Rubin said again. "It's all right. I'm here, I'll take care of this." He removed the security officer's hands from the interloper's arms.

"Here I am, sir," Rubin said pleasantly. "How can I be of service?"

The man stared at Rubin, confused. He tried to say something, but his words caught in his throat and his eyelids fluttered and his large, burning blue eyes were set with fear, and he pleaded with Rubin, at first repeating himself: "I'm here to see Rubin, I made an appointment with him, I've got material for him, lots of material to show him—"

The female security guard standing next to Alon chortled, and Miri the language editor, who was passing by on her way outside from the canteen, a doughnut in her greasy fingers, said, "That's the way psychotics behave. They don't mean anything they say. And if you show them something, they won't see it. That's just Psychology 101."

"That's Rubin," Alon shouted, pointing at Rubin, while Arye Rubin himself, his arm still draped over the man's shoulder, said, "Good, good, very good, nice job," as if he were speaking to a frightened child. "What's your name?" he asked, releasing his grip.

"I . . . my name is David, David Gluzman," the man said, wiping his forehead and his narrow, ashen face with the palms of his hands. "I . . . I have . . . I want to . . . I have a complaint against . . . ," he said, and then fell silent.

The three ultra-Orthodox men standing in the doorway, their identity cards open as if expecting to have to prove their identities once again, moved backward toward the glass doors.

"Where do you live?" Rubin asked. The man stretched his arms at his sides and stood soldier-straight, then recited the details of an address on the far side of town—including the entrance and the floor and the apartment number—like a child in a kindergarten pageant.

Rubin fished around in his pants pocket and extracted a twenty-shekel note, which he placed in the tattered gloves on the man's hands. "You'll need this for the bus ride home," he said quietly as he curled the man's fingers around the money, then placed his hand on the man's shoulder and guided him to the door. "Go home," Michael heard him say. "The best thing for you is to go home."

The moment the double glass doors opened, several yeshiva students standing quite close to Rubin hoisted large placards above their heads: ZIONIST APOSTATE! JEW-HATER! These were written in black, while in red there was a poster that read, ISRAEL TV IS SHEDDING OUR BLOOD!

"Everyone here is nuts," Alon said, "this whole city is full of crazies. The whole country, in fact."

Rubin returned to the building, examined his hands, and sighed. He looked at the clock and said to the security personnel behind the counter, "I've got to go see Benny Meyuhas, I can't leave him alone. If Zadik is looking for me, have him leave a message on my beeper."

Michael looked at the large wall clock and at the monitor hanging opposite the security station, which was broadcasting MTV. A shirtless, rain-splattered young man was kissing a crying girl while five backup singers crooned in the background. Even though the volume had been turned quite low, the backup singers could be heard singing,

*Could you be my girlfriend,* words that would follow Michael up the stairs to the newsroom.

Schreiber the cameraman was standing in the second-floor hallway, his back to the row of offices and his fingers tapping nervously on the railing. On his way to the newsroom, Michael passed a room whose door was halfway open, and when he peered inside, he saw Natasha. Her back was to the door, and she was facing a row of cubbyholes, emptying the contents of one of them and shoving them into her canvas bag. Standing quite close to her was Hefetz, who was speaking to her, his tone imploring. When he noticed Michael, he hastened to say, "I'll be with you in a minute, wait for me in there," indicating the newsroom. Michael continued very slowly down the hallway, managing to catch a groan and some low tones followed by, "Don't you believe I'm looking after your interests?" Natasha's response—if there was one—was inaudible to Michael.

Very few people were in the newsroom, and those who were spoke quietly, as if in the wake of a tragedy. Niva was sitting next to the fax machine extracting page after page and taking notes. "'Haim Nacht . . . receives a stipend . . . has not passed away, H.F.' . . . Does anyone know what the initials 'H.F.' stand for?" A voice from one of the inner rooms responded: "Heaven Forfend!" Niva continued pulling pages from the fax machine, raising her eyes to the monitor from time to time. She watched the start of a live weekly political affairs program, whose regular host had been replaced by a journalist known for his seriousness and restraint, and his slow, careful way of speaking that emphasized every syllable. He told the viewers he wished to say something about the exceptional nature of the upcoming program, and even before introducing the regular participants or the guests, he announced that time would be "set aside for remembering Tirzah Rubin, head of the Scenery Department at Israel Television, who was killed in an on-the-job accident." In a voice choked with emotion, he added, "One could even say she was killed in the line of duty," and then he mentioned Matty Cohen, head of the Production Department, "who, behind the scenes, financed this great enterprise." It seemed that no one in the newsroom was paying attention to the broadcast until one of the regular participants, an old and corpulent journalist whose claim to fame was the vociferous complaints he issued on the program, interrupted the host to mention the sins of the ultra-Orthodox population and the disgrace of Natasha's failure, which he called "missing a rare opportunity, which happens with the Israel Television News all the time." The studio audience applauded, and the journalist looked around with a haughty smile.

Niva raised her head from the pile of papers she was moving from one side to the other. "Oh, shut your face already," she said after glancing for a moment at the screen. "In another minute you'll say something about how you were a kid in the Holocaust." Just then, not a moment later, the bloated face of the journalist grew serious, his haughty smile faded, he cast a dirty look at the camera and once again interrupted the host. "I am very sorry," he declared, "as for me, I'm not going like a lamb to the slaughter again—we've already lived through Auschwitz!" And once again the audience burst into applause, and he bowed his head as though reliving his terrible memories. The camera panned around the table and came to rest on his fat neck. "Shut your big mouth already," Niva demanded. "Someone turn down the sound," she shouted.

No one reacted. "Where's the remote control? Hey, Erez, let me have the remote, will you?" she said as she pulled the remote control from under a pile of papers next to her, and turned off the sound. The man's mouth was still open and his fat lips were moving but his voice could not be heard.

The political affairs correspondent protested. "I need to hear what they're saying. Any minute now they'll mention the Jerusalem murder, and I'll have to report to the studio, too. They'll give me a heads-up, but I want to know what's going on." He took the remote control and increased the volume just as one of the regular participants on the show was saying, "Who says we don't respect Jewish heritage? It's a fact that Israel Television, which everyone would agree is a secular institution, is filming a story by Agnon. What is Agnon, if not Jewish heritage?" she asked excitedly, straightening her pillbox hat.

"Oh, I love this one, too," Niva interjected, "with that upside-down pot on her head, every week a different pot." She stuffed her feet into her heavy clogs. "I've been here for forty-eight hours," she announced. "I've slept maybe two or three. That's enough, I'm closing shop."

"Hey, do you need to interrogate me, too?" Niva asked Michael with a frown, as if a conversation with him was the very last thing she needed at that moment.

He understood, however, that she very much wished to have her say, and since Hefetz was still tied up, he said, "It could be very helpful. I figure that you're the person who knows better than anyone else—"

"So let's go sit over there," she said with false displeasure, pointing at one of the rooms, to which he followed her. Just before she closed the door he could hear a man shouting: "Don't try and sell me Agnon. They only did Agnon because they got a grant. Benny Meyuhas personally received money for this project—"

Michael had not really intended to speak with Niva at this stage, and had in fact thought to pass her off to Lillian, since he assumed that women were more likely to open up to other women (there were those who accused him of being a chauvinist because of this, and Tzilla had said once that it was a primitive assumption that had no factual grounding in his own experience); but Niva clearly wished to speak.

"Listen," she said the moment he had taken a seat, "There's a lot I can tell you. But what do you want to know?"

"First of all," Michael said, "Tirzah's death during the filming of *Iddo and Eynam,* I wanted to—"

"What? The alleged accident?" Niva asked impatiently.

"Why 'alleged'?" he asked, taken aback. "It *wasn't* an accident?"

"No, no," she said quickly, catching herself. "I didn't mean anything by that, that's just what you always hear them say on police shows. So, you want to hear about the accident?"

"The accident, too, but first of all, what . . . did you have occasion to work with her? Did you know her well?"

"Tirzah Rubin kept her distance from all this," Niva said, indicating the newsroom. "It didn't interest her. She really should have been working in theater, but because of Rubin . . . they used to be married. First she was married to Rubin, then to Benny. So it was only natural that whenever Benny had a production, which wasn't all that often, she would work with him."

Michael asked if she was of the opinion, as were many others, that relations between Benny Meyuhas and Arye Rubin had not been damaged by their love triangle.

"Well," Niva said, "that's thanks to Rubin, that he's such a bighearted person and so—how shall I say it—unconventional. He's different, you can't help . . . everyone respects him."

"You, in any event, are a great admirer," Michael said cautiously.

"Yes, absolutely," she gushed.

"How about Benny?"

"He's, well, he's an artist. They're different. He wasn't involved in the news, either, and always . . . for years now they haven't given him . . . he was like the director for religious programming, and programs about language issues, sometimes even children's programming, that sort of thing, where the role of the director is pretty marginal. He just says where to point the camera and that's it, a television director isn't—"

"How did that happen?" Michael asked. "Wasn't he considered talented?"

"Oh, very," she exclaimed. "Nobody said he wasn't. But talented at what? Directing Agnon? That's not for television, he only wanted to direct, well, at the very least, a documentary about some famous author. I remember, even before Zadik's time, something really—who was that author? Maybe S. Yizhar. But they didn't let him do it. And once there was this Palestinian poet, from Ramallah I think, a poet of exile. They didn't let him do that either, and right they were, if you ask me. I mean, what is this? Don't we already have a bad enough name around the world? Do we really need a film about some poet who hates Israel? And anyway—oh, never mind, they didn't let him do it. And then he started coming up with all kinds of weird projects. He wanted to make a film from some new experimental fiction, I don't remember who the author was. They nixed that one too. He always wanted these hoity-toity projects, and it was like they purposely stuck him with all the garbage until finally, after years of sitting on the shelf, they let him do Agnon, and then only thanks to—" She fell silent.

"Thanks to what?" Michael asked.

"I heard they came up with a big sum for this production," Niva said, "like one-point-five million dollars or something like that, from someone in the U.S., some special fund. I don't know any of the details, but something was—they never would have given him a project like this from the Drama Department budget. And still he used up the entire annual budget because he wasn't prepared to compromise on anything. He was just lucky that it was Zadik who made the decisions. If it had been Hefetz—" she said, falling silent again and casting a worried glance toward the newsroom through the glass partition.

"Hefetz would not have approved such a production if he had been director of Israel Television?"

"Never!" Niva guffawed, thrusting her fingers into her cropped hair and swiveling her head from side to side. "Never in a million years." Then she added, with restrained satisfaction: "It was Benny's good fortune that Hefetz didn't get the appointment."

"Did he want it? Did he want to be director of Israel Television?" Michael asked.

"He would have killed to be director," she answered, openly gloating. "I hope he never—if he were appointed, everything would—he doesn't get along well with people like—with him everything's a matter of honor. He's a man with a chip on his shoulder, a guy who thinks he's been exploited by the whole world. But," she said, suddenly snapping out of it, "why am I talking about this? It's irrelevant."

"We were talking about it because of the production of *Iddo and Eynam,*" Michael reminded her.

"Yeah," she said, relaxing. "I think Rubin had something to do with getting that money, set it up for Benny somehow. It doesn't matter. But for Benny Meyuhas, well, he's got this discrimination complex, too. His parents . . . he grew up in . . . well, not exactly with a silver spoon in his mouth. He wished he'd been born to European parents and all that. Never mind, it's not important. This was his big chance to do something that—and then, Tirzah—"

"Tirzah's death put a stop to the production," Michael mumbled, hoping to leave her room for elaboration.

"Yes, exactly. Tell me," she said, bending her head and looking in the direction of the glass partition, "was it for sure an accident?"

"What do you mean?" Michael asked as if he did not understand the question.

"Well," she said, taken aback, "it's just that I heard, I mean someone said to me that there were marks on Tirzah's neck—" She fell silent and wiped her face dry. "Around this place there are always rumors flying. Everyone's saying—"

"You think there were people who did not like Tirzah," Michael noted.

Niva said nothing. Then she looked at him and said, "Yes, there were. But you have to promise me this will remain just between the two of us."

Michael did not react.

"You're not willing to promise?" she asked defiantly. "Well, I'm not willing for people to know that I'm the source of something bad in connection to Tirzah. Especially not me, because—never mind."

Michael nodded.

"What?" Niva exclaimed. "They've already said something to you about me and Rubin?"

"Only about the boy," he answered reluctantly. "About the son you have with—" He pointed vaguely toward the newsroom.

"He thinks no one knows," Niva said. "It's like some state secret."

Michael gazed at her, quite certain that she was the one who did not allow the secret to remain a secret. "So you and Arye Rubin were romantically involved. Was it serious?"

"Yes, like—well, it wasn't very long-term, just, he had this moment of, how shall I say it? Anyway, it just happened. Then I got pregnant, and I thought about not telling him, but I did. Tell him, that is. I don't believe in tricking people. He could have had me fired, but he didn't, he didn't even try. I said to him, 'Arye, I'm thirty-nine years old,' because that's what I was then, thirty-nine, 'and this is my first pregnancy,' which nobody thought would happen, because I have only one ovary. Anyway, I said to him, 'Arye, I have no intention of aborting.'"

"And he didn't put up a fight?"

"He never said a word about it. He said he'd help me any way he could, money and that sort of thing, if I would keep quiet about it, because of Tirzah. Like, not to hurt her."

"But now that Tirzah is gone, things could be different, don't you think?"

Niva shrugged. "I don't know how Rubin feels about it," she said dreamily.

"I would think you know exactly how he feels about it," Michael said quietly. "After all, you've already spoken to him about the boy."

"What? When?" she said, startled.

"A few hours ago, no?" Michael said, taking a chance on the fact that he had seen them chatting in the corner of the hall.

She glared at him, clearly rattled. "People are already talking about it?"

Michael said nothing.

"This building . . . ," she muttered bitterly, hastening to add, "I don't, I don't exactly—we, only for the boy, he's already seven, and I thought—"

Michael said nothing.

"It doesn't matter," she said, biting her lip. "You shouldn't think I would kill Tirzah for that. Do you understand?"

Michael nodded.

"What?" she said, taken aback. "Do you think I would come to blows with Tirzah Rubin in order to have Arye as some sort of . . . some sort of—"

Michael said nothing.

"Well, the answer is no. No," she said definitively. "And it wouldn't have helped me. In any event, he can't stand me."

Michael was hard-pressed to hide his surprise at hearing this. "Is that what he told you?" he asked.

"Of course not. He didn't say anything at all, he's a gentleman. But I'm no fool, even though you can't tell by the way I come across," she said bluntly. "You're surprised, aren't you?" she asked, pleased. "You thought I was figuring Rubin was just waiting for the opportunity—anyway, I didn't mean we should live together or anything, I just wanted—I just wanted him to spend time with Amichai. He's named for a friend of theirs who was killed in the Yom Kippur War, I thought Rubin would appreciate that. I was hoping that at least my kid could know who his father is. At the end of the day I'm doing Rubin a big favor, he doesn't have any other children," she said, blinking. With a half-smile she added, "Anyway, none that I know of. As long as Tirzah was alive, he didn't want to, like, hurt her. But now . . . she's not here anymore . . ."

Michael said nothing.

"Don't look at me like that," Niva said angrily. "I didn't kill her or anything. You can even check, I never left the newsroom until one, one-thirty at night. Everyone saw me. I can't believe I'm even saying this."

"Who is 'everyone'?"

"Everyone. Hefetz, Natasha, the woman who monitors Israeli radio broadcasts. She can even tell you I was here after one, because she came in at ten minutes past to give a news report from Army Radio. What, are you seriously expecting me to answer you?"

"The woman who monitors Israeli radio broadcasts?"

"Yes. Shula's her name. Little tiny woman. She was on duty and she'd just brought her police communications report in. How funny, like you don't know we listen in on your communications twenty-four hours a day. What else could we do? Wait around for you to let us know what's happening?"

"But the monitoring room is pretty far from here," Michael noted.

"Far? So what? There are people wandering around here all the time. I saw the guy who monitors the foreign radio broadcasts in here after one, too, or maybe it was before one. In any event, I never saw Tirzah, or anybody from that production. How could I even get over to the String Building when we're tied up with getting the lineup ready for the next day? What would I have business over there for? Why don't you ask those people?"

"While we're on the subject of Tirzah," Michael was saying when someone knocked on the glass partition. He turned his face to see Hefetz watching him with an expression of curiosity on his face. Michael signaled to him that he would be finished in just another minute, to which Hefetz screwed up his face in complaint, as though he had been waiting hours for Michael. He opened the door and said, "I'll wait for you here, but I've only got fifteen minutes. After that I've got to get to work on tomorrow's lineup." Michael nodded, and Hefetz closed the door.

"There are people," Niva said with loathing, "who are always scheming. It doesn't even matter what or how. You just know that they'll always take care of their own interests." She fell silent.

"Are you talking about Hefetz?" Michael asked.

"No—yeah—no. I don't know. It's not something—"

"Something specific?"

"No, it's just that now he's so full of complaints. He's probably dying to know what information I'm passing on to you. I'm going to tell him you wanted to know where I was when Tirzah was murdered. Otherwise, he'll make my life miserable, he'll be dissatisfied, and when Hefetz is dissatisfied, he's impossible. Beyond impossible. He'll never stop nagging me."

"Does that have anything to do with the business with Natasha?"

"No, forget about it. It's not her. I mean, if it wasn't Natasha, it would be some other girl. He sleeps with all the new ones, he's been hot under the collar for a few years now. And them? These girls think that if the big boss wants to screw . . . never mind. Believe me," she said, leaning forward, her elbows on the table, "I feel sorry for her. All in all, Natasha's a good kid, all alone in the world. She came to Israel from Russia at the age of fourteen, her father stayed behind with some woman. Her mother, at the beginning she neglected her, then she fell in with the ultra-Orthodox and became a born-again Jew and they married her off to a widower with six little kids. So Natasha grew up all alone. Imagine, she finished her matric exams by herself, went to university, came here. She sat around for days, she was willing to do anything, any job. Mop the floors, whatever you asked her to do. I would send her down to the archives or to bring coffee from the canteen, or to fetch the mail. She did it all without a word. Schreiber's the one who brought her here, I think, found her somewhere one night and brought her in like a lost kitten. He dug up a job as assistant researcher for her, he's got good connections in personnel. And now? She's finished, and all because—"

"Does it have anything to do with Tirzah?" Michael asked.

"No," Niva admitted. "Truth is, it has nothing to do with Tirzah. It's just that I feel sorry for Natasha. Even Rubin won't be able to help her now."

"And what about Tirzah?" he asked.

"I just want you to know that it's not true that everyone was crazy about her."

Michael folded his arms across his chest.

"It bugs me that everyone talks about her like she was a saint. It's not true."

"Anything specific?" Michael asked.

"Decent people with high moral standards are not always well loved, if you get my meaning," she said, and her tone of voice surprised him. He had not expected her to sound so quiet and reflective. "You think I hated her because of Rubin, but I didn't, I actually didn't. I didn't have anything against her, but she was annoying, believe me. Decent people with high moral standards," she continued contemplatively, "sometimes go too far. I mean, they become *too* decent. Annoying, if you get my drift."

He raised his eyebrows questioningly.

"They—if they demand a certain ethical standard, let's say they check everything twice, don't report overtime hours, won't let you cheat the government out of a penny. Well, that can get to be a drag. It's so sanctimonious. People like that expect to impose their standards on everyone. So they make enemies. That's what I wanted to tell you, because I heard—" She fell silent.

"Yes?" he asked, his interest piqued. "What did you hear?"

"People are saying it wasn't just some accident, and I felt it too—how can I say it? I heard that someone else was there, in the corridor of the String Building. I heard that Matty Cohen, poor guy . . . and that makes me nervous. Is it true?"

"Is there anyone specific you're referring to when you mention 'enemies'?"

She glanced under the table in search of one of the clogs she had let slip to the floor the moment they had sat down. "I uh, I don't feel comfortable," she said, her eyes on the glass partition. "Hefetz is snooping around like some—"

Michael did not turn his head to look. "Anyone specific?" he repeated.

"No," she said after a long pause. "No one specific."

"But you yourself weren't crazy about her."

She shrugged but did not respond.

• • •

"You want to come to my office?" Hefetz grumbled when Michael exited from the inner office. "Or would you prefer the canteen?"

"Let's sit in your office," Michael suggested. He stood as far away as possible from Hefetz, who was at least a head shorter than he, in order to blur the difference between their respective heights. "If you're ready."

Hefetz led the way through the newsroom, stopping to watch the monitor. "Turn up the volume for a minute," he ordered. The room filled with the voice of one of the inner-circle participants of the live-broadcast political affairs program. A bleached-blond young man was shouting, "She's not even her biological daughter," as he fingered the row of earrings that ran the length of his left ear. "Mia adopted her with her previous husband, André Previn, when she was like eight years old. Woody Allen is absolutely right, in his place I would have left that hysterical Mia Farrow, too." There was applause from the audience, and raucous laughter. "In any event," the young man said, "it's really cool how they got married in Venice, it's so romantic, and—"

"He could be her grandfather," a woman on the other side of the table shouted. "He's thirty-five years older than she is!"

"More power to him!" the young man said. "It's more natural that way. There have been studies that show that an older man with a younger woman—"

"That's a senseless generalization," someone from the outer circle shouted. "Don't make generalizations."

Hefetz waved his hand as if to dismiss them all. "Israel's on fire—the president's brother has been taking bribes, concessions are being granted on Channel Two—and these people are preoccupied with who Woody Allen is screwing. I've never been able to stomach the guy, he's a boring old windbag. Come on," he said, turning to Michael, "we'll leave them to it." At the entrance to his office he was still on the topic. "You see what they're dealing with? And that's a *political* program, not just any old show. Things sure wouldn't look like that if I were in charge. That's—that's the flagship of Israel Television!"

# CHAPTER NINE

How insignificant is a parent's ability to ensure his child's happiness. When they are young, you still have a chance, but at the end of the day—which comes sooner than expected—they must shake off your protection, must stand on their own, both for their own good and for yours. Like Yuval, Michael's only son, who for quite a long time had been disastrously involved with a young woman who was "making his life a misery," but could not or would not break up with her. (Michael often wondered, every time that formulaic expression entered his mind, whether she was really the one who had made Yuval's life a misery; as always, a cloud of distress and sorrow enshrouded his son's name in his consciousness.) No fatherly influence would improve matters in this case; Michael was incapable of helping Yuval, nor could he teach him from his own experience. After all, his own life was no shining example in this sphere, and not just because his marriage to Yuval's mother had failed; since the time of his divorce, eighteen years earlier, he had found no woman he wanted to spend his life with. Not that he had not fallen in love. He had, in fact, and more than once. But somehow it was always with the "wrong" women, love always involved some insurmountable obstacle—an objective one—like the two women who were already married.

The telephone rang, and although it was nearly two in the morning, the ringing did not disturb him. He was happy to be summoned, since he could not sleep. "The torment you're experiencing has nothing to do with having quit smoking; after two or three weeks your body has weaned itself." This was what Emmanuel Shorer, his close friend and boss, had told him. It was Emmanuel who had taken responsibility for serving as a father figure to Michael fifteen years earlier and had brought him to work for the police when he was desperate for money due to Nira's demands for alimony (and thus had in an instant, at a crucial moment, prevented him from completing his doctoral thesis on the relations between masters and apprentices in the guilds of the Middle Ages, and from entering academic life). "Your suffering is psychological. Believe me, I've been there, I know what you're going through," Shorer had reminded him. "Do you prefer to wait until it's too late for you? Until you get a heart attack, like I did? Isn't shortness of breath enough for you?" And yesterday, when Michael had returned to work after two weeks of vacation during which he had spent most of his time flat on his back at home, Balilty, the intelligence officer who fancied himself Michael's close friend, had looked him over. "Having a rough time, are you?" he had asked. "Terrible," Michael had confessed, without—for once—censoring his words, and proceeded to tell him about his difficulties concentrating and his insomnia.

"It's all in your head," Balilty had said, as expected. "Your body is clean, but that's what happens with psychological addiction."

"Well, what about the mind? Doesn't that count for something?" Michael had teased. "Isn't what we *feel* reality?"

If one more person said something to him about psychology, the soul, and the ethereal nature of emotional addiction . . . He had been smoking nonstop since the age of seventeen, more than thirty years, at least twenty or thirty cigarettes a day; he was incapable of imagining himself without smoking. Were it not for his pact with Yuval, that together they would quit (Yuval himself had begun smoking at sixteen; how was it possible to stop your teenage son from making the same mistakes you had?), he never would have managed it. A few times he had been tempted; there were cigarettes in the house, he had not thrown them out. All he had to do was enter the kitchen and, without looking, stick his hand into the back of the bottom drawer. "What's the big deal?" a faint, deep voice full of intelligence and secret echoes whispered seductively. "Just one, your last." But that seductive voice was ignoring the *next* cigarette. "Not even a single puff," Balilty had warned him. "I'm talking from experience. How many times did I quit before I really quit? That one cigarette isn't the problem. It's the *next* one after it. Because what's the point of smoking one cigarette if there isn't another one to follow? There's no point in smoking just one. A cigarette is simply one drag that leads to the next. A cigarette *is* the next cigarette. And that way you find yourself right back where you started in no time." He had inclined his head and gazed peculiarly at Michael, then he had smiled and added, "Just don't get fat. It's easy to substitute food for cigs, and that special look of yours could be ruined. If you get fat, the girls won't chase after you so much. Then again," he said, thinking aloud, "you . . . you don't use artificial sweetener for sugar and you don't drink instant coffee in place of Turkish coffee. What I mean is, you're not the type for substitutes. Maybe you could smoke an after-dinner cigar in another year or two, cigars aren't dangerous because you don't inhale into your lungs."

Well, he was not eating more and had not gained weight, perhaps because he could not fall asleep and had started walking at night. At first it was around the neighborhood, and later it was longer distances; once he had walked all the way to the village of Aminadav, where a night watchman had had to rescue him from a band of wild dogs.

It was the investigations officer who had been summoned to Natasha's apartment by Schreiber who phoned Michael at two o'clock in the morning. "I figured you'd be interested in this because I understand from Zamira that you're dealing with two cases from Israel Television." (Zamira, the division coordinator, knew everything that was going on, since all written material—work schedules, transfers of materials and files—passed through her hands and was under her authority. She was a large woman of forty with especially thick legs who nonetheless insisted on wearing short, narrow skirts topped with billowy blouses, her short blond ponytail swishing from side to side. She always gave preferential treatment to Michael and told him of her woes with men, and especially about the problems she was having with her teenage son.) "We're not talking about tire-slashing like they did to the television crew van when it was parked next to the home of Rabbi Ovadiah Yosef, it's like—well, truth is," the investigations officer concluded, "it's totally fucking insane. I've never seen anything like it. We didn't touch a thing, you'll see it for yourself; even when we didn't think it was connected to anything else, well, if you understand what I mean . . . I don't think it's connected, but after two deaths, well, just in case . . ."

The rain had let up, but a strong wind was blowing. Puddles sparkled on the empty roads, and in the darkness the huge bulldozers that stood in front of the new luxury development being built across from Sha'arei Zedek Hospital looked like enormous, silent beasts. He rolled down the windows of his car and breathed the clean air and the scent of rain and wet earth deeply into his lungs. For a moment, Jerusalem smelled like the garden of his childhood home, the smell of steam rising from wet earth and the smell of darkness that did not threaten but in fact had a calming effect. It seemed possible to believe this was a normal city whose inhabitants were comfortably tucked into their beds and sleeping as if protected from all evil. Because the streets were empty apart from two police vans at the Valley of the Cross and the occasional sauntering taxi in search of customers, he made it in seven minutes, and parked his car where the officer had told him, on Nissim Bachar Street near the Mahane Yehuda farmers' market, facing the stairway that leads to the steep and winding Beersheva Street, which is off limits to traffic. ("There *is* a way of getting your car in," the investigations officer had told him. "Jerusalemites know it, but it'll take me longer to explain it to you than for you to park and walk the distance on foot." Even after living in Jerusalem for thirty years and having completed his high school education at a boarding school there, Michael was still not considered a true Jerusalemite.) He took the narrow stairs two at a time until he reached the floodlight that had been placed in front of the white metal door and found himself facing the head of a sheep hanging from the door frame, swaying in the wind and dripping blood in a heavy stream. The sheep's round, brown eyes stared straight ahead with a look of trust and innocence.

"I'm Yossi Cohen, don't you remember me?" the investigations officer said to Michael, sounding offended. "We met at Balilty's son's bar mitzvah." With one hand he pinched the wet fur collar of his army jacket together. "He's here," the man said into the transmitter he held in his other hand. Returning to Michael, he said, "It's a good thing you came down here. I'm going crazy with so much to do. I woke Balilty up, too. You won't believe it, I've still got to file an eye-rep with the IIO."

"What? What was that?" Schreiber had sidled up to them and had overheard the policeman. "Was that Hebrew?"

"Yes, it was," the officer responded impatiently. "I said I have to file an eyewitness report with the Intelligence and Investigations Office." To Michael he said, "Our friend Balilty is on his way here now. As soon as he heard you'd be here, he wanted to come too. Should be arriving in a few minutes," he added, pleased.

"Aren't you people going to take this down?" Michael asked, indicating the bloody sheep's head hanging from a rope and casting black shadows that danced all around them, even on the dark puddle of slowly dripping blood gathering under the dangling sheep's head.

"In a little while. I didn't want to take it down until . . . the forensics people will be here soon. There was a note attached," the officer said as he handed a piece of cardboard to Michael. Michael examined the drawing of a skull with the words YOUR END IS NEAR printed in red ink in large, distorted capital letters. "Better that Balilty should see this too," the officer said. "If he's on his way anyway, then he may as well see this. But you can wait inside; I'll wait for them here. Outside."

The kerosene heater was of no use; the room was terribly cold. It was a Jerusalem cold—dense, powerful—of old stone rooms. Schreiber stood rubbing his hands over the soot-covered grid of the heater. "She didn't want to call you people," he said casting a look of reproach at Natasha. "It took me a while to convince her, but in the end I told her she could do whatever she wanted, but there was no way I was getting mixed up with them."

"Who's 'them'?" Michael asked.

"These religious fanatics," Schreiber said. He moved to the half-open door and lit a cigarette there. "It's pretty clear they did this, don't you think? Believe me, I know those people."

The room was very small, most of the space taken up by a single bed in disarray. A few sweaters lay in a pile upon it, and at the other side of the room, in a niche in the thick wall, was a clothes hook with several shirts and one skirt hanging from it. There was a pile of books on the floor next to the bed, and perched on a woven-straw stool stood a book in Russian, open facedown. A makeshift kitchen stood facing the doorway; there were water spots and mold on the wall near the electric burner, a single pot and pan hanging there, and a dish rack with three plates, two mugs, a few spoons, two forks, and a knife. Behind a half-open door there was a bathroom: a toilet, a sink, and a faucet with a shower hose.

Michael looked around the room; everything was utilitarian and meager except for a blue vase with a clutch of wilting wild daffodils that stood on the only table in the room, and a long, narrow print in a thin wooden frame hanging over the bed. The print showed a solitary and peculiar tower standing erect in an empty brown field; one side of the tower was brightly lit and the other shaded, the shadow extending from two people, small and displaced, posed in the middle of the foreground. He wondered how it was that in spite of the bright white light on the illuminated side of the tower, the picture exuded the feeling that the light did not have the power to illuminate this world, as though the shadows had overwhelmed it and the blackness in the background was about to flood the entire picture. Four flags blew loftily in the wind from the top of the tower, but even these brought no happiness. The mood of the entire picture was one of regret, of interminable loneliness. Who had painted this picture, he wondered, and why did it disturb him so? Underneath it, in a corner of the bed, folded in between the wall and the simple wooden table on which stood the vase of daffodils and a few plates with the remains of dried-up hummus and pita bread, was Natasha, huddled under a gray army blanket and shaking nonetheless. Michael looked into her clear blue eyes and saw no fear there.

"It's like she doesn't care," Schreiber said, "but at first, from the shock of it, she screamed. After that, nothing. She wanted to clean it up. It took me a long time to convince her to call the police. I didn't let her touch all the blood and filth, I wanted you to see it as it was. . . . Anyway, I took pictures of it all," he said, adding in a faint voice, "It was *her* idea."

"What was Natasha's idea?" Michael asked. From outside the apartment they could hear the forensics people arriving, and Balilty's voice a moment later. "Taking pictures?"

"No, taking pictures was my idea," Schreiber said. "Calling you was her idea," he explained, lowering his eyes. "She said that you—"

"Schreiber, shut up already," Natasha said. Her voice burst forth from between her narrow hands, which were wrapped around her small face.

"What? What did I say wrong? Didn't you tell me to call him? You said he was the only one worth his salt."

"There's no reason to hurt people's feelings," Natasha mumbled, looking out the half-open door. "There are other people here. Everybody needs a good word."

The wives of the striking workers had watched Natasha's flop on television, too. In the living room of the Shimshi household in a town near Israel's northern border they kept their eyes on the enormous television—which took up the entire surface of the glossy brown console—and listened as Natasha at first made her highly emotional announcement (they were waiting for the item about their husbands) and then her retraction and apologies. "Corrupt, the whole lot of them," muttered Esty, Rachel Shimshi's sister-in-law. "Everywhere you look, it's all just filth." She laid her hands on her protruding belly. Rachel Shimshi looked at her suspiciously, as though she were predicting the future.

"I don't want to just sit here doing nothing," Esty said. "If you're gonna put up a fight, you can count me in too."

"A pregnant woman isn't going nowhere," Rachel Shimshi declared, narrowing her eyes as she did whenever she was angry. "That's not what I'm talking to you about. I just want you to get your hands on the keys, that's all." She stood up and went to the kitchen. Esty, too, stood up from the couch facing the television and followed Rachel into the kitchen, where she leaned against the marble countertop watching her sister-in-law slowly soaping dirty glasses of tea.

"You're not gonna leave me at home just when you're standing up to the whole world," Esty exclaimed.

Rachel Shimshi placed the clean glasses upside down on a towel she had spread over the formica table and looked at Esty. "Don't waste your breath," she said quietly. "No chance I'm letting you join us, and that's final."

For the first time in all the years they had known one another, Esty stood up to Rachel, spreading her hands behind her to grab hold of the countertop for support; she refused to accept her sister-in-law's authority. Her heavy breathing resounded in the kitchen. "You're not going to tell me what to do," Esty told Rachel, "I'll decide for myself." She nearly burst into tears because as soon as she had said this she was full of remorse; she had not intended to sound so aggressive, and she most especially did not wish to hurt the feelings of Avram's older sister Rachel, who had always treated her so well. "It's biting the hand that feeds you," her mother would have said, may she rest in peace. Rachel had brought over a big pot of stuffed vegetables, had left Dudy alone at home, and had come to light the candles with her on the second night of Hanukkah. She'd brought doughnuts, too, had done everything as though she had no worries of her own, as though Shimshi were not being held in police custody and all that. Everything just so that she, Esty, would not be alone. And now how was she behaving?

She took a deep breath and continued. "I'm not letting you get into this all alone, you need as much help as you can get. So let's call all the girls, everyone will come with you."

"I don't even have a driver's license," Rachel Shimshi muttered.

"But I do, and so do Sarit and Simi," Esty reminded her. "Lots of them do. For once, let other people handle this. You don't have to do everything on your own. I'll call Tikki, wait'll you see what we'll make of this."

"But how are you going to manage with that belly? How are you going to lug boxes full of bottles? They're heavy, even when the bottles are empty."

"Okay," Esty said while dialing the phone hanging on the kitchen wall. "So I won't do any lugging, other people will do it. Okay?"

"The ultra-Orthodox?" Michael asked. "Because of Natasha's news broadcast?"

"No. That was bullshit. Peanuts," Schreiber said dismissively. "No, I'm talking about something—" He looked at Natasha with apprehension.

After a moment she spoke. "It's something very serious, nothing to do with financing yeshiva students. I was intentionally misled, they wanted to get me into trouble to keep me from pursuing the big issue, and to keep me off the air. Now I really don't know if they'll ever let me broadcast anything ever again."

"Don't worry, they'll let you," Schreiber assured her. "Hefetz will let you, he'll convince Zadik."

"Maybe. Maybe," she said, glancing at the front door. "But who's going to tell Hefetz?"

"I understand you don't wish to reveal your sources," Michael said, "but you're going to have to give us some kind of lead, point us in the right direction, anything. We've got to know at least what the issue here is."

Natasha regarded him with suspicion, then glanced again at the door. Michael hastened to close it. "There," he said, "no one can hear. It's only us."

"It's," she began, hesitantly, "it's that a while ago I heard, it happened that I, well, I came across something really big, I mean big money in the hands of Rabbi Elharizi, and not just him. Others too. Whole suitcases and boxes of dollars and gold, everything. It's being smuggled abroad."

"Do you know where to?" Michael asked.

"We think it's to Canada, but it's not clear—it seems to be for something really huge, but I'm not sure what exactly yet. Some corrupt scheme the likes of which we've never seen before."

"Hard to believe," Michael muttered.

"What?" Natasha pounced. "You don't believe me?"

"No, no," Michael responded hastily. "It's hard to believe that there could be corruption that we've never seen before."

"It's a fact," Natasha said. "And they don't even know how much of this affair I've already uncovered. Me and Schreiber. But today, after we were parked next to Elharizi's house and Schreiber even managed to get inside, they're bound to be suspicious."

"Her life is in danger," Schreiber said. "Believe me. They won't stop at sheep's heads. It's like, well, it's like the horse's head in *The Godfather*. That's probably where they got the idea."

At that moment the door swung open suddenly, and Balilty burst into the room, short of breath, and looked around. "Like college students," he said to himself. "This is the way we lived when we were young. Boy, it's been years. . . . Say, you could catch pneumonia in this place. It's so damp here, aren't you freezing all the time?" he asked Natasha.

She shrugged.

Balilty stood in front of the bed and pointed at her. "Aren't you the one on the news?" he asked excitedly. "Aren't you the one who was talking about the yeshivas?"

Natasha looked out into the darkness—Balilty had left the door open—and Schreiber said, "She was set up. It wasn't her fault, she was set up."

"That was clear right away, you don't have to be some kind of genius to know that," Balilty said. "With those people you've got to check things seven times, they're—" suddenly he looked behind him. "But let's not talk about that now," he whispered, as if in warning. "The guy from forensics—"

Just then a bearded man with a skullcap entered the room. "We took it all," he said to Michael. "We wrapped up the head, we took fingerprints, I'm sure they used gloves. Not a trace here, nothing. We're talking professionals. We cleaned up a little too, but it's hard to see in the dark. I'm ashamed that these kind of people exist," he added on his way out the door. "And they call themselves religious . . ."

Balilty moved the Russian book to the floor and sat on the stool. Schreiber was standing in the doorway, and Michael was leaning on the edge of the table, looking from time to time at the green-black sky and the tower in the framed print hanging above the bed. Distractedly he listened to the questions Balilty was asking Natasha.

"I don't understand," Balilty persisted. "Who gave you the videotape in the first place?"

"A woman. I don't know her."

Balilty pointed at Schreiber. "But he says earlier this evening there was another woman. She was also ultra-Orthodox. And she waited for you too, with another tape, right?"

Natasha did not respond.

Balilty looked at Schreiber. "Was it the same woman?"

Schreiber pursed his lips as if to say, How should I know?

Balilty was growing angry. "You're not going to answer me?" he asked Natasha.

Schreiber began to explain. "She can't reveal her sources on something that hasn't yet—"

"Tell me something, Natasha, haven't you learned anything yet?" Balilty asked. "You've already discovered they screwed you here, didn't you?"

"This isn't the same thing," she said after a pause. She rubbed her pale face, and for a moment her thin, transparent skin glowed pink and a spark of defiance lit the innocent blue of her eyes as she regarded him and answered, "I already told you: this is something altogether different."

"All right," Balilty said with a sigh. "What can I tell you? You make your own bed and you gotta lie in it, isn't that so? Afterward, don't say I didn't tell you so." To Michael he said, "I'm just going to let Yossi Cohen go, and I'll take the cassette from this guy," he said, pointing at Schreiber, "the tape where he filmed the sheep's head." Balilty shuddered. "Never heard of such a thing before. Come with me," he said to Schreiber, and the two left the apartment.

"Maybe you should stay away from here for a few days," Michael said, looking around. "Even if we assume your life isn't in danger, it won't be good for you to come home every evening to something like this."

Natasha pushed the blanket off herself, stretched her legs, and sat up on the bed to look at him. Her blue-eyed look was completely innocent, but the defiant, downward turn of her long, narrow lips gave her face an expression of bitterness and maturity. Her legs dangled—in spite of the cold she was barefoot; wool socks and a pair of boots lay on the floor at the foot of the bed—and he noticed her narrow, naked feet. They looked heartbreakingly vulnerable and delicate.

She bowed her head and examined the exposed stone floor. "I don't know why you people are making such a fuss. Like you've never seen anything like this before. I mean, you see dead human bodies all the time, and here we're only talking about—"

"Right," Michael said, pondering aloud. "But it's the element of surprise. When you're called in to see a body, you know what you're going to see. But this is something out of place. Are you sure you don't want to tell us something? Just the smallest lead?"

"I can't," Natasha said. "It's too . . . not until . . . anyway, it's a criminal offense."

"What is?"

"The scandal I've uncovered."

"And nobody but Schreiber knows anything about it?"

"Arye Rubin knows," she said after a moment. "But he himself deals a lot with dangerous material, I know I can trust him. Nothing ever stops him, he's not afraid of anyone."

"But he's preoccupied right now, what with Tirzah's death—"

"Rubin's never too preoccupied," she said, cutting him off. "Rubin is . . . do you think just because Tirzah died, he stopped working? As we speak he's busy preparing his report on the doctors, and he's working on Benny Meyuhas's film, too."

Balilty and Schreiber appeared in the doorway. "Listen, sweetheart," Balilty said, "there's no way you're staying here. Got that?"

Natasha remained silent.

"Don't you have anywhere to go? Family? Relatives? Friends?"

"No, she doesn't," Schreiber said. "She's 'all alone in the world,' as they say. She can sleep at my place."

"No, sir," Balilty said. "With all due respect, that's a bad idea because from what I understand you're also—"

"Did you tell him?" Natasha said, exploding. "What did you tell him, Schreiber?"

"Nothing, I swear," Schreiber said, his hand over his heart. "He just asked what part of the city we were in earlier today, and I told him. He understood all on his own we were at Rabbi Elharizi's."

"What are you so worried about?" Balilty asked Natasha. "No one is going to hear a word about this from me. But you can't go to Schreiber's place, who knows what's waiting for you there. Maybe they put the sheep's head here and left the body at his place. How about if we drive over and check it out first? That way you won't be waking us up again tonight." To Michael he said, "How about we bring her in to the office? In the meantime she can make a statement."

Schreiber watched Natasha in silence as she put on her socks and boots. Suddenly he asked Michael, "Can you take her with you? I'll be fine," he hastened to add, "I can always go to my sister's, even in the middle of the night. She lives in Sha'arei Hesed, not far from here. But I can't bring a woman with me, even under these circumstances. My sister is super religious, and she has a lot of kids. She wouldn't understand."

"Don't you go setting me up somewhere," Natasha scolded him. "I can take care of myself, and—"

"You'll come with me," Michael announced. "Anyway, we have to take a statement from you. We can do that now."

Natasha silently picked up her canvas bag and tapped Schreiber's arm as he walked toward the door. She waited for Michael to exit, locked the door, and put the key under an empty planter. She followed Michael obediently to his car.

In less than ten minutes they had reached police headquarters at the Russian Compound. Michael led her to his office, first removing the cardboard files piled on the chair facing his desk and then motioning her to have a seat. "Coffee?" he asked, to which she nodded. "Sugar? Milk?"

"Black," she answered. On his way to the hot water dispenser in the hallway, he glanced at her bony hands and her gaunt body and was tempted to say she could afford a little sugar.

When he returned with two cups of coffee, he found her resting her head on the desk atop her folded arms. In the wake of the silence after he closed the door, he listened to her measured breathing; he was certain she had fallen asleep, so he sat facing her as quietly as possible and stirred his coffee. As he peered into the cup, he could not resist the thought that a cigarette would be just the right thing at that moment: desired, craved, long-awaited. It seemed to him that since he gave up smoking, coffee had lost its flavor. Natasha raised her head, her eyes wide open. "I woke you up," he apologized.

"Not at all," she said. "I wasn't sleeping, I was just resting a minute." Suddenly she smiled, exposing her small, white teeth, the teeth of a child. "This is actually a place somebody could rest in," she said with wonder. "You feel safe here."

Michael laughed.

"What's so funny? What could happen to me here?"

"No one has ever said about my office that they feel safe in here. 'Safe' is not a word I've heard used in this room," he said, pondering the idea. "You've got to be really, well, you can't have any misgivings. In short, you can't feel guilty."

"What should I feel guilty about?" Natasha asked with surprise. "What? Did I do something wrong?"

Michael smiled. "Since when do guilt feelings have anything to do with having done something wrong? It's enough to be alive just to feel guilty."

She held the cup of coffee tightly between her hands and stared at a spot on the desk.

Michael said, "A person has to have been wronged pretty seriously in order for him not to have guilt feelings."

"Oh, I'm an expert at that," Natasha said. "But I can't stand when people feel sorry for themselves. You're responsible for most of what happens to you after childhood. I hate it when people bawl about what was done to them without ever considering their own responsibility."

"Even when their lives are threatened just doing their jobs?" Michael asked. He took a sip from his coffee without taking his eyes off Natasha.

Natasha looked into her coffee cup and then peered at him. She said coolly, "What an elegant way to get back to the topic."

Michael spread his hands as if to say there was no choice in the matter. "I said we needed your statement. You can't keep your sources a secret when—"

"I sure can, and I will. I have to," Natasha said. "I have no choice. My career really *will* be over if I say something now. And anyway, what can you possibly do to me? Toss me in jail?"

After a short pause Michael said, "Well, how about at least, without giving away any details, why don't you just tell me who might be interested in leaving you a token of his affection like that sheep's head? Do you have any enemies? Is there anyone who hates you?"

Natasha chuckled. "Who doesn't have enemies?" she said. "It's enough to—how did you say it? It's enough for a person to be alive to have enemies, to be hated. Even if he hasn't done a thing wrong. But if you want to be a journalist and you're, like, young, and you have this thing with the director of the News Department at Israel Television, then, wow—"

"You think you made people jealous?" Michael asked quietly.

"Yeah, but there's no connection to—" she began, then decided against it.

"To the sheep's head?"

"Yes, that's because of, because of the investigation I've been conducting. It's like, they want to scare me off because I'm onto something really important, you know? I'm not afraid. On the contrary: I know I've really got them nervous."

"With that kind of money at stake," Michael said, "I'm really not surprised. We should even consider putting you under police protection."

"Police protection!" she shouted. "Like, a bodyguard? Like someone's going to follow me everywhere and know everything I do every moment of the day?"

"We'll consider it," Michael repeated. "We'll see."

After a quiet moment Natasha asked in a childish voice, "Can I take off my boots in here?"

Michael nodded and watched as she struggled to remove her boots.

"Natasha," he said suddenly. She shifted in her chair and regarded him, her eyes wide open. "Do you think Tirzah Rubin's death was an accident?"

"Me?" she asked, surprised. "I have no clue—I don't know anything about her."

"All right," Michael persisted. "But what do you think?"

She said nothing.

"Because you know Rubin so well," Michael said.

"Rubin, yes, but he—" She stopped, searching for a word. "He is the most, really, there's nobody else like him. Believe me, I know some personal stuff about him," she said with pride.

"Oh, yeah?" Michael asked, like a child on a dare.

"Yeah. Like how he helps Niva out financially. I mean, he couldn't acknowledge the kid publicly or anything, but he didn't abandon the boy either. And then there's Rubin's mother."

"What about his mother?" Michael asked.

"She's in a nursing home in Baka'a. You know the one? On Bethlehem Street? It's like for old folks who came from Europe. You know how much that place costs every month? And who do you think pays for it?"

"He's an only child," Michael noted.

"And there's nobody else, because the whole family perished in the Holocaust. She's not in good shape either, his mother. He has to run over there every day, deal with doctors and all that. Just the other day she ran out of some prescription and he had to dash around—he left everything in the middle, in the middle of preparing his report, and he went over there to bring it to her."

"What was the prescription?" Michael asked.

She looked at him, surprised. "How would I know? What difference does it make? Something for her heart, I don't remember what. Just that it was urgent. I happened to be in his office when they called. Never mind, it's not important. I just wanted to tell you that he's a great guy."

"And what about Benny Meyuhas?"

"I don't really know—but he's Rubin's best friend, so I'm sure he's—"

"And Hefetz?" Michael asked.

"Hefetz?" Natasha rolled her eyes. "He's another story altogether."

"How so?"

"He's a guy who—it's hard to say; he's complex. People will tell you about his drive and ambition, but he can also be really sympathetic and warm. I didn't just—anyway, it's complicated."

"You've had a close relationship," Michael reminded her. "Intimate. Perhaps you were in love?"

"No," Natasha said adamantly. "I never loved him, not for a second. He's just—it's like, if someone so much older and more important than you takes you like seriously—I just couldn't remain, like, indifferent."

"Like, or for real?" Michael asked.

"What?" Natasha asked, confused.

"Did he take you seriously?"

"What do you think?" she asked mockingly. "He's twice as old as me, director of the newsroom, married for about a million years, has grown children. You think he possibly could have been serious?"

"Don't you believe someone could actually, seriously, fall in love with you?" Michael asked.

She stared at him for a while, then lowered her eyes and said, "I have no idea what that is. What does it mean that someone *loves* someone else?"

"How about Schreiber? He seems to look after you, and he's willing to take risks for you."

"Schreiber?" she asked, embarrassed. "It's like, well, mercy on his part. He's this guy with a great big heart. But that doesn't have anything to do with love." She rested her head on her arms again. "I'm exhausted," she said, her voice muffled. "If you want a written statement from me, let's get it done now, before I fall asleep on your desk."

At six in the morning, when the sky was still completely dark and it had begun to rain again, Balilty and Schreiber were already in Michael's office. They were stirring sugar into their coffee when Balilty's ears perked up at the sound of footsteps running down the hall, followed by noise from transmitters and wailing police sirens.

"What's going on?" Balilty asked. "You call your radio monitors, and I'll call mine," he said to Schreiber. "Let's see who gets some answers first.

"Hey, there's no reception here," Balilty said, and walked out into the hallway. Schreiber followed him, and the two returned to the office after a few minutes.

"I don't believe it," Balilty said. He turned to Michael. "What is it you like to say? 'How wondrous are the ways of God'?"

"That's not exactly what I say," Michael corrected him.

"Okay. How does it go again?"

Michael sighed.

"All right, I'm sorry. 'There's no end to miracles.' That's what he says," Balilty expounded to Schreiber.

"Poor women," Schreiber said.

"What? What happened?" Natasha asked as she pulled one boot over a wool sock.

"It's the wives of the fired workers from the Hulit factory," Schreiber said.

"What happened to them?" Natasha asked.

"They're in big trouble," Balilty said, scratching his forehead. "I can sympathize with them, but they're in big trouble. You won't believe this: all the company vehicles, like seven trucks—"

"What did they do?"

"I'll tell you what they did," Balilty said. "They stole them, drove off with seven company trucks all on their own. Then they filled them up with bottles, emptied out all the warehouses. The drivers came to work this morning and found nothing: no trucks, no—"

"Where are they now?" Natasha asked.

"On their way to big intersections, nobody knows which. They're planning to dump the bottles there, block traffic. In short, big trouble."

"Can't somebody stop them?" Natasha asked.

"Nobody has yet, I guess it's still got to be organized."

"Is Danny Benizri with them?" Natasha asked.

"Are you crazy?" Schreiber asked. "You think he's going to get himself into trouble and take part in something like this?"

Natasha shrugged but said nothing.

"Would you?" Schreiber asked pointedly. "Would you go with them, Natasha?"

"I don't know," she answered. "Anyway, it's some story."

"Don't mind her," Schreiber said to Michael. "Ambition has warped her brain."

# CHAPTER TEN

What, should I just start talking? This is hard for me, and with that tape recorder I'm . . . never mind, it's hard for me to talk. Starting this morning when I woke up, I had this bad feeling. It feels like days or even weeks have passed since this morning; look, it's not even dark outside yet, it's only been a matter of hours. All of this has happened in the space of one day, and right from the beginning I had this feeling that I just didn't want to start this day. Sometimes you open your eyes in the morning and before you can even think your first thought, you have a bad feeling, like you do after a dream, a bad dream. I dreamed something, too, I don't remember exactly what. These last few nights I've had trouble—I used to fall asleep in a second. Ask anyone, and they'll tell you that if Aviva has a bed and a pillow, she'll be sleeping like a baby in an instant. That's the way I've been since I was a small child. But I guess this whole matter with Tirzah and Matty Cohen has gotten to me. I, I wasn't particularly close to either of them, but you know how it is when people work together for years. Tirzah was at Israel Television from the beginning, from when it was established, and I've been around for a while too, nearly twenty years, from the age of twenty-two. When somebody dies like that, so suddenly, I just . . . and then all these rumors about Tirzah, if it was an accident or not, well, they set me on edge. But even before, before I saw him, the ultra-Orthodox guy with the terrible burns, standing there next to my desk—I hate when people creep in like that—I was sitting with my back to the door for just an instant, talking on the phone, I had swiveled my chair around for a split second and suddenly there he was, standing next to me. No one can get into Zadik's office without me seeing, nobody. There's no other way into his room, that is, no other way that anyone used, until—okay, you know about all that. But anyway, everything passes by me first: telephones, meetings, people. And I didn't leave my desk for a minute, never even had a chance to drink a cup of coffee or go to the bathroom. I was even supposed to leave early today.

"Nothing's clear to me anymore, nothing. I don't understand anything at all: I mean, how is it possible that someone so . . . so . . . disfigured, so completely burned—burn marks all over his face, his hands, his neck—how could someone like that just pass through unnoticed? Nobody remembers seeing him. How can that be? Didn't he catch anyone's eye? People are telling me that it's winter, everyone's all covered up in layers of clothing. But his hands? I saw them, his hands, and I'm *still* upset by it. And his face! Can you imagine how frightening that is? Here's this bearded guy in a long, black trench coat and a hat, he could fit in in any of the ultra-Orthodox neighborhoods, but his voice sounded like one of ours, I mean, his way of talking was normal, pleasant, no Yiddish inflections, no accent; a real native-born Israeli Hebrew. He came through the security officer, I know this for sure because they called me from downstairs, and they said, 'Aviva, there's somebody here who says he has an appointment with Zadik.' I checked his appointment book, and there it was: Zadik had told me to write the letter S. I didn't ask any questions, I just wrote it in. Afterward the guy left Zadik's office and disappeared as though nobody had ever laid eyes on him. Did you people see him after that? Did you find him? I'm telling you, he disappeared.

"It's been a day of disappearances. Everyone disappeared. You could be sure that if you really needed somebody, they would disappear. It started first thing in the morning, these disappearances. First there was the news about the wives of the laid-off workers, how the trucks with the bottles disappeared and the women disappeared. Have you ever heard of such a thing? Like in Naples. Once I was in Naples, just for a day, but I'll never ever forget it because I was with this guy—I can't tell you who because everyone knows him, and I can't really call him a miser because on the other hand—well, all in all, he *was* a miser. Never mind. Married, a miser, there we are in southern Italy, in Naples for the week-*end,* which is appropriate because it was more of an *end*ing than a weekend. Anyway, why was I talking about this? Oh, yeah, because of the wives of the workers. In the end it turned out they took the trucks, drove them, dumped the bottles, the whole works. That's how it was in Naples, too. There was a train strike. Total anarchy. Take a red traffic light, for example. That didn't obligate you to stop, it was more like a suggestion—so anyway, in the morning they reported, one by one, that the stolen trucks were hitting all the most important intersections: the checkpost in Haifa, and Glilot and Shalom junctions in Tel Aviv, and the entrance to Jerusalem, and Danny Benizri is nowhere to be found. Disappeared. It took four hours to find him and, after all, he's their man, the workers' rep. I still don't know where he was all that time, but it was a sign for what was going to happen all day. The first sign.

"Then Zadik tells me, 'Aviva, get me Benny Meyuhas on the line.' So I started looking for him. I looked everywhere. No luck, the guy had disappeared. Even Rubin didn't know where Benny Meyuhas had gone, and he's his best friend. Even before, before—can I have some water, please? Sorry, with all these pills I'm not sure . . . but every time I picture . . . never mind, Benny disappeared before all that, before Zadik . . . excuse me . . . I'm sorry for crying. It's just when you've been working with someone for ages, and then suddenly he's gone . . . like . . . I still can't believe it. To find Zadik like that, and he's not just some nobody—we're talking about the director of Israel Television! In the office, all that blood. Slaughtered, how can you slaughter a person just like that? He lives a full life, and then suddenly in a single minute . . . Did you see how he was slaughtered? I'm sorry for being like this. All in all he was a good man, not someone who . . . never mind. I swear, from the very first minute I opened my eyes this morning, I was already sure it was going to be a bad day. Do you believe that some people can feel things before they happen? Not everybody, but there are people, sensitive ones, who sense vibrations, and I'm one of them. Call it whatever you like, I felt something. First thing in the morning. I got to work this morning at seven-thirty, because Zadik—excuse me, could I have some more water please? Zadik asked me to come in early because he had his weekly editorial meeting and he was expecting trouble because . . . never mind, it doesn't matter now. Anyway, Zadik asked, and I . . . for years we've been . . . I've known him . . . Don't think this is something dirty, there was nothing between us. It's just, how can I say it? At first his wife was uptight. When I became his secretary, she came around to check me out. You know how it is, I'm, well, not ugly, and his wife . . . anyway, I'm pretty successful where men are concerned, but with Zadik there was nothing. You understand? Still, we've known each other for like fifteen years, I was the secretary of three of his predecessors. I've never gotten it on with the bosses. I'm against that sort of thing on principle, it only brings trouble. I've known Zadik since the time he was just a regular old reporter, I was—oh, never mind, anyway, he asked me to come in at seven-thirty. It's winter, all dark outside, and rainy. On the radio they were already reporting traffic jams, they weren't even talking about the factory women yet. And my car, first it won't start, then it starts, finally, when someone pushes me, but I still made it in by seven-thirty, exactly seven-thirty, you can check to see when I punched in: seven-thirty-seven. I came in the back way, no traffic. I figured there was no getting into the city, what with all the bottles those women dumped. Tell me, how did they manage it? In the middle of the night, and no spring chickens, those women! How did they get those trucks all over the place? You've got to hand it to them, dumping all those bottles and grinding them up in the intersection. Really, you've got to give them credit, it's just like in Naples . . . never mind, they'll have endless trouble from all this . . . I was in the office at seven-thirty, everything dark outside, rain and winter and all that. But at Israel Television there are always people around. You know, not just the security people and the radio monitors. The canteen was already . . . I went down and got a cup of coffee and a hot, fresh doughnut. Not for me, I don't . . . I'm on a diet, I brought it for Zadik. It wouldn't hurt him to take off a little weight either, but never mind . . . it doesn't matter anymore . . . I'm sorry for crying, I can't control myself, it's those pills or the shot, or whatever they gave me. I'm telling you everything, just like you asked, every detail. But it's hard for me to concentrate. And I'd really like to be a help . . ."

Aviva stopped talking for a minute and regarded Michael expectantly. "I can see that it's important to you," he hastened to assure her. "And I understand how hard this must be for you. We really appreciate this very, very much."

She breathed in deeply and exhaled noisily. "You asked for all the details," she said with a pout. "And that takes time."

"We have as long as it takes," Michael said reassuringly, willing himself to sound as fatherly as possible. "You have a terrific memory, and you are clearly a sensitive person."

A cloud of satisfaction passed over her face; as if to conceal it, she sighed and continued talking. "The guy from maintenance showed up at eight, I've been pestering them for a week now, you know how it is: you ask them to come, they say they'll be there in an hour, and then no one shows up, you phone again and again, and in the end they tell you, Stop being a pain in the butt, Aviva. You get that? *They* don't deliver, but *you're* the pest! Anyway, the maintenance man showed up, an electrician, he needed to do something to the outer wall of Zadik's office because it's damp, it's been shorting out the electricity. I called him a week ago, but with maintenance if you don't . . . never mind, it was a new electrician, nice guy, I've never met him before. He seemed pretty young, no older than thirty-something. He wore a wedding ring. The nice guys are always married. So he arrived at eight, well, more like five minutes after eight, I can't be sure about the exact minute, I mean, I had no idea I would need to know later. . . . Anyway, he came in and got started working. And the very minute he started, Zadik opened his door and started shouting. 'What's going on here? Are you people crazy? Stop, stop immediately!' That's the way it was: Zadik shouting at me and at the electrician. So I told him he couldn't talk to the guy that way, like he was some . . . never mind, it doesn't matter. I told Zadik to give the guy a quarter of an hour, until his meeting started. But Zadik said, 'No. Have him go away and come back later.' So this electrician, who had finally gotten started on the job, was already on his way out. He'd managed to open up the wall, and now he was leaving. 'Where are you going?' I asked him. I was pretty worried that the whole thing would stay like that, a big hole in the wall and lots of dust, and then he wouldn't come back. But he laughed. 'Don't worry,' he said, 'I'll come back after eleven. I'm leaving all my tools here, my drill, everything.' What can I tell you, sometimes life is so . . . maybe if he hadn't left his drill and all those tools . . . in the end, it was that drill . . . if he hadn't left it . . . maybe Zadik would still be alive. All that blood. Look how I'm shaking. It's the shock of it. I'll be traumatized for the rest of my life by it. Someone who sees something like that is changed forever. Don't you think so? You can never be quite the same. From now on I'll never be able . . . oh, never mind, it's not important.

"All morning the telephone didn't stop ringing. There were all sorts of calls. Everyone was looking for Danny Benizri. They finally found him. He wasn't at home, he wasn't answering his cell phone or his beeper. His wife told me, 'He came home late and left early, I didn't even see him.' Later it dawned on me he must be with the wives of those workers, maybe they even, like, called him from the beginning, brought him in from the start. I don't know, I heard Zadik shouting at him. The door was open, he was shouting at him over the telephone just before the meeting got started. From Zadik's shouting I understood that Benizri had no clue about what was happening. Still, they managed to get him on toward the end of the morning program. They interrupted the regular program just before nine for a live broadcast. Channel Two scooped us, though, so Zadik chewed him out over the phone. 'A full fifteen minutes ahead of us,' he shouted, 'and you're supposed to be the workers' man!' Of course he was shouting at Benizri; who do you think he was shouting at?

"So anyway, there was this block of time when Benizri had disappeared and nobody knew where he was, but that was before . . . later, they came to interview Zadik about the role of television during a period of financial crisis, with Benizri serving as an example of a journalist who's become more than just a journalist. How did she put it, that interviewer, one of the famous ones, the one preparing the story? She called it journalism that 'takes an active role in influencing reality.' Those words of hers, they stuck with me. I mean, what's she talking about, 'influence'? Like Benizri is really influencing somebody? Some hero he's become! I don't have anything against him—Benizri's a nice guy, a good guy—but I wouldn't want all this to go to his head. She's preparing a character profile of him! So then Zadik says to the electrician, 'That's enough, quit working and come back after eleven. Eleven-fifteen is even better, just to be sure. That's when I have an appointment with the director general of the Israel Broadcasting Authority.' The maintenance man shoots me a look; he's only just put his overalls on, and here he is taking them off again. I mean, it wasn't such a big deal, he was wearing them over his jeans and everything. And a mask, too, to protect his eyes. But still. He shoved the overalls into a corner and left everything there: his tools, the drill, everything. How could I know? Nobody could have known. I even asked him, 'Will you be coming back?' And he said, 'Sure I'm coming back, what're you so worried about?' Truth is, I don't know what was bothering me so much. I was feeling bad, that's it. Justifiably, it turns out. He never had a chance to go anywhere. Funny thing is, he never had to come back from anywhere, either.

"After that—it was around nine o'clock—when all the editors were in their meeting, I slipped in and out of Zadik's office. You know, there are always all kinds of little emergencies that I can't phone in about but that Zadik has to respond to. And in any event, those editors, they're not gods or anything, I've known them all for ages. I didn't exactly hear what they were discussing, but every time I went in, I picked up something else. You may think I'm just some secretary, but I'm not. You can ask anyone about me. Everything I do requires brains, even, oh, never mind . . . I went in and out of the office, I heard all kinds of things, I was sort of generally in the picture about what they were discussing. After all, a good secretary needs to know what's going on. So they're talking about this new television series, *Tekuma,* about the founding of the state of Israel, and Diti, the programming director, says they're not running enough promos for it and she's arguing with Zadik, who reminds her that the show won't be aired for another three weeks and that they're already running nightly promos, which he says is enough. So then they're fighting, I mean, not really fighting, just arguing, but then the argument gets a bit, well . . . never mind, what's important is that I came into the room and suddenly someone asked me, 'Aviva, you tell us: who's right? Are we running enough promos or not?' Well, what am I supposed to say? I mean, I just want to be on good terms with everyone, so I'm sure not going to take sides. That way I'll get myself in trouble with the whole world. Then after that they started up with Nitzan, the scheduling director. He's supposed to meet with Zadik and Diti and fill in all the slots. But then, like, for the cooking slot, which they just replaced with *The Simpsons,* he had no idea, they'd decided without consulting him and he claimed they'd made him a laughingstock and a rubber stamp. They hadn't let him know about the change in time, and not only that: they'd been talking about approving Benny Meyuhas's production, *Iddo and Eynam,* and airing it in prime time, starting with promos already, but had anybody informed Nitzan about it? Nope. All he's been hearing about is that they're planning to put a stop to the production altogether. So who's going to tell him? And then there was the young woman who edits and prints the daily schedules, you know, from six in the morning until programming ends at night. Oh, I can't sit here explaining what every person does at Israel Television—anyway, they started discussing *Iddo and Eynam,* and Rubin opened his mouth, I happened to be there because Diti had a sore throat and I kept bringing her more lemon for her tea. I heard Rubin shouting about *Iddo and Eynam* and then they screened a little of it. They asked me to watch, too, to give my opinion. What can I tell you, it was really impressive. I didn't exactly understand what I was seeing, some kind of ceremony, either a ritual slaughter or a wedding, there was a slaughtered sheep. Yes, a sheep, what of it?! Why are you looking at me like that, what did I say? No, they slaughter a sheep and then this girl dips her . . . no, the girl. I can't do this now, all that blood. But it was all before . . . before . . . never mind. They called me in and asked my opinion. I'm not just some nobody who won't say what she thinks, I have an opinion and Zadik respects it. So I said the film was good. I told them, 'Whatever money has been invested has already been invested, there's so little left to do, why not finish it properly? Wouldn't it be a shame not to?' That's what I think. So then Hefetz said, 'What about the Lavi fighter jet project? Didn't they put a stop to that after spending two billion dollars? Yes, they certainly did.' To which Rubin replies, 'You think this film is no good? How can you possibly think that? When's the last time you saw something of this quality on television?' And Hefetz says, 'We work for Israel Television, not the BBC. This isn't what the public wants, you have to keep the public satisfied. This show will have zero ratings, that's for sure.' So Rubin says, 'Hefetz, so much has already been invested,' and then Hefetz says, 'So what? Since when is that a consideration? Drama sure isn't the Lavi project, and even that they put a stop to after spending two billion dollars. So for sure we can put a stop to this.' See what a great memory I have? That's just the way I am, I remember *everything.*

Tell me something and then ask me tomorrow what it was you said, and I'll be able to give it back to you word for word. After Hefetz finished talking, everyone started shouting. I was the only one who could see that Zadik was convinced. Not by Hefetz, but by Rubin. But he wasn't saying anything yet. He looked at Hefetz and said quietly, so that they practically couldn't hear him, 'If we went according to your standards, then all we'd have here, all day long, would be news and the Eurovision Song Contest.' So Hefetz looks at him and says, 'You got something against the Eurovision Song Contest?' And all this takes place with the door open, because I thought I was coming in for just a minute, but I was wrong, and I had left the door to the office open. So I'm in the office listening to all this, when at last Zadik moves his chair back, angry like, and he stands up and says, 'Aviva, find Benny Meyuhas for me. I want to inform him that he has permission to complete *Iddo and Eynam*.' A few people applauded, not everybody. Hefetz didn't say a word, he just sat there making a face. I've known Hefetz for a long time, too, we've been through a lot together. Anyway, I went to look for Benny Meyuhas. What do you mean, where? Everywhere! At home, on his cell phone, at Hagar's. Only he wasn't anywhere. He wasn't answering his home phone, or the cell, even Hagar didn't have a clue where he was. So how could *I* know? I mean, she was his shadow, did you know that? It's not important, it's just that later, when all the stuff started, before what happened happened, before . . ." She covered her face with her hands and breathed deeply, then removed her hands and looked at him, horrified. "Before I found Zadik lying like that across his desk . . . his head . . . all that blood . . ."

Michael stood up and poured more mineral water into her cup, which he placed in her hand. He touched her shoulder and said, as if to a frightened child, "Drink. Drink a little." She obeyed, drinking a few sips, then wiped her lips with the back of her hand. She raised her eyes and regarded him with gratitude; she wished to please him, and continued talking.

"Hagar came here too. Not here, I mean, there. To my office. Believe me, I'm so confused I don't know where I am anymore. Anyway, she came in, stood next to my desk, and didn't stop talking. She hadn't seen Benny Meyuhas since yesterday, she was already very worried. She was with the actress from his production; all this was before Zadik—the actress, the Ethiopian girl, I can't remember her name. She's Ethiopian, isn't she? I don't care one way or another, but they call her the Indian, Benny's Indian actress, but I think she's from Ethiopia. I think she didn't want to say she was from Ethiopia, she prefers—nobody seems to know anything about her, maybe just Benny and Hagar. Don't think that everyone around here is so open-minded. There are ranks and classes, you better believe it! Especially with the technicians. Her skin is so dark, but maybe not dark enough; I don't know if there are such light-skinned Ethiopians. Never mind, it doesn't matter. The actress said that yesterday, when she was in his house with him, someone came and called for him. She didn't see who it was. She was somewhere else in the house. Maybe the bathroom. She said she was in the bathroom, but I want to tell you what *I* think. Yeah, I think so, it's a known phenomenon between directors and actresses. I'm not saying he wasn't . . . well, with the business with Tirzah and all that. I'm sure that Benny's in mourning. Distraught. But that's got nothing to do with it. You've got to understand, that has nothing to do with it. I remember once when I was really young, I had this relative, an older man, he's passed away since then, poor guy. Well, his wife died—nobody's ever said so, but I'm sure she died of cancer—and two days after her funeral I was visiting the house. Actually, she was my relative, not him, a cousin of my mother's. I was still in the army and my mother, may she rest in peace, said, 'Aviva, go visit him, please, sweetie.' I was my mother's youngest, her darling. I was a good girl and did what she asked. She said, 'Aviva dear, Shmulik is sitting shiva, go visit him and bring him some joy, help him overcome his sadness a bit.' So I went to pay a shiva call, even though I didn't really want to. I didn't want to because I had a bad feeling about it. I told you, some people can feel things in advance. I went into the kitchen for a moment to drink some water or something, and what happens but he followed me in, grabbed me in the corner. In the kitchen, next to the sink. He came up close and started telling me they didn't have a good life together, him and his wife. I mean, his wife's body hadn't even had time to cool off yet—they'd been married for something like thirty years, he must have been well over fifty, with grown children, and I wasn't even twenty—and here he was, grabbing me in the corner during his wife's shiva. I swear it. He's talking to me, and touching me too, at first just my face, and then he's stroking me. And he's not ashamed one bit. Do you think it was from his sadness? Could it be the sadness he felt? In any event, that's what I think about Benny Meyuhas and his actress. I saw her, and she's beautiful, that's for sure, if you like them thin and black-haired. It's a matter of taste. I personally don't . . .

"Where was I? Oh, yeah, Benny's nowhere to be found, and then Rubin says, 'I'll find him,' to which Zadik shouts, 'How is it that you have time for such things? What's going on? Is your report ready?' And Rubin says, 'It's completely ready, including footage of the mother of the guy who was interrogated. I've got it all on film, be prepared for a real brouhaha.' Then Zadik is already sighing because he knows he's going to have trouble on his hands with the hospital spokesman and with the minister of health and all that, but anyway . . ."

In the adjacent room, on the other side of the window covered by a heavy curtain, they could hear the chair being pushed back, the sobbing, the noisy sipping of water. Rafi took the opportunity to change the reel on the recording device. "Whoa, that one's got a real case of diarrhea of the mouth," he said quietly as he pressed a button on the amplifier. "She just keeps talking and talking and talking and you don't even need to ask any questions. I've never seen anyone go on like that."

Again they could hear muffled sobs. Aviva was mumbling, "I'm sorry, forgive me, I can't," followed by deep, hoarse coughing.

"That's because of the shot," a sergeant named Ronen explained. "With some people it doesn't put them to sleep, it has the opposite effect: they become even more wide awake, but without inhibitions."

"I don't know if this one had any inhibitions to begin with," Rafi muttered. "She seems like someone who—"

"Tell me," Lillian whispered when they heard Michael asking if she had the strength to continue, "what about him? Ohayon? He hasn't said a word." She peeked around the edge of the curtain. "How is it that she's going on and on like that when he doesn't say a thing?"

Rafi frowned and, stroking his light beard, said, "You can count on him, that's the way it always is. He just focuses his eyes on her and doesn't lower them. Believe me, that's all it takes."

"Not always," Ronen said. "First he asks a few questions, but sometimes, like in this case, all he has to do is ask what happened. You see how many times he said, 'Don't worry, just tell me whatever pops into your head'? With him, every word is planned: 'Tell *me*.' He puts the emphasis on 'me.' Like he has a special way of listening to her, like he's there just for her. Sometimes that's all it takes. A little personal attention. What more are people looking for? They just want—"

"Quiet," Rafi said, cutting him off. "She's starting to talk again."

"You may as well give me the whole bottle of water. If it's next to me, I won't have to keep asking for it. Where was I? Oh, yeah, people kept coming in and going out. Niva came in looking for Hefetz in the middle of the meeting, and Danny Benizri, and somebody else, I don't remember who. I didn't write them all down, I mean, why would I? The security people downstairs do, they keep track of everyone who comes in from outside the building, but why would I? I just write down the appointments. But I've already given your people my appointment book. The policeman with the green eyes took it. Eli, right? Eli Bachar. Nice guy, but married. I told you, the nice ones are always married. Isn't that true? Never mind, where was I? That's right. So then everyone left, and there was a moment when Zadik was all by himself, nobody else was in his office, and then he made a few phone calls and by then it was already ten-thirty and they hadn't finished with the news yet, and everybody who wandered in stopped to look at the monitor to see what was happening with the wives of the unemployed workers at the intersections, especially that pregnant one. Esty, that's her name, right? The one who chained herself to the steering wheel? And we were looking for the labor minister, who also took a long time to locate. Even her parliamentary assistant didn't know where she was. All that was my responsibility. If someone can't be found, it's like it's my fault. All in all I just want to do my job the best I can and make it home every day in one piece, you understand? I'm clearly overqualified, I've had job offers, I could be—but nothing's worth trading in my job security. When you're a woman on her own, you simply can't manage without financial security. What am I talking about: financial security? That's a laugh, my salary is a bad joke, believe me, the bare minimum, but with overtime and a good pension program and lots of years on the job . . . I can't very well allow myself, as a single woman, to throw it all away. You know what I mean? I'm not exactly looking for adventures, I've learned to hang on to what I've got rather than tossing away something good. Now where were we? Ah, it was ten-thirty and I think that was when I looked up from my work and saw there was nobody around, I thought maybe Zadik had cleared everyone out, I don't know. There was just this moment when nobody was there and I was talking on the phone, not really paying attention, and suddenly I raised my head and there was this guy, this burned man, standing in front of me. I almost screamed! Imagine this: first of all I see his hand, which he had placed on my desk. I didn't even hear his footsteps, I was on the phone. Alon, the security officer downstairs, told me he was on his way up, they told me the guy was on his way, but I didn't know what he looked like. The phone rang. You know how your people were snooping around the other day, how one of the policemen took a bunch of production files? You don't know about it? Whoa, Zadik hit the ceiling about it, threw him out. You didn't hear? Zadik went all the way up to the police commissioner about it. That was yesterday, what a ruckus! Zadik thought that you people were taking advantage of an opportunity to figure out who ratted on that police commander from the Northern District. Anyway, I was on the phone and suddenly that hand, which was sort of brownish red, was on the desk in front of me, like the hand of some Frankenstein from a horror movie. I can't stand that kind of movie because life itself is a kind of horror movie and I don't need to see it in the movie theater, too. Does that make sense to you? So I saw that hand and I almost screamed. But I didn't, I just looked at it. I hope he didn't notice, I don't feel very nice about it even though now it doesn't really matter if he noticed or not. What does it matter now? Just then Zadik opened the door to his office and looked the guy over—the black hat, the beard, the black overcoat, everything. Search me, I don't know anything about the man, but I can tell you this: he had a nice voice, like the voice of a radio announcer. He talked like we do, like a modern Israeli. Zadik ushered him into his office and told me he wouldn't be taking any calls, 'until I come out and tell you so. Don't let anyone interrupt us.'"

"They were talking about you," Rafi whispered to Balilty, who had suddenly appeared in the doorway. "She was telling Michael about how someone walked off with the production files, the ones you pinched. She said you took advantage of an opportunity—"

"So what? Who cares if she said that," Balilty said with a yawn. "That was before Zadik . . ." He fell silent, passing a finger over the folds of his neck as if slicing it.

A light blush rose to Rafi's smooth, freckled cheeks. "Why?" he asked with emotion. "If we'd known about Zadik, wouldn't you still have taken the files?"

"Do me a favor, both of you," Lillian protested. "Don't start up again. I don't want a repeat of yesterday's meeting."

"No, buddy boy, I wouldn't have," Balilty answered Rafi. "But not for the reason you think. If I'd known there was going to be a slaughter, I would have waited, because now, my friend, we'll be able to poke our noses wherever we want in that building and nobody's going to bother us."

"Can you guys keep it down," Sergeant Ronen complained. "It's impossible to hear them."

Balilty kept his mouth shut and looked toward the window. He pushed the edges of the curtain to the side and peered through the one-way glass.

"He asked us to keep the curtain closed," Lillian whispered. Balilty inclined his head and gave her a look, his lips moving as though he intended to say something, but in the end all that came out was "ffffff," like a tire leaking air. Most of those present in the room knew this was Balilty's own personal shorthand for "fuck you."

"Well, it wasn't the first time that Zadik had asked not to be disturbed. About half an hour later—with people coming and going all the time, *everyone* passed through: Hefetz, Niva, Natasha, the guy from the union, the insurance agent who's been after him for ages and made an appointment with him, Shoshana the seamstress, who asked to speak to him—and there I was like a watchdog, making sure that nobody bothered him. In the meantime there was this big ruckus, all the monitors were blaring and you couldn't even hear yourself think. The ultra-Orthodox guy in black, you know, the burned guy, came out after about twenty minutes; you'd think someone like that would wear gloves to hide his hands, but no. It was like he did it on purpose. He said good-bye politely, in a leisurely way, like he had all the time in the world. And boy, what a look he gave me! What can I tell you, I was afraid of him. Not disgusted, afraid. He said good-bye and left. After that Zadik buzzed me on the intercom. No, he didn't leave his office, he spoke to me by phone. Could I have some more water, please?

"I listened to him on the speaker. 'Aviva,' he said, 'don't pass any calls through. Until I leave my office I'm not talking to anyone. Is that clear?' Sure it was clear. Wouldn't it be nice if I had someone to tell not to pass calls through to me, too? Yes, of course it happens sometimes that he sits with someone or has an important phone conversation and doesn't want to be disturbed, so he tells me not to pass calls through. But in this case, everyone was looking for him all the time, phoning: the director general's secretary, the director of the Israel Broadcasting Authority, the head of the labor union at Israel Television, the spokeswoman for the minister of labor and social affairs, the insurance agent, who went to wait in the canteen. It seemed like nobody *wasn't* looking for Zadik. Even Danny Benizri's wife and the lawyer for the Hulit factory workers. Everybody! It's all written down, you can see for yourself, every incoming telephone conversation—even cell phones—they've all been registered. The outgoing ones, too."

On the other side of the window they could hear Michael talking. "Wait a second," he said. His chair squeaked, the door slammed open, and in an instant he was standing at the doorway to the adjacent room. "Lillian," he said in a hush, "do you know if Tzilla has gotten hold of the list of incoming calls yet?"

Lillian nodded.

"On his cell phone, too?"

"The whole works," Lillian assured him. "She's got it all organized, with the times and everything. The two days preceding as well: yesterday and the day before. If you want, she can get the whole week."

"I want to have a look at it before our meeting," Michael said. "Please make sure a copy is waiting for me here when I finish with—" He indicated the other side of the window. "I want to see it, and everyone should have a copy."

Lillian nodded, and Michael examined the toothpick he was holding between his fingers before placing it once again in his mouth and returning to the room.

"People began trickling into my office and standing there, waiting for him. To one he'd said, 'I can see you for two minutes before I leave,' and to another he'd said, 'Come at ten o'clock.' Zadik had promised them all, but who did they complain to? Yours truly, of course. Hefetz shouted at me. Like I really have the authority to tell Hefetz not to enter Zadik's office! I told him what Zadik had told me, so he did me a big favor and walked away. Ten minutes later he was back, that would have been around eleven-fifteen. And Natasha, the silent one, was there, too, just standing in the corner, waiting. They say these young female journalists will do anything to get ahead, but I'm not sure about Natasha. I mean, I don't know, there's something about her—like, she's not a bad sort, really, you know what I mean? Some of them would sell their own mothers, but not Natasha. But boy, is she stubborn! She was there the whole time, from around ten o'clock. After the Orthodox guy left, I don't know when exactly, she came in, took up her position, and didn't move. She was waiting for him, you could say she was ambushing Zadik. Then the spokeswoman for the Israel Broadcasting Authority showed up, and yes, the electrician—the guy from Maintenance—he was funny, and a reporter from the *Times,* I can't imagine how Zadik could have promised to meet him. . . . Anyway, time passed, and Zadik wasn't coming out. It was already after eleven-fifteen, and he had a meeting outside the building. So I rang into his office. But he didn't answer. I got up from my chair and knocked on his door. No answer. I tried to open the door, but it was locked, so I called him on his cell phone. No answer. Eventually, Hefetz looked at me and said, 'I don't like the looks of this, Aviva. Maybe something happened to him.' Those were exactly his words. Truth is, I thought so too. Maybe something had happened to him. Nothing like this had ever, well, it's not like *never,* but for so long? I didn't know what to think, especially since it crossed my mind that two people had already died, one just yesterday, even if it was only a heart attack. And Zadik, after all, was not exactly immune to heart trouble, was he?

"I have no idea if he tried to phone out. He never asked me to get anyone on the line for him. He had his own private direct line he could use without going through me, and his cell phone, too. Maybe he was just sitting there and . . . I mean, I didn't know about that other door. Until you told me about it, I didn't know a thing. I don't even have an idea who knew about it. I've been here fifteen years, and I certainly didn't. Should I go on? Where was I? Anyway, Hefetz called the security officer, and Alon showed up. He tried to open the door, he pounded on it, all that stuff. Hefetz said, 'Let's call maintenance,' and then phoned himself. They showed up pretty quickly, and they, well, they opened the door. That part you know, you've seen it, you were there. But before that, before you arrived, Alon wouldn't let me in. But I couldn't help myself, I couldn't just stand there on the sidelines. I couldn't believe it, so I pushed my way in to have a look. You know, you work with a person for so many years, and you don't even think about . . . and then suddenly . . . and this is the third one, in one week, in three days! Look, you don't know me. Maybe I come across to you as a hysterical woman, but believe me, I'm not. I've seen a few things in my lifetime, in high school I even volunteered at a hospital. I come from a traditional home, that was part of our education, we were expected to be good citizens and all that. So that's the way I am, not hysterical. But something like this, even you, you have seen so much; were you able to just go on as though nothing happened? No way. I'm sure you couldn't. I saw you. Even you couldn't. . . ."

She was right. Even he was not immune to what he saw in Zadik's office. It wasn't just the man's mashed face, an expression of surprise etched around the mouth ("No need to expend much effort on finding the murder weapon, is there?" asked the pathologist with quiet satisfaction, pointing with his elbow at the drill standing in a pool of blood next to the pair of stained blue overalls tossed there). Nor was it just the way the body was sprawled over the large desk. It was all these, along with the blood that had been sprayed about, giving the room the look of a slaughterhouse, that made it hard for him to take it all in. Secretly, pretending to look at the papers strewn on the floor, Michael had turned his head away from the body while the forensics people worked energetically, collecting fingerprints and scraping samples onto glass slides. Only a moment before they wrapped Zadik's body and placed him on the stretcher did he come close and take a careful look. Blood had stained everything: the light blue carpeting, the wall, it had filled the room—the windows were closed—with the sour smell of rust.

"No one knew about that door," Aviva repeated, full of respect and humility, "until you discovered it." Her voice trembled.

It is precisely those things you discover by chance, not by strenuous effort or resourcefulness but by diverting your attention, that often wind up leading to rare achievement and bring you a rather embarrassing notoriety. Embarrassing because you did not really earn it; rather, at a certain moment, in the middle of carrying out the job, just as the forensics people were busy examining the initial data, bending down next to the body, preparing samples for testing blood and tissues, taking photographs, marking things—just then you had to excuse yourself for a moment, get some fresh air, and that's when you discovered what no one else had bothered to notice. How had no one noticed? How was it that no one had attempted to open that door from the outside? They had thought it was a locked closet, ancient; they explained again and again that the metal cabinet that had stood in the hallway for years had concealed the wooden door. No one had noticed that the cabinet had been moved from its place, and for the time being no one could remember how much time had passed since it had been moved, or how long the light-colored door had been exposed, for all to see. Was it truly possible that people working there for years had no knowledge of a second door leading into Zadik's office?

"Once I tried opening it, years ago, but it was locked," Hefetz had told him, while Arye Rubin had regarded Michael with surprise when asked about it. "A door? A hidden door?" He nearly smiled when he said, "Believe me, in this building there are so many alterations and tack-ons and hallways and stairways and basements and doors and windows that have been blocked up that nobody can really know."

And then there was Niva. "Show me," she demanded. "I have to see this. I don't want to see the inside of the room. Have they cleaned it all up? No? Then I'm not looking, I just want to see if there's really a door, and where it leads." He brought her to the hallway and showed her; she stood in front of the door in absolute amazement and disbelief. When she placed her hand on the round doorknob and turned it, and the door opened without a sound, she looked at him again, dumbfounded. "It even works," she said in a feeble voice. "I've been here for twenty years, and I thought there wasn't an inch of this place I didn't know. Not just here, but the String Building as well. And suddenly, a door! Right in the middle of the hallway! Where has it been hiding all this time?"

Hefetz was the one who told him the tall, narrow metal cabinet had been leaning against the door all those years, causing everyone to forget about its existence, and that the cabinet had only recently been moved. "They forgot about it?" Michael asked. "Forgot? I mean, they knew about it once and forgot?" Hefetz squirmed under Michael's scrutiny and spread his arms as if confounded. "I don't recall that I knew about it, maybe I did once, I can't swear by it. But even if I did, I didn't *know* that I did."

Rubin intervened. "You don't pay close attention in a place you know really well, someplace you walk around every day. Whatever you take for granted ceases to exist. A cabinet has been standing here for years, but if you ask us what's inside it, we won't have a clue because it's not in use. Once upon a time office supplies were stored there, I only just remembered that now; paper, staples, that sort of thing. It was kept locked then. Now too, no? It was your people who opened it up, right?"

"Yeah, it was us," Eli Bachar confirmed. "But nobody had a key. Not for the cabinet, and not for the door."

"I'm sure nobody saw it, the cabinet was hiding the door for years," Niva said. The conversation took place just after Zadik's body had been removed by stretcher; before the investigation at police headquarters they sat in Hefetz's office, near the newsroom. "But I'm telling you," she said excitedly, "we didn't even notice that someone had moved the cabinet, even though there are plenty of observant people around here. I couldn't tell you whether that cabinet was moved yesterday or today or even a week ago. I simply didn't notice. My eyes are always on the ground when I walk, and how much do I actually get around here?"

"That's just it," Arye Rubin said. "Paradoxically, it takes someone from the outside to discern details that we are blind to. You see," he said to Michael in wonderment, "it was a good thing you were wandering around the hall."

Inside Zadik's office there stood a bookstand on which were arranged trophies and a number of collections (flags, matches, wine corks) and a shelf that held bottles of alcohol—not a proper bar, just a shelf; behind this was a curtain, the bottoms of which had been shoved aside as if someone had pushed the bookstand from its place and neglected to straighten the edges of the curtain. When Michael had bent down and looked from down below, he noticed suddenly a light-colored wood surface and the hint of a door frame. He exited the office and walked down the hallway, opening door after door and looking in. The narrow metal cabinet stood quite close to one of the doors, very nearly hiding it. When he pressed on the doorknob, he did not expect anything to happen, when suddenly a small space opened in front of him, a square niche that led to another door. He tried opening that one, too, but something was blocking it. He pushed hard against the door and felt something on the other side moving. All at once he could hear the voice of Yaffa from forensics on the other side of the door. "What's going on?" she called, taken aback. "Someone—who is it, who's there?"

"Hang on a minute," Michael had said, dashing back to Zadik's room. Together they moved the bookstand and pushed the curtain to the side, revealing the other door.

"Wait," Yaffa said quietly. "Excuse me for a moment." She nearly toppled him while she dusted the doorknob and the bookstand for prints.

"They used this door," Michael said. "They opened this door, didn't they?"

"Sure," Yaffa said, eyeing him with frustration. "They probably opened it today, otherwise we would have found something, at least some dust, cobwebs, something. Look, nothing," she said scornfully. "Not even—well, what did you expect? Maybe you hoped that someone would enter, kill a person, and then leave signs on the door and the knob? At least a palm print, a thumb. Something."

"Nothing at all?" Michael asked.

"Nada," Yaffa mumbled. "There are prints on the bookstand and the bottles and all that, but not on the door. In any event, not fingerprints. But we'll find something else, don't worry, something will turn up. Just like they taught us, 'Every time you touch something . . ."

". . . you leave a trace,'" Michael completed the sentence in a near whisper, and sighed.

"Why can't you believe that?" Yaffa insisted as she bent down to the foot of the bookstand and carefully lifted a single hair from the floor with a pair of pincers. "Do me a favor," she said before he had a chance to answer, "bring me a small plastic bag from the sack next to the door, or tell Rafi and he'll give you one." He hadn't even moved a muscle when she called out, "Rafi, anybody, I need to bag a hair," and Michael, who was standing between Yaffa and a young man he did not know, was handed a bag, which he passed on to Yaffa. "You haven't answered me: do you or don't you believe it?" Yaffa sat down on the rug, placed the hair in the bag, and sealed it, then looked at him expectantly.

"What? That every time you touch something, you leave a trace? Experience shows that's true, generally," he said pensively. "But we know that often it's just a matter of luck, and—"

"When's the last time we didn't come up with something for you?" Yaffa said, offended. "If you consider all the times we've worked together, I would have thought you'd—"

"No, no, no," Michael hastened to appease her. "That's not at all what I meant. You're a terrific team, there's no question about it. It's just that there's always—"

"It's true that things are tough at first," she agreed; even though she had not let him finish his sentence, she knew what caused his doubts.

"Until you make some sense of it all, until you get a handle on all those details, it seems like you'll never get any real answers. But something turns up, it always does," she concluded, though it was unclear whether she was trying to convince him or herself. Her long ponytail bobbed up and down when she added, "At least in this case we were very lucky to get here so quickly, before anyone could . . . it's lucky they called you so fast. Who called you? Ronen?"

"Yes."

"Was he a plant here? Gosh, now I understand why he hasn't been at work. Did Zadik know about him?"

"He did," Michael said with a sigh. "He agreed to it because of Matty Cohen."

Although little time had passed since he had spoken with Zadik, it seemed to Michael as though their conversation about the results of the postmortem performed on Matty Cohen had taken place eons ago, and that ages had passed since he had told Zadik about the excessive quantity of digoxin found in his body. "What's digoxin?" Zadik had asked. "Isn't that something given to heart patients? I think I've heard of it, I think I even saw Matty taking it. Or maybe he just told me about it."

Michael had explained to him that the popular medication, produced from the digitalis plant and sold commercially from as early as the beginning of the eighteenth century as an efficient way of increasing and stabilizing heart rate, was also a dangerous drug. "Medical professionals and heart patients alike know," Michael said, explaining to Zadik what he had learned from the pathologist who had performed the autopsy on Matty Cohen, "that the main problem with digoxin is the narrow range of proper dosage and the fatal side effects the drug produces when just a little too much is consumed." He thought to himself about the name of the plant—digitalis, responsible for the digital beat—and a digital ticking began resounding in his ears. Zadik had sat up straight in his chair and, clearly rattled, placed his hand over his chest, then stretched his fingers to feel his left arm. Michael added that for that reason, the level of digoxin in Matty Cohen's blood had been constantly monitored, and shortly before his death it was found to be fine. The autopsy, however, had revealed that the quantity of the drug in his bloodstream was four times normal.

"Four times?" Zadik said, horrified. "How could that be? Does that mean he took too much by accident? Or not by accident?"

"It's hard to know," Michael said. "It's hard to know whether he ingested it himself, accidentally or not, or whether it was given to him." He imagined the sound of different heartbeats, the normal and the abnormal—terrifying, galloping, exaggerated.

"What does that mean, it was given to him? Are you saying someone poisoned him?" Zadik was astounded. "Don't joke about this—what do you think we do here, poison people? Anyway, you're just talking off the cuff, there's no proof, is there?"

Nonetheless, Zadik did not put up much of a fight about approving Sergeant Ronen for "employment," and Ronen started work immediately as a temporary electrician for the Maintenance Department ("Only because you gave me your word of honor that he won't go near the files, trying to figure out who our informer was," Zadik had warned Michael, "and because I trust you, and because of this business with the digoxin, even if you can't pin anything on anyone"). So that was how Ronen was able to contact Michael the moment Aviva alerted the security officer; thanks to Ronen, Michael had managed to arrive on the scene before the doctor and before the forensics team.

Now he was looking at the mass of blond curls on Aviva's head as she leaned forward, her hands over her face. He noted the bright red of her long fingernails against the background of her starkly white hands. In his head her voice resounded—not the feeble, lifeless tone she had been using for the past hour, but the nasally, whiny voice she had used to repeat, over and over again, what he had heard her saying after they broke into Zadik's office as she stood near the desk: "How can this have happened? I never left my desk, and nobody . . ." She kept repeating this until the moment she collapsed, as fate would have it into the arms of the director general of the Israel Broadcasting Authority, who had been summoned, and before they could get a tranquilizer into her. "Just so you know," the doctor had told him, "she could sleep for hours now." But only one hour had passed before she opened her eyes and sprang to her feet, so they were able to bring her in for the prolonged questioning that was just now coming to an end. Afterward she was completely exhausted, her limbs sprawled limply. She said, leaning over the desk, "Now I'm simply tired, I don't even have the strength to get up from this chair." She lowered her head to her folded arms and fell fast asleep.

He continued sitting there for a moment, facing her, reliving the ruckus that had taken place in her office even before they had completed their investigations. The police commissioner and Emmanuel Shorer, who was serving as Jerusalem district commander, had asked him to sit with them in the little room next to the secretary's office; a moment later they were joined by Natan Ben-Asher, director general of the Israel Broadcasting Authority, who was wearing a dark pinstripe suit, the corner of a handkerchief poking out from his breast pocket. His hair was dark ("You think he dyes it?" Yaffa had asked in a whisper before he entered the room) and shiny and combed back from his high, prominent forehead and his puffy cheeks. He looked around, removed a checked handkerchief from the pocket of his trousers—which he used to meticulously wipe clean one of the empty chairs in the room—hiked up his trousers, and sat down, muttering all the while, "What a terrible disaster, simply horrid, I have no idea . . . ," and then fell silent. He regarded them and added, wagging his finger, a nervous quiver to his voice, "First you must investigate the security angle here. I have no doubt this was an assassination, it has to do with the political situation." He repeated this assertion several times. When the police commissioner wondered whether they might need to close down Israel Television, Ben-Asher flew out of his seat to point at the monitor, which was broadcasting there, just as in every room in the building. "The nation's official television station will not be shut down!" he declared. Ben-Asher raised the volume on the monitor and said, "Do you see what's happening here? Look!" They watched a live broadcast as Danny Benizri climbed the metal steps of a semi trailer; on the top step he stopped to interview Rachel Shimshi, who was sitting in the passenger seat, leaning toward the steering wheel, her hands cuffed to the wheel. "I'm not unlocking them!" Rachel Shimshi shouted hoarsely. "I'm not taking off the handcuffs, and I'm not getting rid of the metal chain. Tell everybody that I'm . . . that we're . . . we have nothing more to lose!" Ben-Asher said, "You want Channel Two to report this?" In the background they could hear Danny Benizri talking to Rachel Shimshi. "You're desperate, you've lost all hope—" Rachel Shimshi said, "I want everyone to know, I want our husbands to know, that we're with them one hundred percent. Everybody else left them alone to rot, but we wives believe what they did was right. *We're* not going to leave them alone to rot."

"If you think about it logically," Danny Benizri tried to say, but she cut him off in an instant. "Don't talk to me about logic," she shouted. "Don't try to find any logic in the way people behave when they're desperate. You can't ask desperate people to behave logically. That's the way it is all over the world, this is a democratic country, with justice and all that. We're not going to move the trucks. Only way I'm leaving here is if someone takes me by force," she cried, looking to Esty, who was sitting in the driver's seat. "You can't move her without using force either," she announced and pointed at Esty's protruding belly. "We'll see how you guys manage with a pregnant woman. What are you going to do with her?"

"They interrupted regularly scheduled programming for this live broadcast," Ben-Asher told them with satisfaction, as though a body had not just been removed from the adjacent room. "One does not shut down this kind of work." He hastened to add, "There is no time to lose; as tragic as the circumstances are, it will be necessary to appoint a replacement for Zadik to ensure continuity here. We shall endeavor to do our jobs, and you shall endeavor to do yours. As for Zadik, I feel quite certain you will find his untimely death is due to the work of terrorists. Awful, this is simply awful. Just two months ago he became a grandfather—"

"Eighteen months ago," Emmanuel Shorer corrected him.

"What was eighteen months ago?" Natan Ben-Asher asked, confused.

"His grandson was born a year and a half ago," Shorer said, looking past Ben-Asher. "Do you have a candidate to replace Zadik, someone who can take over immediately? Who would it be? Say, Arye Rubin?" he guessed.

"No. Not Rubin," Ben-Asher said quickly. "We need Rubin to continue with his reports." Slowly, carefully emphasizing every word, he added, "Rubin is proof that we are a democratic state, even if he is quite radical.

I told Zadik, may he rest in peace, I talked to him about Rubin's one-sided reporting. After all, any other institution would have—"

"Who were you thinking of?" Shorer asked pleasantly, looking straight into the small eyes of the director general of the Broadcasting Authority, who was wiping his face with his handkerchief.

"I will tell you whom I've been considering," he said, "and with the authority vested in me I will carry out this appointment immediately. I have the full backing of the communications minister and the prime minister himself."

The police commissioner expressed astonishment. "You mean to tell me that the prime minister and the communications minister already know about . . . this situation? When did you have time to inform them?" he asked.

"First of all, I spoke with the cabinet secretary from the car on the way here," Ben-Asher said coolly, clearly self-satisfied. "I didn't want them to hear about it from leaked information. And I explained to them that we need to mobilize immediately. Beyond that, I have had discussions with the prime minister about general policy with regards to Israel Television . . ." Suddenly a note of hesitation crept into his voice and he added, as though walking on eggs, that "Zadik—how shall I say it?—was a dear man, truly, but rather impulsive. That was certainly, for me as well, part of his charm—"

Emmanuel Shorer tugged at the ends of his ample mustache and let out a sigh. "I had no idea," he said dryly, "that Zadik had any sort of charm at all, as far as you were concerned. I do believe I heard rumors of a threatened dismissal—"

"No, no, certainly not," Ben-Asher said, smoothing his hair back and removing an unseen speck from his trousers. "Perhaps there were differences of opinion, but he had, in any event, reached the end of his contract, and—"

"Ahhh," Shorer exclaimed, "so in fact you had no intention of extending his contract."

"Well, that decision was not solely mine," Ben-Asher said, shifting uncomfortably in his chair. "There had not even been any sort of formal discussion of the matter, though now—"

There was silence in the room for a long moment before the police commissioner asked, "So how do you envision the ongoing work of Israel Television in the near future?"

"You mean, until you people solve this conundrum?" Ben-Asher inquired, sitting up straight in his chair.

"Let's say," Shorer said expectantly, "that in an atmosphere of panic and mistrust, when everyone is suspicious of everyone else and people are afraid—afraid in general and afraid to enter the building—well, how do you intend to—"

"Why should people be suspicious of others?" Ben-Asher asked, astonished. "It seems perfectly clear that this is not someone from inside Israel Television, that we're talking about a security issue, maybe even the Jewish underground movement. If I were you, I would assign police protection to Arye Rubin and the entire building. Naturally, you have a free hand and any assistance you—"

"And who is going to fill in for Zadik?" the police commissioner asked.

"I am hereby appointing Hefetz to replace Zadik as director of Israel Television," Ben-Asher announced as he rose from his chair and opened the door. "Call Hefetz," he said authoritatively. "Where's Hefetz?"

"Our people are speaking with him," Shorer told him.

"He's under investigation?" Ben-Asher asked, rattled.

"Everyone's being questioned," Shorer responded. "We're not calling it an investigation yet. This is only an initial clarification of the facts."

"So have them bring him here for a moment," Ben-Asher demanded. "Israel Television is the flagship of the state of Israel, we cannot leave it for even a second without a captain," he proclaimed dramatically from the doorway. "We cannot tolerate anarchy in this institution. My motto is, 'A guiding hand at every moment.'" He called out, "Bring Hefetz, where is he sitting? In his office?"

The police commissioner looked at Ben-Asher as though he were about to say something, but instead he remained silent, looking expectantly at Emmanuel Shorer, who was drumming his fingers on his knees. Shorer shrugged and said, "All right, there doesn't seem to be any choice in the matter. If the prime minister—if it's necessary, then it's necessary. Can you call him, please?" he asked Michael, who hastened to bring Hefetz in from his office near the newsroom.

"Clear everyone out of the secretary's office," Ben-Asher ordered. "Have them wait somewhere else, there are too many people here. And turn the volume down!" he commanded, pointing at the television monitor; half of the screen showed trucks blocking various intersections, while the other half featured the minister of labor and social affairs holding an unscheduled press conference in the lobby of the new Hilton Hotel. She kept smoothing her mussed hair while speaking with emotion about the importance of obeying the law. "If every disgruntled citizen of Israel takes the law into his own hands . . . ," she was heard saying before someone turned down the volume on the monitor. No one, however, suggested turning it off altogether.

Someone shouted, "Israel Television should be shut down right now, and everyone should be sent home. It's dangerous to be here!"

A woman's voice rebuked him. "Are you crazy? Israel Television should never be shut down. That would be like we were at war or something."

Ben-Asher rushed to the door of the office and opened it. "I would ask of everyone to clear the area," he said imperiously. "Allow the police to carry out their task quickly. Please, all of you, clear the area." People regarded him, then turned silently to file out. "We'll be needing a policeman on this floor," he told the police commissioner.

"We've already sealed off the hallway," the commissioner retorted. "I don't understand how—" He whispered something to Shorer, who quickly left the room.

"Ahhh, here you are, Hefetz," Ben-Asher said, stretching his lips into a smile that exposed two rows of large, bright white teeth.

"Mr. Ben-Asher," Hefetz said, his voice trembling, "look at what—"

"What do you mean, 'Mr.?' Hefetz, my friend, that's not the kind of relationship you and I enjoy. I have always been Natan to you. Why suddenly 'Mr.?'"

"People here are in a panic, Natan," Hefetz explained. "They want to close down Israel Television. They're shouting at me as if I could—what can I do about this?" he asked.

"Have a seat, my friend," Ben-Asher said in a fatherly manner. "Sit, drink some water, settle down. You need to be relaxed to set a good personal example. Here, look at me: do you think this isn't difficult for me? Didn't I work for years with Zadik? Way back from the days when I was director of personnel, when this whole business was brand new. We go back a long way, had our share of arguments and disagreements and differences of opinion. Zadik was a great man, head and shoulders above the rest."

Hefetz nodded in rapid agreement with every word, and looked around the room.

"There are people who will say," the director general intoned, "that Zadik and I were enemies because of the petition. You remember the petition?" Hefetz nodded. "And because of the letter of resignation he handed me a year and a half ago. But it isn't so. You, Hefetz, my friend, you know the truth: that I held Zadik in high esteem. Didn't I?"

"Absolutely," Hefetz said. He bowed his head like a scolded schoolboy.

"And, I believe, he held me in high esteem as well, did he not?"

"Sure he did," Hefetz said, raising his head to look at the police commissioner.

"And I think that he would agree with my decision if he were to know that I am requesting you to serve as his replacement," Ben-Asher concluded, carefully examining his polished fingernails. "What do you say to that?"

"I . . . I . . . ," Hefetz stuttered. "Whatever it takes, I . . . if there's no choice in the matter . . ."

"Why, Hefetz, do you have a problem with it?" Ben-Asher asked in wide-eyed surprise. "Do you feel incapable of the task of commanding this ship? Do you fear you will be unable to steady it?"

"No, no," Hefetz responded quickly. "I . . . it's just that, I haven't yet . . . I'm still in shock about—"

"Because people have raised the idea of shutting down Israel Television until a proper assessment of what's going on here can be made," said the police commissioner. "How do you feel about that?"

An expression of piqued interest crept across the face of Emmanuel Shorer, who had in the meantime returned to the room and resumed his position. After years of working so closely together, Michael often knew exactly what was passing through Shorer's mind, as he did now. If asked, he would have said the look on Shorer's face was one of ironic detachment, the look of a man watching a play performed by inept and amateurish actors. Only recently Shorer had told him—thanks to information passed on by his daughter-in-law, who worked as a makeup artist for Israel Television—about the differences of opinion ("They're calling it 'war' over there," he had said) between Zadik, the director of Israel Television, and Ben-Asher, director general of the Israel Broadcasting Authority. Zadik had issued a complaint about arbitrary cutbacks the director general had made in the budget, and that Ben-Asher had torpedoed a program he particularly disliked, had even made drastic reductions in wardrobe and makeup. He talked of Ben-Asher's plans to turn Israel Television—with the backing of the communications minister and the prime minister—into an entertainment channel, the bullhorn of the administration. Shorer had also brought to his attention the article published several weeks earlier in a Jerusalem daily titled, "Left-Wing Wasp's Nest or Citizen's Revolt?" Shorer had mockingly quoted the article, which claimed to take readers "behind the scenes at the IBA," conjecturing about the source of the animosity raging between Zadik and Ben-Asher by mentioning Ben-Asher's demand that Zadik resign of his own free will, since he had "dragged Israel's official television station down to a level of complete lawlessness by failing to maintain a balanced picture of events." Michael and Shorer had been having this conversation late one night in the Mahane Yehuda farmers' market, in a restaurant Shorer particularly favored because the owner, a guy named Menash who roamed from place to place opening a new restaurant every few years, tended to cook the food himself in huge aluminum pots, "Just like the ones my grandmother had," Shorer told him. Menash prepared Sephardic classics, his specialty being calzones, little turnovers made with a very thin dough just like his own mother would make for Rosh Hashanah, but filled with meat instead of cheese. "They tell me that the Russians call it piroshki, but that's something altogether different," he had told Michael. Michael, who was only then considering giving up smoking, had dared to mention it toward the end of the meal. "No question about it," Shorer had said, "you've got to stop. Look at the color of your face, it's gray. Your face is gray. Have you had any tests done?" Michael had shrugged in response. "Do me a favor," he had said, "let's talk about something else," and so, in order to take his mind off the smoking issue, Shorer had regaled him with stories of the director general's policies at the IBA, how he was demanding the use of a new broadcasting lexicon, having proclaimed, in the latest Director General's Directive, that use of the expression "the other side" was no longer acceptable. "You know why?" Shorer had asked him, and then, without awaiting an answer, explained: "Because we can't let 'the other side' write history for us. That's why it's no longer permissible to use the term 'Intifada,' only 'uprising' will do. Same with 'territories,' only 'Judea, Samaria, and the Gaza Strip' is acceptable now. Taste this, Michael, take a taste of this *matboukha,* he learned to make it from his grandmother. Right, Menash, this *matboukha* is your grandmother's recipe?" Menash was standing next to the table, rubbing his palms together. "Pour yourself some more *araq,*" Shorer instructed Michael, "it'll make you feel better. Listen to me, I'm talking like Balilty. How's Balilty? I haven't seen him for a few days . . ."

They drank to Menash's health and to a successful marriage with his new, third bride. "She's Russian," Menash told them, "but she's got the soul of a Sephardic Jew. None of this liberated woman stuff, look at her back there in the kitchen." Proudly, he pointed to a very young woman with golden hair standing behind the wooden counter, watching them.

"Zadik may not be the genius of his generation," Shorer had told Michael when Menash took his leave of them, "but he's got a lot of integrity. And balls, too. I sat with him at the Peleds' one Friday night, just after the article came out. He tells me, 'They may be able to control the use of this word or that in radio news broadcasts, but do they really expect me to instruct people what not to say on a political affairs program? Can you imagine everyone sitting around the table shouting, and we'll stop the discussion to remind them not to say 'the territories,' but rather, 'Judea, Samaria, and the Gaza Strip'? Now Zadik may not be the genius of his generation, but there's something very true about his practicality, his sincerity. So then Aliza Peled, you know her, the one with the white hair, teaches at the Hebrew University? You met her at Mumik's wedding"—Michael nodded—"so she says that her friend, a language editor, told her that in written Hebrew you're not supposed to write *Palestinian* with the letters *samekh* and *tet* but with the letters *shin* and *taf,* so as to recall the ancient Philistines."

"That's all they talked about the whole evening." Shorer sighed. "You go out for a nice dinner, hoping to have a good time, and these people can't let it rest, they get right to politics. We were four couples sitting around the table, and Zadik started talking about the cutbacks, complaining how Ben-Asher wasn't even willing to pay for taxis for guests anymore. How can you invite someone to appear on your program when you can't even send a taxi to fetch him? No wonder everyone's making a beeline for Channel Two."

"We'll announce it on the evening news," the director general was telling Hefetz. "You'll deliver a eulogy, say whatever you want to, but I want a copy beforehand. And then you can announce that you've taken it upon yourself . . ." Michael clamped down on the toothpick in his teeth and was staring at Shorer, when suddenly there was a sharp rapping at the door to the office and Eli Bachar stepped in. He motioned to Michael to come with him. Michael hurried out of the room and returned a moment later, his eyes on Shorer and the police commissioner.

"What is it?" the commissioner asked impatiently. "What else could possibly have happened?"

"Benny Meyuhas has disappeared," Michael said. "They can't find him anywhere."

"Meyuhas the director?" Ben-Asher wished to clarify. "He's the one they can't find?"

"He's been missing since yesterday, nobody's seen him," Michael said.

"So this could be our man," the police commissioner said. "We've got to put out an APB on him and make a public announcement, don't you think?"

"Yes," Shorer said. "Absolutely."

"What?" Hefetz said, taken aback. "You mean like, 'Israel Police requests assistance in locating'—and all that?"

"More than that," Shorer responded. "We've got to get his picture out there. You must have a photograph we can use. We'll need you to put it on the news, too."

"The news?" Hefetz exclaimed. "The news? Do you really believe— Maybe something's happened to him!"

Natan Ben-Asher said, "They don't believe any such thing, my friend." He glared at the police commissioner. "We will not present him as a suspect, we shall simply announce that he has disappeared and that we are requesting assistance in locating him. That is what we shall do."

# CHAPTER ELEVEN

Michael sat in Arye Rubin's office at the end of the second floor, slowly stirring coffee in a pale yellow mug. "I used to smoke," Rubin said wistfully as he moved an ashtray full of cigarette butts aside. "These belong to an editor who was sitting with me. It's been four years and two months since I quit." Arye Rubin sat in a chair next to the large table, his back to the wall, and stretched his feet out in front of him. Facing him, Michael was afforded a view of the wall and the large corkboard hanging on it, which was covered with photographs, clippings, and notes held up by red and blue thumbtacks. In the hours that had passed since Zadik's body was removed from the building, Michael had managed to pore over the secret files that had been found in a locked drawer of the dead man's desk, and while the forensics team was busy emptying the contents of Zadik's office into large black bags, he had examined the safe that had been opened at his request and in which he found additional files, files absolutely no one knew a thing about. Michael had taken these and sequestered himself for a while in the little office next to Aviva's. He flipped quickly through the thin plastic files: in one he found a copy of a secret personal contract between the Israel Broadcasting Authority and Hefetz; in a manila envelope he found the results of Zadik's medical examinations; and finally he came across a yellow file—nothing was written upon it—sealed with masking tape. He carefully slit the tape and found a single page, handwritten in a tiny print on both sides, detailing the budget for producing *Iddo and Eynam,* as well as the donation that made it possible. He had just managed to finish reading the document and examining the signatures, and had his hand on the phone, poised to share his findings with Balilty, when he was summoned from the end of the hallway. Eli Bachar informed him that initial questioning of Arye

Rubin had been completed, and that Rubin had been unable to shed any light on the disappearance of Benny Meyuhas. He claimed not to know a thing about his whereabouts ("He sounds trustworthy," Eli Bachar said reluctantly. "That doesn't seem logical, but when he talks to you, he's very persuasive") but expressed willingness to do anything to help find Benny, including accompanying Michael to search his home.

An atmosphere of anxiety and distress pervaded the building, along with an unnatural hush; among the staff, people spoke quietly if at all. Even the newsroom, which Michael passed on his way downstairs, had been quieter than usual. In the canteen—now bereft of employees—sat a dozen policemen, listening to Yaffa from forensics describe the circumstances surrounding the murder "from the traces left behind." Several times she stated that because of the manner in which Zadik had been killed, it was highly likely that they would find—"If we are diligent in our pursuit"—clothing spattered with blood. Policemen could be heard in every corner of the building—employees were forbidden from entering rooms that were in the process of being searched; indeed, the entire area surrounding the site of the murder had been sealed off—and their footsteps resounded down empty hallways as they searched through closets and cubbyholes and storerooms and rubbish bins, increasing the paralyzing anxiety that had settled on the staff, who left their offices only when absolutely necessary and only with police approval. No one left or entered the building without the permission of Michael, Balilty, or Eli Bachar.

After being investigated and providing an initial, unsigned testimony, Arye Rubin had accompanied Michael to Benny Meyuhas's home, where Eli Bachar, Sergeant Ronen, and two people from forensics were already well into their search for some finding that might explain what had become of Benny Meyuhas. Rubin had shown no outward sign of shock at finding the house in disarray—drawers overturned, large black bags stuffed with anything that had aroused suspicion—and Michael, secretly observing his reactions for some sign that Rubin did know what had become of his friend, had been impressed by the man's self-control. He knew by Rubin's strained posture, by the repeated spasms of his left eyelid, and by the fist his hand kept forming and unfurling that Rubin was actually under intense strain. He knew from experience that tension and anxiety cause many people to jabber compulsively and associatively without inhibition, especially if you kept quiet and ignored their distress. Thus, he tended to silence in Arye Rubin's company, not speaking to him apart from relevant and necessary questions, like asking for Rubin's help in deciphering Benny Meyuhas's handwriting as he paged through the small appointment book he found on the nightstand in the bedroom, or basic details about meetings that had been scheduled the week before. Rubin, however, had not been tempted to ease his burden by talking; on the contrary, the longer they stayed in Benny Meyuhas's house, the more tight-lipped he became. They had made their way back to Israel Television in silence; even now, as they sat in Rubin's office drinking the coffee he had prepared for them, they did not speak. Rubin's face projected something deep and serious, his expression that of someone who had witnessed a disaster involving someone close and dear to him and been powerless to help. It was Michael who disrupted this silence as he raised his eyes to the corkboard and the enlarged black-and-white photographs posted there. "Is that one from World War Two?" he asked, pointing at a photo of Japanese soldiers standing in tight rows, their hands raised high in a sign of surrender.

"Yes," Rubin answered, regarding the corkboard as if noticing it for the first time. "I have a whole collection. Like that one," he said, pointing at another photograph, this one of soldiers in gray uniforms sitting on barren desert ground, their heads bowed. "It's from World War I, enemies of the French army. And this one," he announced, drawing Michael's attention to a midsize color photo of soldiers in camouflage in a tropical jungle. "Americans in Vietnam," he explained. "I have a whole collection, but there's no room for them all here."

"It's not a very uplifting collection," Michael noted. "In fact, a bit odd, wouldn't you say?"

Rubin shrugged. "It's what interests me. Why should I worry about whether it's odd or not?"

"There are no Israelis here, no Arabs," Michael observed, surprised. "No Egyptian soldiers. You know, the classic photos." He placed his empty mug on the table.

Rubin stretched his lips into a mirthless half-smile. "No need for those here, they hit too close to home," he said quietly. "I carry *those* around in here," he explained, pointing to his head.

"I've heard that you yourself were a prisoner of war during the Yom Kippur War," Michael stated.

Rubin frowned, passed his hand over his face as if to erase it, and gazed at the wall facing him. "Forget about it, that's a kind of myth, it's not worth talking about. I wasn't really a prisoner of war. . . . If it's all the same to you," he said quickly, pressing the start button on a nearby monitor, "I'd prefer to keep this thing on." A portrait of Zadik in a black frame appeared in the upper corner of the screen, while in the center of the picture, against a background of old black-and-white photographs of Zadik from his childhood and more recent color snapshots taken with the American president and with the head of the union at Israel Television, stood Giora Ilem, known for facilitating songfests and sing-alongs and for writing particularly sad lyrics. Dressed in a black shirt, the buttons of which seemed ready to pop off, he repeatedly slicked back what had once been a healthy forelock of sand-colored hair but now looked like a coil negligently stuck to his forehead. There was a grimace on his blotchy face, the pinkish tones of which no makeup could conceal. His stubby fingers were clasped, the palms of his hands resting on his chest, and he quickly noted, with suppressed sadness, as if squelching his tears, the names of the people in the photographs with Zadik: Yitzhak Rabin, Golda Meir, Shimon Peres, Ariel Sharon (in the uniform of a brigadier-general), Abba Eban, President Gorbachev, U.S. presidents Carter and Clinton, the author Günter Grass, an aging Yves Montand. He dwelled on one particularly radiant photo, of a young long-haired Zadik smiling broadly, his arm around Sophia Loren's shoulders, and ended with Zadik in the company of Israeli singers Arik Einstein and Uri Zohar. He told of Zadik's love of Israeli music, especially songs from the pioneering early years of the state, and with a big smile in spite of his sadness, explained that anyone who knew Zadik had to have heard his off-key renditions of "Ammunition Hill" or "The Two of Us Hail from the Same Village" at one time or another.

"Will you look at this," Rubin muttered. "This is what they have a budget for, the sky's the limit for Giora Ilem, the National Sycophant." Michael noted that it was the first time he had heard Rubin speaking maliciously offscreen. "Some people just glide through life like first-time skiers," Rubin said, and without taking his eyes from the screen, added, "Nice guys, the kinds that get along with everybody. Who doesn't love Giora? Who could say a bad word about the guy? But what is he if not a collection of clichés and interminable niceness, a guy who resolutely stays clear of all confrontation in order to preserve his popularity? I can't stand these nice people who haven't got an enemy in the world." Rubin turned the volume down but left the monitor running. "I have to keep on top of things," he said by way of apology, "even if for the time being they're only dragging old stuff out of the mothballs. Pretty soon there'll be a special broadcast with an official announcement about Zadik and Israel Television."

Michael looked at Rubin's dark gray eyes and the fine web of wrinkles surrounding them, at the deep line between his gray brows, at his narrow nose with the small hump that lent it a fascinating presence, at the deep twin creases running the length of his cheeks, which hinted at torment, at the full lips that, surprisingly, did not suggest hedonism, at the short-cropped gray hair. "What a good-looking man, a real hunk. He's even better looking in person than on television. You can see how tall he is and all that. He looks like Paul Newman, don't you think?" Yaffa from forensics had asked him this the day before as they stood in the hall in front of Michael's office, just before a short meeting on the results of Matty Cohen's autopsy. "You can be sure he's the type who gets any woman he wants. If he's interested," she added in a whisper. After a moment of reflection, she said, "But he doesn't look like someone who's particularly interested. I'd say he's not a happy man, and I doubt he'd put much effort into it. There's even something, well, dead about him, you know? Anyway, he's in mourning right now, they say he really loved Tirzah, even though they were divorced. What do you think of him?" she asked Tzilla, who was standing next to her, one hand on the doorknob.

"Yes," Tzilla said, distracted. "He looks like a real Don Juan to me, but I understand there aren't any women who haven't—"

"There are guys like that," Yaffa said, thinking aloud. "Guys who can't say no to a woman. If she's hot for him and wants him, he'll go along with it. That's the kind of face he has."

"What a great setup," Tzilla said with sudden bitterness. "Really wonderful. The man gets to screw around but at the same time bears no responsibility and carries no guilt." Yaffa regarded her in wonder. "You can even have a kid out of wedlock," Tzilla added, "no strings attached. What can I tell you, it's paradise! What a great guy he is!"

"I really do think he's a pretty great guy," Yaffa said. "Maybe his character's a bit weak, but he's got—they say he's a really good guy, like the kind who helps people out."

"We've heard all about it. I'm sure he's a real saint," Tzilla muttered, pressing the doorknob and entering the room. She slammed the door shut without waiting for Michael and Yaffa.

What's her problem?" Yaffa asked, shaking her ponytail. "She's become some sort of man-hater on us. What's going on? Has she been having problems with Eli?"

Michael shrugged his shoulders. "Who hasn't?" he said, though his meaning was unclear. He opened the door and waited for Yaffa to pass inside. He, too, had noticed Tzilla's unusually ugly mood and, lately, Eli's restiveness. Although he was very involved in their marriage, their lives, their relations with their children—after all, he had been their principal matchmaker and godfather to their eldest son—he did not dare ask them anything directly. At best he would say to Eli Bachar, "How are things?" and gaze at him intensely with the kind of look intended to make Eli squirm and ask, "What?" But lately Eli had simply dodged his stares. Before going on vacation, Michael had twice invited Eli out for a quick cup of coffee down at the corner, just the two of them, and had asked, "What's happening?" and "How are you doing?" with great feeling, and he had felt certain Eli understood he was really taking an interest, had hoped to hear what was bothering him. But then, too, Eli had evaded him. Once he said, "Everything's fine. Why?" and the second time had even answered, "Not so great," but had held back any details and hastened to change the subject.

Yaffa is right, Michael thought now as he looked at Rubin. His face had a certain Bogartian severity, the kind that women supposedly love because in their eyes it is only a mask for potential gentleness. It was clear both from the quiet way Rubin had spoken to Yaffa the day before on his way out of police headquarters and from the way he had looked into her eyes until you could see her melting, that Rubin knew well the impression he made on women, though it was not clear whether he derived any special pleasure from that. There was a certain generosity in his eyes, which might have been vulnerability or weakness, but there was no escaping the powerful emotion that flowed from them.

"Are you generally in good health?" Michael asked. Rubin flinched, and cast Michael a look of surprise. "I mean, your heart, blood pressure, that sort of thing. According to this," Michael indicated a form he had removed from a manila envelope containing a signed statement by Rubin taken during the investigation of Tirzah's death, "you are fifty years of age, born in 1947. Is that correct?"

"Yes. I'll be fifty-one in another two months," he said, once again stretching his lips into a distorted smile, while his soft gray eyes suddenly clouded over. "Why are you interested in the state of my health?"

"It's a standard question," Michael explained. "We don't wish to put people under unnecessary strain, like with Matty Cohen."

"You people also believe Matty Cohen had a heart attack because of the investigation, and all the tension?" Rubin asked. "In his condition he shouldn't have agreed to undergo the investigation. I specifically told Zadik—oh, well, what does all that matter now?" Rubin waved his hand dismissively and looked with anticipation at Michael.

Michael did not respond; instead, he repeated his question, while pretending to give his undivided attention to the papers in front of him. Did Rubin have any special health problems?

"No. None," Rubin answered.

"Do you take any medications on a regular basis?"

Rubin flashed him a guarded look. "No, I don't. Sometimes I take an aspirin for headache or back pain, and something for allergies when the seasons change—I'm allergic to cypress trees—but nothing out of the ordinary. How does all this concern Zadik?"

"We're asking the same questions of everyone," Michael stated, "just as we asked everyone where exactly they were this morning when Zadik . . ."

"Yes," Rubin said distractedly. "Eli—is that the guy's name?—he already asked me that during questioning. That was considered an official interrogation, was it not? I told him I was right here, with Dr. Landau from B'tzelem, the human rights organization. We were working on the report for Friday's program. Don't you have that information?"

"Apparently I do," Michael said, mimicking Rubin's own distracted tone of voice. "But I don't have all the reports in front of me at this moment, I only have—" He dug around inside the manila envelope and fished out a small spiral notebook. "So I've been asked to question you again."

"I was here the whole time, as I told them," Rubin said.

"And you're certain—sorry for asking this again—you're certain that you had no contact from here with Benny Meyuhas?"

"Absolutely positive," Rubin answered, his body tense. "I wish I had—this whole situation is completely out of hand, believe me. I was looking for him like crazy before this, before they found Zadik. I wanted to tell him his production of *Iddo and Eynam* had been approved—that is to say, that he can complete it—but I couldn't find him anywhere. I haven't heard from him since yesterday. It just doesn't make any sense to me, I'm worried about him. I can't understand how he hasn't even called me, at the very least—"

"And you have no idea who this person was who allegedly took him away?"

"Why 'allegedly'?" Rubin asked, incredulous. "That's what Sarah said. She was there in the house, wasn't she?"

"Benny Meyuhas and Sarah have a very close relationship," Michael noted.

Rubin shrugged. "Who knows?" he said. "People say that the relationship between a director and his actors is always close."

"Oh, come on," Michael said, "we're not children here, you know what I mean."

"Are you asking me or telling me?" Rubin countered.

"I'm asking you," Michael said. "I'm asking you whether he spoke with you about this young woman, Sarah, and I'm asking you to tell me anything that comes to mind about the man who picked up Benny Meyuhas—who you think that could have been, even if there doesn't seem to be any grounding in fact for your ideas. And I'm also asking you about Benny Meyuhas's relationship with Zadik, and where you think he might be, because under the present circumstances he is not only a suspect, it's also possible that his life is in danger. You certainly understand that he is very shaky right now, that he could harm himself. You two are very close friends; this is no time to conceal things."

"That's true, we're very close friends. Even more than that," Rubin said. "We're brothers. Benny Meyuhas is my brother."

"You're speaking metaphorically, right?"

"A brother you've chosen to be your brother is often closer than a biological brother," Rubin said, lowering his gaze.

"You've known each other since you were kids," Michael stated, his eyes on a photograph in the right-hand corner of the corkboard. It was the same photo of a school field trip he had seen, framed, at Benny Meyuhas's house, featuring a youthful Benny and Rubin and a third friend, along with Tirzah.

"Since we were kids," Rubin said, following his gaze. "I'm an only child, Benny, too. My parents were old: Holocaust survivors. My father died when I was twelve. My mother is still alive. Benny's folks were old, too, I think one side of the family came from Turkey, and the other—I don't remember, maybe Bukhara. Things were pretty tough in his home. His parents didn't have any children, and after ten years of marriage his father took another wife and had three daughters with her. Then suddenly Benny's mother got pregnant and he was born. The father divided his time between the two houses and ran around trying to make a living to support two families. They were poor, we weren't. We had reparation payments from Germany, they got welfare. Benny would come to my house, I would help him with his homework. We played soccer, that's how it all started. We became inseparable."

"And what about Sroul?" Michael asked, gazing at the photograph.

After a long pause Rubin sighed. "Yeah, Sroul, too. Who told you about Sroul?"

Michael did not respond.

"We met Sroul when we were fourteen, in the ninth grade. He was . . . he came from a Revisionist household, his father had come from Iraq and married a Polish Jew; in Israel he was part of Menahem Begin's inner circle, a member of the Irgun . . . I don't remember exactly, I think he was in the Jewish Underground; wherever Begin was, he was there too. After that Sroul came along with us to the youth movement and the immigrant camps. Caused a big scandal in his house, they wanted him to be in the Beitar Youth Movement and all that. . . ." Rubin fell silent, then after several seconds, added, "But he doesn't live in Israel any longer."

"He left after the war," Michael said. "Because of his injury."

"He lives in Los Angeles, became ultra-Orthodox," Rubin said bitterly. "At first we kept in touch, but it's been years since . . ." Rubin's voice faded out but Michael waited in silence. "We haven't spoken in years," Rubin said.

"Only Tirzah did," Michael said simply, as if stating a fact. "She's the only one who kept in contact with him all these years."

"Tirzah!" Rubin said, astonished. "No way! What did Tirzah have to do with—"

"She was your girl, not just yours but Benny's and Sroul's too. That's her in this photograph, isn't it? The Three Musketeers and all that?"

"Sure, she was once, when we were young, but—"

"A month before her death, she visited the United States," Michael said. "We think she might have gone to meet him."

"No way!" Rubin said, visibly agitated. "She went for work, two weeks on a business trip. Most of the time she was in New York, she had meetings with producers—I don't know, I suppose she could have been on the West Coast too . . ." A note of caution crept into his voice. "I don't know the details of her trip, I never had a chance to talk to her about it afterward," he said.

"In fact, she spent three days in Los Angeles," Michael informed him. "We know this for sure. We have the details on her hotel and her meetings there," he said without altering the expression on his face; in actual fact, he had no such information. "Don't you think she would have met up with Sroul there?"

"No, I don't," Rubin said. "Do you want some more coffee?"

"Why don't you think so? Don't you think that if she'd gotten as far as Los Angeles—even if she was on business—she would have taken the time to try and find someone who had been so very important to her in her youth? In her place, wouldn't you have tried?"

"If that's true, she didn't mention it to me," Rubin said flatly. "Not to me, and not to Benny. Benny would have told me about it."

"Do you have Sroul's address?"

"Why are you so interested in him?" Rubin asked in a tone of wonder, though Michael thought he could discern a hint of agitation, too.

"It seems fairly natural that we would be interested in him, especially since the last person who saw Zadik alive was an ultra-Orthodox man whose skin was badly burned. It only seems natural to think it was your friend Sroul, don't you think?"

"That's impossible," Rubin said after a short silence. "Sroul didn't have any connection to Zadik, he never even met him. Why would . . . ? And if Sroul had come to Israel, don't you think we would have known about it?"

"I'm asking you that very question," Michael said. "That's exactly what I'm asking you: if he were to come to Israel, would he contact you or Benny Meyuhas?"

"There's no question about it," Rubin said. "I would know about it in advance. No question."

"Tell me," Michael said slowly. "Sroul's well-off, isn't he?"

"How should I—I think he's done well for himself, maybe in diamonds," Rubin said reluctantly. "He married an American woman, ultra-Orthodox, her father was in the diamond polishing business. They were rich. She, the eldest daughter, was born with some kind of birth defect; a paralyzed hand or something. I don't know all the details, but they married them off to one another because, well, she was the kind they had to find someone for."

"You've never met her?" Michael asked, surprised. "Didn't they invite you to their wedding?"

"No, I've never met her," Rubin said. "I met up with him only twice, years ago, in Los Angeles. He didn't even bring me to his home, I didn't understand why. That is, I *did* understand why. It was because he had a new life, he didn't want to remember who he had been before. It was strange between us, he . . . he wasn't the same person I'd known. He'd become this Orthodox Jew in the full sense of the word, saying blessings before taking a bite from a piece of fruit, or when he came out of the bathroom. You know what I'm talking about?"

Michael nodded. "When was the last time you saw him?" he asked.

Rubin thought for a while before answering. "Seventeen years, I think. I'm not sure," he said, shifting uncomfortably in his chair. "It's hard to keep in touch after so many years. We didn't even exchange greetings at Rosh Hashanah, or talk on the phone for that matter. I felt he wasn't interested in keeping in touch. That was the feeling he gave me. And he didn't like what I do for a living."

"Why not? Because of your politics? Is he politically right-wing?"

"Not exactly," Rubin said, restless. "He was . . . he became anti-Zionist. I mean, in his opinion he became a *true* Zionist, like the Neturei Karta sect, the ultra-ultra-Orthodox kind who don't think a Jewish state should even have been established in the Land of Israel before its time, before the arrival of the Messiah. Sroul said it was a profanity, that sort of thing. It was unbelievable. Suddenly someone you knew as well as you knew yourself was talking like some evil spirit had gotten inside him. I saw there was no sense talking to him. Our second meeting was a disaster."

"And what about Benny?"

"What about him?"

"Was he in touch with Sroul?"

"Not at all. Just like me. He met with him more often than I did, maybe four times, because Benny's stubborn and thought maybe he could change Sroul's mind. But they broke off contact ten years ago or so, and Tirzah, too."

"And yet," Michael said, glancing down at a pile of yellowing newspapers, journals, photographs, and cassettes stacked nearby, "and yet he was the one who financed the production of *Iddo and Eynam,* and you are the one who solicited the money from him, right?"

Rubin sat up straight in his chair. For a long moment he did not speak, then, clearly rattled, he regarded Michael. "That's . . . Benny can't ever know about that," he said, his voice choked. "I don't know how you got hold of that information, nobody in the world knew about it but Zadik and me. And Sroul, of course. Even Tirzah didn't know, and certainly not Benny or Hagar or anybody else. That was my secret with Zadik; Zadik was a man of his word, he would never have leaked that to you people. Benny's ego completely depended on the belief that finally his talents had been recognized. You think they would have ever let him do a project like this without outside funding?"

"But it wasn't seventeen years ago that you were in contact with Sroul, it was more like a year and a half," Michael stated dryly. "This isn't the time to hide things like that, and I am asking you to tell me exactly what and how, all the details. And for that purpose," he said as he placed a recording device on the table, pushed the play button, and stated the date, the hour, and the name of his interviewee, "I will record this conversation."

"You think the Orthodox Jew who visited Zadik was Sroul," Rubin said ponderously. "I can't say I didn't think of that, but I prefer—"

"I will ask you to tell me in detail how you made contact with him and what monies were transferred for the purpose of the production *Iddo and Eynam,"* Michael stated pointedly.

Rubin looked around as if hoping to gain time, though this time he did not try to offer refills on coffee. "Okay," he said at last, "I thought somebody had to help Benny express his full potential. He's fifty, like me. If a man can't do what he's been dreaming of all his life by the time he reaches fifty . . . you have no idea how many people he approached to produce the Agnon story and how many times he was rejected. I wanted—I'm telling you, Benny is like a brother to me. My only brother."

"Sroul, too, if brothers are measured in their willingness to come up with two million dollars," Michael noted.

"In that sense, yes," Rubin said. "I knew that if I asked him for the money, and if it was for a story by Agnon and not some of the usual political stuff or something too contemporary, that he'd give it."

"You met with him," Michael said as he consulted the spiral notebook in his hand, intentionally taking his time; he recalled exactly the dates marked in the secret files from Zadik's office, but he was listening to Rubin's heavy breathing and sensed the tension in his body even before Rubin stretched his legs. "You met with him exactly two years ago during Hanukkah, in Los Angeles."

"I went to his house," Rubin admitted. "Without phoning in advance. I waited for him, ambushed him really, I had the address from . . . from family of his in Israel, he had this relative in—never mind, I don't even remember. I knew he had five kids, I knew all along what was happening with him . . . you could say I'm the sentimental type, I couldn't accept the way he'd cut himself off. I don't take no for an answer, as you know from my work, from my program. My whole life, I've set my mind to something—anyway, I went there, waited for him, ambushed him, pleaded with him. He agreed. Even an ultra-Orthodox Jew can perform a good deed for a secular Jew! That's how he came to be the secret, silent producer. Nobody knew about him, our shadow producer. The agreement was that no one would ever know, and I had no intention of talking about it with anyone, but you already—I don't know how you found out—"

"You of anyone should know about that sort of thing," Michael said, indicating the pile of cassette tapes by the foot of the table. "Your work is also based on investigations, and you've been at it for a while. You yourself told me how you'd latched onto that doctor, and about the family of that Palestinian kid who was tortured."

"That's true," Rubin said with a sigh. "But I really didn't want Benny to know about this. Not Benny or anyone else because—you have to understand what a humiliation it is for a director of Benny Meyuhas's caliber to be dealing with the junk he does here. They've given him the worst: religious programming, entertainment, kids—all of it. And once in a few years a film, usually a documentary, something neutral, meaningless, and he's—"

"How did that happen?" Michael wondered.

"That's Israel Television for you," Rubin answered bitterly. "This isn't exactly Cinecittà here, this place has really come down in the world. . . . Benny started working for Israel's official television station right at its inception, and he had high hopes, he thought—at first he really did get to direct a few things, you can see for yourself in the archives, I even have a few of them—there was no video then, no video cameras, so I had them transferred to videocassettes just a few years ago. I can show you what a talented guy he is. But then little by little he got pushed aside, it's been years since . . . He wasn't capable of leaving, he wasn't the self-starting type. He needed security, he'd pretty much given up; he was just sitting around waiting to retire. You can't imagine how happy he was when Zadik called him in to inform him about *Iddo and Eynam*. Suddenly he'd reverted to what he'd been once, like when we were young, it was—"

"So he had no reason to bear a grudge against Zadik?" Michael asked.

"None whatsoever," Rubin insisted. "On the contrary. I've already told you and I've told the district commander, Shorer, and I've told the police commissioner himself: no one in the world knows Benny better than I do. It's not just that he could never harm another human being; he wouldn't even hurt a fly! He didn't have any reason to kill Zadik, it makes no sense for him to do something like that. There's no way that Benny's a murderer, he'd be incapable in any situation. He'd prefer to kill himself before killing anyone else, in fact—well, anyway, in light of the circumstances and everything you know about him, I guess I can tell you that he did try to commit suicide once. He swallowed pills because he thought he was about to be fired. He almost succeeded. You have no idea how worried I am about him right now because—" The telephone rang, putting a stop to his nervous prattle. Rubin fell silent and wiped his face; he stared at the phone, shrugged his shoulders, and let it continue ringing. "In any case, it's not Benny," Rubin said to the room at large. "If he calls, it will be to my cell phone."

"Who exactly was responsible for . . . failing to make use of Benny's talents, or, as you see it, for his humiliation?" Michael asked.

"There's no one person," Rubin said after a long moment of silence. "Certainly not Zadik, if that's what you're hinting at. It's more a matter of the state of the world today and the powers that are at work in it, not really about specific people here at Israel Television. It's a question of ratings and money and compromises and power struggles and the nature and meaning of this medium—television—which has so much power, both to destroy and sometimes to build. And it's about what's happened to how Israel sees itself, and what Israel thinks about literature and art, about the writers Bialik and Agnon. And it's about the fact that Israel Television has become so closely aligned with the government, which wants to believe that most Israelis are stupid and soulless. It's a good thing that the current director general of the Israel Broadcasting Authority was not in charge when the money came in, he never would have given it—he would have confiscated it and used it for some *grand spectacle*, a big variety show. Or some big Hanukkah party. Oh well, I guess it's stupid to expect—after all, there's no real affinity between television and art in the commonly accepted meaning of the terms."

"Really?" Michael asked. "Do you really believe that? On principle? What about the BBC? What about people like Dennis Potter?"

"No, of course you're right," Rubin answered, then added, sadly: "Television can certainly be an incubator for great art. The problem is what's become of us, and television is the symbol, the place where you can sense it most clearly, the nation's conscience. Anyone sitting here like me can see it: our conscience has totally calcified."

There was silence for a moment, then Rubin said quietly, "I don't know why I'm telling you all this, it's all obvious. Did you learn anything new from what I've just said?"

"Zadik ran Israel Television for the past three years," Michael said, "but before him there were—"

"It didn't work," Rubin declared. "People want to survive in the system, they can't push for a production that uses up the Drama Department's entire budget. They told him to do something less . . . less bombastic; that was one of the terms they used to describe it. They told him, 'Adapt a short novel, some contemporary short story, something like what Uri Zohar did with *Three Days and a Child* by A. B. Yehoshua, or Ram Levi's *Khirbet Khaza'a*. A short film for television, thirty, forty minutes tops.'"

"That didn't suit him?"

"Actually, it did, and he made a few attempts: a story by Yaacov Shabtai, an independent screenplay. I can show you. But his dream was—" Rubin opened a side drawer in his desk and removed three cassettes held together with a rubber band. "This is the unfinished material, I'm keeping several copies of it."

"*Iddo and Eynam,*" Michael pondered aloud. "Ultimately, it's the story of a love triangle. One woman and two men who compete with one another in every sphere."

"You're familiar with the text?" Rubin asked, dubious. Michael nodded. "It's probably been a while since you read it," Rubin said. "If you read it now, you would read it differently. In any event, Benny saw it in a completely different way, in his eyes it was a story of . . . you know? He wrote something about it, let's see if I can find it—" He emptied the drawer. "I'll find it," he assured Michael. "He sees it as a story of Eastern Jewish heritage and how civilization—the power of the intellectuals, the academics—has suppressed the originality, the spontaneity, the spirit and the sentiment of the people. That sort of thing. He thinks that Zionism made a huge mistake by aligning itself with Western civilization. But if you ask me what I really think, I'll tell you it was the mystery, the conundrum, the depth of the story that caught his eye from a visual standpoint. He simply wanted to deal with the greatness of it. . . ." Rubin's voice slowly faded. He shrugged instead of attempting to explain.

"Allow me, for a moment," Michael said slowly, "to be conventional."

"Be my guest," Rubin said. "Would you like some water?" Without waiting for an answer, he rose from his chair and pulled a bottle of water from under his desk, along with two Styrofoam cups. "It could be refreshing," he said, then chuckled softly. "I don't mean the water, I mean that if you don't ask me some kind of conventional question, you'll totally ruin my stereotypes about the police."

"We're talking about a man who for the past few years lived with a woman you loved your entire life, a woman who was once your wife but who abandoned you. That didn't affect your relationship with Benny Meyuhas?"

"No," Rubin said. "I keep hearing that question over and over these past few days, ever since Tirzah . . . is no longer with us. There hasn't been a policeman or a doctor or a colleague who hasn't asked it, either directly or indirectly, it's really amazing how . . . how unimaginative people can be. Truly, people can only imagine themselves, their own lives. They can't fathom that human beings are varied, different, that they think or feel in ways different from their own."

"There were no strains in your relationship at all?"

"I can't explain it," Rubin said, fatigued. "I have no explanation. Do I need one? I loved them both, Benny and Tirzah. My marriage to Tirzah ended because of things between the two of us, which I have no desire to discuss right now, and in any event you've undoubtedly heard . . . I saw you talking with Niva, and she doesn't exactly keep the matter a secret," he added bitterly.

"You're referring to the boy?" Michael asked.

"Tirzah didn't know about that, I *hope* she didn't know about it, I only wanted . . . I wanted to save her the grief." It seemed as though Rubin's cheeks suddenly sank, that his face had caved inward in pain. "But there were other matters. You stand there facing your wife, time after time she wants to know. She's heard rumors, she's seen things, she's felt things. You answer. You lie, of course you lie, what else are you going to do? In the end you get to the point where even when you *haven't* done anything . . . She asks you where you've been, with whom, when . . . in a line of work like mine, try explaining that you weren't . . . After all, I'm a man with a past, and Tirzah, I can understand . . . being in the position of the suspicious wife who spies on her cheating husband, well, there's something humiliating about all that, that role didn't suit her. In the end we split up, we couldn't find another way. So then . . . Benny had always loved her. I prefer . . . I preferred that she be with someone who really loved her. He'd remained faithful to her all through the years, without hope or expectations, he simply never married, even though he had plenty of opportunities." Rubin's voice faded to nothing, but Michael remained silent until he resumed. "He had girlfriends, women, but nothing ever worked out. He waited and waited, and in the end he got Tirzah. I've already told you, he's not a flexible person. He can't compromise. On anything. He prefers having nothing at all to compromising in order to survive. This isn't something he'll tell you himself, but I know what I'm telling you is true. I know the man. Believe me, he hasn't harmed anyone."

"What about Sroul?" Michael asked.

"What about him? If he's in Israel, I don't know anything about it. He hasn't made contact with me."

"According to our records," Michael said on a hunch, pretending to read from the spiral notebook, but in fact watching Rubin tense up from the corner of his eye, "he entered Israel two days ago, the day after Tirzah was killed."

"Maybe he wanted to come to the funeral," Rubin said. "I have no idea how he would have known about it, maybe from the newspaper—but I didn't see him there, at the funeral. You can check the video, since the funeral was filmed—"

"Did you inform him about Tirzah?"

"The truth? No, I didn't," Rubin said, looking very guilty. "I didn't have time. I didn't manage it—"

"But somehow it seems he heard about it."

"Maybe from Benny," Rubin said, openly doubtful. "I don't see how . . . Benny wasn't in touch . . . but maybe if Tirzah was in touch with Sroul, then Benny might have phoned him."

"Why, in fact, was she in contact with Sroul?" Michael asked.

"No idea," Rubin responded. "I swear. Maybe to get money from him to finish the film up. Don't forget, she was in effect Benny's wife. I think she loved him, too."

"Did she know that the funding for the film had come from Sroul?"

"No way," Rubin answered emphatically. "No chance, she didn't know a thing. But maybe she got it into her head. Wait a minute," he said as he looked at his watch and turned up the volume on the monitor. "I'd like to see this, not on the screen but live. Come with me downstairs to the studio if you want to or if you have to. They're making the announcement about Zadik, and Hefetz will speak. I want to watch it in the studio. Why not join me if you're planning to stick around?"

They stood waiting for the elevator, but Rubin quickly grew impatient and was about to take the stairs when the elevator arrived, and Rubin flung open the narrow door. Inside stood Hefetz, bare from the waist up, just shoving his arm into the sleeve of a dark blue shirt. Next to him stood a wild-haired, blushing young woman, a man's dark suit jacket flung over her shoulder and a makeup kit in her hand. "First put your shirt on," they heard her saying before Rubin waved the elevator on and closed the door.

"Let's take the stairs, that thing's only got room for two people anyway," he said to Michael as they ran down the stairs. Out of breath, he added, "That wasn't what you think, if you thought Hefetz was fooling around. He's going on air, he was getting dressed, she was putting his makeup on, that's the way it happens sometimes in an emergency, you get dressed on the way." When they reached the ground floor Rubin turned toward the canteen, stopped at the doorway, and watched the monitor hanging there. The canteen was nearly empty except for two tables in opposite corners: at one sat a group of workers in blue overalls eating quietly, and at the other, Natasha and Schreiber watching a soundless monitor broadcasting the five o'clock Channel Two news. As the broadcaster mouthed his lines, a picture of Benny Meyuhas appeared with the caption: BENNY MEYUHAS, DIRECTOR. THE POLICE REQUEST PUBLIC ASSISTANCE IN LOCATING HIM. When she spied Rubin, Natasha let her small hand drop from her chin and rose from her chair, but he signaled her to wait. "Later," he called to her quietly. She returned to her chair and sat down and only then nodded hello to Michael.

"If the canteen is that empty, and there are still doughnuts to be had, then the situation really is awful," Rubin said as he walked slowly toward the stairs. "This is where you really get the feel for what's going on—the canteen is the heart, the very center, of this place. Everything happens here. Everything. Since Israel Television began. See that wall over there? It was built while we sat here eating. I remember it like it was yesterday, Zadik—" Suddenly he coughed as though choking, and his eyes filled with tears. He slowed his steps, and Michael followed him to the studio.

Rubin instructed Michael to take up a position in the lighting technicians' room, where he stood sandwiched between the computer and the desk and watched through the glass partition. The communications minister sat in the studio, having her face made up; Hefetz sat to her right, nervously tightening his dark blue necktie. Karen, the anchorwoman, sat to the left of the minister, who was now answering a question: "Israel Radio and Israel Television do not stop broadcasting except on Yom Kippur," she responded fervently. "Shutting down Israel's official television station in the event of a disaster—and murder is certainly a form of disaster—would only be giving in to . . ."

Michael had left the lighting technicians' room and gone to stand in a corner of the control room just as the director was saying, first to himself and then into a microphone, "Come on, get her out of there already, we're done with her, Karen, tell her, 'Thank you very much, now shut your face.'" That was why Michael failed to hear the end of the communications minister's sentence. "Ready with camera two," Tzippi the assistant producer said, her hand on her huge belly, rubbing.

"Someone turn on the upper monitor! Ready with camera one, Danny," the director shouted. Erez, the editor, stood silently in the back. He shot an openly critical look at Danny Benizri, who had come racing into the control room, torn off his sweater, shoved his arms into a black shirt he removed from a hanger, and turned his face to the makeup artist, who was on her way out of the room. She frowned—"You've already been made up," she said—but powdered his forehead nonetheless. "He thinks he's some American movie star," Erez muttered to himself. "Runs around all day, shows up at the very last minute, does his little striptease, undress and dress, undress and dress." "Are we finished with the videocassette?" asked a young man sitting at the video machine as he switched cassettes. No one answered him.

"Ready camera two, Hefetz," the director said. Hefetz felt for the transmitter behind his ear through which he could hear the instructions and took a sip from his cup. The atmosphere in the studio reminded Michael of an operating room or a command room in wartime. It's easy to forget that no lives depend on what happens here, he thought to himself as his eyes carefully scanned the people in the room, all of whom were tense and nervous and wasted no words. "Thirty seconds . . . final words 'can continue . . . cannot continue,' ten seconds on the word," said the producer to Karen. "Can I have a profile over the window?" the director shouted. "I told you, get her out of there already," he repeated, angry that the interview with the communications minister had not yet ended.

Three television cameras were pointed at Hefetz, and in spite of the fact that the makeup artist had applied more powder to his forehead and chin just before the lights went on, his face was shiny with perspiration. On one side of the monitor Michael watched still photos of Zadik flash one after the other from a prepared videocassette, pictures from his childhood and his youth, pictures of him in the white dress uniform of the Israel Navy, a picture of him in the news studio. In the background Hefetz's shaky voice could be heard: "Today we have suffered a great loss. A terrible loss. For me, this is a personal loss. I have been together with Shimshon Zadik from the beginning of his career as a junior reporter through his job as editor of the News Department"—on the screen appeared a photograph of Zadik leafing through papers and talking on the telephone at the head of the conference table in the newsroom—"all the way up to the position he held for the past three years as director of Israel Television. Shimshon Zadik was a man of vision who enjoyed everyone's trust and confidence." Behind Hefetz there appeared a photograph of Zadik shaking hands with two men in jeans and polo shirts, underneath which ran the caption, SHIMSHON ZADIK, DIRECTOR OF ISRAEL TELEVISION. One of the men had a false smile, as though he was making an effort not to let the cigarette between his lips fall to the ground; the other had removed a video camera from his shoulder and the caption changed: SIGNING OF AGREEMENT WITH TECHNICIANS' UNION. At that moment Michael's attention was caught by the entrance of Elmaliah the cameraman into the studio. He noticed with astonishment the huge tray of doughnuts Elmaliah carried in one hand, and the single doughnut he was shoving into his mouth with the other, oblivious to the anxiety and shock of everyone else in the room. "I have taken it upon myself to replace Zadik temporarily, until an official appointment can be made," Hefetz was saying, Zadik's face framed in black behind him. "I pledge to continue his path and his creed . . ." Elmaliah nodded and, with a full mouth, said, "Got his wish, didn't he, this is what the guy's always wanted."

"Shut up, fool," Niva whispered from the doorway of the control room, wiping her eyes. "Don't you have any respect for—"

"What's the problem?" Elmaliah protested. "Like I said something so terrible?" He looked around, wiped his lips on the back of his hand, and set the tray on the counter behind which Erez the editor was sitting. "Okay, I didn't notice," he said after stealing a glance at Michael. "But it doesn't mean anything, does it?"

Erez seemed about to say something, but just then Eli Bachar entered the control room and scanned it until his eyes met those of Michael, who made his way over to him. "We found Benny Meyuhas," Eli Bachar said quietly. "They're waiting for you upstairs." All eyes followed them out of the room as they left, and no one said a word.

# CHAPTER TWELVE

On the stairs, on their way to the entrance of the building, Eli Bachar managed to recount to Michael how he had been standing there by chance ("I let Sasson go home, his wife was home alone with the flu and he's been here since this morning, he promised her he'd be home by eight to light the Hanukkah candles with the kids, and it was already a quarter to eight. So I let him go and I was standing there explaining to Bublil who was allowed to enter the building and who was allowed to leave, you wouldn't believe what a pressure cooker it was around there—we're holding all these people here, the staff of Israel Television, from eleven o'clock this morning, just like you said, nobody coming or going, and even though we've brought them sandwiches and stuff, well, they've got plans, they want to get out of here"); and how the taxi had stopped in front of the door and a short man in a heavy khaki army jacket and beret had stepped out of it. "I was just, like, glancing outside, not really thinking about anything, not really paying attention, just watching how he paid the driver and looked toward the front door of the building. Then he caught sight of the death notice about Zadik and turned completely white, really frightened, you would think he hadn't known a thing about it," Eli Bachar whispered to Michael as they stood near the security officers' station in the foyer. "You should've seen his face when he saw the picture of the religious guy," Eli Bachar said, referring to the drawing that police artist Ilan Katz had composed according to Aviva's muddled description, which they had hastened to post everywhere, including next to the death notice at the entrance to Israel Television. "He walked up close and touched it; he looked like someone had whacked him on the head with a club. And I'm looking at him through the glass window, and it's not registering who I'm looking at until suddenly it dawns on me. I figured out who he was even before the security officer, who had his back to the entrance and hadn't even noticed him. So this Benny Meyuhas just strolls in like, like he hasn't done a thing wrong, like he hasn't been missing or anything and nobody's been searching for him. What can I tell you, I think the guy's a bit of a wacko, totally out of it."

While Eli Bachar continued talking quietly, Michael contemplated the expression on Benny Meyuhas's face from a distance. Meyuhas was standing just inside the building, near the entrance, handcuffed and surrounded by policemen and security guards; he was staring straight ahead as though looking at nothing. Just then Arye Rubin dashed in from the control room, nearly knocking them over as he pushed into the throng toward Benny. "Are you crazy? Take these things off him!" he shouted, grabbing the handcuffs. "What's going on here? He's no criminal!" Rubin placed his hands on Benny's shoulders. "Benny," he said, "what's happened to you? Why didn't you . . . Where have you been?" He peered into Benny's face as if able to gauge what he had been through. Benny Meyuhas was leaning against the wall next to the security guards' station, his face averted; he did not answer, and avoided looking at his good friend. In fact, he looked at no one, his eyes half closed and the expression on his face one of extreme fatigue. If he had not been leaning against the wall, or if the guards had not been holding him up, it seemed he would simply collapse.

"Are these handcuffs absolutely necessary?" Arye Rubin protested. No one paid him any attention, partly because at that very moment Hagar came racing down the stairs. It seemed that the rumor that Benny Meyuhas had been found had spread through the building, and she had rushed to see him. She spread her arms to embrace him, but the look on his face caused her to hang back. She did not touch him but said, "Benny, Benny, where have you been? Where did you disappear to? Are you okay? Why didn't you—"

Michael followed Benny Meyuhas's gaze as it rose to the monitor. Hefetz's face was being broadcast in close-up, a photo of Zadik bordered in black in the upper right-hand corner of the screen. Hefetz was saying, ". . . the decision not to suspend Israel Television broadcasts is due in part to the devotion and courage of employees at all levels, who have decided to honor and acknowledge Shimshon Zadik—may his memory be a blessing—by following his example, by continuing along the course he charted, by upholding his motto: You cannot stop the news."

Benny Meyuhas's eyes blinked rapidly. He lowered them from the screen, then shut them. He grimaced, a look of disgust on his face. The picture on the screen had changed, and under the caption WANTED was a police composite sketch of a man in ultra-Orthodox garb, while a broadcaster droned in the background: "The Israel Police request assistance in locating the whereabouts of the man shown in this picture. He is approximately feet five nine inches tall, medium build, with brown eyes. His hands and arms show burn marks . . ." Someone lowered the volume.

Eli Bachar was standing quite close to Benny Meyuhas, and he gently led Arye Rubin and Hagar away from him, ignoring their pleas to remove the handcuffs. Rubin appealed directly to Michael. "What is he, some criminal you have to detain?"

Distracted, Michael ignored him by turning his head as if he had not been spoken to.

Rubin's face was confused, as though he had lost his confidence in the secret covenant he had imagined existed between Benny Meyuhas and himself. He fell silent and stopped protesting against the policemen who were pushing him away from his friend.

"Where are you taking him?" Hagar cried out as she ran after Eli Bachar and Sergeant Bublil on the stairs. They were quickly ushering Benny Meyuhas to the second floor; Hagar ran past them, bursting into the newsroom and shouting, "Benny's here, he's fine, they're taking him to Hefetz's office for questioning." At once people sprang to their feet and raced to the doorway: Zohar, the military correspondent; David Shalit, the correspondent for police affairs; Niva the newsroom secretary; and Erez, the editor.

"Benny!" David Shalit managed to shout before they led Benny Meyuhas into the office of the newsroom department head, which had been temporarily commandeered for interrogations. The newsroom staff that had gathered stared at the policemen in silence. Hagar and Arye Rubin stood by the office door. "Should we wait here?" Rubin asked.

Michael shrugged his shoulders. "No need," he said. "This could take quite a while."

"If that's the case, I'm going up to the editing rooms," Rubin stated. "If you need me, I'm in the vicinity." He hesitated for a moment, then added obstinately: "In any event, you can give me a call."

Michael nodded vaguely and entered Hefetz's office. Sergeant Bublil looked at him and asked, "Would you like a cup of coffee, sir? Three teaspoons of sugar, right?"

"No, no, not for me, thanks," Michael said; coffee suddenly had no taste without a cigarette. Then after glancing at Benny Meyuhas's face, he said, "On second thought, bring in a nice big cup of coffee with milk," to which Bublil nodded as he left the room, returning from the newsroom a minute later with a large, steaming mug. Bublil set it on the desk, removed three packets of sugar from his pants pocket, and placed them alongside the mug. From his jacket pocket he extracted a spoon and laid that, too, on the desk before going out to the hallway to deter curious onlookers from besieging the office.

Eli Bachar seated Benny Meyuhas in the chair facing the desk and without saying a word pointed to the mug of coffee and removed the handcuffs. He went to stand in the corner of the room, near the door. Michael sat across from Benny Meyuhas, who tore open each packet of sugar, one by one, spilling the contents of each into the mug, stirring slowly, without raising his eyes.

"Where have you been?" Michael asked. Benny did not so much as glance at him.

After a long silence, Michael asked, in the grave, quiet voice one would use for a terminally ill patient who had disobeyed his doctors' instructions, "Don't you have anything to tell us?" Benny Meyuhas stared at his coffee mug and said nothing.

"You know, in the end you'll talk," Michael said, struggling to maintain his composure in spite of the anger that Benny Meyuhas's passivity provoked in him. "Don't you think this is a waste of time?"

It appeared as if Benny Meyuhas had not even heard the question. His hands were wrapped around the mug of coffee, and he leaned over it, inhaling the vapor without raising it to his lips.

"For thirty-six hours you've had the whole world concerned,"

Michael said, as Benny moved the mug to his mouth slowly and sipped. "Quite a few people were worrying about you. At the very least, we want to know where you were."

Benny fixed his gaze on the darkened window behind Michael's back and remained silent.

"You don't want to tell us where you've been?" Michael asked, adding, "We want to know, for example, whether you were in the building this morning, or next door at the String Building, or anywhere in the vicinity, for that matter."

Benny Meyuhas did not remove his gaze from the blackened window. Aside from rapid blinking, there was no sign that he had heard what had been said.

"Are you aware that Zadik was murdered?"

Silence.

"Didn't you hear about that?" Michael asked.

Benny Meyuhas said nothing, but the twitch in his eye and the sudden shiver that passed through him made it clear that he knew. It was impossible to know whether he had only learned about it upon seeing the death notices.

"Do you know where and how he was murdered?"

Benny Meyuhas covered his face with his hands, rubbed his pale cheeks, closed his eyes, then opened them and stared once again at the window. Lightning illuminated the darkened skies, followed by a single burst of thunder, and for a moment the bluish light given off by the round neon lamp was blurred, imparting a jaundiced hue to his pale face.

To Michael it was clear that Meyuhas was aware of his surroundings, perhaps even more intensively so than everyone else. He understood from the strange dichotomy between the frequent changes in Meyuhas's expression and his slow hand movements that this highly sensitive man was gripped by great turmoil or extreme anxiety. "All right," Michael said with a sigh, "for the time being I am going to have to put you under arrest. We're going to bring you in for questioning under oath. You have the right to request legal representation." He paused for a moment, waiting to see Meyuhas's reaction. Benny Meyuhas seemed completely at ease, and Michael added, gently, "I'm sorry. If you were willing to talk, to cooperate, we could . . ." Again he looked into the face of this man who looked as though his soul had taken up residence elsewhere, far away.

Eli Bachar waited for Benny Meyuhas to return his mug to the table, then handcuffed his wrists and led him downstairs to the police van. Michael accompanied them to the ground floor, where Hagar placed herself in front of Eli Bachar and said in a shaky voice that rose suddenly to a hysterical shriek, "If you take him, I'm coming with you, I don't care what you—"

"You are welcome to come along," Michael said, cutting her off. "Your turn would come up sooner or later anyway. But just take into consideration the fact that you'll be interrogated now, too."

"You people don't scare me," Hagar grumbled, frustrated at being denied a good excuse for an outburst. She rushed over to Benny, nearly grabbing his arm, but one look at the somber expression on his face caused her to lower her hand. The van was already waiting outside; Bublil escorted Benny Meyuhas into it. Hagar bent over as if to enter the van as well, but Bublil stopped her, casting a questioning look in Eli Bachar's direction. Eli waved his arm to say it was all right, and Bublil, with a shrug, climbed into the van and sat in the driver's seat.

In the hallway, on his way to the canteen, Michael saw Hefetz and Natasha, deep in conversation. Hefetz extended his hand to touch Natasha's cheek, as if trying to remove a mark or a crumb in a familiar, friendly manner. Natasha brushed his hand away. As he drew near, Michael could see the anger in the burnished blue of her eyes, could hear the venom in her words: "Ah, I get it. You're taking *care* of me, is that it? Looking out for me? Who else would take care of me, if not for—" At that moment she caught sight of Michael and fell silent.

Hefetz, whose back was turned to the hallway, turned his face to Michael, casting him a look of utter helplessness. "I don't know what to do with her," he complained, as if speaking about a child who was their mutual responsibility.

Natasha grabbed a lock of her hair and gave it her full attention. "You get it?" she said to Michael. "He's taking care of me, looking after my well-being, making sure nothing bad happens to me. You get that?" Then she added, without looking at Hefetz, "Well, if that's the way it is, why doesn't he just bring me home with him? How would that be? At least there, nobody would lay a hand on me, and he'd be looking after me, right?"

"That's not funny," Hefetz said in protest. "I really *am* concerned with your welfare. Why don't you believe that? Why do you treat me like I'm some kind of . . . of criminal?" He appealed to Michael: "She doesn't believe me, she thinks I just want to clear my conscience or that I only act in my own self-interest. But really, like I told you before, I just want to know what I can do. . . . I hear about this slaughtered sheep hanging in front of her door, at night, twenty-four hours later, and even then only by chance, thanks to a couple of policemen I overheard talking. Nobody thinks to tell me these things, and she? She treats me like a stranger. When all is said and done, what do I want? I know her so well, like . . . we're so close . . . we're . . ."

"Hefetz," Natasha said quietly, emphasizing each syllable. "I've told you a thousand times, Hefetz, there's no more 'we.' There's me and there's you, each of us completely separate. You know that expression, Two of us together, each of us apart? Well, that's us to a tee. Believe me, not just us. And if you, if you think that—" She turned to Michael. "He says he loves me," she said with wonder mixed with open desperation. "So what does that mean? What does it mean to love somebody?"

Hefetz shifted his startled gaze from Natasha to Michael. "Natasha . . . ," he said in warning, "Natasha—"

"Don't *you* . . . I'm asking you what it means to love someone. Answer me." To Michael she said, "I'm asking you, too. Two men, older and smarter than I am, I'm asking you what it means to love somebody."

Michael said nothing, but looked at Hefetz, who was shifting his weight from foot to foot and wiping his brow. It seemed he was about to answer, but instead he merely said, "Natasha, do me a favor—"

"Does loving someone mean wanting the best for him?" she said, persistent. "Yes or no?"

Hefetz cleared his throat but said nothing.

"So you can help me. You can give me permission, you can help me. . . . I want to get that report on the air, that's the only thing—"

"Do you hear her?" Hefetz said to Michael, deeply disturbed. He took hold of Natasha's arm. "Don't you understand how dangerous it is right now?" He lowered his voice to a whisper. "After everything that's happened, can't you give up on that story about the ultra-Orthodox? Why are you hanging on to it? Do you really want to get involved with those people?"

"What?" Natasha said, shaking off his arm, her lips in a pout. "Because of a sheep's head? That's what's got you so uptight?"

"No, not only that," Hefetz said. "I mean, that too, that's pretty scary, at night, no? It's not frightening to come home and find that thing swinging over your front door? Of course that's scary, isn't it? But not just because of that sheep's head. It's because of Zadik, too. I saw him after he was murdered. Believe me, Natasha—" Hefetz's voice cracked.

"There's nothing to fear now," Michael said quietly, "since you're all being taken over to police headquarters. Nothing will happen to you between now and the time we take your testimonies."

"You're taking us *now*?" Hefetz exploded. "We have to go to police headquarters now? We're in the middle of—we have—" He nodded in the direction of the canteen, where the newsroom staff sat talking excitedly around three Formica tables that had been pushed together. "We have an urgent staff meeting, there's nowhere for us to meet since the police have—so this is the only place for us to sit and there are a few matters we have to—I haven't even decided who's going to run the News Department, I'm all alone now—Rubin isn't willing to fill in for me even temporarily, says he doesn't want any administrative jobs and there's nobody—" Michael shrugged, and extended his arm to invite Hefetz to enter the canteen. He followed Hefetz inside just as Niva was shouting, "We can't very well announce on the news that one of our colleagues has been arrested as a murder suspect, can we?"

"Calm down already," Erez grumbled. "Why are you shrieking like a little girl, don't you know anything? We won't use the word 'arrested,' we'll just say he's been detained. But we have to report it; do you think Channel Two is going to behave in a polite and friendly manner and just leave it out of their broadcast entirely?"

When they noticed Michael among them, they fell silent. For several long seconds they stared at him until Niva, shaken and hostile, dared to speak up. "Is it true that you've arrested Benny Meyuhas and that he's your main suspect?" Without waiting for an answer, she added, "I can't believe it! You've got to be completely blind to see that Benny Meyuhas—he wasn't even here, how could you?"

"We've got to get a few things wrapped up quickly," Hefetz said. "They want to take us to police headquarters to give testimony."

"Now?!" Erez protested. "After they've been driving us nuts all day? As if this trauma, this disaster with Zadik, wasn't bad enough—what have we been doing here all day if not giving testimony?"

"What, are we suspects too?" Niva demanded to know. "Is everyone at Israel Television considered a suspect?"

Michael regarded her silently, then glanced at pregnant Tzippi, who sighed, spread her arms out on the table, and laid her head down on them. When his eyes met those of David Shalit, the correspondent for police affairs shot him a questioning look. Shalit stood from his place and approached. "I'd like to have a word with you, Chief Superintendent Ohayon." In a whisper he said, "I've got to know how many—"

"Forget about that for now, Davey," Hefetz said quietly. "Nobody's gonna talk to you about that right now, they've got . . . slightly more important matters to attend to. Wouldn't you say that's true?" he asked, turning to Michael. "How long do we have to wrap up?"

"Another half an hour or so," Michael answered after consulting his watch. "And I hope that we'll be finished by morning. That depends on how things develop."

"What about the late-night news?" Hefetz insisted. "You can't take the folks from the late-night news, somebody's got to be around for the broadcast."

"Prepare a list for me," Michael said. "Name all the people who are absolutely essential, but I mean essential, the ones that you can't do without, and we'll—"

"But that's almost all of us," Hefetz protested. "Erez, and the anchor and the late-night production assistant, and the researcher and the reporters—Danny Benizri and Rubin—and Niva—"

"I don't have to be here," Niva said.

"You draw up a list, and we'll come for those people with the van, after the late-night broadcast. I want to see that list. As for the others," Michael said, "they'll have to come with us now, no arguments. Anyone who doesn't come in at nine-thirty will be questioned after midnight. No problem."

A uniformed officer entered the canteen. "Sir," he said breathlessly, "we . . . wanted . . ." He indicated that he would prefer to speak to Michael outside the canteen.

Michael rushed over to him. "What is it, Yigael? Anything new?" he asked.

"A couple of things, sir," the policeman answered. "First of all, there's this guy at the entrance to the building with a special delivery for Hefetz. They wouldn't let him in, but he's got this envelope in his hand and he won't let anyone see what's inside. He says, 'I'm only giving this to Hefetz, that's what they told me, the editor told me.' So we decided to ask you, sir, if—"

"Hefetz," Michael called out, and Hefetz hurried over. "Tell him, Yigael, let him decide," Michael said to the policeman.

"I woulda let the whole thing go, sent the guy packing," the policeman said apologetically, "but he was so insistent, and I thought—"

"You did the right thing," Michael said. "In these situations you never know." In fact he was thinking about Natasha; he wondered whether those pages meant only for Hefetz were about her.

The policeman explained the matter to Hefetz as the three progressed together to the main entrance. Michael and Sergeant Yigael stood next to the stairway and watched as Hefetz approached the messenger, who was holding in one hand a scooter helmet and in the other a yellow envelope, which he handed over silently to Hefetz and then made to leave. "Hang on a minute, hang on," Hefetz called after him. "I haven't signed for this," he said, but the young man had already disappeared from view.

"What's the second thing you had to tell me?" Michael asked Yigael as he watched Hefetz holding the envelope as though weighing it. On their way back to the canteen, Hefetz began ripping it open. Michael considered asking him to open it in his presence, but the police sergeant distracted him when he said, "Sir, you'd better come with me to the second floor, where the newsroom is, we found something—They're waiting for you there."

A policeman was stationed at the entrance to the newsroom as well, while inside there were three members of the forensics team. "Yaffa will show you," one of them told him as he walked into one of the rooms. "It's in the third room down, in the room marked FOREIGN CORRESPONDENTS."

"We found it!" Yaffa informed him triumphantly. "What was it we said? That 'every time you touch something you leave a trace.' So here you are." She pointed with a finger wrapped in a silicone glove at the front of a light blue T-shirt spread over a computer printer standing under the window. "You see this stain?" she asked him. "Looks brownish, right? Well, that isn't brown, it's red. Someone tried cleaning it but didn't manage. Whoever it was didn't know you need cold water in order to clean blood at first." She smiled, clearly pleased. "They worked on it with boiling hot water, maybe from the teakettle"—she pointed at an electric kettle in the corner of the room—"or maybe from somewhere else. In any case, they tried to get rid of the stain with hot water, but all they did was turn the stain brown."

"You're sure that's blood?" Michael asked, hesitant.

"I'm not sure of anything," Yaffa answered. "That'll only be after we run some tests. But I'm willing to bet. When someone gets slaughtered like that, there's bound to be blood, and nothing can cover it all up."

"With you I don't place bets," Michael said as he bent down for a closer look at the shirt. "Every time I've made bets with you in the past, I've felt like—hey, what's written on the label of this shirt? This shirt is—"

"Excuse me, sir," Yaffa dared to interrupt. "This shirt is filled with signs. You could call it a miracle. First of all, if it's blood and if this shirt is connected to the crime scene—note I said 'if' twice—then it's sure not a woman."

"Why? Because the label says LARGE?"

"No, not necessarily. Plenty of women like loose-fitting shirts, big roomy shirts. Maybe that's another reason. But getting back to what I said about working on a bloodstain with boiling water—"

"Not every woman knows how to clean stains," Michael protested.

"Aha!" Yaffa said, openly triumphant. "Not every woman knows how to clean stains, and not every type of stain, but if we're talking about blood, well, that's a different matter. Every woman knows that blood comes off first of all with cold water. If you'd ever gotten your period, you would have known that too."

Michael raised his hands as if giving in. "Hmmmm, menstrual blood. If we're talking about the menstrual cycle, then I really can't—who am I to stand up to the cyclical forces of nature?" he said without smiling. "But what about the size?"

"As you yourself said, sir, it's a men's size LARGE," Yaffa confirmed. "But here we're in luck. If it's connected to this case, then we've had a lucky break. If this turns out to be Zadik's blood, then we've got a real lead, because this shirt is unique. I don't think you can find it in Israel. Maybe one of the fancier shopping areas in Tel Aviv, Gan Ha'ir or Kikar Hamedina. Look," she said, showing him the label. "See that? Brooks Brothers, made in the U.S.A., really expensive store. It's only for men prepared to pay a lot for everyday clothes. I happen to know about it—I'm telling you, you never know what you remember and when you'll make use of it one day: not long ago there was this woman at work who brought a pair of socks in for her boyfriend. But the guy's married, and he asked her, 'How am I supposed to bring a pair of Brooks Brothers socks home with me? What am I supposed to tell my wife? I mean, she knows I wasn't in America, so who could possibly bring me something like this?' Anyway, the fact that he was such a coward about the whole thing really made her mad, and she decided not to give him the socks—she'd brought him three pairs—so instead she gave them to Rami. You know Rami, don't you? I heard this story by chance. I'll bet you that the person this shirt belongs to has at least another one, along with a few pairs of Brooks Brothers socks. If you find somebody with Brooks Brothers T-shirts or socks, well, we'll be on our way to wrapping up this case, you know what I mean? You can only get these things in America; a present for yourself or someone you love. You should know that, I mean, in life in general. And look what else I found," she exclaimed, waving a tiny, sealed plastic bag in front of him that held a single gray hair. "It was on the shirt. Inside it. If this is blood, and if this shirt is connected to the scene of the crime, then this hair could be the key to the whole case."

"Who found this shirt?" Michael asked.

"Yigael did, right here between the computer table and the wall, all bunched up. What do you say about that?"

"Good job, Yigael," Michael said, causing the sergeant to blush.

"Who's been in this room today?" Michael asked Yaffa. "Have you checked it out yet?"

"Excuse me, sir," Sergeant Yigael interjected from his spot near the door, "but everyone's been in here. Turns out that the whole staff comes in and out of the foreign correspondents' office, not just the foreign correspondents themselves: graphic artists, and people who need the computer, and just about anybody who has business in the newsroom. They all come in here."

"So you haven't checked who exactly was in this room today?" Michael asked.

"Sure we checked, sir, of course we did," Yigael said, slightly offended. "But . . . ," he said, hesitating, then fell silent.

"But?"

"But look at the list," he said as he removed a folded sheet of paper from his shirt pocket, which he then proceeded to unfold. "There are like thirteen people on this list that said they were in the room or that someone else said they were here. Look. And we haven't even finished yet, there were more people walking around, we only just got started because we only just found the shirt about half an hour ago . . . anyway, sir, Yaffa says that anybody could have come in, thrown the T-shirt behind the computer, and left immediately, and nobody would have known the difference."

Michael perused the list of names, which included the assistant producers Tzippi and Zivia, and Karen the anchorwoman, and Hefetz ("What business did Hefetz have there?" he asked the sergeant, who scratched his forehead. "I don't exactly know, sir, he says he only popped in for a second") and Rubin ("He came in looking for Hefetz") and Eliahu Lutafi, the correspondent for environmental affairs, and Elmaliah the cameraman, and Schreiber. Natasha had been there, and Niva, and even Zadik had passed through at around eight in the morning—in several instances Yigael had noted the times as well—and there were three names Michael did not recognize. "I haven't had a chance to talk to everyone yet," Yigael said, "but, say, Danny Benizri was in here with somebody, a cameraman, and they worked on something on the computer. You can talk to him, sir, he's in Editing Room 8, he's been sitting there for the past hour and he didn't want to—he says to me, 'If you people are going to shut me in here, at least let me work.' What was I supposed to do, put up a fight? He said, 'Call me when your boss gets here.' What could I say to that? Arye Rubin's there, too, in the editing rooms. He also said if you need him—"

Michael refolded the sheet of paper and, glancing at the sergeant, said, "Good job, Yigael. Now you've got your work cut out for you: I want you to fill in the missing information, find out exactly when—and for what reason—these people were in the foreign correspondents' room, and whether they noticed anyone else entering."

"Yes, sir," the sergeant answered, his round brown eyes shining brightly with the compliment.

"How long will it take for you to get the results?" Michael asked Yaffa.

"About the shirt? The blood?" Yaffa answered distractedly. "Not long, maybe by tomorrow already, but the hair will take longer, that's more complicated. You know how long it takes with DNA . . . I hope we'll have the results by the day after tomorrow, but we'll get the blood test back first."

"I'm going upstairs for a minute," Michael said. "If Eli Bachar or Balilty are looking for me, that's where I'll be."

Sergeant Yigael nodded vigorously, and Michael raced up the stairs, in part, perhaps, to test his breathing, to see whether the pressure he had felt in his chest over the previous few months, mainly when dashing up stairs—the chief reason his family doctor had insisted he quit, describing in lurid detail the effects of several lung diseases—had dulled or disappeared since he had quit smoking. Now it seemed as though the pressure had not decreased at all and that he could still hear a whistle in his breathing; he asked himself why he should suffer so, why he should give up smoking at all. Anyway, there was a NO SMOKING sign at the entrance to the editing rooms, so at least he was spared having to search for somewhere to smoke, or to break the rules, which he had done so often in the past.

Danny Benizri was sitting in front of an editing table, his black button-down shirt open to reveal a white T-shirt underneath. At the sound of the door opening he raised his face from the monitor and stopped the film; frozen on the screen was a picture of Esty, pregnant behind the wheel of the truck, her hand on her stomach, writhing in pain and gesturing to something or someone beyond the camera, while Rachel Shimshi, on her knees next to Esty in the truck, was tapping her cheeks. She was clearly rattled.

"This is the report about the wives of the laid-off workers for tonight's broadcast," Danny Benizri explained before being asked. "It's . . . it's really awful, what's happening there. This one," he said, pointing at Esty, "she lost her baby today. First pregnancy. Today's a terrible day, with everything that's happened. I just need another couple of minutes to finish." Michael approached the monitor for a better look at the picture Benizri was describing. "With everything that's happened through this whole affair," the reporter said, "I just don't understand how Rachel Shimshi could have let Esty come with her, pregnant like that. And it took her a while to get pregnant, too. Believe me, I'm well informed, I know this story from the inside. She had so much trouble, lots of fertility treatments, you name it. And for what? To lose the baby? That was the only reason Rachel Shimshi agreed to leave the truck. She took off the chains herself, put a stop to the whole operation. The other women didn't even know a thing about it. We called an ambulance, there was so much blood. Don't even ask what went on there. She'll be fine, but not the baby. What a huge mess from all this."

The telephone rang, and Benizri sighed. "Yes?" he answered, impatient. "Sorry, I thought it was my wife. . . . Okay, I'll be there right away."

"You're going somewhere?" Michael asked. "Because I was planning to ask you—"

"That was Hefetz," Benizri explained. "He told me to get down there right away, I've got to—he says it's urgent."

"It'll only take a minute," Michael said, "and we can leave together. When exactly were you in the foreign correspondents' room?"

Benizri, who was occupied with removing the cassette from the editing machine and turning it off, stopped what he was doing and gave Michael a confused look. "The foreign correspondents' room?" he asked with feigned innocence. "I wasn't there, no way. When? Who said that?" A moment later he remembered: "Oh yeah, I was there with the graphic artist, just for a little while around noon. I remember that now, because from there I dashed out for a bite to eat, I was famished. Why do you ask?"

"How long were you there?" Michael asked.

"Maybe twenty minutes. I was talking with the graphic artist and . . . not very long." Benizri placed the cassette into his travel bag and moved toward the door.

On their way to the elevator, Michael asked, "While you were there did a lot of other people enter the room?"

"As usual," Benizri said. The elevator door opened. "The foreign correspondents' room is not exactly a private place. Sure, people came and went. I think maybe even the correspondent for foreign affairs stepped in"—he smiled awkwardly at his own joke—"and so did the foreign news editor, and . . . I don't remember who else. We were standing over in the corner."

"Next to the computer?" Michael asked as they stepped into the elevator.

"Yeah, how did you know?" Benizri asked, surprised. "Why is that important?"

"And you didn't see anything special or unusual? Nothing strange?"

Benizri shrugged. "I didn't see a thing, strange or otherwise. Do you have any idea how many things I've been dealing with today?" The elevator stopped, and Michael followed him to the canteen. From the end of the corridor he could see Hefetz standing in the doorway. In one hand the acting director of Israel Television was holding a cup of coffee and in the other a yellow envelope. Hefetz cast a stern look at Danny Benizri and said, "Listen, Danny, I've just received—" He cut himself off when he noticed Michael.

"What? What did you just receive?" Benizri asked, glancing at the envelope.

"I . . ." Hefetz started, embarrassed. He loosened the knot in his tie, unbuttoned the top buttons on his shirt, and passed his hand over the gray chest hairs sticking up from his collar (he was not wearing an undershirt, and Michael made a mental note to verify his dress habits with someone in Wardrobe). "Not here, not like this, I didn't intend . . . but because of the police there's nowhere for a little privacy in this place."

Michael ignored the reproach in his voice. "It's not that there's no *physical* location for privacy, Hefetz, you've got to be more precise: it's that there's no more privacy at all, and that's that. Very simply, the director of Israel Television was murdered here this morning. I need to know what's in the envelope too, because it may be connected to this case."

Hefetz looked at him, disquieted. "I can promise you there is no connection," he said faintly.

"Okay already," Benizri said impatiently. "Tell us what this is all about, and let's get it over with. I mean, what could be so bad?"

"Fine," Hefetz said. "Don't say I didn't warn you." He handed the envelope to Benizri.

Danny Benizri opened the envelope and removed a stack of photographs. Unsuspecting, he looked at the first of them; a moment passed before he realized what he was looking at. He shoved the whole stack back into the envelope, looked around, and said, "God . . ."

"Exactly," Hefetz said. It seemed to Michael that he could detect a faint echo of pleasure in his voice, maybe a dash of schadenfreude. "That's just what I said. This is the last thing we needed right now."

"May I?" Michael asked as he reached for the envelope.

Danny Benizri moved his hand behind his back. "It's irrelevant, believe me," he demurred.

"There's no such thing as irrelevant," Michael said. "I am truly very sorry, but I must see what's in those photos."

"It's nothing . . . pictures of . . . how could intimate photos of me with a woman have anything to do with Zadik? Something to do with blackmail, I guess."

Michael extended his hand again, and this time Benizri placed the envelope in it.

Slowly, Michael removed the photos and looked at them. Danny Benizri scanned the corridor, terrorized, but for the moment no one was passing by.

"These certainly are intimate photos of you with a woman," Michael said. "But this isn't just any woman, and it's pretty clear who she is, don't you think?"

"Believe me," Danny Benizri said, pleading, "this has nothing to do with any of this, and it will only ruin everything. She . . . the minister . . . Mrs. Ben-Zvi . . . she had no intention . . . oh, my God, how could I not even have suspected . . ." He fell silent, watching Michael with a plaintive look on his face.

"If photos like these arrive here on the very day the director of Israel Television is murdered," Michael said, "and if they are used to blackmail a senior correspondent at Israel Television and the minister of labor and social affairs, then there is no way *not* to make a connection between these matters."

"There was only the photographs in the envelope," Hefetz said. "No note, no mention of blackmail."

"Who brought them?" Benizri asked.

"A guy with a motorcycle helmet or something," Hefetz explained. "Young guy. He gave the envelope directly to me, thank God."

"What do you mean, 'thank God'?" Benizri interjected, his hands shaking and his face pale. He retrieved the photos from Michael and looked quickly through them. "Don't you get it? If there are photos like these of us—of her and me—next to her house, in the lobby of the hotel, in—look at this! It's like they shot us with a telescope, right there in the room! How could they have done this so quickly? It's just . . . this'll be the end of me, and not just of me—"

Michael stuck his hand out again, and Danny Benizri handed over the photographs. "Black and white," Benizri said bitterly. "In black and white, a few in color. You know, for variety. What are you going to do?" he asked Hefetz. "Broadcast this on the evening news?"

"Are you asking that seriously?" Hefetz said, shocked.

"Of course," Benizri answered. "I don't know anymore."

"Are you nuts?" Hefetz protested. "What do you think I am? Do you think I'm running some lowlife rag of a newspaper, some—of course I'm not going to broadcast this! But I don't know what the big papers will do with this. With your luck, this could make the front page of *Yediot Ahronot* or something."

"I've got to make a phone call," Danny Benizri said in a whisper, beads of sweat gathering on his upper lip. "Excuse me, please," he said, turning away as he removed his cell phone from a pocket and dialed. "It's me," he said quietly before walking away.

Hefetz peered into the canteen. "Look at that," he muttered. "Quiet as a cemetery. You can't even open your mouth around here anymore, everything you say . . . I've never, ever seen the place looking like this, not even during the Yom Kippur War. And believe me, I've been around. This canteen's been here for as long as Israel Television. The wall over there was built while we sat here eating. In 1969, right after Israel Television got its start, there were two groups that kept apart from one another. There were class distinctions here, not like now: there were the Poles, who had only just come to the country after they'd been tossed out of Poland, disgruntled Communists with cigarettes constantly in their mouths. They walked around with their noses in the air, laughing and making fun of everything around them, snobs who had worked in the Polish film industry and thought they knew everything. But ultimately they were refugees. On the other side of the canteen were the Israelis. We were all young, we didn't know a thing . . . in the seventies I would arrive from the army, from reserve duty—I was an officer—and I would show up at the canteen and I wouldn't know where I belonged. I mean, who should I sit with? The young people or the editors? With the Poles or—none of them are left, the Poles. They died, they left. Who knows where they went. But there was always shouting, there was never quiet like there is today. You could never hear the monitor like you can right now, and nobody's asking for it to be turned down. I see they've put on some rerun, I asked them to find something for the time being. But I didn't think . . ."

Hefetz entered the canteen and regarded the two tables around which people were sitting, then raised his eyes to the monitor. Michael followed suit. "What, then, is your opinion on the role of the author?" a young interviewer was asking with exaggerated emotion, his bald head and round face shining. He touched his small, dark beard. Two panelists began speaking at the same time, then both fell silent. They looked at one another, embarrassed, then one of them, the younger one, pointed to the other, inviting him to speak, and so the other—

whose pinched face and narrow lips gave him the severe look of a monk—leaned forward and explained that the present era and the media had completely undermined the status of the artist in general and the writer in particular. "People no longer read," he exclaimed bitterly. "If you don't give them soft porn or some story about incest in the family—"

"Incest is always in the family, isn't it?" said a woman on the panel, smiling slightly as she tossed her reddish curls, while the second man, the younger one, said, "I've actually noticed that readers—personally, I've had lots of feedback on my book *The Gypsy from Givat Olga,* and lots of excitement. Readers have written me quite positively about the erotic bits in the book." On the screen there appeared three books, the camera focusing at length on the book he had just mentioned.

"What is this? Where did they dig this up?" Hefetz shouted as he rushed to the telephone. The woman on the screen was saying, "You asked about the role of the author? Well, the author's role is to see the truth and to tell it; sometimes she even has to lie in order to tell it beautifully, effectively, but—" Hefetz slammed down the receiver just as the broadcast was cut short and in its place appeared a caption: OUR REGULARLY SCHEDULED PROGRAMMING WILL RESUME IN JUST A MOMENT. Niva rose from her chair in the corner of the canteen and approached them with heavy, shuffling footsteps, her clogs dragging.

"Here's the list you asked for," she told Michael with open animosity, handing him two sheets of paper. "All the names and their jobs and their reasons for needing to be here. That's what you wanted, wasn't it?"

Michael ignored her question, eyed the pages she had handed him, and said, "If this is the case, then all the people listed in the left-hand column should be available for questioning now."

Niva nodded.

"And where are they now?"

"In the newsroom, like we were told. They're waiting for you to take them in. Isn't that the way it works?"

Michael left the canteen and went up the stairs to the newsroom. Sergeant Yigael was waiting for him in the doorway and informed him excitedly that Tzilla was looking for him. "She says they've given you a cell phone, sir," he said, unsure how far he should push this. "She says you never have it on. But I told her there's no reception in the canteen." Michael fished around in his pockets; his phone had remained with Eli Bachar, who undoubtedly had left it off. "She asked for you to call her," the sergeant said. "She said it was urgent."

Yaffa dialed her own cell phone for him, mumbling something about intelligent people with no technical sense at all, and handed it to him. Without fanfare or small talk Tzilla told him he would need to attend a meeting of the Special Investigations team "before police headquarters turns into a madhouse, what with everyone being investigated." She added, "Everyone's already waiting for you. There's a van outside waiting to bring you here."

"There's so much material that it's hard to know where to begin," Tzilla complained when everyone was already seated, busy eating and drinking. Only after eight o'clock, during a scheduled break in the investigations and searches, was she able to gather the entire team for a meeting. "In any event you people need to eat something," she had claimed to Michael. "After such a long day and being involved with investigations you couldn't very well have had time to eat. Balilty's brought pita bread and hummus and fixings"—she pointed to the table in the corner of the room—"we've got everything, coffee, too, just get Eli here for me since he hasn't been answering his cell phone or his beeper, and bring Balilty back from wherever he popped out to for a minute, I have no idea where, but that minute has stretched into half an hour just like always with Balilty: if you manage to catch the guy you can never let him go." While she was talking she opened the door and looked out into the hallway. "Danny Balilty," she called out. "Has anyone seen Danny Balilty?"

Two doors opened, and in one stood Balilty. "What are you shouting for?" he asked, feigning innocence. "I told you I'd be there in a minute, didn't I? Geez, what's the big deal? Are you people waiting for me? Everybody else is already there?"

Michael smiled as he listened to Tzilla assure Balilty that they were waiting only for him, but at that moment he heard Eli Bachar's voice as he entered, breathing heavily, asking, "Is there coffee?" He sank into a chair, then noticed the Hanukkah menorah in the corner, three candles burning. "What's going on here?" he bellowed. "Since when do we celebrate Jewish festivals around here, like little kids or the Orthodox?"

"As long as we're on the topic of children," Tzilla said, "why don't you pop home sometime? The kids haven't seen you for two days and I can't leave here. Your mother brought them in earlier to light candles and we tried to find you, but there was no reaching you. Anywhere."

"So that's it," Eli Bachar mumbled. "I knew that menorah looked familiar. Isn't that the one Dana made in kindergarten?"

Michael sighed and fished a new toothpick from his shirt pocket.

"Try a cigar," Balilty counseled him. "Hold an unlit cigar in your hand and see how satisfying that is."

Michael regarded him for a moment, then shook his head. "Too soon," he said. "Too soon, too close to when I gave up smoking. Try me again in another month."

"If you haven't gone back to cigarettes by then," Balilty teased him. Michael ignored the comment, Balilty's invitation to a duel.

"Let's get started," Michael said. In a quiet voice he read out the known facts from a summary prepared by Tzilla, mentioning the two previous deaths and Matty Cohen's digoxin, and emphasizing that Zadik's murder removed any possibility that the other two deaths could have been accidents. "The assumption under which we are working—until we have reason to believe otherwise—is that we're talking about a single murderer," he concluded.

"About the digoxin," Lillian asked, crinkling her forehead, "did Matty Cohen take too much of it, or what?"

"Four times too much," Tzilla said. "He took four times what he should have."

"On purpose?" Lillian asked.

"He neglected to inform us," Tzilla answered coolly.

"I'd like to suggest," Balilty interjected, "that we deal with Zadik first and move backward, because with Zadik the case is clear. We're talking about half an hour, hour maximum. Pretty tight alibi."

"It only looks that way, like it's really clear," Eli Bachar said. "Lots of people were in the building, dozens of them. Do you have information on everyone who was around?" he asked Tzilla. She explained that there was no list of the employees, only the guests, who were made to show identification before entering the building.

"First of all," Michael explained, "it certainly seems we're looking for someone on the inside, I'd say someone *very* much on the inside. Not a guest."

"Because of the door," Lillian noted.

"Because of the door," Michael agreed. "It's clear that if the murderer entered from the hallway door, then it has to be someone who knew about it, which in my opinion narrows the possibilities considerably."

"Not only that," Balilty said. "The person who knew about the door also had a key to enter through the back of the String Building without passing through security the night Tirzah was killed. I'd also like to remind everybody that I spoke with the guy who oversees the broadcasts—write that down, will you, Tzilla?"

"First tell me what it was about."

"I talked to the guy who oversees the broadcasts," he repeated, making himself sound important. "You've got to talk to the behind-the-scenes people, it's a no-brainer talking to the VIPs, it's the ones who aren't in the spotlight that—"

"Balilty," Tzilla said impatiently, "what did he say?"

"The guy's in charge of all the technical matters, decides if something gets broadcast or not, and he sits in the central control room, it's like the master control center. All the satellite stuff passes through there, so, for example, broadcasts from the Knesset on Channel Thirty-three come through master control. What's important to remember here—write this down, Tzilla—is that there's nobody there between one and four in the morning. The room is open, and anyone can just walk in. At night all kinds of equipment goes missing over there." Balilty spread his arms as if to say, Voilà!

"So?" Tzilla said. "How does that connect to our case?"

"It means," said Balilty vaguely, "that there are all kinds of hiding places, limitless possibilities. It's impossible to know who has access to what."

"Even who might have had access to Matty Cohen's medicine," Sergeant Ronen noted. "We'll never solve that riddle, you can be sure of that. If a guy takes a prescription on a regular basis, how can you prove that someone sneaked him an extra dose?"

"Nothing's impossible," Balilty said as though speaking from experience. "But let's start from the end and work backward."

"The end," Michael said, "already presents us with an enigma: the Orthodox Jew with the burn marks who disappeared as though he'd never existed. Nobody saw him or heard him."

"We've put together a composite of him," Tzilla reminded them all. "It's been distributed, there's not a squad car in the city without one. And they broadcast it on the five o'clock news. Did you see it?"

"I was busy," Michael answered, "but I was thinking that maybe—"

Balilty was staring at him, concentrating hard. Suddenly he sat up straight and said, "Forget about it, I already thought about that, and it won't work."

"How do you know what he's talking about?" Eli Bachar sputtered furiously. "Why don't you let him finish?"

"I know what he's going to say," Balilty bragged. "Because great minds think alike, okay? He's thinking that maybe the burned religious guy is really Benny Meyuhas, right?"

Michael nodded.

"Why, so they'll think he's Sroul?" Balilty asked for clarification. "As if their friend Sroul had come back to Israel?"

"Who's Sroul?" Ronen asked.

"You mean like a disguise?" Lillian asked.

"Why not?" Tzilla interjected. "After all, we're talking about a director here, he's got access to all kinds of costumes. He's also knowledgeable about the possibilities."

"The Border Police have no record of his entering the country, at least under that name," Eli Bachar said.

"That's fine," Balilty said dismissively, "but he could have entered with a different passport under another name. With an American passport and an American name."

"We haven't managed to make contact with his family in Los Angeles," Eli Bachar said. "We've been trying since this morning, but there's no answer, only an answering machine."

"But directors really got all kinds of possibilities," Tzilla persisted.

"They *have got* possibilities, not *got*," Emmanuel Shorer said from the doorway.

"I was talking about Benny Meyuhas," Tzilla said, glaring at Shorer as he entered the room, closed the door, and took a seat. "And the burned guy," she added.

"All right," he said with a wave of his hand. "Don't mind me, I'll try to follow along."

"There are two things that stand in the way of this hypothesis," Balilty said. "One is the difference in height, which is of course possible to change. Benny Meyuhas is a lot shorter than Sroul, according to Aviva's description. But the other—and this I do not believe can be changed, it depends on Aviva's hearing—is the voice. She talked at length about the guy's voice, said it was a different voice, the kind you can't forget. And she knows Benny's voice really well. She's certain it's a different voice."

"Okay, that just reinforces what I said before, that we've got to get something out of Benny Meyuhas," Rafi said. "In my opinion he suits our criteria to a tee."

"We've been putting more and more pressure on him, and he still won't talk," Lillian said. "What more can we do?"

"Dig around like Eli did today," Michael said. "What came out of all your investigations, Eli?"

"Not much," Eli Bachar answered. "I put tape recorders on your desk, but we really didn't get anything new from them. That actress just keeps repeating her version of events, that she was with him at his house. In the end we got it out of her that she was with him in the bed—'for the purpose of consoling him,' she says—and then somebody rang the doorbell and at first he didn't want to answer but the person kept ringing and ringing and so finally he went to open it, told her not to leave the bed, to wait for him there and not to move, and she was afraid it was Hagar, her producer."

Balilty snorted. "Producer? More like guard dog, shadow, always at his side, dying to have him for her own. If she'd found that little actress in his bed, that would've been the end of her. It was hard enough on her that he was living with Tirzah; but if she'd found him with some young actress? Whoa! That wouldn't have been a pretty sight."

Eli Bachar said, "At first she said she didn't hear anything, said the bedroom door was closed because Benny had closed it on his way out. So we did an experiment, went there to try it out."

"Good job," Balilty said. "You're a pretty thorough guy."

There was hostility in Eli Bachar's green eyes as he stared at Balilty. "I stayed in the bedroom while Coby went to the front door and spoke in a normal voice. I could hear him—not the words, but I could hear his voice. On a hunch I told her she may not have left the bedroom, but she certainly must have opened the door to listen. At first she said, 'No way,' and denied it, but eventually, when I put some pressure on her—"

"Pressure, hah!" Balilty grumbled. "What kind of pressure? You couldn't exactly threaten to arrest her!"

Eli Bachar ignored Balilty. "So then she says, 'I cracked the door open a tiny bit, just to know who it was,' and she told me it was a man's voice, one she'd never heard before. Then she heard Benny Meyuhas—he sounded all excited—and the other guy's voice again, then the door slammed and that was that. He didn't come back. Time went by and he didn't return, so she got up, got herself dressed, and waited in the living room. Eventually she went home."

"Hang on a minute," Rafi said. "He never came back to the bedroom? He didn't get dressed first? It's winter—the guy couldn't have gone out without shoes. I mean, he was in the middle of f—"

"We asked about that," Eli Bachar said, cutting him off. "You better believe we asked about that. She said he'd left his clothes in the living room, that's where they'd gotten started—"

"Every man has his own style," Balilty muttered.

"No," Eli Bachar said. "This guy isn't that type. He's no philanderer. I understand that he was showing her unedited clips from their film, it wasn't . . . she'd come to offer her condolences, I don't know exactly—"

"It always starts somewhere," Balilty concluded. "Some people learn from the experience of others. You bring a pretty young woman home with you, show her some film clips, you're an important director. What's the big surprise? Then things move into the bedroom. Doesn't surprise me in the least."

"We don't have time for your pearls of wisdom right now,"

Emmanuel Shorer said bluntly. "He went to get dressed in the living room? He left the house without stopping to talk to her, without a word? What do you people make of that?"

"That he was in a big hurry," Balilty summed up flatly. "That he didn't want the little actress to see who'd shown up at the door."

"Let's get back to the murder itself for a minute," Michael said, reminding them it had been determined that it was during the half hour Zadik was alone in his office that someone had entered through the side door. He suggested they name the prime suspects and check their alibis.

"All the longtime employees of Israel Television are suspects," Balilty said, "all the people with keys to the back entrance of the String Building, the old-timers."

"Okay," said Eli Bachar. "What about the head seamstress?"

"Who?" Balilty asked.

"The head seamstress, Shoshana Shem-Tov. She's got a key, and she's been there since Israel Television was founded. She's due to retire in another two years," Eli Bachar said as he glanced at his lists.

"What kind of motive does she have?" Balilty asked. "Why bother with her? Did she have issues with Zadik? Did he mistreat her?"

"Not Zadik, but Tirzah Rubin," Eli Bachar said calmly.

"What kind of problems did she have with Tirzah Rubin?"

"Benny Meyuhas, too. Don't you get it? The head seamstress, the head of the Scenery Department, the director—she was always—"

"Okay already," Balilty said, "what kind of clashes did they have?"

"None, in fact," Eli Bachar said. "Truth is, I just wanted to show you that just because someone's been there a while doesn't mean they're a suspect."

"Gentlemen!" Shorer cried out. "Is this the way things work around here? As if this were a kindergarten?"

Silence fell on the room until Eli Bachar cleared his throat and began speaking again. "Let's say we want to start with people with keys. So we take Max Levin, for example, a guy who's responsible for having planned and built most of the String Building. He's got a key to the back entrance, and there's reason to believe he knew about the door in the hallway."

"So?" Michael said. "Let's say we start with him. What have we got on him?"

"He was in the String Building at the time Zadik was murdered, never left his office from eight in the morning until they called to tell him about Zadik. He'd been sitting for at least three hours with the security officer, whose name was"—Eli Bachar flipped through his notepad—"Ziko. Yeah, I remember it was a weird name."

"It's not *weird,* it's probably Bulgarian," Shorer muttered. "Ziko is a common name among Bulgarians, a nickname for Yitzhak. But that's not important. Go on, go on."

"They were working on the problem of theft. Seems there's a huge problem, equipment gets stolen all the time over there. Here, I've got a complete list; a television camera was stolen, and now it turns out it was passed over to the Palestinian Authority. They suspect a building contractor who was doing some renovations there, and maybe a cleaning contractor, too. The investigation into the stolen camera took on pretty big proportions, nobody suspected the damage to be so great—it led to the discovery of a whole series of thefts, all kinds of things: spotlights and video cameras and lighting equipment, lots of stuff."

"I noticed they're pretty sensitive about all that right now," Rafi said. "I talked to the guy in charge of maintenance, and he says that for the past couple of days, ever since the business with Tirzah Rubin, people have been bringing stuff in like crazy. Turns out they were hanging on to cameras and all kinds of things at home. So now they're bringing it all in before somebody starts hunting them down."

"In any event, Max Levin seems clean, along with a list of other people who weren't alone at the time," Eli Bachar concluded. "Hefetz says he was wandering around the building, everybody saw him. He was in the canteen and the archives. Everywhere."

"We're talking about half an hour," Michael reminded them.

"Okay. He says he wasn't looking at his watch all the time, but he was in Aviva's office twice trying to get in to see Zadik. I don't know if—"

"What about Rubin?" Shorer asked. "What about him?"

"Rubin was in his office, working on his report for Friday's show. He was writing text—that's what he told us—and never left his office."

"Any witnesses?" Shorer asked.

"No," Eli Bachar answered. "Nothing specific. He interviewed some doctor in his office, a guy who's working with him on a report about doctors who cooperate with the Israeli secret services."

"Oooooh," crooned Balilty, "how I love those bleeding-heart liberals who— What? Why are you looking at me like that?" he asked Michael. "I can't stand those self-righteous leftists, they're out of touch, living in a dream world, they think—"

"Not now, Danny," Shorer said quietly. "We've got a lot of work to do."

"Well," said Lillian, "I'd like to tell you about my talk with Natasha concerning Rubin."

"Really?" Tzilla said, resting her chin in her palm and staring at Lillian in an aggressively expectant manner.

"I had a chat with her in Rubin's office while he was in the editing room," Lillian explained.

"And who asked you to converse with her?" Tzilla asked, raising her voice in anger. "Did someone ask you to? Do you think there's some connection between the sheep's head she found at her apartment and these murders? Do you think that—"

"Tzilla," Michael implored her, "enough of that. I've already spoken to you about it."

Tzilla regarded him with mistrust but said only, "All right. So what's the deal with Natasha?"

"I recorded it," Lillian said, clearly pleased with herself. "Here's the cassette. Do you want to watch it?"

"Before we get to that—" Balilty said as Tzilla inserted the tape into the machine and removed a remote control from the right-hand drawer of Michael's desk. "Wait a minute, don't start it yet," he instructed her. "I just want to say about that sheep's head, you should know that it doesn't appear to be connected to the case."

"Which means?" Shorer asked.

"Which means," answered Balilty, "that I have my sources, especially among the ultra-Orthodox, and I spoke with Schreiber the cameraman, and I have a pretty good idea—never mind, what's important is that she's onto something pretty serious. I have a few plants, a mole, okay? They tell me the sheep was meant solely to convince Natasha not to continue investigating the matter. All right?"

"What's the matter in question that she has information about?" Lillian asked.

"Listen, honey," Balilty said with a cool look. "When the time comes to know, you'll be told."

"That means," said Eli Bachar by way of explanation, "that Balilty simply doesn't know. Have you people noticed that he doesn't know everything?"

Tzilla cast a protective look at her husband, nodded her head, and turned the volume on the monitor up before Balilty had a chance to respond.

"This is in Rubin's office, okay?" Lillian said. "It was Yigael who set up the camera for me." They watched Natasha remove her red scarf and look around. She took stock of the walls and the papers scattered across the desk, then turned over one upside-down photograph, looked at it, and frowned at the portrait of a man in a doctor's white coat with a stethoscope dangling from his pocket. She tossed the photo into a corner. Lillian's voice could be heard on the tape. "Please sit down," she said. "It's not exactly the first time you've ever been in this room, is it?" A hand removed the stack of cardboard files sitting on a chair and patted the chair, signaling to Natasha to take a seat.

"I don't come here all that often," Natasha said, her gaze straight and steady at the camera. "Usually I sit with him in the editing room or the canteen."

"What's wrong? Don't you like all these photos?" Lillian goaded her. The camera panned to the corkboard overhanging the desk, to which were pinned rows and rows of black-and-white photographs: hundreds of uniformed Japanese soldiers, their hands held high over their heads in surrender; seated Wehrmacht soldiers, hands on their heads; in the corner of the corkboard, a large photo of dark-skinned soldiers sitting in the sand, their feet bound; American soldiers, their heads bowed, facing Japanese officers.

"Check it out," Balilty hooted. "What an album he's got! He should collect them into a book."

Michael, too, watched the film and thought about *The Family of Man,* a collection of photographs he had encountered in his youth and which Becky Pomerantz, the mother of his good friend Uzi from high school, had particularly liked. She was, as well, the first woman to seduce him, teaching him to love music and good books like *The Family of Man,* with its impressive photographs. Becky Pomerantz had taught him to smoke, too, when he was seventeen. How he wished he had a cigarette now. If only he had a cigarette, his powers of concentration were certain to improve greatly. Maybe he should take up smoking again, just for the duration of this investigation, then he would give it up for good. He wished someone could approve such a plan, where he could smoke just for a few weeks. But then he'd have to endure this torment of quitting all over again. He passed his fingers over his face and touched his bottom lip lightly, just at the most comfortable spot for a cigarette, and resumed watching the cassette.

"That's Rubin's collection," Natasha was explaining defensively. "He calls it his 'pacifist's collection.' What's wrong with it? Would you prefer naked girls?"

Lillian's face appeared on-screen, watching Natasha with heightened interest, giving her her full attention. "First of all," she said, "of course naked girls would be better. They're lots prettier, don't you think?" She smiled mysteriously. "Second of all, I thought you had something going with Hefetz. Are you involved with Rubin, too?"

Balilty glanced at Lillian and whistled. "Good job, Miss Lillian," he said. "I see they taught you something over in Narcotics."

"I'm not involved with Rubin," Natasha said quietly on the screen as her pale face—especially her cheeks and chin—turned deep red, bringing out her bottomless blue eyes. "And it's all over with Hefetz."

Michael noted that she had not bothered to ask Lillian how she knew about Hefetz and that she accepted as a given the fact that Lillian knew everything about her. Nor did it seem that she cared. "Rubin is just nice to me, he was nice right from the beginning, and it doesn't have anything to do with . . . nothing to do with . . ." Her voice faded, and Lillian waited a moment before asking her next question.

"Nothing to do with what?"

"Sex," Natasha said, then covered her face with her hands.

"How about we get right to business," Lillian suggested. "We don't have all the time in the world for this. The question is, where were you between, say, ten and eleven o'clock?"

"I was . . . I was with Schreiber. First I went to the bathroom, then I was in Aviva's office—I took over for her for a few minutes so she could go to the ladies' room or something—and after that with Schreiber. I was waiting for Zadik . . . I was hoping to talk to him," Natasha said.

"You were in Aviva's office?" Lillian asked. "Right at the scene of the crime, no?"

"I didn't budge from there," Natasha said. "Everyone saw me there. You can ask anyone."

A loud knock on the door could be heard from the monitor, then the door opened and the film ended.

"That's all?" Tzilla asked, disappointed. "That's all there is?"

"That's all," Lillian affirmed. "After that Benny Meyuhas turned up, and things got crazy. But I checked out her alibi, and it's all true. Aviva confirmed it, Hefetz saw her—"

"Hefetz! Oh, that's a good one!" Eli Bachar said mockingly.

"Okay, there were others. Schreiber told me they were in a side office, not far from the hallway door that—"

"Schreiber's crazy about Natasha," Eli Bachar told them. "We have to take that into consideration."

"What's going on over there? Is everybody nuts for that scrawny little chick? She looks like a famished orphan," Balilty said, astounded.

"Some guys like that type," Tzilla assured him. She stole a glance at her husband. "There are some guys you can't even know what's going to turn them on."

"Was there any time you had the feeling she was covering something up?" Michael asked Lillian. "With your experience dealing with drug addicts, you must be an expert on liars."

Lillian smiled. "I can tell you that Natasha did not seem like an addict or a liar. Schreiber seemed pretty high the whole time, but I don't think it's anything more than ordinary dope."

"And neither of them—Schreiber or Natasha—has a motive," Balilty pondered. "Rubin either, for that matter, don't you think?"

Lillian nodded.

"Anybody want more pita bread or something?" Tzilla asked. No one responded. "Then I'm going to get rid of all this, it's making me gag."

"Let's get back to the murder itself," Michael said, reminding them that someone could only have entered the room through the secret door during the half hour Zadik was alone, unless the murderer was the ultra-Orthodox Jew who had entered and exited through Aviva's office. "We've already determined the guy was wearing a maintenance man's coveralls," Michael said. "The coveralls remained in the office, and the forensics people are certain they'll find some evidence on them, but even if they don't find anything but Zadik's blood, we still have—"

"The T-shirt," Tzilla said.

"But doesn't that mean that the person who put on the coveralls knew that the maintenance man would be working in Zadik's office?" Lillian asked. "Did he come in wearing coveralls, or did those belong to the maintenance man? I don't understand."

"Apparently he entered in street clothes," Eli Bachar said. "In any event, no one recalls having seen a maintenance man or technician in the hallway."

"At Israel Television that doesn't mean a thing," Balilty noted quietly. "Those people don't seem to notice anything: who shoved Tirzah Rubin, the Orthodox guy with the burns—"

"So he used the coveralls that some maintenance man had left there earlier?" Lillian persisted. "Then he must have known they'd be there. Or how about this, which is even more confusing: he told Zadik, 'Hang on a minute, let me step into these coveralls before I bash your brains with a drill.' Like, 'Let me just put these clothes on so I won't get myself all messed up.'" She glanced around with the air of a little girl showing the grown-ups how smart she is.

"No, darling." Balilty sighed. "Don't you remember what we said about Zadik's autopsy? I mean, we discussed this this afternoon, and you were certainly there: we said that the pathologist found a large bruise on the base of Zadik's skull, near the neck, which indicates that he lost consciousness first, and only then there was the business with the drill. *Capisce?*"

"The guy rammed him with the tool, he didn't drill a hole in his head. That's why there was no noise," Eli Bachar explained.

Lillian hung her head. "The official results from the pathologist haven't come back yet," she claimed. "I don't remember all that because I haven't seen it in writing."

"So you're going to have to take my word for it, sweetheart," Balilty said softly. "First the guy cracked him over the head, then, when Zadik lost consciousness, he pulled on the coveralls and creamed him with the drill. Got it now?"

"Do me a favor, Danny," Tzilla said as she wrapped her arms around herself, "spare us the gory details, will you?"

"So did he know or didn't he?" Lillian persisted.

"Did who know what?!" Balilty shouted.

"The murderer," Lillian said. "Did he know about the maintenance man or not?"

"Even if he didn't know," Tzilla said impatiently, "even if it all developed spontaneously—let's say it wasn't premeditated—then the scenario could have been something like this: you enter the office, something happens that makes you need to eliminate the other guy, you whomp him without giving it much thought, then you notice the work clothes and the tools and you get a great idea. What difference does it make if he knew or he didn't know?"

"Nobody knew that a technician was supposed to come," Michael announced. "Only Aviva. Zadik himself had completely forgotten about it. Aviva had set it up in advance, and it was penciled in to her appointment book, but in a way nobody from the outside could have understood. We checked it out."

Lillian, however, was not appeased. "How? Did she write in code? In a secret language?"

"You'd be surprised," Tzilla said, a note of victory in her voice. "You'd be very surprised. She writes first names only or even just initials and a phone number and nothing else. She says she got used to setting up meetings that way when she managed the office of a division commander during her army service, since everybody was always walking in and taking a peek."

"That's also not a bad method for making sure your boss is completely reliant on you," Balilty added. "It's typical of single women who have no lives and no family and their work is their whole life. They make sure the boss can't manage without them."

"Not everyone is like that," Lillian said. She threw him an offended glance. "Some women—"

"Let's get on with it," Michael said. "Do you have the list, Eli, the one with who entered and exited the building, and when? Rubin's doctor friend, for example. Is that marked in? Hand the list over to Tzilla and just tell us who the problematic people are."

"No one," Eli Bachar answered. "No one's problematic. On the face of it nobody's . . . everyone . . . the time span is just too narrow," he explained.

"I would get back to the question of motive," Michael said.

A ruckus broke out in the room. "Whoa, pipe down," Michael said. "Let's discuss motives with regards to the murder of Zadik."

The room fell silent.

"What's so difficult here?" Shorer asked. "There's no man alive without enemies. A man without enemies is a dead man."

"Even dead men have enemies," Balilty muttered. "Believe me, my sister-in-law's mother—" He glanced at Michael and shut his mouth.

"All right," Eli Bachar said. "The director general did not like Zadik."

"Let's get serious," Rafi said irritably. "The director general didn't like Zadik? Oh, come on!"

"I'm just doing what I was asked," Eli Bachar said with mock innocence. "But if you're asking for my impression, I'd say that folks at Israel Television really liked Zadik. All of them, even in the canteen. They're bawling down there like—"

"Fine," Michael said. "Then we're asking for your impression."

"You see, that's something else altogether," Eli Bachar said. "My personal impression, no basis in fact for this whatsoever, is that, well—did you see the five o'clock news? When they announced Zadik's death?"

"Yes," Michael said. "We saw it and recorded it. We recorded it, right, Tzilla?"

"That's why we're sitting in this room," Tzilla said, inserting a cassette into the VCR. "Should I start the video?"

"Pay close attention to Hefetz's speech," Eli Bachar said. "I was there when he was giving it. Not in the studio but in the newsroom. We all stopped what we were doing for a minute."

Tzilla started the tape. Hefetz's full, round face filled the screen as he proclaimed, with a grave expression, "It is with great sorrow and deep regret that the board of directors and employees of the Israel Broadcasting Authority announce the untimely—"

"He's totally over the top," Lillian called out. "Those are the same words they used to announce—I mean, we're not talking about the prime minister here."

"Never mind, that's not important," Eli Bachar said, shutting her up.

Michael, distracted, caught fragments of sentences: ". . . employees of the Israel Broadcasting Authority announce . . . all the citizens of the state of Israel . . . lucky that . . ."

"Wait, quiet." Until now Emmanuel Shorer had been sitting quietly, watching. "Listen carefully to what he is saying here. Tzilla, rewind the tape, please."

Tzilla pressed the button on the remote control and rewound the tape. "Here," Shorer said. "Stop here. Now listen up, everybody."

". . . to carry out the principles established by Shimshon Zadik, may his memory be a blessing," Hefetz began, his trembling voice full of emotion. "The news must go on, . . . I have taken upon myself to fill in as director of Israel Television and hope to function according to the will of my superiors and to express faithfully the policy of the government, to which the Israel Broadcasting Authority is subject—"

"Stop!" Shorer cried. "Stop the tape, Tzilla."

"What happened?" Balilty wondered. "I didn't hear anything too remarkable."

"You didn't?" Shorer marveled. "'To express faithfully the policy of the government.' We've never heard anything like that before: that man should *not* be serving as director of Israel Television under any circumstances! That is certainly not what Zadik would have done."

"So what does it *mean*?" Balilty asked, his face openly astonished. "Are you suggesting that's a motive for murder? That maybe it was all a plot, that somebody ordered Hefetz to—you mean to say that somebody wanted to shut Zadik up so that Hefetz could take over for him and become the government's mouthpiece? That's what you mean?"

"We have learned," Shorer said placidly, "from years of experience, that in a murder case every odd detail, every exception to the rule, can turn into a lead. Do you not think this speech is quite exceptional?"

"Well, it's certainly not standard issue," Balilty said, squirming in his chair, "but what does it, like, mean? Do you think it's connected to the whole issue with the ultra-Orthodox and Natasha's investigation?"

The door opened, and a uniformed police officer stood in the doorway. He was breathing heavily, his breaths loud in the ensuing silence. "Excuse me, sir," the policeman said, then, noticing Emmanuel Shorer, turned to him and excused himself again.

"What's going on, Davidov?" Shorer asked. "Has something happened?"

"They dispatched me to tell you . . . a body's been found in an apartment near the Oranim gas station. They couldn't phone in because you're in a meeting—nobody's answering their cell phones or beepers—so they sent me. It's the body of a man."

"Why the—" Eli Bachar began, irritated. "Is that any reason to—" He fell silent when Shorer raised his arm.

"Why was it important for us to know this immediately?" Shorer asked. "Who thought it was something we needed to be disturbed about?"

"They say, sir," Davidov explained from his position in the doorway, "that the guy fits the description in the composite we've been passing around."

"What? What did you say?" Balilty shouted as he jumped to his feet.

"They're saying that the guy's the right age, with burns, and dressed like an ultra-Orthodox Jew," Davidov said, rolling the hem of his windbreaker between his fingers. "They phoned from the site by telephone—they didn't want anyone to listen in over the transmitters or cell phones—they asked for you to get down there right away," he said to Michael.

"Where is it exactly?" Michael asked, rising from his chair. Eli Bachar and Sergeant Ronen rose to their feet, too. Michael's eyes were locked on Emmanuel Shorer's face.

"Here, I've got it all written down," Davidov said as he handed a large piece of paper to Michael on which was written an address in thick pencil. "It's in the Mekor Haim area, two buildings behind the Oranim gas station. Second floor, the top floor of the building. The entrance is from the rear. The names of the policewoman and the investigator who found him are written on the side, but they asked you not to talk to them by transmitter, only by cell phone if you absolutely have to. The number's on the paper, too."

Balilty peered at the paper. "Nina Peretz? You know her?" he asked Michael over Shorer's shoulder as they raced from the room. Michael had already reached the stairs.

"I know her, and you do too," Shorer said. "Nina, the redhead. The one with the . . ." He drew narrow hips with his hands in the air.

"Ah, *Nina*!" Balilty exclaimed, his eyes lighting up. They were on the stairs heading toward the entrance to the building. "The redhead, from Hatzor Haglilit, right? Wasn't she relocated to the southern district? I heard she was sent south because—" He looked to the left and right, but one look from Shorer made him shut his mouth.

"They moved her and then moved her back again," Shorer said. "There's a new police commander, so she came back. Why are you so surprised? She was going nuts down in Beersheva. She said there was no one she could relate to, said she didn't get to meet anyone interesting. She requested a transfer, and we moved her back. Are you riding with me or with Ohayon?"

"What kind of a question is that?" Balilty asked. "With you, of course. You can tell me all about Nina the redhead; what great news that she's . . ." He fell silent while Shorer removed the blue flashing light from his car and affixed it to the roof, then sounded the siren and raced after the squad car ahead of him transporting Michael, Eli Bachar, and Lillian, who had somehow squeezed in without being invited.

"Great news? What's the great news?" Shorer asked in a loud voice to overcome the noise of the siren. But Balilty waved his hand dismissively and said, under his breath, "Nothing. I didn't say a thing."

# CHAPTER THIRTEEN

While the south Jerusalem street that curved away from the gas station was quite dark, the front yard of the dilapidated building, surrounded by towering old cypress trees, was illuminated by two spotlights that had been placed in the entrance. One after the other, the cars driven by Emmanuel Shorer and Michael Ohayon pulled up behind the forensics van that stood by the ambulance in front of the crooked, rusty gate. Jumping out of Shorer's car, Balilty complained about the bitter cold and raised the fur collar on his jacket. "Check it out," said Sergeant Ronen, who emerged after Balilty from the car, "a real Jerusalem winter." A band of children appeared from behind the gate and quickly dispersed. "Anybody who hasn't been here can't know how cold it can get," he said. Shivering, he glared at the one child who had not run away and was now standing next to the van, hiding behind a group of adults undeterred by the light rain. "Tell me," Ronen said to no one in particular, "what are these kids doing out here? It's after ten o'clock; don't they have parents? Don't they have to get up for school in the morning?" He watched the children run away and entered the front yard of the building.

Several bearded young men wearing skullcaps and dark clothing stood huddled together under two black umbrellas. "Hey, Mr. Policeman," one called out to Shorer as he emerged from the car and looked around, "what happened here? Is it true there's a dead body inside? Is it a murder? Did somebody get killed?" Shorer did not even look in their direction; he simply walked quickly inside, his head bent against the rain.

"We're from the yeshiva next door, we're the neighbors. We'd like to know," said another, stepping out from under the umbrella.

"Go on, get lost," Balilty chided them. "Go back to your yeshiva," he said with obvious loathing. He added, when he saw that the young men did not budge: "Like it's really *your* yeshiva, like you really own the place. In fact you just move into a place that's slated to become a neighborhood clubhouse, and then you call it your yeshiva. Take off, get out of here now!" He was shouting. "Go ruin some other part of the city, go fill the place with yeshivas. You've already destroyed Jerusalem, the whole city you've ruined."

Michael placed a hand on Balilty's arm. "Not now, Danny," he said quietly. "You've found just the time to repair the world."

"Who's talking about the world?" he grumbled. "They've ruined the Mahane Yehuda market and everywhere else they go. Property values tumble to half wherever they show up."

Michael sighed. He almost said, How many times a day do I have to listen to your lamentations about how religious people have ruined the real estate market in Jerusalem? Instead, he remained silent, watching two women who had rested plastic shopping bags filled with groceries on the fence, close to the narrow path that led from the sidewalk to the entrance of the building, and also the portly man near them with the loud cough. "Please clear out, people," he told them. "You're making things difficult for us." He waited a moment, until one of the women stooped slowly to retrieve her two large bags with a sigh. Without waiting to see whether they had really left the premises, he followed quickly after Balilty and Shorer along the stone path lit up in bluish light by the spotlight.

A policeman stepped out from inside the building. "Over here, sir," he called to Shorer, who was near the head of the line. "And watch your step. Make sure you walk along the stone path, it's muddy on both sides of the pavement." To Michael he said, "There are stairs at the back of the building that lead straight up to the second floor." He watched as Eli Bachar hesitated at the end of the path before leading them to the narrow staircase.

A large flashlight had been placed next to the last door on the second floor as well, and it was lighting up the rusty, crumbling banister and two large plants placed on the landing in front of the wide-open door. The harsh light painted the sole surviving geranium a bright bubblegum pink and illuminated the doorbell, which had been ripped from its place and was dangling from an electrical wire next to the door frame, banging occasionally in the cold wind.

Nina the redhead, in tight blue jeans, was already waiting in the doorway. She's no longer a redhead, Balilty thought to himself; her hair had been cut short and in the pale light of the hallway he could make out highlights of platinum blond. Balilty also managed to whisper—perhaps to Michael, perhaps to himself—that she seemed to have put on some weight, which did no harm to the charm of her sturdy little body.

"Nina, sweetheart, long time no see," Balilty said, pressing in before Michael. He patted her shoulder and stooped to kiss her cheek. But she turned her face away, a frown on her full lips, and gently pushed Balilty aside with a small hand sporting a large diamond ring on one finger.

"What have we got here, Nina?" Shorer asked.

"Please step inside, sir, see for yourself. The body's in the first room on the right." A moment later she noticed Michael, and her lips widened into a half-smile. "How are you?" she whispered.

He nodded, then shrugged. "You can see for yourself," he said.

"Tell me about it," Nina said, casting a furtive glance at Lillian, who had already entered the apartment and was following Shorer toward the room where the body was. She added, "In fact, you look quite good. I've heard you've given up smoking. Is it true?"

Eli Bachar, who entered at that very moment and heard her question, laughed quietly. He turned to a member of the forensics unit who was leaning over a large bag lying on the floor near the front door, and tapped his shoulder.

"I see rumors reach all the way down to Beersheva," Michael said, drawing close enough to take in the heavy scent of her sweet perfume, a fragrance that had annoyed him back in that short period of time when she had taken to consulting him on personal matters, when she was still married to a man she despised but from whom she refused to separate for reasons that were never clear to him. Michael had bought her a bottle of perfume then, something light and lemony, but she—after thanking him, her eyes teary ("You have no idea how touching it is when a man thinks to bring you something")—had sprayed a little onto her wrist, frowned in her typically doubtful manner, and said she could not dream of giving up on her Estée Lauder.

"You'll give up smoking, too, when you get to be my age," he said.

"My *ripe old* age," Balilty said. "Don't forget to say, 'my *ripe old* age.'" He approached Nina, took her hand in his own, and examined the diamond. "So what's this all about?" he asked. "Have you gotten engaged?" The look in her eyes, which lit up in shades of brown and green, was enough to make him stifle his smile; he clucked in sympathy when she told him the ring had belonged to her mother, who had died several months earlier.

In the meantime, they entered the first room on the right, which, due to its low ceiling, appeared small and oppressive. The forensics expert explained that this was one of three rooms, and that it appeared the man had not been in the apartment for very long: the kitchen was nearly empty of food and the rooms nearly bereft of furniture. He told them that the fully dressed body of a man had been discovered on the narrow bed pushed up against the wall. An overcoat had been found hanging from a simple wooden chair next to a bare table, and the fringes of a gray wool scarf that had apparently been draped around the dead man's neck had been moved aside by the doctor, who was at that moment examining him. The forensics expert told Shorer, "I'm pretty certain he was strangled, like this"—he grabbed the ends of the scarf—"with hands and perhaps the scarf. Can you see?" he asked, turning to Michael. "Even under the beard and the burn marks you can see—on his neck, on his forehead, under his eyes, wherever you get a glimpse of his skin—that the coloring and the spots indicate this is the face of a man who has been strangled."

Michael glanced at the gaunt body; rigor mortis was already setting in, and he turned his gaze to the bare walls instead. The room was damp and smelled of mold. Emmanuel Shorer shoved aside an electrical cord that extended from a space heater near the bed. "Didn't they even turn it on?" he asked, to which the doctor shook his head.

"It's thanks to the cold that his body is so well preserved," the doctor explained. "However, this didn't happen days ago, it's only a matter of hours—six or eight, perhaps—there are all kinds of signs. We'll only know after the autopsy." He rolled back the sleeve of the dead man's sweater and also that of the gray flannel undershirt beneath it and carefully examined his arm. The inner forearm was full of red and blue bruises. "Hemorrhages," the doctor told Michael. "It seems he was receiving injections. Look here," he said, as Michael drew near and bent down to the bed. "On the one hand it doesn't appear . . . but he was also very thin, there's no question about it. We'll be a lot smarter after the autopsy. But there's something else here—"

"He could have simply rotted here," Nina said, cramming her hands into the back pockets of her tight jeans as she approached the bed.

"Is that how you dress for work?" Balilty asked from where he was standing in the doorway. He pointed at her black leather boots with stiletto heels.

"I was on my way out on a date," she explained testily, "when I was called here. You see what a responsible person I am? Anyway, as I was saying, the person who strangled him was counting on the fact that the apartment was empty and no one was expected here. The guy would have rotted here for a few days, that was the idea. But thank God the neighbor found him. If she hadn't—"

"Doesn't anyone live here?" Balilty asked. "This place is completely empty. I looked in the kitchen, the fridge looks about a hundred years old."

"Does he have a name, this man?" Shorer asked. "Is this the person we've been looking for or not?"

"It is," Nina confirmed. "We know it not only from the composite drawing but also from his passport, which says his name is Israel Hayoun, I'll show it to you in just a second—" She hurried from the room, returning a moment later with a brown envelope wrapped in plastic. "He had two passports, one Israeli and one American. He entered the country on his American passport. Here's the stamp from two days ago, look right here." Then she pointed to a corner of the room. "Those were his belongings, there's his suitcase, we've had an initial look through it all." Michael thought there was something heartbreaking about the old brown suitcase, the kind he had not seen for years, similar to one he had found in the attic of his former father-in-law, Yuzek. That one had been tied with rope, and now, just as then, images of detachment, expulsion, and loneliness rose in his mind. "Two shirts, a sweater, a pair of trousers, underpants, undershirts, socks, two of everything; a Bible he got in the army—the date's written inside—a prayer book, two old photos in frames, and this book of poems. You understand poetry, right, Michael?" she asked as she handed him a thin brown volume with yellowing pages that was falling to pieces and held together by a thick rubber band. "Look, there's a dedication. I don't know anything about Israeli poetry," she mumbled. "Only Russian." She watched as Michael carefully removed the rubber band and gazed at the first page. Underneath the title *Stars Outside* was written, in black ink, "To our Sroul, on the occasion of having completed seventeen winters. From Tirzah and Arye."

Michael intended to say something about the poet Natan Alterman and how an entire generation of Israelis had grown up with his poems—as he himself had—and he very nearly recited the line, *Even in that which is old and familiar there is a moment of birth*. But one look at the impervious expression of this lonely, abandoned man—even the word "abandoned" seemed too festive, too pretty, too Alterman-like in the face of the emptiness and neglect surrounding them—caused him to change his mind. Instead, he said, "Have you checked it all out already? Have the forensics people been through his belongings? May we handle them?"

"Yeah, they've been through it all," Nina confirmed. "They're in the bathroom now, checking . . . what is it you want to look at here?" she asked as Michael knelt down to the pile of clothing in the corner and extracted two photographs he found underneath a few shirts. He studied them for a while, then passed one to Shorer, who was standing over him, asking to have a look.

"All right," Shorer said as he gazed at the stained, yellowing photograph that featured the gang they recognized from the photo in Benny Meyuhas's house and on the corkboard in Arye Rubin's office at Israel Television. "There's no question about it, this is our man."

"You mean the name on the passport and the burn marks on his face and hands weren't enough for you people?" Nina asked. "I knew this was the guy from the minute I laid eyes on him. I was sure of it, even though he doesn't look exactly like the composite. How many men could possibly fit this description?"

"One in Jerusalem, maybe two in all of Israel," Balilty remarked. He was standing in the center of the room, staring at the body. "Tell me what gives with this apartment. There's nothing here, just a couch and space heater in the living room, a few pieces of furniture in here, and a nearly empty fridge. What is this place? Who found him, the neighbor? Where is she, this neighbor?"

Michael listened to Nina explain that the apartment had remained empty because of a legal entanglement due to a divorce: "The owners of the apartment—his sister and her husband," she said, indicating the dead man, "can't reach an agreement. Believe me, I know how that goes: the apartment gets stuck, it's neither for rent or sale. The neighbor told me that this guy's sister lived here until just two months ago, didn't want to leave because she was afraid if she did he would take control and walk off with everything. So what happened was that they both lived here. They didn't talk to one another, but lived together. He was on the living room couch, she was in here, in the bedroom. They didn't utter a word to each other, made one another's life hell but neither one gave in. Finally—this is what the neighbor says, she's on good terms with the sister . . . Hey," Nina said to Shorer, "do you want to hear it from the neighbor herself? She asked that if you do, we should go over to her place because it's pretty hard for her to look at . . . him . . ."

"He, she, them," Balilty complained. "Don't these people have names?"

"Why don't you just tell us for the time being, later she can come give her testimony," Shorer said, looking at Michael. Michael nodded, then stepped aside and motioned to Eli Bachar.

"What? You want *me* to go down and talk to her?" Eli Bachar said, casting a look of animosity in Balilty's direction.

"Take Lillian along and get the woman's testimony," Michael said. "In any case there are too many people hanging around here."

"But do they get to stay?" Eli Bachar asked, looking at Balilty and Sergeant Ronen. He muttered something else, but Nina flashed him the look that a teacher gives a pupil who is disturbing the class, then spoke in a loud voice, as if to cover up his disruption. To Shorer she said, "The lawyer told Dalia—Dalia Gottlieb, sister of Israel Hayoun, the dead man; her husband is called Eldad, he's an accountant, the neighbor says he's a real sleazy guy—so the lawyer told her she could leave the apartment without losing her rights to it, there's some kind of . . . I didn't really understand, even though I went through it once.

Remember that?" she asked Michael suddenly; in fact, he had no recollection, and gave an indecipherable wave of his hand which he hoped she would not put to the test. "Whoa, what crap that guy gave me! Do you remember how, after we'd already decided to get divorced and he'd left, then he showed up, went to sleep on the couch so he wouldn't lose his rights to the house? His lawyer put him up to that. Good thing we didn't have any kids. But this Dalia has two kids, grown and out of the house. Now she's living on her own in Pisgat Zeev, waiting for the sale of this apartment. You wouldn't believe it, but there's demand for apartments around here," Nina prattled on. "This neighborhood isn't much of anything, but it's accessible to everywhere and—" She stopped talking and stood pondering the single bed in front of her, where the dead body of a man still lay.

"Nina," Shorer said, "we're waiting for you to explain how he was discovered."

"Oh, sorry, I thought . . . The neighbor, Iris Marciano is her name, has a key. Her sister and brother-in-law came for a visit from up north in Maalot with their two children and she needed an extra mattress. So she went upstairs to fetch the mattress from the living room couch. Dalia Gottlieb didn't even know her brother was in the country, and she certainly didn't know he was here; even the neighbor, Iris Marciano, didn't know he was here. She never heard a thing. Can you imagine what a shock it was for her to find him like that? She didn't touch anything, she ran straight out and called us. I came right away and found him just like that, just like he is now. He never even told his sister he was coming, didn't phone her or anything. He just showed up, and that's all."

"What about other neighbors, in the next building?" asked Shorer. "How could they not have seen light in the apartment or heard voices or steps or noises? Didn't they hear anything at all?"

"No, nothing. She was sick, the neighbor," Nina said, "she had the flu. Her son was on a youth movement field trip. After all, it's Hanukkah vacation. She's a single parent, her husband left her two years ago. So she was alone, sick with the flu. She had a high fever for two days, she didn't hear or notice a thing. That's what she says. You can ask her again," said Nina, as she licked her full lips, then bit the lower one. "If you ask me, there are a lot of strange things here, any way you look at it."

"Okay, we're asking," Michael said, his interest piqued. "What, for example?"

"Well, for one thing, what was he doing here in the first place? There's no sign that he's been here for two days. Maybe he drank a glass of water or made himself a cup of coffee, but when did he arrive? Did he sleep here? The neighbor says she knew Dalia's brother lived in America, that he was a rich man. He even helped his sister pay the divorce lawyer and all that. That's what the neighbor says. So why did he hole up in this dump? Why didn't he go to a hotel?"

"Do me a favor and show me the rest of his things, the documents you've got stashed in the brown bags," Shorer said, and Nina handed them over without a word. He leaned over the table and went through the papers in a rush, stopping when he came across a clipping from a newspaper stuck inside Sroul's American passport. "What do you say about this?" he asked Michael, handing him the clipping. Michael glanced at the obituary announcing Tirzah Rubin's death.

"You think he saw the obituary and got right on a plane?" Balilty wondered aloud. "That's the way it is with old friends: there's no replacing them, that's what I've always said. These were his school chums, he'll never have better friends than that, no way. They're like family, especially in this country. That's so Israeli, you know? It's what's so nice about life here, what with youth movements and field trips." Motioning toward the photograph resting on the table, he said, "Look at that smile. How much do you want to bet that he didn't smile like that too often after that?"

No one responded, but everyone looked at Michael, who was sitting on the wooden chair next to the table, going through the papers. "This is all you found?" he asked, and Nina nodded. "There's no wallet here, no credit cards, no cash. Did you find any of those elsewhere, like in his suitcase or his pockets?"

"No," Nina said. "We didn't."

"But we're not talking about a robbery here," Shorer mumbled. "No one here has mentioned that possibility, have they?"

"No," Nina responded. "The place wasn't even broken into. Everything points to this guy having let in someone he knew. In the kitchen there was—there is—an electric kettle, cups with coffee in them. The cups were washed, but in the sink there is evidence that they drank coffee."

"He was hosting someone here," Lillian interrupted. "The forensics people say that there was at least one other person in the kitchen besides *him,*" she said, pointing toward the dead body. "We don't know yet whether it was a man or a woman."

"So there's no money. Nothing, in fact, except the passports and airline ticket?" Michael asked.

"I wouldn't say that," Balilty muttered. While they were talking, he had bent down next to the narrow bed holding the dead body, looked underneath it, thrust his hand beneath the decrepit mattress, pulled out a purple, oblong plastic folder—the kind distributed by travel agents, the tickets and itineraries inside—and ran his pinky over what remained of the gold lettering, nearly erased by time. From inside the folder he extricated an old, yellowing newspaper clipping along with a few letters in their envelopes, held together by a small rubber band. There was silence in the room until Balilty broke it. "Most important thing is that the forensics team has finished their work," he said mockingly. "They're done searching," he said, looking around. He called out, "Joe! Joe, Joe! Where are you?"

A member of the forensics team appeared in the doorway. "What is it now?" the man asked, fatigued.

"I understand that you people have finished up in here, right?" Balilty asked, waving the purple ticket folder.

"What's that?" the forensics expert asked as he drew near, examining the folder. "Where did that pop up from?"

"Right here." Balilty pointed to the bed. "He put the things most important to him under his head, and guess what? It wasn't money or credit cards; it was something completely different, something that could provide a lead for us. That is, it *could* provide a lead, but only if we actually find it, if we're not told that 'we've finished with this room.'"

"What I meant was that we finished dusting for fingerprints and all that," Joe explained, wiping his forehead with his arm, careful not to let his latex gloves touch his skin.

"That's not fair," Nina interjected. "How could he have looked there with the body still on the bed? The doctor only just got started—you yourself heard him say that they're ready to break down the bed just as soon as the body's been removed. They simply haven't gotten to it yet, that's all."

"What's important is that we've gotten to it now," Shorer said, flashing a look of warning at Balilty, who was poised to answer him.

Michael examined the tabletop. Joe from forensics said, "We've already taken prints from there. Only thing left is the bed," he said, motioning toward the doctor. Michael made a quick swipe of the table with his forefinger and spread the newspaper clipping on it. Nina and Balilty drew near.

"I don't understand this," Nina said. "What is it?"

"What's the caption underneath the photo?" Balilty asked.

"Nothing," Michael answered. "No caption. Just the date, written by hand: the twelfth of October, 1973. That's all."

"What do we have here?" Shorer asked, only now joining the others.

Balilty bent his head and examined the photographs from up close. "Hang on a minute," he said. "Look over here, Jo-Jo. And bring your magnifying glass." Joe left the room for a moment and returned immediately, handing a magnifying glass to Balilty in silence.

"It's a photograph of prisoners of war," Balilty said after a moment. "Looks to me like Egyptians, in the Sinai." He lifted his eyes from the photo. "That's what it looks like to me at first glance. Probably from the Yom Kippur War," he said before examining the date.

"How's that relevant?" Nina asked.

"I heard they spent a few days as prisoners of war in Egypt," Balilty said as he returned to studying the photograph, using the magnifying glass. "Here, the date's written on it," he mumbled.

"Who? Who were prisoners of war?"

"These three guys, the ones in that other photo, the ones who were together in the army—"

"That's not exactly the way it was," Michael said, "but that's not important for the moment."

"What else did you find?" Shorer asked.

"Letters. Three, I think," Michael said. "I need to read them carefully. Not here," he added, though while he was talking, he removed each from its envelope and unfolded them. "One is from 1975, the second from 1982, and the third is dated one month ago. They're all," he said, riffling through them, "from Tirzah. Here at the bottom, signed, 'Love, Tirzah.'"

"Tirzah Rubin met up with him in America a few weeks before she died," Balilty explained to Shorer. "We think it was about *Iddo and Eynam,* the film Benny Meyuhas was making. You know, the one they ran out of money for? We think she might have contacted him to ask for backing."

"I suggest," Michael said, looking at Shorer, "that we bring Benny Meyuhas here. Right now, before they remove the body."

Shorer was silent a moment, then said, "That may just do the trick. I don't get the impression that something else will cause him to talk, and we can't—you don't want to wait until after the autopsy?"

"No," Michael answered. "I want to see him look at the body. I want to watch him when he sees it."

"Now?" Balilty asked. "You want him here now?" He removed his cell phone from the inner pocket of his jacket.

"No, no, Danny," Michael said. "I'm going to bring him here myself."

"Yourself?" Balilty said, astounded. "Alone? I can get someone to bring him here—"

"No. Me, by myself," Michael insisted.

Puzzled, Balilty regarded him until suddenly his eyes lit up with comprehension. "I get it," he said, pleased.

Michael nodded, though his intention was unclear. He himself did not know precisely why he was insisting on bringing Benny Meyuhas there himself from police headquarters. When he had seen the expression on Benny Meyuhas's face, that deadened, absent look—as if some great terror had frightened all expression away—he had ordered that special surveillance be placed on him, had instructed them not to let Benny Meyuhas out of their sight for even a moment. And now, when he pictured Benny Meyuhas's face, he believed that only under his own surveillance, on the way back to this apartment and in the apartment itself, would he manage to prevent the impending disaster he could not stop feeling was headed their way.

Shorer said, "Michael's afraid that no one else will take care of him like he will. Isn't that so? Do I know who we're dealing with here, or what?"

Embarrassed, Michael nodded inconclusively again. He did not feel comfortable forming the words, in front of everyone, that would describe the strange feeling he felt throbbing inside him for this odd creative genius, Benny Meyuhas, a man who had expressed something so meaningful about Agnon's story *Iddo and Eynam*, perhaps the most meaningful thing he had heard for a long while; and this had turned him instantly, in Michael's mind, into a precious and vulnerable creature.

"I'm sure you'll be safe," Balilty assured him, "but I'm coming with you anyway."

Michael thought to protest but could not find anything to say. In any event they had nothing more to do there until the body was taken away. "Good idea," he said at last. "Come with me and start searching for a new lead on this case."

"What, like—" Balilty was confused. He made a circular motion with his hand that Michael did not comprehend. "Like you want me to ask who left the Israel Television building? I mean, they haven't been letting anyone in or out. Nobody left without us knowing about it. Only with our permission."

"Nevertheless," Michael insisted, "there are always exceptions. You know as well as I do that the minute we start checking, we'll find that quite a few people left the building. Even Hefetz went out to eat with the director general, and I doubt it was in some hole-in-the-wall right next to the building, like he's sure to tell you. You know it's easy to say one thing and do something else altogether. I don't need to tell you it's possible to go places without moving your car, so that also proves nothing—there are plenty of taxis around. In short, everything needs to be looked into all over again, and anyway, most of these people are being questioned right now at headquarters."

"Are you sure this is connected to what's been happening at Israel Television?" Nina asked. "I know I'm not involved in all that, but—"

"Oh, come on!" Balilty cried out maliciously. "This guy, what's more or less the last thing he did in his life? He visited Zadik. Right? And when he left Zadik's office, Zadik was slaughtered like some . . . that much you know, right? And we have the composite drawing of him, okay? And now he's been knocked off, too. I mean, what more do we need to know? This isn't some kiddies' game!" Nina glared at him and Balilty snorted, then settled down a bit and continued. "There's no sign of a break-in or a robbery here. He was hosting someone, and if you ask me it had to be Meyuhas, and I'd bet Meyuhas was also the one . . ." Balilty's voice faded and then, uncharacteristically hesitant, he added, "But blow me down if I can think of a motive."

"Oh, there is one," Shorer insisted. "We simply do not know yet what it is."

"How do you see it, sir?" Nina asked Shorer. "Do you believe all these murders are connected?"

"Of course!" Balilty shouted. "How could they not be?"

"It certainly appears that way," Shorer replied, plucking the ends of his mustache. "They seem to be connected. In fact, they seem to have grown one from the other."

"How so?" Nina asked as she leaned over the table in what appeared to be an innocent pose, though Michael suspected there was something provocative, some taunt aimed at Balilty, about the way her oversized sweater clung to her breasts.

Shorer did not look at her. He was staring at the dead body when he said, "Naturally, we'll be smarter when Benny Meyuhas and the sister provide positive identification of the body. Maybe Aviva should, too. But assuming this is Sroul, it seems fairly clear that he came to Israel in the wake of Tirzah's death. Matty Cohen was murdered because he saw something, Zadik was murdered because of something that *this* man apparently informed him, and then this man, if he is indeed who we think—"

"That's him, no doubt about it," Balilty hastened to interject. "No question at all. Does anybody doubt it?"

Shorer laid a hand on Balilty's arm, silencing him. "If he is indeed who we think, then we can assume he was—if you'll forgive me—the man who knew too much. And this was why he had to join the others."

"That means," Balilty explained to Nina, "that what we need to clarify here is why Tirzah was murdered—that is to say, who did it and why—and then we'll know all the rest. But that's not easy at all, because Benny Meyuhas was up on the roof with an entire crew when she was killed."

"That's not entirely true," Michael said, turning to the door. "Not at precisely the hour she was murdered. Don't forget they took a break just then. They were waiting for the sun gun, they needed the light—"

"Okay," Balilty admitted, displeased. "So there was a little bit of time that he left the roof to search for the sun gun in the warehouse, before he sent the lighting technician to find it. But he wasn't alone. Schreiber the cameraman went with him, that's what I understood."

"But they weren't together the whole time," Michael said. "Schreiber isn't the type of guy who can stay obediently in one place for any length of time. You can imagine him getting antsy and wandering around. After all, there are all kinds of tunnels and hallways around there, right?"

"So what are you trying to tell us?" Balilty baited him. "That at the very minute Schreiber took off, Benny Meyuhas—a real superhero, that guy—pounced on Tirzah, who just happened to be standing there next to some columns, and then raced back up to the roof as if nothing had happened?"

"That's just it," Michael said, "I'm not saying anything at this point because I simply do not know." He stopped for a minute, then repeated himself. "I simply do not know. And what about you? Do you know something that the rest of us don't?"

"In the meantime, no," Balilty admitted, chagrined. "But give me another day or two, and I'll—"

"All right," Michael declared, "I'm going to bring him here. Please leave everything as it is, don't touch a thing. Danny, are you coming with me?"

"He is," Shorer said. "He's going back with you, and he'll stay at headquarters to do some questioning."

Balilty looked around, displeased. "And are you staying here?" he asked Shorer.

"For the time being," Shorer replied with forced pleasantness. "And if I decide to leave I will do so, according to whatever needs to be done. It's not a matter of ego or prestige. Or do you think otherwise?"

"No way, not ego," Balilty muttered. "I'm in favor of solving this case."

"I'll be back with Benny Meyuhas within half an hour," Michael summed up. "Nina, please let them know we're on our way. Have them wake Benny up if he's sleeping."

Next to the front door, on his way out, Michael heard Shorer ask, "Nina, do you think you could arrange a little cup of coffee for us?"

# CHAPTER FOURTEEN

The moment Michael entered police headquarters, he realized he would not be returning to the scene of the crime within half an hour. Echoes of the tumult could be heard all the way to the front door, and they grew louder as he climbed the stairs. Outside his office a crowd had gathered; people were jammed together in a circle around Hefetz and Danny Benizri, who were standing within inches of one another. "You think I can do whatever I want?" Hefetz shouted as he reached for the collar of Danny Benizri's army jacket. However, in view of the look he got from Benizri—who was watching Hefetz's hand approach as if it were a poisonous snake—Hefetz thought better of it and returned his hand to his side. "I told you," he said, though his heart did not seem to be in it, "I received an order from the director general! Just stay out of this whole matter, I told you—" Just then, Hefetz noticed Michael and fell silent. When he resumed talking, he was no longer shouting; instead he drew even closer to Danny Benizri and spoke in a near whisper. He watched Michael from the corner of his eye, tensed up in anticipation of his reaction and awaiting it all the same. "We're not socialists here," Hefetz said. "Try to understand: those are yesterday's cold noodles. You want to bring me a character profile of Shimshi's wife? What could possibly be new about *that*? In any case, they've all been arrested! You already filmed them on their way in to jail, what more could you show? You want to show the empty factory? The trucks? The bottles? All of it's been all over the news for days, people are sick of seeing it, especially your pessimistic take on it!"

"Do you hear what you sound like?" Benizri shouted. It appeared he had not spotted Michael, or if he had, he was unconcerned about him or about Eli Bachar, who was standing guard, observing them from the small office at the end of the hall. Eli Bachar motioned to Michael, to which Michael responded with a nod of his head and a look that meant Eli would have to wait a moment. "What are you anyway," Benizri spat at Hefetz, "the director general's mouthpiece? And how about the director general himself? He's the *government's* mouthpiece! You should be ashamed of yourself! This'll be the downfall of the country!" Benizri nearly choked on his anger; his face was scarlet, and veins protruded from his neck. "What do you think, they didn't put pressure on Zadik, only on you? Don't you remember how he'd complain about those phone calls? But he never—"

"Danny," Schreiber said from behind as he tugged at Benizri's arm and glanced suspiciously at Michael, "calm down. It's not worth the—"

"Leave me alone!" Benizri shouted. "All of you, just get off my back! We don't get any support at all around here: on the one hand somebody's knocking us off like flies, and on the other hand—" Suddenly, shaking, he smothered his face in his hands. Schreiber took hold of his shoulders and pulled him out of the fray.

"Listen, Hefetz," Rubin said from behind, "I don't know what's happened to you, and I don't understand anything anymore. I don't know if you thought that if you told us here—at police headquarters, before we're all questioned—about your plans for cutbacks, we'd shut up about it for a while. Well, I'm not buying it. Just so you know," he said, planting himself in front of Hefetz, "you can't just cancel overnight a show that's been running for years and years. Not today, not just like that, not when Zadik's body is still warm. I mean, I don't mean that literally . . . But he's barely dead, and you're off and running to please your master."

"Just so you people understand: our ratings are zip!" Hefetz cried. "The public has had it, I haven't even been given a hundred-day grace period. Do you get it? The director general, Ben-Asher, today he—they want things that are more . . . entertaining . . ."

"Did you hear what Benizri was saying?" Rubin said authoritatively. "People are dropping like flies. And you? You people—" Michael noted that this was the first time he had heard Rubin's voice rise to a near shout.

But Rubin did not finish what he was saying because just then Benizri shook himself free of Schreiber's grip and attacked Hefetz, grabbing his arms and shaking him violently. "You want entertainment? Tomorrow the labor minister is giving a press conference, won't that be a riot? People's lives are in ruin. So what are we doing—giving the public some live flesh to chew on, some blood! Some great gossip! Hasn't enough blood been shed?"

"The gossip will come out in any case, Danny," Hefetz said quietly, and Benizri let go of him at once. Hefetz wiped his brow. "It'll appear in the papers no matter what you do, prepare for that."

"I'm already prepared. But I'm not the problem," Danny Benizri said in a parched voice. "You want to talk to me now?" he asked Eli Bachar. "Because if you do, that's fine with me." Eli Bachar nodded and motioned to Benizri to join him in a small office at the end of the hallway.

Rubin approached Hefetz once again. "I want to understand something," he said, looking straight into Hefetz's eyes. "You're telling me right here, after one meeting with the director general, on the very day that Zadik was murdered in his own office, that you're immediately pulling my show off the air? The show that's won so many prizes, that . . . that . . . and I even have a whole program ready to be screened, completely prepared. That's what you're telling me?"

Hefetz stepped backward and glanced at Michael, who neither averted his gaze nor moved from where he was standing. "What the director general meant," said Hefetz to Rubin, clearly shaken, "was not that the program has been canceled but that you will no longer be hosting it." Silence fell on the people gathered in the hallway. Hefetz adjusted his glasses, pursed his lips, and suddenly seemed to have lost all inhibitions. "He meant that someone else would be hosting it," he said quietly, "and that you are simply suspended. For the time being you are suspended because you have failed to raise the ratings on your show. Now do you understand? Suspended. Benizri, too. If you want an explanation, I'll be happy to—"

A harsh laugh escaped from Rubin's mouth like a convulsion. "I know the official explanation," he said coolly. "What could you possibly tell me? All you could do would be to recite the director general's words. Your master's voice. What could you tell me? That Benizri has been suspended because he 'exchanged critical remarks about the minister of labor and social affairs with the laid-off workers' wives during a live broadcast'? Or that he didn't always know how to behave himself in the face of authority? You think I don't know what the director general's complaints are? Zadik stood up to the guy day in and day out. Every day he would say, 'Let them fire me, as long as I'm in this position I'm not going to—'"

"If you'll pardon me," Hefetz said, calmly cutting Rubin off, his face emotionless, "Zadik is no longer with us to make matters right for you people. With all due respect, I am now the boss."

Rubin regarded him for one long moment in silence. "I knew it," he said at last, under his breath. "I knew that as soon as you got a little power, you would become a paradigm of the arrogant upstart slave. But I never believed it would happen so quickly. Perhaps you yourself made it happen—"

"Watch it," Hefetz said. "Just watch it, Rubin. Be careful what you say. There are witnesses here, and I have full backing from the director general—"

"Full backing!" Rubin said. "There's no connection at all between my ratings and suspending me, none whatsoever! There's no connection between Benizri's supposed infraction and—but never mind, that doesn't matter. When we're talking about tyranny, the authority of a despot, there doesn't *need* to be a connection, or real reasons. Ladies and gentlemen," he called to the small crowd gathered around him, "please welcome the new tyrant, the Despot of Israel Television! Please welcome the little dictator, welcome—"

"I don't need to listen to this bullshit," Hefetz said with loathing. "Did you want to talk to me?" he asked, turning to Michael. "Here I am. Where do you want me?" Before Michael could answer him, Hefetz looked at Rubin and said, "The show's over, and the good life, too. Not everybody around here is going to get to do whatever he pleases. This is a new era. Do you understand that? Do you or don't you understand that?"

"And what's going to happen with *Iddo and Eynam*?" Hagar blurted. "Are you planning to dump that too?"

"Don't worry, Hagar," Hefetz said in a fatherly manner, "we're planning to honor all existing contracts. Let's wait and see how things fall when matters quiet down a little. In the meantime you should know that the director general is very much in favor . . . he even said—"

"Hefetz, excuse me, excuse me," said Eliahu Lutafi, the correspondent for environmental affairs, who had pushed himself from the crowd and readjusted the skullcap on his head. "Don't you think you could wait to the end of the thirty-day mourning period, or at the very least until the seven-day shiva for Zadik has ended? There's something not quite—"

"Lutafi," Hefetz said, his face pinched and drawn. "Now you're starting up? What are you worried about? You're staying right where you are." Without waiting for an answer, he looked to Michael, who motioned Hefetz to join him in his office.

"Tzilla will be questioning you," Michael told Hefetz. "She'll be in in a moment and she'll speak with you, and you'll sign a statement, and then you'll be free to leave."

"Not you?" Hefetz asked like a child expecting to speak with the principal and instead getting the very last of the substitute teachers. "I thought that you yourself—"

"Tzilla," Michael said into the intercom, "Hefetz is waiting for you in my office."

After listening to Tzilla for a moment, Michael said, "I'm coming to get him, I've wasted enough time here. You can divide up the people waiting next to my office. I want signed statements by the morning." To Hefetz he added, "Wait here, please. Don't move until she arrives," and with that he left the room without waiting for a response.

"He hasn't said a word, sir," said the policeman on duty outside the interrogation room on the ground floor. "He's just sitting there, hasn't even lifted his head. Maybe he's sleeping, I'm not sure. Peretz is in there with him, but—"

Michael nodded. "All right," he muttered. "Don't worry about it. Go drink something, eat something. Your shift is already over." The policeman curled his lips into an awkward smile and made way for Michael to pass by.

Michael opened the door in one swift motion. Benny Meyuhas did not even lift his head, but Peretz, the interrogations officer, jumped up from his seat, startled. Michael placed his hand on Peretz's shoulder, and the policeman sat back down in his place. He tugged at the sleeve of his thin blue sweater, frowned as if to say he had failed, and said, aloud, "He won't eat or drink. Or talk. I don't—"

"You're doing fine," Michael said encouragingly. He approached Benny Meyuhas, who was sitting at the opposite side of the table. "Benny," Michael said. "You're coming with me now. We're waiting for you." While speaking he took hold of his arm, and Benny Meyuhas looked up at him, heaved himself to his feet without a word, and followed Michael out. "Come along with me, Peretz," Michael said to the policeman. Without speaking they ascended the stairs and exited to the parking lot, where Michael's car was waiting.

"You drive, please," Michael said to the policeman, bending toward him and whispering the address. Peretz sat behind the wheel, and Michael opened the back door and invited Benny Meyuhas to have a seat. Benny Meyuhas did not budge for a moment, but Michael held the door open and gave him a gentle shove, causing the director to bend down and fold himself into the car. They drove the whole way in silence, Michael's eyes constantly on Benny Meyuhas; he paid special attention as they passed the Oranim gas station. It seemed to him then that Benny Meyuhas sat up in his seat, but he did not shift or raise his head or look out the window. Only when Michael told Peretz to stop the car next to the apartment building and then said to Benny Meyuhas, "Here we are, Benny, you can get out of the car now. You know this building," did Benny Meyuhas raise his eyes for the first time. As if the spotlights were blinding him, he shut his eyes and covered them with the palms of his hands.

"Yes," Michael said sympathetically, "I know you're familiar with this building. Sroul is waiting for you inside."

Benny Meyuhas regarded him with wonder. "Sroul?" he blurted suddenly. "He's still there?"

"Why?" Michael asked with forced affability. "Where did you think he would be?"

Benny Meyuhas did not answer, and Michael stepped out of the car, leaving the door open for Benny to join him.

After several long minutes, Benny Meyuhas emerged from the car, his body stooped. He did not completely straighten up even when he raised his head to look at the building. "I'm waiting here," he said to Michael. "Tell Sroul to come to me."

"He's waiting for you inside," Michael said softly. "He can't come outside to meet you just now. Don't you know that?"

"Why not?" Benny Meyuhas asked. "Is he too weak?"

Michael looked into the man's face in search of a trace of sarcasm, but the bluish light of the spotlights showed only a tortured face outlined in deep creases that seemed to have deepened in the two days since Michael had first met him, giving him the look of a man filled with so much pain and sorrow that Michael found it hard to keep his eyes on him. Benny Meyuhas gazed up toward the second floor. "He was feeling better," he said. "He told me he'd be fine, well enough to speak with you people."

Benny Meyuhas began to speak again, then fell silent, pursing his lips like a small child who refuses to eat another spoonful of soup and shaking his head stubbornly.

"Come with me," Michael said, pulling him gently toward the building. At one point it seemed as though Benny Meyuhas's legs would give way and he would collapse, but Michael, who was tensed in anticipation of any possibility, held his arm tightly and coaxed him toward the path.

Balilty, who had returned ahead of Michael, was standing with Shorer at the entrance to the apartment. They nodded in Michael's direction but did not look at Benny Meyuhas as they made room for the two to pass by on the way into the bedroom. Nina was waiting just outside the room, a smile forming at the edges of her lips until she caught sight of Benny Meyuhas's face, and she stepped aside. "Ronen's in there," she warned Michael quietly, and Michael nodded, pulling the director into the room after him. Inside the room, quite close to the door, Benny Meyuhas stopped in his tracks and gazed at the bed. Without a word he drew closer and looked. He knelt down and pressed his face into the dead man's arm. A moment later he lifted his head and looked at Michael, who nodded in affirmation, but Benny Meyuhas continued to regard him with a questioning look.

"He's dead," Michael said after a long silence.

Benny Meyuhas jumped up and threw himself on the emaciated body, then burst into a loud and piercing wail. In the midst of his crying he called out, "Sroul! Sroul! It's all my fault! My fault!" He continued to sob, his voice now faint and stifled as though bubbling up from the depths of his body. Sergeant Ronen looked at Michael in shock, poised to pull Meyuhas from the bed, but Michael held his hand out to stop him. They stood waiting: Nina near the door, Sergeant Ronen in the corner, and Michael next to the bed, waiting for the wave of sorrow to subside.

They waited in silence as Benny Meyuhas pulled himself up from the body and knelt next to the bed. He covered his face with his hands as though in prayer, until finally he stood up, with great difficulty, turning around to look at Michael, his eyes drained of color as though they had suddenly been gouged out, leaving only emptiness behind.

"When was the last time you saw him?" Michael asked.

"Today," Benny Meyuhas responded hoarsely, though now he seemed grounded and completely in focus. "This afternoon, late, just before I came to the television station. He told me to come and tell you . . . he wanted me to . . . but I couldn't do it . . ." Again, sobs emerged from the depths.

Michael led him out into the hallway and toward the living room, where chairs had been set up, along with a table with a recording device on it.

"Where do you want this?" Balilty whispered from the doorway, where he was standing with a video camera. "We set it up in here because there's a door between the rooms," he explained. "This way it's easy, or relatively easy, since you insisted on doing this here instead of back at headquarters, and Shorer says—"

"You people decide," Michael concluded. He looked at Nina as she got Benny Meyuhas settled on one of the chairs and pointed the microphone at him. "You're better at that than I am," he said distractedly. "But I don't want you people in the room with us."

"That's the whole idea," Balilty said in a stage whisper. "We'll be in the next room listening to every word, and we thought we'd put the camera next to the window."

Michael nodded, entered the room, and sat facing Benny Meyuhas. He motioned to Nina to leave, pressed a button on the tape recorder, quietly mumbled the date, time, and name of the interviewee into the microphone, then looked at Benny Meyuhas and said, "Are you ready to begin?"

Benny Meyuhas pressed his hands into his face and from behind them said, "I have no one left . . . I have nobody left to protect." He sat up straight in his chair. "What do you want to know?" he asked.

# CHAPTER FIFTEEN

"*You*?" Rubin said, surprised to find Lillian standing in the doorway to Balilty's office. "Where's the big boss? I thought that he would—"

Lillian straightened the sleeves of the long green men's shirt she was wearing, sat down across from Rubin, and placed an orange file on the table between them. "For the time being, *I'll* be asking the questions. Do you have a problem with that?" she asked, inclining her head. With artificial affability she added, "I've heard you have nothing against women, but suddenly it would seem—"

"No, no, no, perish the thought!" he said with elaborate formality, a smile on his face. "I've always said that women constitute the *better* part of the world."

"So," Lillian said, an inquisitive look on her face, "you've been sent a woman, and what do you do? Complain!"

"No, that's not what I meant," Rubin apologized. "It's just . . . surprising. I had understood that . . . oh, never mind; as far as I'm concerned, you're welcome to begin whenever you're ready."

"Ready I am," Lillian said, and she pressed the button on the recording device. For a quick moment she turned her head to the back, toward the wall and the window, which appeared completely dark and was covered by a curtain; from the other side one could see everything that was taking place in Balilty's office.

Rubin followed her gaze; his eyes skittered from Lillian to the recording device until finally he aimed a bluish, focused stare at her. "I would like to speak with Benny," he said as if sharing a secret. "I've already requested permission several times. Chief Inspector Ohayon promised me that—"

"No problem," Lillian said pleasantly. "We'll just finish up here, and then we'll see. By then, Chief Inspector Ohayon may be able to escort you himself."

She gestured to the door, implying that Michael would soon return, but Rubin looked toward the door and said hesitantly, "I don't feel comfortable talking with you people before I—" Lillian flashed him a look of anticipation, forcing him to finish his thought: "First I want to speak with Benny to make sure he's all right."

"Why? Why is the order of events so important to you? Do you need to coordinate your stories?" Lillian asked teasingly. Rubin chuckled, as though she had been joking, but then she grew serious and added, "Right now this has nothing at all to do with Benny. I won't even ask about him for the time being, okay?"

"Okay," Rubin said. "What would you like to know?"

"First of all," Lillian said, getting straight to business, "we're checking the issue of physical presence."

"'The issue of physical presence'?" Rubin said mockingly. "What kind of pompous expression is that? You mean, where was I and what was I doing?"

Lillian stretched her lips into the likeness of a smile and said, "The question, to be more specific, is whether you left the building today."

"Today. You mean after . . . after Zadik—"

"Yes," Lillian said with exaggerated friendliness. "Let's say, between eleven o'clock and eight."

"Eleven o'clock this morning?" Rubin asked, wrinkling his brow.

"Until eight this evening," she offered cheerfully.

"Twice," Rubin said. "Both times with permission."

Lillian opened the orange file, flipped through several pages, and perused the information written there. "Is that so?" she asked. "And who gave you permission?"

"What is this?" Rubin asked. "Are you keeping a file on me?"

Lillian placed her elbows on the desktop and rested her chin in her hands, then stared at Rubin in anticipation, completely ignoring his question. Rubin glanced at the file and began talking. "All right. The first time, early in the afternoon, it was our security officer who gave me permission when I explained to him about my mother," he said impatiently. "The second time would have been around six this evening, with permission, I believe . . . I can't be certain, I can't recall if I got permission myself or whether it was my producer, or perhaps Hefetz. Believe me, I don't remember."

"Was this after Benny Meyuhas arrived, or before?" Lillian asked.

"After," Rubin said after pondering the question for a moment. "Yes, absolutely, it was after he arrived. I remember, God, it's hard to believe it was just—" He glanced at his watch. "It's already one in the morning, that was seven hours ago, I can't believe it. It feels like a century ago."

"So you left twice. For how long each time?" Lillian asked sweetly.

"The first time it must have been . . . what, about eleven o'clock?"

"Twelve-forty-seven," Lillian told him after glancing at the page on the table in front of her. "Precisely. You said you'd been summoned to the old-age home where your mother lives. Someone from the facility called us to confirm this."

"Well, then," Rubin said, "since someone called, you know it's true. I don't understand where the problem is."

"No." Lillian shrugged. "There's no problem, it's just that—"

"What?" Rubin asked irritably.

"It came up in the conversation," Lillian said very slowly, "that your mother takes digoxin, doesn't she?"

"I don't know," Rubin said, perplexed. "I don't know the exact medical names . . . I'm not a doctor. But—"

"They told us you went to bring a prescription for her, something urgent. Did you not? Is it not true that she needed to have a prescription filled?" Lillian asked with mock innocence. "We understand the prescription was for digoxin. If you had to ask the pharmacist for it, then you certainly know—"

"Who says I asked the pharmacist for it?" Rubin asked irritably. "Listen, young lady," he said—Lillian blinked but said nothing—"my mother is eighty-three years old and has serious health problems. Why don't you verify *that* over the phone? Why don't you ask them at the old-age home? And anyway, what does all this have to do with—?"

"Well, that's just it," Lillian said, still with the sweetness of a diligent little girl eager to cooperate. "In fact we did verify it, and what we discovered was—" She stopped as if to check her papers and secretly glanced at the curtained wall; for a moment she imagined how they would all be sitting there critiquing her performance, how Tzilla, who was interrogating Hefetz at that moment, would take issue with this and that when she watched the video recording later, using her criticism to vent her frustrations. But Lillian managed to continue: "What we discovered was that she does, in fact, take digoxin, and that she should have had eight ampoules in her cupboard. But there were only four."

Rubin spread his arms in an elaborate gesture of surprise and helplessness, then let them fall noisily to his lap. "I certainly have no control over that," he said as though registering a complaint. "Is that my responsibility, too?"

"Well, we figured you could surely help us out," Lillian said. "We wondered how it could be that two evenings ago you visited your mother," she said, glancing at her papers as though she did not already know what was written there by heart. "It says here you saw her the day before at seven o'clock, and then suddenly, the next morning, the digoxin had disappeared."

"I don't know anything about that digoxin," Rubin said impatiently. "And when exactly was I at my mother's at seven in the evening? Which day?"

"No," Lillian hastened to amend, "not seven in the evening. Who said evening? Seven in the *morning*. You were there at seven the next morning, the night after Tirzah was killed."

"All right," Rubin conceded, "I visited her in the morning on my way to work. I wanted to see if she was . . . she loved Tirzah, my mother was very attached to her. I wanted to know, I was afraid they would tell her about Tirzah or she'd hear about it on the news—"

"No, you're misunderstanding me," Lillian persisted. "Not only did you visit her, but after that visit the ampoules of digoxin suddenly disappeared. So we were thinking—"

"I don't know what you want from me," Rubin said, annoyed. "What would I want her digoxin for?"

Lillian sat up straight in her chair, her hands clasped on the desk, her fingers interlaced. "Matty Cohen was taking digoxin, too, just like your mother. Matty Cohen died of an overdose of digoxin. Did you know that?" Lillian asked with sincere interest, just as she had been taught.

"No," Rubin answered, furious, "I did not know that. Sorry if that surprises you. Is digoxin such a rare drug?"

"No, I wouldn't say it was," Lillian said, "it's a drug that regulates heart rate, the drug you purchased for your mother and which you now suddenly don't know anything about."

"It could be that I got mixed up," Rubin admitted.

"And what about at six in the evening, or whenever it was?" Lillian asked.

"What? What about six in the evening?" Rubin asked, completely confused. He glanced at his watch. "Why don't you tell me where Benny is? Why don't you answer my questions about him? I want to speak with Benny, and at the rate you're going—"

"No, I'm talking about the second time you left the building with permission," Lillian said, ignoring his outburst. "You said it was at six o'clock?"

"What do you want from me?" Rubin exclaimed with the obvious antagonism of a person being pursued. "God," he cried out in anguish, "it was with a whole crew: a cameraman and a soundman, everyone. We went to Umm-Thuba, do you know about Umm-Thuba?" His tone shifted from nervous agitation to condescension. ("Pure aggression," Tzilla would call it later when they listened to the tape and watched the video featuring Rubin's face, drained of color, and Lillian's back. "She made him completely lose his composure," Tzilla would say with admiration and not a word of criticism against Lillian.)

But throughout the interrogation Lillian was tenser than ever at the thought that Tzilla would join the group behind the curtain, watching her every move, eager to see her fail. It wasn't that the process of interrogating a suspect was foreign to her, not only in her position as an investigator for the Youth Department as an expert on drug users, but also since she had interrogated dealers and parents and anyone else who passed through Narcotics. But now they were listening to her from the other side of the wall. (Tzilla had told her, without looking her in the eye, that this was a "crucial interrogation." This made Lillian regard her and think, I'm sure you don't want me to be the one doing it, but she did not say a word; "I'm also sure they forced you to take me on here," she thought, mortified, until she reminded herself that no one here, not even Tzilla, could read her mind. Even Michael Ohayon could not do that.)

"Of course," Lillian said shortly to Rubin, as though they were both aware that he was needlessly wasting their time. "But after all, you sent the crew back, and you returned alone. You weren't with them the whole time."

"After we made our inquiries and completed the filming," Rubin said, "I wanted time to speak in private with the mother of the boy from that village. When you talk with someone in private, without a crew and away from the cameras, everything looks different. She cooperated completely, it was very important for the report. I didn't know then that they would be relieving me of my duties on the show—"

"So you stayed on to speak with the mother of the boy who's the star of your report?" Lillian scanned her papers to verify his statement.

"Yes, it's a program about doctors who cover up for—"

"Yes, I know," Lillian said. "We are well aware of which program you were filming, the one about the Palestinian youth tortured by the Israeli secret services. That's what you've been spending all your time on lately, isn't that so?" She was trying to sound provocative; while Rubin remained silent, she could not help noticing the slight twitch in his eye. (Earlier, Balilty had told her, "Don't forget to rile him up a little, that always brings out the best in them.") "We know how deeply devoted you are to the struggle for human rights, that's your big issue, isn't it? You're pursuing justice in the case of a Palestinian youth who threw a Molotov cocktail—"

"He's a child, not a youth," Rubin protested.

"Sixteen is a youth, nearly the age of an Israeli soldier," Lillian insisted. "Tell me, when they attack Jewish citizens of settlements over the Green Line, are you this perturbed? The truth: if they had picked on a sixteen-year-old settler youth, would you have made a program about *him*?"

"You're mixing everything up," Rubin complained. "That's cheap demagoguery. But I'm accustomed to that nonsense, I hear it all the time. It's like I've already said twice before: first of all, we're not talking about picking on someone here, we're talking about very serious physical torture. You don't even want to know the details, believe me. . . . Furthermore, if the settlers weren't occupying territory, if they were living on land that belonged to them, inside the Green Line, then nobody would toss Molotov cocktails at them. And anyway, my program deals in a general manner with human rights abuses and the resulting injustices perpetrated on—"

"—the Palestinian people," Lillian said, completing his sentence. "Human rights abuses and the resulting injustices perpetrated *solely* on the Palestinian people, and not on anyone else; that's what the viewer sees when he watches your show."

"Can I go see Benny now?" Rubin asked, repulsed. "I think this argument is—this is not the reason you brought me here, is it?"

"No, it isn't," Lillian admitted. "It's to find out about that missing hour and a half."

"What hour and a half?"

"From six-thirty until eight," Lillian said. "From the time the crew departed from Umm-Thuba, when you told them you would follow them later. And that's exactly what you did. You returned an hour and a half later."

"I just told you," Rubin said, exploding, "that I stayed to talk to the mother. And the boy's sister, too, you can—"

"—ask them?" she said, smiling sweetly. "They're already here, under interrogation. Don't concern yourself about it. But we want to ask *you,* not them."

Rubin stood up and pushed his chair back. At the same moment, the door flew open, and Tzilla was standing there, pale-faced. She signaled to Lillian to join her in the corridor. Lillian stepped outside, leaving Rubin alone. The video later showed that he did not move from his place, did not even try to look at the papers on the desk; it seemed as though he felt he was being watched, and he sat down and covered his face with his hands. After that he stood up again and paced the room as though taking exercise.

"There's something going on," Tzilla told Lillian. "They phoned from the scene of the murder, in the middle of interrogating Benny Meyuhas. They're on their way here right now, and they're asking for you to get him to talk about the business with Sroul by the time they arrive."

Lillian returned to the office, closed the door very quietly, and took her seat, expecting Rubin to do the same. But Rubin was not eager to sit down. "I asked to see Benny," he said, his voice threatening. "I don't understand—is he being detained without rights? What is this here, how can you forbid me from—"

"Not now," Lillian said. "First we'll finish what we started: this hour and a half, of which you sat with the mother of the Palestinian boy from Umm-Thuba for about ten minutes and then disappeared. Doesn't anybody, like, know where you were?"

"Like? Like? Or really?" Rubin asked, mocking her openly. He sat down and said, "I'm really interested in knowing what you're thinking."

When Lillian spoke next, her expression had totally changed; the false sweetness and artificial affability made way for a no-nonsense austerity she had developed over years of working with drug dealers. "Tell me," she hurled at him, bringing their banter to an end, "how is it that you never mentioned the ultra-Orthodox guy with the burns, the one who visited Zadik? How is it that you never told us he was your friend Sroul?"

Rubin looked at her without blinking. "I did not know that that was Sroul. As far as I know, he's in America. I for one have not seen him here in Israel."

"What about the police composite we've been passing around?" Lillian persisted. "You could certainly have known from that. Even just a word, you could have said something. Anything. I mean, if a composite like that is so very similar to someone's childhood friend, a person so dear to him that he keeps a picture of that person in his office, the person Tirzah went to visit before—"

"Who says?" Rubin interjected. "Who says she went to visit him? She went to the U.S. on business. Maybe she saw him there as well, and I've already told you people, I told Ohayon earlier—don't you people cross-check your information? Don't you update each other?—I told him that she wanted to raise more money for producing *Iddo and Eynam*. But that's none of your concern."

"Everything," Lillian said, "but every little thing, as you have already been told, is now our concern. What I am asking you is, how is it that you did not tell us that the person in the composite was your own friend Sroul?"

"Believe me," Rubin entreated her, "it never entered my mind. It's that simple. . . . You know how it is when you just don't think about something? It simply wasn't in my head. I've been so confused lately, and worried about Benny. And don't forget, my wife's body was—"

"Your *ex*-wife's body," Lillian corrected him. "And as far as work is concerned, you seem really quite clear-headed to me."

"Work is something else entirely," Rubin said, leaning forward. He looked intently into her eyes. "Believe me," he said, "I had no idea he was in Israel. Even now I'm not entirely certain it's Sroul. Just let me speak with Benny, and perhaps—"

"So where *were* you during that hour and a half? On your way back to the television station from Umm-Thuba?" Lillian asked. She maintained an impenetrable expression, careful not to give herself away.

"I've already told you," Rubin said in exasperation, "I was in the village with the mother of that boy. Do you have any idea what they did to him?" he asked with dramatic restraint. "Maybe if I tell you a little bit, you'll understand why I had to sit with the family in private. What would you say if I told you they stuck a pole in his rectum? Do you think the family would be willing to discuss that sort of thing in front of a television camera?"

"So what you're telling me is that for the entire hour and a half that you were missing, you were in the village?" Lillian asked. She riffled through the papers in front of her as though she did not know what her next question would be.

"Yes, that's what I'm telling you," Rubin said, calmer now. He leaned back in his chair like a person who has done his job.

"If that's the case," Lillian said, "how do explain that you were seen at the Oranim gas station?"

"Ahhhh," Rubin said with a smile, "now you expect me to report every time I fill my tank with gas? The tank was low, and I—"

"No, no, no," Lillian said, cutting him off, "I'm not just talking about the gas. First of all, since when does it take an hour and a half to fill your tank? And second, we know for a fact that you didn't fill your tank up. Don't forget, your face is known all over the country. People recognize you. According to our information, you were seen in the vicinity of the Oranim gas station, and you stopped at an auto supply shop to pick up a flashlight. It was already dark by then, and rainy, no? Do you remember now? It wasn't all that long ago," she said, glancing at her watch, "just seven hours ago. I'm sure you remember stopping there to buy a big flashlight. Where is it now?"

"Yes, that's right, I'd forgotten," Rubin muttered. "I bought a flashlight, I needed to check the . . ." He fell silent.

"How long did it take?" she asked, staring intently at him. "How long did it take you to buy that flashlight?"

Rubin shrugged. "I have no idea," he said. Then after a long pause, he added, "It took as long as it took."

"And after that did you come straight back to the television station?"

"Absolutely, yes," Rubin said, blinking several times. "If you'd like to know what I needed a flashlight for, well, I should tell you I've needed one for weeks now, and suddenly I found myself passing by—"

"Suddenly passing by?" Lillian exclaimed. "On the day that Zadik was murdered? And Benny Meyuhas was arrested? And Sroul's picture was plastered everywhere? Just then you needed to buy a flashlight? Please forgive me if I'm just the slightest bit skeptical about all this."

Rubin studied her closely and frowned. A moment later he said, "What does it matter now what I say and what you find skeptical? Believe me, it doesn't interest me in the least. That's how it was, pure and simple. What are you trying to do here, frame me?"

"No," Lillian said sedately. "I am not trying to frame you, please believe me. I simply wish you would tell me what you were doing in the Mekor Haim area of Jerusalem in an apartment that belongs to Sroul's sister. Here's what I would like to happen: you'll tell me all on your own, without me having to milk you for every bit of information. So perhaps now, after all this is finally becoming clear, you're prepared to explain what you were doing there?"

Rubin folded his arms over his chest and ran his tongue over his chapped lips. For a long moment he sat looking at her and finally said, "Don't forget that in my line of work I often find myself in situations such as these, on the other side of the table—where you're sitting—and I know all the tricks of the trade. What I'm saying, my dear," he said, unfolding his arms and placing his hands on the desk, then leaning toward her, "is that I know this gimmick you're using, so I can tell you with absolute certainty that nobody saw me in Mekor Haim in an apartment owned by Sroul's sister. You know why nobody saw me there? I'll tell you," he said, speaking slowly and emphasizing every word. "For the simple reason that I was not there. Do you understand? It's quite simple: I was not there. Not today. Not yesterday. Not the day before that. In fact, it seems to me that I've only ever been there once before, about ten years ago perhaps. So no one could have said a word to the contrary to you. That's all I wanted to explain to you. And now I have no intention of speaking with you any longer until I am taken to see Benny Meyuhas. I want to talk to him. I have the feeling that without me around, they'll harass him until he says something . . . never mind, I demand to see him right now, and I will accept no excuses. Either that, or you'll be hearing from me in the future. I'm sorry I have to resort to such threats, but there is a limit to the foolishness I am willing to endure. At the end of the day, we live in a democracy, not under Saddam Hussein!"

The two sat for a long moment without speaking. Finally Rubin said, "We're wasting time here, your time. I refuse to continue our conversation until you've kept your promise and let me speak with Benny Meyuhas."

"Wait," Lillian said, and she left the room.

Tzilla was already waiting outside the room, and she pulled Lillian quickly to the far end of the corridor to fill her in on the latest developments in the apartment in Mekor Haim. She suggested having Rubin wait in the hall and recited—with the help of the note she had jotted down—the question Michael had asked her over the phone.

"What? What was that?" Lillian asked. "What are we talking about? What doctor? The one from his interrogation?"

"Believe me, I don't have a clue what he's talking about. He didn't even ask you to wait for an answer," Tzilla said. "He only requested that you ask the question, right before you send him out of the office. We need it on video, that's what Michael said."

"Okay," Lillian said uneasily. "I just don't like asking what I don't understand myself."

"Who does?" Tzilla countered. "But after this we'll be waiting for you with coffee and sandwiches in the little office." Lillian was about to return to Balilty's office when Tzilla called after her. "Wait a second, wait until I'm behind the wall." Lillian watched as she hurried down the hall, her long silver earrings—which had become her trademark over the years—swaying from side to side.

"Okay," Lillian said to Rubin when she returned to the office. He looked at her with anticipation. "He's still in conference"—Rubin guffawed at her use of the word *conference,* though she ignored him—"but it'll be over soon, and you can . . . in the meantime you'll have to wait outside the office until Chief Inspector Ohayon is available."

"I insist on speaking with him," Rubin proclaimed. "I have all sorts of . . . I request . . . no, I'm not requesting, I am insisting on speaking with Ohayon as well. Would you let him know?"

"I already have," Lillian said in a strained voice. "He knows."

"And?" Rubin asked. "What did he say?"

Lillian sucked air into her lungs and filled her cheeks, then exhaled noisily. "He asked me to ask you," she said, standing next to the door, her hand on the doorknob, "if you know who shot the doctor in the back."

Afterward, when they watched the video, the members of the Special Investigations Team argued among themselves about the meaning of the expression on Rubin's face when he heard the question. "The fear of God nabbed him," Balilty claimed, while Eli Bachar opined that Rubin's face was apathetic and that his expression gave nothing away. As for Lillian, she thought fear and apathy produced similar reactions, especially where facial expressions are concerned. She felt that Rubin was stunned and had not actually comprehended what she was asking, at least for the first minute.

# CHAPTER SIXTEEN

Just before dawn, Michael brought Benny Meyuhas back to his office at police headquarters in the Russian Compound and told him to wait there with Sergeant Yigael, who had suddenly turned up. (Ever since finding the bloodstained T-shirt in the foreign correspondents' room at Israel Television, he had attached himself to the Special Investigations team like a small boy trailing after a gang of boys older than himself, ready and willing to be of service at any time.) After providing them with coffee and hot pita bread, Michael joined the rest of the team for an emergency meeting in Balilty's office.

At two in the morning Michael had stopped his interrogation of Benny Meyuhas and had holed himself up with Shorer in the kitchen for more than an hour. When they emerged, the district commander instructed Balilty, Sergeant Ronen, and Nina to return to headquarters with him. Balilty, who was eager to hang around until the interrogation was completed but was compelled—by the unmistakably decisive look in Michael's eyes—to obey orders and return to the Russian Compound to take part in interrogating Hefetz, was now opening the meeting with a report to all the assembled, including Tzilla (and her lists) and Eli Bachar, whose green eyes were ringed in red from fatigue, and Lillian, who seemed wide awake and was standing behind Sergeant Ronen's chair, expertly massaging his neck and shoulders; she desisted only when Balilty began recounting how Hefetz had secretly slipped out of the building.

"He left after it was already dark, after six o'clock; that's always a kind of dead time over there before the shit hits the fan," Balilty said. "I found out about it completely by chance," he muttered, though no one in the room fell for this offhand remark that concealed a declaration of his own special talents; by his own testimony, he could "squeeze juice out of rocks." "You see, I was talking with Ezekiel the auto mechanic, the guy who takes care of Ruta's car"—the tribulations of Ruta, Balilty's wife, and the old Fiat she refused to part with, were known to all—"because I stopped by to settle an account with him. He'd stayed late at the garage, he was sitting with his bookkeeper in the back, must have been about seven o'clock. Or seven-thirty, I can check. Anyway, Ezekiel tells me that a little while earlier, an hour or two, he saw Hefetz ducking into the Iraqi hummus place. You know which one I mean," he said, turning to Michael. "We used to go there, over on Jeremiah Street, behind the junkyard. Little place, they cook the hummus on an old paraffin stove, like in the Old City. Do you remember what I'm talking about?" Michael swiveled his head, though it was not clear whether in confirmation or merely to encourage Balilty to get on with it. "In any case," Balilty continued, "Ezekiel the mechanic sees Hefetz stealing into the Iraqi place 'like a thief,' that's what he said about Hefetz: 'He looked to the right and looked to the left and dashed in like the place just swallowed him up.' That's how he described it. But it gave me the tiniest lead, something I could hint at with Hefetz to let him know I was aware he'd left the building. And that's not all: I told him that this was exactly the same time another murder had been committed and that he, Hefetz, could be considered a suspect. That's when everything turned smooth as butter with him. Could I have another cup of coffee?"

"But he closes up at three-thirty, four o'clock, the Iraqi," Eli Bachar remarked as someone passed Balilty a half-full cup of Turkish coffee.

"Most of the time that's true," Balilty said, "but if you're an important guy," he said with a sigh, "or if you're coming to meet the director general of the Israel Broadcasting Authority on the sly, then the restaurateur himself—if you consider the Iraqi hummus place a restaurant—opens up for you, actually waits there for you till you show up."

"Hang on, I don't get it," Sergeant Ronen said. "Who does the Iraqi guy know? Which one was he waiting for?"

"Both of them," Balilty answered impatiently. "Hefetz and Ben-Asher. He's known them both since they were kids. They were in school together in Baghdad, then they were neighbors in Israel, in the camps for new immigrants. All three of them, or maybe just two of them, I'm not clear on that. Anyway, what's important here is that they're some kind of gang, the three of them, since way back," he said, holding his hand just above the floor to indicate how small they were back then, "and together they hated the whole world: the camps and the European Jews and the teachers and the Jewish Agency. Everybody! So the Iraqi opens up his place specially for them. He has this room in the back where he lives. Did you people know that?" Everyone waited with anticipation, hoping he would reach his point soon, but Balilty would not be rushed. "With me, if I go there after, say, three o'clock, I don't have a prayer in hell of even getting a crumb of pita bread. 'Kitchen's closed,' they tell me. But Mr. Hefetz and Mr. Ben-Asher? Whatever they want. That's the way it is, not that I care, I mean we're just talking about a lousy hummus joint, but—"

"Tell me, Balilty," Eli Bachar said, "why can't you just get to the point? Just for once!" Michael flashed him a look—fatigued but austere—and Eli Bachar shut his mouth, pulled his cooling mug of coffee toward himself, and stared at the window facing him, outside of which the sky was still dark.

"I already told you the point here: he left the building. It's recorded in the security officer's ledger, he was out for an hour and a half," Balilty said. "And he was sitting with the director general. They're making plans: cutbacks, savings, stuff like that. If you ask me, it's an ass-licking, ball-busting plan. Seems like Zadik's death saves the director general a lot of trouble."

"So what do you make of all this?" Shorer asked him.

"It's all pretty clear," Balilty said as he looked with disgust into his Styrofoam cup before slurping down the rest of the coffee. "This Ben-Asher, I don't need to tell you his whole life story, you can read about it in the papers. But what's important to keep in mind about him is how much he wants to screw the European Jewish establishment, the people he thinks screwed him. Nobody knows exactly how he worked his way into the system; he started off at Israel Radio in the Arabic Department and moved over to television, first on the station that broadcasts from the Knesset—the one nobody ever watches—and then later he was in charge of bringing Egyptian films for screening on Friday afternoons. Sometimes I used to watch them myself because of Hanna, my sister-in-law, my little brother's wife. And then suddenly, I don't know how—what do I mean, 'I don't know how,' that's the way everything works around here—suddenly the guy's director general of the Israel Broadcasting Authority. Ever since then, the gig's up, nothing's going to remain the same, you'll see. A real upstart, that Ben-Asher. Between him and Hefetz there's going to be a lot of score-settling to come. They've already informed Rubin that he's been relieved of his duties."

"All right," Shorer said, "but you're not implying that Hefetz is in some way involved in Zadik's death, are you?"

"No, I'm not implying any such thing," Balilty said with a smile. "It doesn't seem that way. He would have been named director of Israel Television at some stage anyway; believe me, that was part of the plan. No way that Hefetz could have done it: he was in the newsroom when Tirzah Rubin was murdered, there were witnesses, except for a couple of minutes when he was with Natasha. But even then what's-her-name—Niva—saw them."

"So what are we wasting our time on this for?" Eli Bachar asked, enraged. "Don't we have enough work to do as it is?"

"First of all," Balilty said, "I'd like to point out that if Hefetz could leave the building so easily without anyone noticing, then other people could too. Not just today—I mean yesterday—which was a particularly tough day, but on other days, too. And anyway, it's just a side story, you know, so we won't get bored. We all already know the story of Zadik's death, right?"

"Right," Michael said, "but we don't have enough—for the time being, we don't have enough of a case. Maybe when forensics gets the DNA results—"

"But it's clear we're talking about Zadik's blood on that T-shirt," Lillian reminded them. "It says so in the preliminary report."

"The blood is one thing," Balilty was quick to point out, "but we still don't know who the T-shirt belongs to. And there's that gray hair that could be—"

Michael's beeper sounded. He looked at the display screen and said to Tzilla, "It's from the forensics lab at Abu Kabir. Give them a call, would you, and see what they have to say."

"Already?" Eli Bachar asked, incredulous. "What could they possibly find that quickly? It's only been three hours since—"

"First of all," Balilty said, "three hours is a pretty long time, and second of all, maybe they found something really important."

Tzilla dialed the phone, and when she was put through to the pathologist, she handed the receiver over to Michael. He listened for a long moment, then said, "Hang on a minute, I'm going to put you on the loudspeaker, we're holding a short team meeting right now." Everyone in the room could hear the distraught voice of the pathologist: "Final stages, spreading, terminal," he was saying.

"What?" asked Lillian, alert and tense. "What was that?"

"Cancer, that's what. Our Sroul had cancer," Balilty announced. Into the loudspeaker he said, "Dr. Siton, can you tell us where? Which kind?"

"Lung cancer." The pathologist's hoarse voice crackled through the speaker. "It seems he only had a few weeks left to live. When a person's living, you don't make such predictions, because you can never really know, but since this man is no longer with us, I can tell you—off the record, it won't appear in my autopsy report—that it was only a matter of weeks. Incidentally, in America they tell the patient the truth to his face because they're afraid of being sued for malpractice."

Shorer stood and approached the loudspeaker. After informing the pathologist who he was, he asked, "What does this mean physiologically? How would it have affected him? I mean, is it right to assume that strangling him would have been quite simple, since the illness itself involves difficulty in pulling air into the lungs?"

"Yes," the pathologist answered, a note of sarcasm in his voice. "It's easier to strangle someone who is about to stop breathing anyway."

"Excuse me for a moment, Dr. Siton, this is Michael Ohayon again. I have a question: in the state he was in, wouldn't he have required assistance of some kind—an oxygen tank or something?

"Naturally," the pathologist said through the speaker. Michael gave Nina an inquisitive look; she shrugged as a way of saying she knew nothing about it. "There must be some sort of oxygen tank in the vicinity, no doubt about it."

"There was nothing of the sort there," Nina said, a look of panic spreading across her face. "We took apart the entire apartment, there was nothing—the only place we didn't touch was under the sink, it appeared nobody had touched anything there for ages."

"Impossible. There must be something," the pathologist declared. "He could not have managed without oxygen—take a better look around. It won't necessarily look like an oxygen tank, there are small models—something called a cannula, looks like a pair of eyeglasses. It's two holes in a tube that you wear on your nose like a small mask, with a pipe running from it to the patient's back, where a little tank—which looks like a thermos—sits in a backpack. There must be one somewhere in that apartment, and a tank, too, even a small one. Didn't you find anything that even—"

"Yes!" Nina cried suddenly. "There was a thermos! Silver, I didn't understand . . . it was in the kitchen, I thought . . . we checked for fingerprints, but we only found the dead man's. Nothing else. The thermos was in a kitchen cupboard, looks like some futuristic soda-making machine. Is that right?"

"Send somebody to bring it in," Michael told Tzilla. "Right away." Turning to Nina, he said, "What about those glasses? Wasn't there a pipe attached to a mask that looked like a pair of glasses?"

"No," Nina said. "But we weren't able to check the surroundings because it was dark. Maybe it's outside. We'll be able to search as soon as it's light outside and the rain has let up."

"How could a man in his condition," Shorer asked the pathologist, "manage such a long flight?"

"I'm sure he was given steroids. We haven't checked his blood yet, but I'm certain we'll find steroids. Lots of them, and strong ones," the pathologist said. "There are anabolic steroids that can keep you on a constant high for days. They give you the false impression that you have strength. Afterward you crash, if the steroids don't finish you off first."

"Excuse me," Sergeant Ronen asked when the doctor had finished speaking, "but why are we so concerned with lung cancer and oxygen masks? The guy was strangled to death, there's proof of it. So why is it important—I mean, isn't it more important for us to finally hear what Benny Meyuhas had to say?"

"We'll get to that," Michael assured him, "in just another minute. But first of all this is of the utmost importance, since we did not understand until now what it was that prompted Sroul to come forward *now* and tell Tirzah Rubin a few weeks ago something that had been bothering him for more than twenty years."

"What, you mean like because he was going to croak?" Eli Bachar asked. "Like he wanted to confess before he died?"

"But he was religious," Lillian said. "Don't you people know that religious Jews don't do confession before they die? I mean, what are we talking about here, gentiles?"

"Every person confesses in one way or another before dying," Shorer said. "Especially if something is weighing heavily on his conscience."

"What was weighing heavily on his conscience?" asked Tzilla. "Do we know yet?"

Michael looked at Shorer. "We don't yet, but perhaps we still will."

"Did Meyuhas know?" Balilty asked. "I mean, about the cancer? Do you think he knew about the guy's condition?"

"We'll have the answer to that question very soon. If you'll excuse me for a moment—" Michael rushed to his office.

He flung the door open and startled the two men sitting across from one another at his desk, but still managed to hear Yigael ask Benny Meyuhas, "So he came to your house by surprise to pick you up?" To Michael the sergeant said, "We're trying to formulate a testimony. I thought it would help if we worked on his statement together."

Michael sat down next to Benny Meyuhas and signaled to Yigael to keep silent. "Tell me," he said to Meyuhas, "was Sroul a healthy man?"

"What do you mean?" Benny Meyuhas asked Michael. "Apart from the burns and all that?"

"Yes," Michael said, "apart from his injury."

Benny Meyuhas frowned in bewilderment and said, "Yes, you know, like the rest of us, I guess. We're not getting any younger . . ."

"No, no," Michael said. "I'm asking whether he discussed his condition with you. His medical condition."

"His condition?" Benny Meyuhas asked, confused. "I mean, he wasn't looking so good, but I thought it was because of the flight or the circumstances. I have no idea what medical condition you're referring to."

"When I asked you why Sroul suddenly told Tirzah his big secret," Michael said impatiently, "you explained that according to what Tirzah had told you, he'd said that you were all growing older and there was no way of knowing what the future holds and that therefore he had decided to tell her. I asked you about it, remember? It's written in the brief, and we've got you talking about it on film. I asked you why he waited so many years and suddenly—"

"Yes, you asked, but I really don't know," Meyuhas said. "I told you that I don't know, that I don't have any explanation other than the fact that he had great faith in Tirzah, and it turns out they spent a fair amount of time alone together. You know how it happens sometimes that people suddenly tell a secret they haven't shared with anyone for years? Tirzah told me he'd said that we're all growing old. But I've already told you that, haven't I?"

"So you don't know anything about a fatal illness, any difficulties breathing?"

"No," said Benny Meyuhas. "I'd noticed how thin he was, but it had been years since the last time I'd seen him. As for his breathing, well, he was once a very heavy smoker. But why are you asking?"

Michael looked at him in silence. "It's not important at this moment," he said. He was just about to return to Balilty's office when the intercom rang and he hastened to lift the receiver. He heard the voice of Yaffa from forensics on the other end of the line. In a subdued voice—quite unusual for Yaffa—she said, "Listen, Michael. Are you listening? I've been trying to reach you on your beeper for over an hour."

"What? What is it?" Michael asked, low on patience. "Have you finished?"

"Listen," she said, clearing her throat. "I don't know how to tell you this, I've never had a thing like this happen before . . ." She hemmed and hawed, until finally Michael lost his patience completely and demanded that she tell him whatever it was immediately. As he listened, he felt his leg muscles go limp suddenly, and he grabbed the edge of the desk and slumped into the chair next to Benny Meyuhas, aware of the puzzled looks he was getting from Yigael and from Benny Meyuhas. "I have no idea how something like could this happen," she said, her voice muffled. "There's no point in putting the blame on someone, the responsibility is mine in any case: it simply disappeared. There's no plastic bag. Do you remember how we put it in a small plastic bag next to the shirt? Well, we've got the shirt, but we're still searching for the bag with the strand of hair. Don't worry, though," she said, quick to make up for it, "we haven't given up. It's just that I can't give you the answer you're waiting for yet."

Michael hung up the phone before he could hear any more of what Yaffa had to say and raced back to Balilty's office, where he found his Special Investigations team embroiled in an argument. Balilty's voice could be heard right through the closed door as he shouted, "How am I supposed to work like this if I'm not told the complete story? In the middle of the Meyuhas interrogation I'm booted out, sent back urgently to work on Hefetz. What are you hiding from me? Our whole team is meant to be involved."

"All in good time," Shorer said as Michael took his seat. "It is not possible to know everything all at once, believe me."

"You're the boss," Balilty said, openly hostile. "You get to decide. Just don't come complaining to me that I neglected to tell you something important or that we didn't solve this business quickly enough."

"Benny Meyuhas did not know about Sroul's lung cancer," Michael said quietly. "He had no idea about it."

"How about Rubin? Did he?"

"That," Michael said, "we'll know in another couple of hours, I hope."

"Where is Rubin anyway?" Lillian asked. "I told him to wait on the bench, and then they told me *you'd* taken him," she said, looking at Balilty.

"He went home," Balilty said. "He's waiting for a phone call from his friend Benny Meyuhas, who's supposed to call him when we're done with him, right?" he asked Michael.

"Yes, exactly," Michael said.

"You let him go home?" Lillian cried out. "I thought he was . . . I told him to wait outside until—"

"It's all right," Balilty said, trying to calm her down. "I told him to go home, don't worry." He chuckled. "He may think he's alone, but he's not, not for a single minute. His telephone is—"

"Without a court order?" Eli Bachar asked, worried. "Nobody's asked for a court order. So we're doing without it?"

"Believe me," Balilty assured him, "it'll be fine. I'm telling you, on my honor."

"With all due respect," Eli Bachar said, "when we bring this to the prosecuting attorney's office so it can be considered legally binding in court, your promises and your word of honor won't be worth shit."

"Gentlemen," Shorer cried, giving them both a look of reproach, "how many years is this business between you two going to continue? You should both be ashamed of yourselves, two grown men. Balilty, do you have a court order to tap that phone or not?"

Balilty said nothing.

"I see," Shorer said.

"There wasn't enough time. Until I get the duty judge out of bed and all that—"

"I see," Shorer repeated. "So it's not for use in court; whatever it is that we'll hear over the phone will be for our use only, which is still something. How long will it take you to get a court order?"

"I've got someone already on the way to the duty judge," Balilty said, "and he should be back any minute now, I promise. I didn't want to go there myself, I would have missed this meeting. And I didn't want to miss this meeting because I thought we'd finally get to hear what it was Tirzah came back from America with, what it was she learned there."

"Not now, Danny," Shorer said, shutting him up. "That's not material for now."

"Anyway," Balilty said, "I told Rubin to phone here at eight this morning and that we'll be able to tell him then what's happening with Benny Meyuhas, so that then he can, like, talk to him."

"People," Michael said to the room, "we've got two hours until eight o'clock rolls around. You can take a short rest, after that we've got a production that needs—" He looked at Shorer and fell silent.

"Needs what?" Tzilla asked. "I've got to have the details."

"You'll get them soon enough," Shorer reassured her. Turning to Michael, he asked, "Where do you want to do it?"

"At Israel Television, I think," Michael said, examining the toothpick he had removed from his shirt pocket.

"In Rubin's office?" Shorer asked.

"No," Michael answered after careful consideration. "In the String Building, near the scene of the first murder."

"Well, Monsieur Poirot, this is genuine Agatha Christie, isn't it?" Balilty muttered. "That's where you think we'll have the fatal meeting that'll get him to talk?"

"It's worth trying," Eli Bachar said. "And it'll give us the chance to—"

Shorer flashed a concerned look at Michael.

"So, you need all of us there?" Nina asked. Michael glanced at Shorer, placed a hand on his arm, and said, "We'll know that in a little while. In the meantime, you're all on standby. Everyone."

"Hey, look, it's already getting light outside," Nina exclaimed. "And it seems the rain has cleared up, too."

In place of a response, there was a knock at the door. In the doorway stood Elmaliah the cameraman. Bleary-eyed, he asked when they would finish up with him; behind him a curl of smoke rose in the air, and he made way for Hefetz to enter the room. "May I have a word with you?" Hefetz asked Michael. "I've got to talk to you about something." Looking at the assembled team, he fell silent.

Michael stepped outside and motioned to Hefetz to follow him to his office at the end of the hallway. He removed a pile of cardboard files from one of the chairs and, in silence, offered Hefetz a seat. When he sat down, Michael felt for the first time just how very tired he was. He could not decide, however, whether it was the hair that had disappeared from the forensics lab—about which he had told no one, not even Shorer—that had broken his spirit, or whether it was this interminable contact with life and death for days on end without sleep that had caused his limbs to feel so very weak. Or maybe it was having given up smoking, that strange mourning he felt inside: true mourning. What was he mourning, anyway? That faithful convoy of cigarettes that had suddenly been stopped short after so many years? Or was it that multitude of times and people and loves and essential life moments that were hanging from that priceless chain of cigarettes?

Quitting smoking—which he was supposed to regard as the "beginning of a healthy life"—seemed merely to be the end of many lives and the start of something detached, severed, and there was no way of knowing what new spark would come along to carry it forward. He wondered how he could ever make anyone understand how those little creatures made from paper, tobacco, and a flame had become the pillar of fire that had led him on his long journey through the wilderness. He was stunned by this train of thought; perhaps even this tendency to exaggeration stemmed from the extreme fatigue brought on by giving up smoking.

"Is it okay if I smoke in here?" Hefetz asked as he looked at the plume of smoke rising from the cigarette in his hand. "I'd actually given it up, but yesterday I couldn't take it anymore. This is my first in more than three years," he said, taking a heavy drag. "They tell you it's not good for your health, but in the end you die of something anyway, right? If not a heart attack, then somebody comes along and kills you."

"How can I help you?" Michael asked, snapping the toothpick between his fingers into two.

"I don't know what to do about Meyuhas," Hefetz said. "I don't know what to tell people, how to deal with it on the news, whether or not to announce that he's been detained on suspicion of murder. And the worst of it is . . ." He fell silent and stared at the butt of his cigarette.

"The worst of it?" Michael asked after a long moment of silence.

"The worst of it is what people are saying. . . . Balilty told me I should announce, on the same morning that Benny Meyuhas has been picked up, that his production of *Iddo and Eynam* will continue as though nothing's changed. But how can I say such a thing after what's happened? The guy is a suspect for the murders of two, no three, people, and I—"

"The matter necessitates some discretion," Michael warned him. "If you can promise to keep a secret."

"Of course. I mean, I don't have to give anybody a full report," Hefetz said, inflating his chest. "I can . . . even the director general doesn't need to know yet."

"I'm talking very seriously about complete secrecy," Michael warned him again.

"Come on," Hefetz said, offended, "what do you think? That I'm going to run around shooting off at the mouth? You think I can't be trusted? You think I was just handed the position of director of Israel

Television because there was nobody else who could do it after Zadik?"

"The truth is, we are not holding Benny Meyuhas as a suspect for murder," Michael declared. "He's not a murderer, and he's not an accomplice to murder; in fact, he's about to help us clear up the whole matter. But we have to pretend that he is still a suspect, so therefore I am asking for your cooperation." Michael looked into Hefetz's frightened eyes, which were darting around the room.

"So what do I need to do?" Hefetz asked as he stubbed out his cigarette on the sole of one of the cowboy boots he was wearing.

"You've got to act as though you yourself don't understand, as if he's a suspect but temporarily free. You should treat him for the time being with compassion, like someone quite ill, if you understand what I'm getting at. Let's say, you shouldn't express astonishment if he returns to work on his production, and you should probably let people know he's coming back to work on *Iddo and Eynam.*"

"Where?" Hefetz said, alarmed. "What people should I tell?"

"Nobody special," Michael advised him. "Just act normal. At the morning meeting, when you go over your daily schedule, you should say something noncommittal about his being a suspect but out on bail, or something like that. Give people the feeling that for the time being, to make life easier for him, you've decided to let him continue with his life's work. Is that clear?"

"Yeah," Hefetz said. "I hope I can pull it off successfully without understanding what . . ." He glanced at Michael, who maintained a neutral expression. "But thank God," Hefetz hastened to add, "you have no idea what a burden you've lifted from me to know that he's not a suspect." He sighed, then, tense again, he asked Michael, "Why can't we just announce that he's been found alive and well and that he's not a suspect for murder?" When Michael rose from his chair and walked silently to the door, signaling him to follow, Hefetz stopped in the doorway and said, "So if it's not Benny Meyuhas, then who's been . . . Who *is* the murderer?"

# CHAPTER SEVENTEEN

At seven-thirty in the morning, just as a sharp-tongued anchorwoman interviewing the minister of labor and social affairs tossed her long hair away from her face and boldly asked her interviewee whether her private affairs had perhaps clouded her judgment with regard to the future of the unemployed workers from the Hulit factory—the camera tarrying over the minister's face, beads of sweat already shining from her powdered upper lip—Tzilla appeared in the doorway to Michael's office to inform him that Rubin had arrived.

"Hang on a second," Michael said without moving his eyes from the screen on the small television set that had been placed in the corner of his office. "Look what's happening," he muttered. The minister could be heard saying, "I don't know which private affairs you are referring to, but the matter of the Hulit factory workers was in my mind—"

"I'm speaking about a romantic relationship that had already begun," the anchorwoman said, twirling her hand in the air, "before the tunnel hijacking."

Tzilla was watching the screen now too. "Oh, my gosh, I don't believe what's going on here!" she exclaimed.

"That's because of the photos, they got caught in the act," Balilty offered from the doorway. "She's been blackmailed, and this is even before the press conference. I've seen the front page of the paper," he said, waving the rolled-up newspaper in his hand, then spreading it out for them to see. "Look." Balilty was beaming as he pointed a thick finger at the huge photograph at the center of the page, which featured the minister of labor and social affairs at the entrance to a building, with Danny Benizri standing close behind, his hand on her shoulder. "This pushed everything else aside," Balilty proclaimed, "even the murder of some burned-up Orthodox Jew. See?" he asked, showing them the lower right-hand corner of the paper. "There's nothing hotter than a steamy, forbidden new romance: the media and politics, super-sleazy. Great, isn't it?" Balilty said mockingly while the minister droned on in the background: "Whoever believes that my private affairs have any influence on my professional judgment . . ." Tzilla turned the television off.

"I'm off, going to set everything up," Balilty said. "Your client couldn't wait. He didn't phone, he came in himself, so you can have a quick word with him yourself. Maybe we'll get something new out of him."

"Show him in," Michael instructed Tzilla. He pushed all the papers on his desk into a single pile.

"You're going to give me a heads-up beforehand, right?" Balilty asked.

"Rest assured, Balilty," Tzilla teased him. "Rest assured and get out of here already. I've got it all under control, so you can relax." She took his arm and pushed him away from the office, then returned a moment later with Rubin.

Rubin muttered a hesitant hello from the doorway, and Michael motioned him to sit in the seat facing him. Rubin seated himself and gazed at Michael expectantly. After a moment of silence he said, "I've come to take Benny, and I don't know what I need to—"

"I have a few more small questions for you," Michael said absentmindedly as he flipped through the papers. "Questions that arose during the interrogations through the night. Ah, here are the papers I was looking for," he mumbled, as if chastising himself. He held his pen as if ready to write and said, "In the matter of the digoxin, we wanted to—"

"Again?!" Rubin exploded. "This business with the prescription again? I told that young woman, Lillian, I told her that—"

"Please," Michael said in a fatherly manner, "there is no need for anger. You must admit there is something peculiar here: as you know, Matty Cohen died suddenly, and we found—"

"I don't want to hear this nonsense anymore!" Rubin said, cutting him off resolutely, emphasizing every word. "It's a waste of everyone's time, and I feel like some sort of scapegoat here. What's wrong, you can't find anyone else to pin things on, so it's either me or Benny? Is that the way things are shaping up? Simply because Tirzah was . . . Look here, are you prepared to arrest me?" He held his hands in front of him, his fingers clasped and his wrists together. "I do not belong in this place, and you know it, but if you wish to arrest me, then be my guest, go ahead."

Michael said nothing.

"And if not, then please tell me what's happening with Benny Meyuhas and where you're holding him so that I can take him with me, because he doesn't belong here either. This country is still a democracy, and in another minute I'm going to phone up a top-notch lawyer. Do you understand?"

Michael said nothing.

"So if that's the way you want it," Rubin said, rising from his chair, "I'll simply be on my way, with or without Benny. I'm coming back with my attorney." He moved to the door; Michael made no move to stop him. Next to the door, his hand on the knob, he turned around and said, "Just tell me where you're holding Benny. That much at least you owe me."

Michael shrugged, glancing at the papers in front of him. "We're not holding him anywhere," he said as if surprised. "He went back to work hours ago."

Rubin froze in his place, let go of the doorknob, and stared at Michael in shock. "Work? What work?"

"Filming missing scenes from *Iddo and Eynam,*" Michael said, as though the matter were clear.

"Now?" Rubin asked in a shaky voice. "He's gone back to *Iddo and Eynam*?"

Michael shrugged again. "We told him he'd been given the go-ahead, and he said he only needed another week to wrap up shooting. He said every minute they weren't working on it was a waste of time, and his producer was waiting outside . . ."

Rubin stared at Michael for a minute, then opened the door and stepped out of the office.

Michael waited a moment, then dialed the phone. "Can you hear me?" he asked into the receiver. He listened, then continued. "Rubin left a minute ago, so the time has come." Again he listened, adding, "There's nothing we can do about it, we've spoken about this. You've got to phone him right now. Now. Ring him on his mobile phone." After another pause he said patiently, compassionately, "I know. I know. But you've got no choice. You've got to phone this friend whom you love—or loved—and take him with you. Right away."

After that Michael glanced at the door to his office and at the receiver of his telephone, now resting in its cradle, and allowed a few minutes of inertia to pass before instructing Tzilla to continue as planned.

"Seems funny to bring our cameramen and equipment in there," Balilty whispered to Tzilla.

She ignored him, speaking instead into the transmitter. "Everything's ready, everyone is in position."

Once again, the illusion that the whole world can turn into one huge ear appeared in Michael's mind. But in this case there was an eye, too: his own, as it peered, alongside Shorer, whose noisy breathing he could hear (and which made Michael feel safe and protected for a moment, the way it had fifteen years earlier when Shorer had brought him to work with him and had kept him nearby while they were on duty) as they stood next to one another in one of the nooks used for scenery storage. They were watching Benny Meyuhas, who was kneeling down and cupping his hands around a low, quivering flame in one of the memorial candles placed by the seamstresses and the members of the Scenery Department near the spot where Tirzah's skull had been crushed. Balilty had been in charge of clearing the building of people and instructing Benny Meyuhas exactly where he should wait. First they heard the ringing of a telephone and then the sound of Benny's hoarse voice as he said, "I'm here, in the String Building, by the scenery flats. Near where Tirzah . . ." After a moment they could hear him continue: "So I'll wait for you here, of course I'll wait."

Michael knew Balilty was responsible for the dimness in the corridor—the nook where he and Shorer were hiding was completely dark—and this was why Rubin's voice sounded hesitant and anxious as he called out to Benny Meyuhas.

"Here I am," they could hear Benny answer him in a feeble voice. "Arye, I'm over here, near where . . ." He stood up. "Where the candles are."

It seemed to Michael as though Rubin's heavy breathing was audible through the whole corridor; a moment later they could hear him cry out in a surprised, nearly mocking voice, "*This* is where you are? Lighting candles like some teenage girl on the anniversary of Rabin's death?"

Benny Meyuhas returned to his kneeling position on the floor, and Rubin bent down, leaning on his heels, beside him.

"They told me you'd returned to work," Rubin said, astounded. "That they'd let you go. Is that true?"

"They let me go, but I haven't gone back to work yet," Benny Meyuhas said, his head bent. "I only said I'd come back here."

"I see," Rubin said. A long silence stood between them, until suddenly Meyuhas said, "Tell me, Arye, do you ever think about that doctor?"

"What doctor?" Rubin asked, taken aback. A moment later he said, "Oh, the doctor. The Egyptian one. No, never. What made you think of him?"

"I think about him a lot, I've been thinking about him all through the years. I can't seem to forget him," Meyuhas said, his voice cracking. "I think about who shot him in the back as he started walking away."

"Benny," Rubin said, sounding worried, "why are you . . . all these years we haven't said a word . . . we haven't said a single word about it, we never talked about it. And now suddenly you're thinking about it? What's it got to do with anything?"

Benny lowered his head and said nothing.

"It was only us there, Benny," Rubin said imploringly. "We're the only two left. Sroul's dead—if we keep our mouths shut then it's all over, they don't have a case against us. Why did you have to go and bring up that Egyptian doctor?" He glanced around the area.

"There's no one here, Arye," Benny said. "It's just the two of us, alone. How did you know Sroul's dead?"

Rubin did not answer.

"Who told you Sroul's dead?" Benny Meyuhas insisted.

"I'll tell you in a minute," Rubin promised; the deep tremble in his voice betrayed his horror and fear. "But before that, you tell me why you suddenly remembered that Egyptian doctor. What's that got to do with anything?"

"I'll tell you what," Benny Meyuhas said, suddenly rising to his feet. "I'll tell you what it's got to do with anything: there's no room for you and me to form some sort of conspiracy now. It's all over. I know that you . . . that you murdered Tirzah. That much I'm sure of. I knew it right from the start. And from that moment I didn't care about anything else anymore. I have nothing more to lose. Did you know Sroul was dying of lung cancer? He had nothing more to lose, either. You did him a big favor, you know?"

"Tell me," Rubin said coming closer to Benny, the threat in his voice supplanting the fear. "Did you say anything to them?"

Benny Meyuhas backed away. "To who?"

"Them. The police. Ohayon, Balilty. Whoever. Did you tell them about what happened back then?"

"I . . . I . . ." Benny Meyuhas stuttered.

"Did you tell them or not?" Rubin demanded in a threatening whisper. "Just answer me straight, no bullshit."

"Sroul came to Israel to talk about it, did you know that?" Benny Meyuhas asked him hoarsely. "He told Tirzah about it, she was planning to leave me. She said, 'You're murderers! I can't live with a murderer!'"

Rubin placed his right hand on Benny Meyuhas's shoulder. "I know what she said to you, Benny. Look at me," he said quietly. "Look at me, I know very well what she said. She said some things to me, too. But I didn't run to the police to tell them, you know."

Benny Meyuhas smothered his face in his hands. "I can't look at you, Arye," he said, sobbing. "You went too far, you should have . . . we should have, right from the beginning . . . now you've become like some . . . like Macbeth, you're wandering around spilling everyone's blood. That's what Sroul said, and he wanted—"

"I know what Sroul said, too," Rubin told him, placing his left hand on Benny's other shoulder. Now they were facing one another, very, very close. "Which means you don't leave me many options," he said, pulling Benny toward him.

The Special Investigations team heard Benny whisper into his transmitter. "I don't care," he said, "I have nothing left to lose. In any case I can't—" At that moment Michael came out of his hiding place at a run and entered the wide corridor where they had found Tirzah. Arye Rubin spun around in surprise, and just then all the lights came on and Benny Meyuhas, who had collapsed as though he could no longer support his own body, was pulled out of the way and handcuffs were snapped on Rubin's wrists.

"Where do you want him?" Balilty asked Michael quietly.

"Leave him here for a minute, leave me alone with him," Michael said. "Before we take him out of here, I want . . . I've got to hear the whole story, before the lawyers move in and all that."

"You'd better take legal admissibility into account," Balilty reminded him. "Remember that without a lawyer you can't use this stuff in court."

"Yeah, I remember," Michael said.

"What's this story about the Egyptian doctor?" Balilty whispered. "Some kind of skeleton in his closet, as they say? And all this time I was thinking—"

"Get everyone out of here," Shorer ordered. "Remove everyone from the vicinity and leave him"—he indicated Michael—"alone with the suspect, as he requested."

And so it happened that Rubin, in handcuffs, bent down to sit with his back up against the wall of the corridor, facing the Wardrobe Department, and Michael flopped down next to him.

A very long silence passed between them before finally Michael said, "People spend their whole lives worrying their wounds."

"You don't say!" Rubin cried, though the irony in his voice failed to drown out the grief. "What a discovery! Excuse me if I feel compelled to inform you that you don't have to be a genius to understand that," he said, and then fell silent.

"I'm talking about with work as well," Michael said quietly. "A lucky few hit on the opportunity to work in what it was that wounded them early on."

"What are you talking about?" Rubin asked in quiet wonder. "I don't understand you."

"Don't you think that the whole business of repairing the world that has become your life's work has to do with what happened to you back then? Tell me," Michael said, "who was it exactly who shot the Egyptian doctor in the back?"

In one swift move, Rubin stood up and looked around him. "Who told you about the Egyptian doctor?" he asked in a hoarse voice. "You just repeat what you've heard from others like a parrot, don't you?"

Michael did not answer him.

"Was it Benny who told you?"

Michael said nothing.

"I've never talked about Ras Sudar with another living soul. Never. Not even with Sroul or Benny," Rubin said, his voice muffled. His blank expression did nothing to keep the immensity of his sorrow from his face.

Michael glanced at the stairs leading to the roof and at the strip of light that emanated from there.

"What is it you want now?" Rubin asked. "You want a story from history? From twenty-four years ago?"

Michael said nothing.

"Benny's already told you," Rubin said. "Why are you asking me?"

"Everyone's got his own version," Michael said after a long pause. "And every person's got the right to tell his own version. The differences are more meaningful than the similarities. In any case, that's surely true here."

"That means he told you," Rubin said, his voice filled with contempt. "I always knew he would. He's weak, there are no two ways about it."

Michael said nothing.

"All right, you want my version?" Rubin asked. "So you'll get it. Exactly as it happened," he said, and his voice had altered as though it really mattered for him to tell these things to, of all people, Michael Ohayon.

Michael sat up straight, and Rubin sat back down next to him. Both sat with their backs to the wall, staring straight ahead. Later, when Emmanuel Shorer asked him why Rubin had agreed to talk, Michael told him that more than all the crimes that had been committed here, there was one wound that was so huge it dwarfed the rest of Rubin's life. The murders that were intended to quiet the voices and heal the wound did not quiet or heal; instead, they opened the wound even further. And Rubin felt it more than all the others, heavier and more violent than the crimes themselves and all the accusations about to come his way . . .

"It's not like it seems," Rubin said, turning his head to look at Michael's face. When he saw that nothing had registered there, he continued. "It wasn't just the two of us or the three of us; we were eight: Benny, Sroul, me; Bin-Nun, who's since died of a heart attack; David Alboher, downed by a sniper's bullet; Shlomo Zemah, who left for Brazil, and I for one have never heard about him since; Itzik Buzaglo, killed in a car accident; and Sasson. I have no idea what ever became of him."

Michael stretched out his legs out in front of him and laid his hands on his knees.

"What do *you* want?" Rubin asked in a harsh voice.

"Me?" Michael responded. "I want to hear about Ras Sudar during the war, from your own mouth, without any mediators."

And so they were, at that moment—the killer and the hunter—complete partners in one matter; and this matter was infused more than anything with grief and disappointment.

"Okay," Rubin said peacefully, his voice now distant and detached. The words seemed to float up to the surface one after another, as if a boulder had been lifted from above them. "We were paratroopers," Rubin said, "each one a great guy, real quality; idealistic and all that. You and I are about the same age, right?"

Michael nodded silently.

"So you know what I'm talking about," Rubin said. "You know very well what I mean. Paratroopers, great guys to the last of us. Back then, thirty years ago, I don't know, it's tough to explain. What can I tell you? That I wanted to be an officer? That I was filled with militaristic ambitions? That that's the reason I carried out an order? Was it even possible to disobey an order? Maybe it all happened because of the heat, because we'd already lost so many of our comrades; who knows the real reason why someone does something at a given moment? This is the way it was: they brought us in to guard Egyptian prisoners of war. There were maybe sixty, seventy of them, they were subdued, quiet. They were at our mercy, as the saying goes, bound at their hands and feet. The heat that day in Ras Sudar was insufferable, even though it was October." Rubin fell silent, then after a moment let out a sound like a moan. "I can see it all now, just like it was yesterday or an hour ago," he said. "Their eyes were blindfolded. Maybe that was why . . ."

"That was why . . ." Michael's voice echoed Rubin's, urging him on.

"That was why," Rubin said, "all of us afterward were able . . . they were sitting the whole time, we couldn't see their faces. We gave them water, and that was all. The only one we talked to was the doctor, and that was why we couldn't . . . that was why we told him to walk away. And only when he was at a distance . . . only then, we shot him in the back. I swear I don't know who it was. We were told, 'The tanks are on their way.' We thought that meant Egyptian soldiers were on the hilltops surrounding us. The commander of our platoon, Sasson—there was this command—I don't know why we refused to carry it out, I don't know why. The whole affair was so unnecessary that it's hard for me even to describe it: in the hills there were thousands more Egyptian soldiers, like the sixty or seventy we were guarding, but nobody did a thing about them. Our prisoners? They sat for half a day in the sun, and we gave them water. Then came our orders to move out. 'Head up north,' we were told. We said, 'What are we supposed to do with *them*?' So over the transmitter and not . . . can you believe it, over the transmitter they tell us, 'Solve the problem.'" Rubin fell silent, staring off into space, while Michael rested his chin on his arms and waited patiently. He caught sight of Shorer's silhouette at the end of the corridor, listening to every word. Michael had a sharp sense of the gap forming between himself and the observers standing behind the wall as he bonded with Rubin. Rubin was not mistaken in feeling that a deep affinity was forming between him and Michael as he told his story. While he did not forget for a moment that he was a killer only just apprehended, there was something else—no less important—that begged to be said, to be heard by someone who could understand all these matters that perhaps no one would ever understand again.

"Sixty or seventy men were sitting cross-legged in the desert sand, and I'm telling you"—his voice suddenly cracked, and he whimpered—"that this action, having them get to their feet and hustling them into three rows; I can't forget how they shook their legs after all those hours of sitting," Rubin said, hiding his face in his hands and sobbing. "It was terrible, terrible to see that. After that we carried out the order and mowed them down with their hands and legs bound and their eyes blindfolded. And after that . . ."

"After that?" Michael prodded him gently, amazed at the tone of his own voice.

Rubin exhaled noisily, then speaking quickly, said, "After that our tank corps arrived, along with a bulldozer, and they plowed all the bodies into a pit. And the doctor . . ." He covered his face with his hands again and spoke from behind them. "He . . . he . . . he was . . ." He moved his hands away and looked at Michael. "He was the only one I'd spoken to. In English. The rest of them were faceless . . ."

"So someone shot him in the back? Who was it?"

"We couldn't shoot him in the face," Rubin said, as if he were offering condolences. "He had a face . . ."

"So who shot him?" Michael persisted. "Sroul?"

Rubin's head drooped. "No, not Sroul," he said after a pause. "Sroul didn't shoot anyone. He didn't shoot anyone, except for . . . except those prisoners, the faceless ones, the ones we all shot. Afterward, when Sroul got burned—it was that same night—he thought it was divine punishment, and that's why he became religious."

"And no one knew about this whole affair?" Michael asked. "Not even Tirzah, until her last meeting with Sroul in Los Angeles?"

"We never spoke about it," Rubin said. "Benny and I. Not a word. Not with Sroul over the phone, either, or when I visited him there two years ago. Nothing. Not until Sroul told Tirzah. Because he was sick. He knew his days were numbered. Sroul told her, and when she came back from America, she said, 'You have a week to get organized. If you don't come clean with this story on your own, *I'll* tell it. To the whole country, on television, in the papers. I won't let it remain buried under the sands of Ras Sudar.'"

Michael stared at length at Rubin, then said, his voice full of compassion, "She wasn't prepared to keep quiet. So you had no choice, you had to kill her."

"I told her," Rubin continued, as if he had not heard what Michael said even though he had heard him clearly, "I told her, 'Tirzah, look what I've done with my life since: I've been atoning for twenty-four years—twenty-four years! Do you want to turn my whole life into dust? A huge nothing? Completely annihilate me? Don't you understand what damage you'll do to everything we've been fighting for? You'll turn us into a laughingstock!'"

"But she wasn't prepared to keep quiet," Michael said.

"I came to the Wardrobe Department to persuade her," Rubin explained. "But she was—how can I put it?—well, it's well known: she was very stubborn. She was so pure, that Tirzah. She'd started telling things to my mother. My mother's a Holocaust survivor. 'You did to them what was done to your mother,' Tirzah screamed at me. And then I saw red," Rubin said. "I didn't want her to . . . I had no intention . . . I didn't want her to die, it was an accident. Something huge and terrible, much bigger than me, suddenly came into the picture. I'm not talking about anger or fear. Not at all. But this huge thing that Tirzah had bungled into so stupidly and innocently—my mother, the Nazis, the murder at Ras Sudar—those are the things that my whole life, our whole lives, are built on—our roots. No one would ever understand that. It was bigger than me and us back when we were ten and twenty years old. It dwarfed us back then when we were supposedly so strong . . ."

In the blink of an eye Michael could picture, with startling clarity, the line of Rubin's thought. He shivered suddenly, and just as a feeling of alienation tends to explode into one's awareness during the greatest moments of ecstasy, so, suddenly, did this thought push its way into Michael's mind: "And so, in old age, you finally understand what it is to identify: To identify is a moment of identity."

"We," said Rubin. He could see clearly the ring of hostility and utter emptiness encircling him, at its center the tiny bubble of light and warmth that had formed between Ohayon and himself. "We, we, we were we, and if you shred this us-ness, all that's left on each one's shoulders is a burden too great to bear, literally too great to bear. In this us-ness of ours as the children of parents who came out of the concentration camps and this us-ness of ours as young men standing in the middle of the Sinai Desert facing helpless Egyptians, there flowed something that robbed us of ourselves. When we cried as we listened to 'The Song of Camaraderie,' we cried for ourselves and for the lies the song told us. The 'camaraderie' we sing about every Remembrance Day, the camaraderie the song tells of, which we 'Carried without words / Gray, stubborn, silent,' is what this country and this people saddled us with. We'd thought that the State and the People were a sort of mother and father, when really, no one was there but us, and our own broken-down parents.

"My whole life, our whole lives, are a cover-up for this truth, a cover-up for the murder of our mother and father, and for the murder we committed. It wasn't exactly a lie; the fig leaf was not a lie, but a culture, a way of life. It was all we had. In fact, what Tirzah wanted to do would have been anarchy. What she was preaching wasn't even post-Zionism; it was failing to understand the destruction out of which we arose and are, in fact, made. In her purity, Tirzah had preserved that Zionism, that constructive lie. Woe to that purity, that once I was married to, which I loved more than I loved myself. Woe to that purity; now it has overtaken me."

And he fell silent.

"You pushed her, and the column fell?" Michael asked suddenly.

"I don't remember exactly," Rubin said. "I shook her. I held her by the shoulders, and then I grabbed her neck. She wouldn't shut up, I wanted to shut her up. I wanted her to stop saying that nonsense."

"And that's what Matty Cohen saw," Michael reminded him.

Rubin said nothing.

"He saw you," Michael said. "At first he thought it was an argument, but in the morning he heard that Tirzah had died, and then he understood the connection to what he had seen. It was only in the morning that he figured it all out, right?"

Rubin said nothing.

"That's when you put the digoxin in his coffee. Or was it in something else? Did you switch his ampoules? I haven't figured out exactly if—"

Rubin said nothing. He felt sharply that the bubble of light and warmth between Michael and himself had dissolved. He acknowledged the gravity of the reality that had turned the tables on the feelings of friendship that had brought them close to one another for a moment, but he did not begrudge Michael returning to himself and his duties.

Rubin's utter loneliness seemed to him more appropriate now than it had ever been before.

"You left the building to meet Tirzah?" Michael asked. "Was the meeting planned?"

Rubin's head bobbed; it was unclear whether he was affirming Michael's question.

"When?" Michael asked, persistent. "When did you leave the building? Before midnight or after?"

"Before," Rubin said in a hushed, muffled voice. "At a quarter to twelve. She was waiting for me."

"And no one saw you?" Michael asked.

"No one was there, nobody was in the editing rooms; the place was empty except for the newsroom. But they were all busy . . ."

"What about the guards at the entrance? How did they not see you leave the building?"

"Maybe they did. Sure they did," Rubin said pensively, closing his eyes, "but there was a basketball game on, and they weren't paying much attention. I come and go all the time, it wasn't like someone unfamiliar. I left and returned."

"How did you get into the String Building?" Michael asked. "From the back entrance?"

"Yes. I have a key."

"And that's how you met up with Tirzah, killed her, and managed not to be seen by a soul."

"No one. There was nobody around," Rubin said.

"Except for Matty Cohen," Michael reminded him.

"Yes," Rubin said, his voice breaking. "He passed by, and I wasn't sure if he'd . . . I hoped . . . I went back to the editing rooms. It was raining, I'd gotten wet. I told them I'd needed to fetch some stuff from my car. In fact, I myself don't know where I got the resourcefulness from—is that what you'd call it, resourcefulness?" he asked bitterly. "The whole time I kept thinking that . . . and then Natasha came along . . . I know," he said, suddenly coming to life, "you think I'm some kind of monster: kill someone, commit a murder, then go back to work like . . . like nothing had happened."

"And in fact that *wasn't* the way it happened?" Michael asked matter-of-factly, trying to disguise any trace of irony.

"It was . . . it was as if I hadn't been there, as if it weren't really me," Rubin said. "I can't explain it."

"And what about Zadik?" Michael continued. "Did Sroul tell Zadik?"

"Zadik called me in to his office," Rubin said, as if stunned by Zadik's intervention, as though he thought of Zadik as unconnected to the affair; a stranger, a disturbance. "Sroul had been to see him in the morning, and Zadik told me . . . by telephone, he phoned my office—it was an internal call, which is why you have no record of it, why you knew nothing about this—Zadik called me to his office, and I knew Sroul had been to see him, and I already knew what Zadik wanted to say to me. That's why I entered through the door from the hallway. I didn't want Aviva to see me going in, even if I didn't know beforehand that I . . . I didn't know I would need to . . . but anyway, I entered from the hallway. He told me . . . he told me I would have to tell the whole world . . . and suddenly he sounded just like Tirzah. Suddenly . . . you would think that Zadik . . . after all, he was such a pragmatist, a guy with no principles. There's no way of knowing about people. . . ."

From the end of the hallway came the sound of footsteps. Michael could make out the silhouette of Emmanuel Shorer; Rubin fell silent.

"What actually happened with Zadik?" Michael asked. "What was with the drill? Where did all that anger of yours come from?"

"It wasn't . . . I . . . I had no choice," Rubin explained in a choked voice, averting his gaze. "He sent me into despair, I simply went berserk—that's the only way to describe it. He'd told me over the phone that Sroul had been to see him, he said, 'I've got a clear picture of what's happened here, Rubin. Come in to my office right away so we can decide together what to do.' Well, I understood that was the end of me. I didn't mean to . . . I didn't know how . . . on a hunch I entered through the door from the hallway, I didn't want anyone to even see me going in there. Only when I was already in the office, at first from behind, with the big ashtray . . . and when he fell, I bashed him again. It was only after that that I put on the technician's overalls and picked up the drill. I didn't have a . . . I can see exactly how you're taking all this in. I think I can even explain it all, but never mind, it doesn't matter. In any case, nobody's going to think they have anything to learn from me anymore." He fell silent, and his head drooped.

"And what about Sroul? Your childhood friend Sroul?" Michael asked. "Was he asphyxiated when you took away the oxygen mask, or did you actually have to strangle him?"

"He was already dying," Rubin said in a voice that rose from the depths; "it wouldn't have made any difference."

"So, we started with three great guys of real quality," Michael said as though reciting "Ten Little Indians." "One went on to be a defender of the weak and disenfranchised, one became an Orthodox Jew, and one brings the stories of Agnon to the screen."

He looked up to find Shorer standing in front of him. "Did you hear all that? Did you get it?"

"No," Shorer said quietly. "That's not the story. It just seems to you as if that's the story."

"What?" Michael asked, astonished. "I don't get it. What do you mean?"

"I want to give you both, now, the official version of what happened. Do you understand me?" Shorer said, looking at Rubin. Rubin averted his gaze. "The way I'm going to tell it to you is the way it happened. The true story is that Rubin killed Tirzah because he was jealous, he couldn't live without her. He pleaded with her to come back to him, but she refused. Matty Cohen saw the whole thing, saw him push Tirzah, knock her down, all the things we already know . . . so he poisoned him. We don't yet know all the details, but we will. Right, Rubin?"

Rubin's head swiveled, his intent unclear.

"We're going to bring him in now for a proper interrogation, and we'll hear about how Zadik found out about it and then had to die. And that's all. No Ras Sudar or any of the other stuff. Do you understand me?" he asked, turning to Rubin. "Do you understand what I'm telling you?"

Rubin nodded.

"Do you think something like this can be kept a secret?" Michael queried, astonished. "Why do you even *want* to—"

"We have a police commissioner and a state and an army and censorship and enough troubles already right now without riling up the Egyptians with this story," Shorer said, glaring at Michael.

"Forget about the moral aspect for a moment," Michael said in a shaky voice. "Let's be practical here. Do you really believe something like this can be kept secret now, after everything that's happened?"

"No question about it," Shorer declared resolutely.

"And what about *you*?" Michael exclaimed. "Will *you* keep quiet about it? *Can* you keep quiet about a story like this? And me? Am I capable of shutting up about it? Because what—"

"Of course you can!" Shorer said, grabbing Michael's arm and lifting him to his feet to look closely into his eyes. "Look at me," he commanded when Michael avoided his gaze. "Don't you treat me like some war criminal. The good of the nation is as important to me as it is to you. Or do you think you've been appointed Guardian of the Truth?"

Michael said nothing.

"How many years have we known one another?" Shorer asked, but he did not wait for an answer. "Your uncle Jocko, my best friend—who brought you to me—what did he tell you? In my presence he told you to trust me like a father. And hasn't that been true all these years? Have I ever let you down? Did I ever fail to back you up?"

Michael bowed his head.

"So, what? Suddenly I've turned into a villain? You yourself in another few days—maybe before that even—you'll discover for yourself . . . After all, you studied history, didn't you? What are you going to do with this truth we heard here today? Do you believe that every wrong can be righted? That the truth is always the highest value, that the truth wins out over life itself even? Do you know what kind of material we'd be handing over to . . . to everyone! To the Palestinians and the Egyptians and to . . . to us, ourselves. There is no question about it; in any event the Censor's Office would never allow this to get out. . . . It's just a waste of time, do you understand me?"

After a pause, Michael said, "I don't know if I can keep quiet about this. I don't know how a person can live with a secret like this."

"Oh, yes, you do!" Shorer said sadly. "You most certainly do. You'll keep quiet, and how," he said, his grief deepening. After a brief silence, he added, "We're evolving, you see? We're learning to keep quiet about bigger and bigger matters."

Afterward, everything took on a quality of unreality. As though weightless, Michael followed the policemen who escorted Rubin to the police van, and as though in sleep he heard bits of a news broadcast from car radios in the parking lot: ". . . he shot his wife, fatally wounding her," came the broadcaster's voice. "The couple's two children were in the apartment at the time. . . ." And when Michael entered Shorer's car—the radio was on there, too—he heard that seventeen women had been murdered by their husbands or partners during the previous year, and heard, too, the item about Shimshi and the other workers who had been brought to court for a hearing to extend the period of their arrest.

Natasha was awaiting their arrival at the entrance to police headquarters. Her gaze followed Rubin as he stepped out of the van, his hands in cuffs. She moved the canvas bag from her shoulder, ran a hand through the lank locks of her hair, and tugged at the ends of her scarf. She approached Rubin. "Rubin!" she exclaimed. To Michael, who was plodding heavily nearby, she said, "What's going on here? Why is he—" When Michael said nothing, Natasha said, "It's a mistake, a *big* mistake. Rubin is the kind of person . . . what, are you really arresting him?" She choked on her words.

Michael did not answer her.

"I came here for a totally different reason," Natasha mumbled, her eyes on Rubin's back. "Now I really don't know what to do, because . . ." Something in her lost expression prevented Michael from telling her to go away, to leave him alone. She stood next to him talking, though only fragments of her sentences reached his ears. "Now Hefetz is no longer willing . . . I told him you knew . . . I told him . . . that you would help me bring it to air . . . the State Prosecutor's Office . . . if you saw the video you'd know . . ." And without knowing how it happened, he found himself following Natasha up the stairs, her light-colored, dirty canvas bag bouncing against her gaunt thighs as she led the way to his office. "Do you have a VCR?" she asked, winded. "Because if you don't—" He opened the office door; he still had not spoken, or at least that was the way it seemed to him. Then again, several minutes later Balilty entered the room carrying a VCR. He inserted the cassette into the appropriate slot, and without intending to, Michael heard the sounds and viewed the scenes that flooded his office, and noticed Tzilla, too, who had entered his office by pushing the door open with her foot—her hands occupied with three mugs—and was now watching the screen. They were looking at aerial shots of a green city on the banks of a river, Natasha's voice in the background explaining that this was an area, not far from Montreal, to which Rabbi Elharizi had smuggled the money and gold bricks he had gathered from his followers. "Two days ago," Natasha's voice proclaimed, loud and clear, an image of Rabbi Elharizi on the screen, "I fell into a trap, I let myself be led blindly by facts that were fed to me in order to keep us from seeing what was really going on. And *that* begins with this," she said as the film skipped to Rabbi Elharizi, standing at the entrance to Ben Gurion Airport dressed as a Greek Orthodox priest, his head bent but the hood covering his face slightly pushed to the side, exposing him. "What is Rabbi Elharizi doing at Ben Gurion Airport in the garb of a Greek Orthodox priest?" Natasha asked. "What is he doing? He's preparing the groundwork for realizing his vision; in order to bury this scoop of ours, I was led astray two days ago. But now there are no more diversions. Let's watch a snippet from a secret cassette distributed by Rabbi Elharizi among his believers." Again the film skipped to Rabbi Elharizi, speaking as if possessed: "The Holy Land of Israel will be laid to waste, the destruction of the Third Temple is near. Soon, no stone will be left unturned and all will be ashes and dust. Our Arab enemies will lay our cities to waste and run our fields asunder. Jewish women will fall prey to them, our homes will be set aflame and our children annihilated. Destruction and desolation, my brothers! But we, we wish to keep our breed holy! Let us depart for the New Jerusalem!"

"Stop, stop the tape!" Tzilla shouted. From inside that same weightlessness Michael watched as Balilty's finger moved to the VCR and pressed the button, freezing the frame.

"What is this?" Tzilla cried out. "Call everyone, they've got to see this. They're running off with the taxes we've paid! Everyone's got to see this, these people are skipping out on us!"

"As far as I'm concerned," Balilty proclaimed, "they're welcome to leave yesterday, along with all their corruption. Come on, let's keep watching," he said to Natasha. To Tzilla he added, "You want us to call Eli?"

"Eli's with the kids now," Tzilla said as she sat down. "Go on, go on," she told Balilty. "This is something that you just can't—something everyone needs to know." She lowered her voice to a whisper. "I've got to keep watching even if it makes me sick."

Michael thought that on any other day he would have been shocked by this cassette tape, he would have been highly disturbed by the insult of it and overcome with nausea at these scenes of the rabbi's "vision" and the Jewish way of clinging to exile and boxes of gold. But today these images were simply floating in the chasm of grief that had opened up inside him these past few hours.

Balilty pressed the button, and the film lurched forward, Rabbi Elharizi's voice echoing in a closed room. "Unlike Rabbi Yohanan Ben Zakkai, who was smuggled to Yavneh in a coffin when Jerusalem was under siege by the armies of Vespasian," cried the rabbi prophetically, "we shall leave proudly in an aerial convoy, my brothers, every hour another plane departing. These ships shall transport you to the land of water: Canada. Pack your belongings; no redemption, no revival, awaits us here. A voice came down from on high in the still of the night and visited both me and the mystic Rabbi Bashari. And it said, 'And I will make them as a vexation to all the kingdoms of the land . . . and the carcass of this people will be as food for the birds of prey and beasts of the field. And there shall be no succor, for the land shall be laid to waste.' Soon it shall come to pass! Rise and depart! Depart! Depart before the destruction! There will be seventeen meeting points," the rabbi said before Natasha's clear voice interjected to read a list of the names of towns in the Negev and in the north of Israel, as well as the names of the rabbis in charge at each point. This was followed by the continuation of the rabbi's speech: "We must save the souls of our brethren, our fellow Jews," Rabbi Elharizi intoned, behind him the wizened old mystic himself, struck dumb years earlier and exploited now by his sons and followers at festive gatherings for the purpose of dispelling doubts on questionable matters. "Canada!" Rabbi Elharizi cried, and the head of the old mystic, who sat sunken into a velvet armchair and propped up by huge pillows, lolled backward. "We shall build the New Yavneh there, we shall save our race before—" Suddenly the speech was cut short, and the film showed Rabbi Elharizi humming a tune from the Neilah prayers of Yom Kippur: El Norah Alilah, which Michael, like any traditional Eastern Jew, recognized from his own childhood. The rabbi sang, "Judge them now, in the hour when the gates of repentance are closing," while a choir of ultra-Orthodox men carrying suitcases and boxes joined in for the chorus: "Oh Lord of deed and action, provide us with forgiveness." And with that the picture was cut off, the voices fell silent, and the screen was blue and empty.

"What . . . What are they planning?" Tzilla whispered. "They're taking all their—"

"They're leaving for Canada," Natasha explained. "A whole city is being built for them there. All the government allocations they've received, all the contributions from wealthy benefactors, it's all been converted into gold bricks. I've got pictures of the boxes, and Schreiber's testimony. He's seen it with his own eyes."

"But what's he talking about?" Tzilla cried. "Why are they leaving Israel?"

"Why?" Balilty chuckled. "Because they're jumping off a sinking ship. I've known about this for a while, we've collected quite a bit of material. This tape you've brought can certainly help us," he told Natasha, "you've done a great job, no question about it."

"Please explain to me," Tzilla interjected, "do me a favor; I don't know whether to laugh or cry."

"There's not much to explain here," Balilty said dispassionately. "Rabbi Elharizi himself dealt with transferring the money. He's not just any old rabbi, he's a rabbi with vision! Wouldn't you say that's true?" he asked, turning to Michael, who was sitting the whole time behind his desk, at his usual place, feeling the weak December sun penetrating the room through the dirty window and waiting, resigned, for his room to empty of people.

"It's very simple," Balilty continued. "Brilliant and simple. All the brilliant ideas are ultimately simple, don't you think?"

No one answered him.

"And it's not Rabbi Elharizi on his own," Balilty proclaimed, "he's got Rabbi Bashari the Cabalistic mystic with him. You saw him in the background, didn't you, sitting in his armchair? We think of him as a puppet, but his followers believe he has supernatural powers. Don't ask! No outsider could ever understand it."

"So, like, he's going to bring whole families to Canada?" Tzilla asked.

"Tens of thousands of them," Natasha said, her eyes flashing. "There's already a whole settlement set up there, they've got . . ."

"Not tens of thousands," Balilty corrected her, "it's more like *hundreds* of thousands." When he saw the look of disbelief on Tzilla's face, he hastened to add, "We're talking about *vision* here! This is *prophecy*! There were doubters in the distant past, too, but believe me, we're talking about a prophecy of destruction and redemption here! Our people have attended rallies, and I've heard all about this from them, but we didn't have any concrete evidence before. We weren't able to get our hands on a videocassette or a finger on all that money. I still haven't figured out where this young lady here got it all," he said, glancing at Natasha, "how she managed to come up with all the material we couldn't—"

"There are about one hundred seventy-five thousand believers at present," Natasha said.

"Anyway," Balilty continued, "whole families are going to emigrate to this Canadian New Yavneh. Rabbi Elharizi himself said that Jerusalem will soon be laid to waste, that's what he saw in his vision. And here," Balilty said, pointing at the empty blue screen, "will be the New Yavneh. Is that all, Natasha?"

"There's just a little bit more," she said humbly. Balilty extended the remote control to her, and she fast-forwarded the tape until the screen showed Rabbi Elharizi, once again in the hooded garb of a Greek Orthodox priest. Natasha's voice intoned, "Rabbi Yohanan Ben Zakkai was smuggled in shrouds and a coffin out of besieged Jerusalem, but Rabbi Elharizi has made do with a different disguise . . ."

"Great work," Balilty mumbled. "That's first-class journalism, honey. Come with me, we'll take this film to where it needs to be. What do you say?"

Natasha looked at Michael. He intended to nod in affirmation, but just then the telephone rang, and Tzilla rushed to answer it. While she chattered happily into the receiver, obviously talking with someone she particularly cared for, Natasha followed Balilty out of the room, closing the door behind her.

"It's Yuval," Tzilla said with a big smile, handing him the phone. "He's in Jerusalem, arrived here half an hour ago. He wants to know if you have a little time for him. Did you even know he's doing a stint in the army reserves? He's barely got half a day off before he has to go back."

Michael took the receiver, wondering from where he could draw the strength to sound normal, but his son, uncharacteristically agitated, did not even ask how he was, only whether Michael could meet him. "Are you all right, Yuval?" he asked, startled; abruptly, he snapped out of the state of floating he had been immersed in.

"Yeah, I'm fine," Yuval reassured him. "I just wanted . . . I've got a couple of hours, I wanted . . . I was hoping that if you had a little time . . ."

Michael recognized the budding disappointment he remembered so well from his son's childhood, which had affected Yuval each time like a slap to the face; time after time he had let the boy down by failing to keep their appointments. So Michael hastened to name a place they could meet.

Pale rays of sunlight filtered through the glass-brick walls of the coffee shop, where large gas heaters warmed the room, illuminating Yuval's whiskers and the dark eyebrows he had inherited from his father.

"Let's have breakfast," Yuval said, and Michael, nodding, signaled to the waitress. She hastened to inform them about the healthy-breakfast special. "It's new," she told them, "not on the menu yet."

"I'd like a three-egg omelet and a big salad," Yuval said. "How about you?"

"The same for me," Michael told the waitress.

"And we don't smoke," Yuval announced to the coffee shop at large, which at the time contained only the two of them, an older man reading a newspaper, and a young woman who continually looked at her watch.

"I didn't know you were doing reserve duty," Michael said. "How come you didn't tell me?"

"Didn't have a chance," Yuval said. "It's just an exercise. It was supposed to be a regular three-day exercise, but—never mind, it's not important . . . I wanted to ask you something," he said hesitantly, glancing away as if uncomfortable.

"I'm listening," Michael said, simultaneously thanking God for installing in children the mechanism that prevents them from discerning that something has befallen their parents.

"It's something we almost talked about once," Yuval said, "when I was doing my regular army service." He fell silent for a moment, then said, "Back then I had—I don't know if you remember, but—I had thoughts about . . . you probably don't remember—"

"I'm going to need some kind of clue, some kind of a lead. Anything," Michael said apologetically. "There were a few things that . . . how can I know if you don't say anything?"

"Tell me," Yuval said, leaning forward, "without making fun of me"—Michael was about to assure him he would never dream of making fun of him, but Yuval did not wait for his reassurance—"and don't tell me this isn't the kind of question a guy who's one year away from finishing his bachelor's degree should be asking, okay?" Again, he did not wait for an answer: "I wanted to ask you—but really now—if you're a Zionist. Are you a Zionist, Dad?"

The arrival of the waitress with a tray upon which stood their mugs of coffee and a basket of fresh rolls, and her setting of the table with plates and forks and knives and spoons and napkins, delayed Michael's response and restrained the astonishment he was about to express. Of all the things in the world he was preparing himself for—problems with a girl or a crisis at university or even waffling thoughts about the future—he had never imagined that this was the matter about which his son would ask to meet with him so urgently.

"Why are you asking?" Michael was trying to gain time; finally the waitress left them alone.

"First answer me," his son said as he pulled a fresh roll from the basket, tore it open, and smeared it with butter.

"True, it's no longer the clear and simple question it was once,"

Michael pondered. "What exactly are you referring to? The need for a Jewish state?"

Yuval nodded. "I guess," he conceded.

"If that's the issue, then yes, I suppose I am a Zionist. Sure, Zionism has brought on tragedy—both sides are its victims—but what can you do? I . . . if Zionism means a home for the Jewish people, then you could say I am a Zionist."

"Why?" Yuval exclaimed. "Like, you really care if you live in a Jewish state?"

"I guess I do," Michael said after several moments. "Jews, too, need their own homeland. Where else would your grandparents have gone after the Holocaust?"

"But why here, in Israel?" Yuval demanded. He lay the buttered roll down next to him, as yet uneaten, and opened three packets of sugar to pour into his coffee, then handed three more to his father, who absentmindedly poured them into his own mug. Yuval watched him, alert with anticipation.

"It's our home, no?" Michael asked at last.

"Why? Because of the Holocaust?" Yuval argued.

"Not just because of the Holocaust," Michael answered, thinking of Yuzek, Yuval's grandfather, a Holocaust survivor who had been preaching against gentiles, and the anti-Semitism he believed to be globally pervasive, ever since Yuval was a small child. "A long time before that, in fact. Since the Bible."

"The Bible!" Yuval screeched, then looked around. "Now *you're* talking like that, too? About that fairy tale? It's just a myth, isn't it?"

"What's so disagreeable about myths?" Michael asked, turning his head away from the sunbeam that was threatening to blur his vision. Suddenly his son's agitated excitement and doubts flooded him with unexpected joy. "It's a serious claim, certainly no less serious than the Muslim claim to the Temple Mount, and just as fair. If not more so."

"Tell me," Yuval said, pushing away the plate holding his roll. "Is Judaism a religion or a nation?! I mean, after all, it's a religion!"

"No, that's not true," Michael said, breathing in deeply. "In Judaism, the religion *is* the nation. Which means that being Israeli is also being Jewish."

"But what do I need the Temple Mount for? I don't want it at all!" Yuval cried.

"There's nothing you can do about it," Michael said. "I don't think we need the Temple Mount for the time being, at least not until the time of redemption; there's no reason to get mixed up with the Holy Temple: at the End of Days when the redemption comes then the Holy One, Blessed be He—as they call him—will take care of that himself. So for the time being the question of the Temple Mount is only theoretical."

"Listen," his son said as he took a sip from his coffee, grimaced, glanced into his mug and then at his father. "That's the reason I don't want to take part in guarding their outposts or dismantling them, either. I think it's completely insane that in this country—*Zion!*—all the guys my age walk around with rifles and have to defend these thickheaded Jews who have settled on Arab land."

"What are you talking about? The entire land of Israel, or only the territories?"

"Well, even during the War of Independence Arabs were driven away and their lands confiscated," Yuval claimed.

"Now it's clear that we settled land that had been previously occupied, but there's nothing we can do about that today. And anyway, do you know of any people in the world that has attained its place without conquering someone else? The Arabs who came here did it too, that's the human condition," Michael said, eyeing the waitress as she approached with a large tray. "The problem is that as Jews we had expectations of ourselves, that we would be more moral, more understanding of others. Turns out we're just like everyone else, and nothing more."

"But it's like dogs, dogs establishing their territory," Yuval muttered, then fell silent watching the clumsy maneuvers of the waitress as Michael lifted the salad and one of the plates, bearing an omelet, from her hands.

"Eat up while it's hot," Michael said, glancing at the omelet in front of him. It smelled great, but for some reason did not awaken any desire in him to touch it.

"Like dogs," Yuval repeated with disgust after the waitress had left them.

"Maybe that's true," Michael conceded, "but that's the way it is: a person is obliged to maintain a territory in order to protect his home and children. There's nothing shameful in that. On the contrary. But I completely agree with you that the manner in which we conduct these territorial matters of ours here in Israel since the Six Day War is ugly, and very bad. Disgraceful, in fact."

"It was ugly from the very beginning," Yuval protested as he cut a piece of omelet and pierced it with his fork, "because there were Arabs here from the start, and the land was theirs."

"But there's nothing we can do about that now," Michael reiterated. "We simply have to acknowledge the fact that we took their land and expelled them; there's no way of giving it back. What would you have us do, put Jews out of their homes? When there's a Palestinian state and peace reigns, we can discuss it—or at least acknowledge it . . ."

"But there's no chance of living here in peace," Yuval claimed with a mouth full of omelet as he piled finely minced salad onto his plate. "Or what do you think about that?"

"There was a chance," Michael said, stabbing a small piece of omelet, "and I think there still will be a chance. But the hatred around here, on the part of the Arabs—some of them, at least—it's so strong, you can't ignore it."

"I don't want to live in such an insane place," Yuval said. "Do you know what the guys from the Nahal Brigade are doing in their regular army service while they guard settlers in the area around southern Mount Hebron?"

"What?" Michael asked, finally shoving a piece of omelet into his mouth, amazed to discover that he could actually taste it. "What? What are they doing?"

"They're knitting! Believe me, you've never seen anything like it: twenty, thirty guys guarding the Hebron area, combat soldiers from the Nahal Brigade! They sit around a stove heater knitting hats, scarves, socks. It's unbelievable! Guys who studied in my high school! I've seen pictures with my own eyes, I swear!"

Michael smiled.

"Don't laugh," Yuval said. "Think about it: it's serious, a rebellion against Israeli machismo, don't you think? It's a rebellion that's very, very . . ."

"Constructive," Michael offered.

"That's just it," Yuval said as he shoved the last bite of his omelet into his mouth and prepared to attack the salad and cheeses. "But I don't want to live in a place like this. It would be better . . . maybe I'll take off, I want to go abroad."

"To where?" Michael asked, holding his breath for a moment. Then he reminded himself that these were, for the time being, nothing but words, and he focused on his roll and cream cheese.

"Maybe Canada?" Yuval pondered aloud.

Michael stifled a horrified chuckle before asking why.

"Because," Yuval answered with a full mouth, "we're living in a crazy place where the price of life is higher than life itself. You get it?"

Michael nodded.

"That means," Yuval continued, "that the price this country collects from its citizens is higher than the value of life itself here. That's what I think, for the time being. Anyway, it's true for the way things look right now," he concluded, dunking a new roll into the olive oil from the minced vegetables, which were referred to as "Arab salad" on the menu.

"Maybe you're right," Michael said. "And I'd like to tell you something, too, but promise me you'll—"

"Is everything okay?" the waitress asked with exuberant diligence.

"Everything's just fine," Michael assured her.

BATYA GUR's stunning novels probe the depths of human emotion in one of the richest, most fascinating parts of the world. Giving the reader a glimpse into the troubles and triumphs of Israel's land and people, they tell of the contradictions and conflicts that pull it apart on a daily basis, yet at the same time "reveal the incredible love of life in this little country that dances on a volcano" (*Elle* magazine [French edition]).

---

Turn the page for a glimpse into other wonderfully complex and absorbing books in Batya Gur's Michael Ohayon mystery series, including:

*The Saturday Morning Murder*

*Literary Murder*

*Murder on a Kibbutz*

*Murder Duet*

AND

*Murder in Jerusalem*

# *The Saturday Morning Murder*

In *The Saturday Morning Murder*, the first in Batya Gur's beautifully written series, the reader meets Chief Superintendent Michael Ohayon, as he investigates the shocking murder of a Jerusalem psychiatrist. Dr. Eva Neidorf was set to deliver a lecture on the ethical problems in psychoanalysis—making her murder quite opportune for some of her colleagues, and the investigation quite complex for Ohayon. The list of suspects is long, and Ohayon follows a trail through the psychoanalytic community—patients as well as analysts—as well as the bustling Jerusalem commercial district and the Israeli military. In this "flawless" (*Publishers Weekly*) debut, readers are treated to a complex plot, an intelligent and compassionate detective, and a beautifully realized description of Jerusalem.

Michael Ohayon looked at his watch and saw that it was eleven o'clock. A strong wind was blowing, blotting out the sound of the rain. He rose from his seat, and the old man stood up, too, and asked him if he was going to go to Neidorf's house now. Michael took the hint and asked if he would like to accompany him, adding something about the lateness of the hour and the bad weather. Hildesheimer brushed his reservations aside with a sweep of his hand and said that he had already lived quite long enough, in his opinion, and that in any case he would not be able to sleep tonight. As he spoke, he led Michael to the coatrack in the corner of the long hallway, took down a heavy winter overcoat, and put in on. The house was dark and silent, and the two of them let themselves out. Outside it was very cold. Michael, who had kept his jacket on all the time he was sitting in the study, felt the wind like an icy blow and was glad to get into the police Renault.

He activated the radio, which responded immediately. Control tried to tell him something in a tired female voice; he listened patiently. Everyone was looking for him, everyone said it was urgent. "Okay; tell them I'll be in touch later. And tell my team that I'm in the middle of something." Control sighed and said, "Will do."

Hildesheimer sat next to him, sunk in thought, and Michael was obiged to repeat his question twice before the old man nodded and gave him Dr. Neidorf's address, the same address that Michael had seen on the identification card in her bag in the course of his repeated rummagings through its contents that morning.

It was a little street in the German Colony. Almost every time Michael passed Emek Refaim Street, he thought of the Knights of the German Templars who founded this neighborhood in 1878. How pathetic were their hopes for redemption, symbolized by the remnants of their flour mill, still visible on the corner. Michael maneuvered the Renault through the narrow alleys and parked carefully. He opened the door for Hildesheimer and helped him out of the small car. The two of them went through the little gate and walked up the path leading to the front door, where the old man stepped back to let Michael open the heavy wooden door.

Michael tried all the keys, at first in the light of the streetlamp and then in the light of all the matches left in the box, which Hildesheimer lit one after the other with an admirably steady hand. Finally they both resigned themselves to the fact that the key to the house was not on the ring. Neither said a word about where it might be.

Michael went to his car and came back a few seconds later, a sharp object in his hand. He mumbled something to Hildesheimer about the skills one acquired during the course of one's life, then he set to work on the lock. Hildesheimer went on lighting matches—Michael had brought a new box from the car—and ten minutes later they were standing in Eva Neidorf's house.

Michael shut the door.

In the bright light illuminating the entrance hall, he saw the old man's pale face. His grimly pursed lips expressed what they had both already realized: someone had preceded them.

# *Literary Murder*

The next book in this engrossing series once again finds Chief Superintendent Michael Ohayon investigating a crime among insular intellectuals. In *Literary Murder*, two rival literature professors from Hebrew University in Jerusalem are murdered on the same weekend. The upstart Iddo Dudai is poisoned while vacationing in the beautiful beach town of Eilat, and the prominent poet Shaul Tirosh, whom Dudai had recently challenged in public, is found bludgeoned in his office. Since each of the victims would have been the most obvious suspect in the other's murder, Ohayon must divine whether these two rivals' murders are a coincidence, or the result of a conspiracy. And when he uncovers a love triangle and a profound betrayal, the chief superintendent learns that the dark secrets of a respected literature department run deep.

When he woke up that morning, he had told himself that the first day was safely over, that Uzi was taking care of Yuval personally, that he had the finest apparatus available, that there was only one more dive to go, and that tomorrow it would all be behind them and he would be able to drive home with an easy mind.

But then he saw the title "Do You Have a Regulator?" and he began to read the article below it. "There are no rules governing the examination of the tank valve and the regulator; the sole responsibility belongs to the diver," it said. He went on reading to the end of the article and decided to show it to Yuval as soon as he came out of the water. ("During the dive, immediately after the diver had executed the underwater somersaults, a fault in the air supply was discovered, necessitating an emergency haul to the surface, while I gave him buddy-breathing," reported the diving-instructor author of the article, and Michael found himself reading with intense concentration. "Observation of the underwater pressure gauge showed a drop in atmospheric pressure from 100 lbs to close to zero, during inhalation from the regulator.")

Michael Ohayon looked at his watch: the practice session was due to end in fifteen minutes. He stood up and approached the sea. The Diving Club was crowded. No father had ever abandoned his son to his fate like this, he thought in a panic, and then he saw the figure in the black rubber suit being carried from the boat by two people and laid on the beach.

The first thought, of Yuval, was immediately dismissed, because the youngster removing the diving mask from the supine figure was not Guy, the diving instructor who had gone out with Yuval, but Motti, to whom he had been introduced the previous evening. With him was a woman in a diving suit, one of the students in the course, Michael thought. From where he was standing he was unable to see the expressions on their faces, but something in their movements, as they bent over the figure in the diving suit lying on the sand, proclaimed catastrophe.

The premonition of disaster immediately turned into a certainty when he saw Motti rapidly pulling out his knife and ripping open the recumbent figure's diving suit. The woman ran in the direction of the office, a small stone building on the beach not far from where Michael had been lying.

Motti began mouth-to-mouth resuscitation, and Michael couldn't take his eyes off the spectacle. Without knowing how he got there, he found himself standing next to them, waiting for the chest to rise and fall. But nothing happened. Together with Motti, Michael counted the breaths to himself.

It was a young man. His face was pink and swollen.

Superintendent Ohayon, who had seen a lot of corpses during the course of his career, still hoped that one day he would achieve the callousness of the police investigators and private detectives on television. Every time, he was astonished anew, always after the event, by his feeling faint, by the nausea, the anxiety, and sometimes the pity too, that he felt in the presence of a corpse, precisely when scientific detachment and attention to detail were called for. Nothing at all would be demanded of him here, he consoled himself when he realized that all the attempts at resuscitation would be unavailing.

The woman came running back with a young man who held a doctor's bag. Michael drew closer, silencing the inner voices reminding him that he was on holiday and that it was none of his business.

## *Murder on a Kibbutz*

The third book in the Michael Ohayon mystery series, *Murder on a Kibbutz*, is another "meaty story, dense with character and plot" (*Chicago Tribune*). Chief Superintendent Ohayon is seasoned at penetrating complex and insular societies, but when a secretary is murdered on a kibbutz, he encounters barriers that even he has never seen before. The young victim, Osnat Harel, was carrying on an affair with an outsider, and the jealousies, prejudices, and inflexible attitudes of the agrarian kibbutzniks, along with their general distrust of outsiders and their fear of losing their toehold on tradition, make this the determined superintendent's most difficult case yet.

THE KIBBUTZ ITSELF WAS NOW FIFTY YEARS OLD. A half century had passed since the oldest members had settled on this land. It was not the oldest kibbutz in Israel, but it was certainly well established. The atmosphere today was festive, but at the same time it was clear that nobody was taking the celebration too seriously. Only the children looked excited, but they were drawn to the lineup of agricultural machinery, and none of them paid any attention to the platform and the little choir standing on it. And apart from the members of the choir, hardly anyone was wearing blue and white. Not even the kindergarten children, Aaron noticed with a trace of disappointment that then amused him, and there was no sign anywhere of the national flag. He would have to ask Moish about that too. And at the same moment he thought of the nostalgia that would overcome him on national holidays, and of the excitement with which he would look forward to Shevuoth, the Festival of Weeks, in particular, the feeling of participation in great and important events that had really and truly pervaded him then.

He could not entirely suppress the feeling that once you took away the blue and white and the flags on the Caterpillar, the whole ceremony seemed archaic and foreign, as if it were taking place on a collective farm in Soviet Russia. And yet, he thought, chewing a straw reflectively, he felt that time had stood still, as if he were watching documentary footage from a movie about early Zionist history. But now it was the farce of an agricultural ceremony in a place where agriculture was almost bankrupt—a kibbutz, a Zionist agricultural commune, that derived its income from an industrial plant that, of all things, manufactured cosmetics, having given its name to an international patent for a face cream that abolished wrinkles and rejuvenated skin cells and was advertised in all the newspapers with two photographs of the same woman captioned "Before" and "After." No one else seemed to be showing any recognition of the absurdity of celebrating an agricultural rite where only the manufacture and sale of face cream made it possible to go on working the land. It could, he thought, be why Srulke hadn't appeared. When Aaron had looked for him in vain in the dining hall in order to greet him, Moish had assured him that he would show up for the ceremony, "if only," he said, grinning, "to inspect what they've done with his flowers."

As he looked around, ostensibly keeping an eye out for Srulke but actually trying to catch a glimpse of Osnat, Aaron concluded that at least one sector of the kibbutz economy was blooming: There were so many children that a stranger might be excused for wondering how anybody had time for anything else. The products of this intensive reproductive activity scampered about, and the apparent contentedness and good humor of the large families gave him a pang of vague longings. But his other voice nipped them in the bud. The little devil inside him immediately scoffed at his wish to belong, and the skeptical inner voices that had grown louder over the years now asserted themselves and conjured up the image of a herd of placid Dutch cows, spoiling his sense of festivity beyond recovery. He tried to suppress the feeling that there was something stupefying about the tranquility here, recalling the rage that would seize hold of him in the past and that had attacked him today too, on his way to the dining hall with Moish for lunch.

It was only a short distance from Moish's room to the dining hall, but it had taken a long time to get there, what with having to greet everyone they met and with Moish's delaying them by remembering one little chore after another, stopping at the children's houses to see if a dripping faucet had been repaired and the sandbox in the kindergarten refilled with fresh sand, and then at the secretariat to find out whether someone who was supposed to phone had phoned, and only after he had studied the notices on the bulletin board, extracted the newspaper from his pigeonhole and read all the notes he also found there, and answered the phone ringing in the big lobby on the ground floor—only then did the two of them climb the stairs to the building's second floor, to the dining hall itself.

At the door, Moish lingered to take in the scene, and an eternity seemed to pass before he picked up a tray. As they stood before the trolley holding the trays, Aaron suddenly felt fatigued and impatient with the waste of time, the idleness. He summed it up for himself: The minute you walk into the door of the dining hall, your oxygen supply drops, your productivity declines; that phlegmatic calm, that slowness, they're enough to drive a person crazy. He retreated behind the protection of the guessing game: who was who, who belonged to whom. He succeeded in identifying members of three and even four generations standing together in groups, the youngest children on their fathers' shoulders. Which of the adults had been born on the kibbutz and which had married into it he couldn't guess, but he could tell at a glance which of them were guests like himself.

## *Murder Duet*

Jerusalem is rich with cultural history, and Chief Superintendent Michael Ohayon, an avid classical music lover, revels in the world-class performances of the ancient city. In *Murder Duet*, the solitary Ohayon crosses paths with his neighbor Nita, an accomplished cellist, when he stumbles upon an abandoned baby and takes her into his care. Nita is from a family of musicians, and her own experience as a single mother is invaluable as Ohayon scrambles to find the baby's parents, and keep her safe from harm. But when Nita's father is murdered, and her musician brother is also murdered soon thereafter, Ohayon must share his attention with the bereaved Nita. Delving deep into the competitive and complex world of the classical music community, while struggling to keep his own life together, and the baby out of harms way, Ohayon must penetrate a reticent and layered community of musicians in this "virtuoso performance" (*Booklist*).

THE TRAFFIC JAM HAD BARRED HIS WAY through King David Street and obliged him to turn on his siren at the Mamilla traffic lights. As he had pushed on toward the concert hall, he had stared, as he always did now, with astonishment at the frameworks of the luxury buildings that were replacing the razed old neighborhood, and then pushed on toward the concert hall. His astonishment—sometimes accompanied by revulsion—at the changes in the view emerging beyond the traffic lights returned whenever he stopped at this intersection. After glancing, with a sense of relief at their survival, at the Muslim cemetery on his left and the "Palace"—the imposing round edifice that housed the Ministry of Commerce and Industry—on his right, he looked straight ahead. For months he had been contemplating the systematic destruction of old buildings. They had left a building once visited by Theodor Herzl untouched, like a single tooth in an old person's mouth, while, like a set of gleaming white false teeth, the new buildings now stood behind a big sign announcing "David's Village."

They had called him on the police radio when he was already on his way to the Russian Compound, after depositing the babies with the afternoon babysitter. At that moment he was at the Mamilla intersection, staring at stickers proclaiming THE PEOPLE ARE WITH THE GOLAN and JUDEA AND SAMARIA ARE HERE on the back window of the car in front of him. The driver was hastily shutting his window in the face of the barrage of curses let loose by a woman in rags, the beggar woman known as the Madwoman of Mamilla, who plied her trade among the cars stuck at the traffic lights, thrusting a filthy hand at the drivers, grinning or growling with her toothless mouth. The address given him by the dispatcher on Shorer's orders filled him with terrible panic. "He tried you first at home," she said, and her voice—a familiar froggy croak—sent a shiver down his spine, as if she had scratched with a stone on a pane of glass.

"I was on the way," he said into the two-way radio, mainly for the sake of saying something, and he turned into the right lane. The chill that had flooded in him, that had filled the pit of his stomach at the sound of the address, had not been dispelled even by the words "the body of a man" the dispatcher had added, as if urgency justified her lack of caution about reporters listening in to the police frequency. The chill increased the closer he got—speeding past the long row of cars drawn up at the seemingly unchanging traffic lights—to the concert hall.

He was chilled, his knees felt weak, and his teeth chattered. How could Shorer find him if he spent his days waiting for babysitters? he castigated himself. He speeded up. The afternoon babysitter, the one they had taken on specially for Nita's rehearsals, had been half an hour late. "Because of the traffic," she had said angrily. The bus route had been changed for the visit of the American secretary of state. "And the day before yesterday it was because of some rabbi's funeral," she panted. "Three hundred thousand Hasidim for a rabbi nobody's ever heard of! It's impossible to live in this city anymore—it's either terrorist attacks or Hasidic funerals or state visits with limousines and motorcycles. Even if they're only going from the King David Hotel to the prime minister's house on Balfour Street, they shut the whole damned city down because of them. What do they care? They're not in a hurry to get anywhere."

Between waves of the shivers he heard himself asking the dispatcher about whether Forensics had already been informed and sent to the scene. He heard his calm, matter-of-fact voice, the familiar voice routinely and automatically on tap for such occasions. Nevertheless it sounded strange to him now as he asked whether the pathologist had already been sent to the scene. When he had parked at the rear entrance of the concert hall, he turned to the radio again and asked that Tzilla be sent to the scene.

The young Magen David Adom doctor stood next to the skinny pathologist, whose checked shirt emphasized his concave chest and his thin, hairy, white arms. Polishing the lenses of his round spectacles punctiliously, he questioned the doctor briefly in his singsong voice, the silences punctuated by constant humming. He sounded as though he were practicing an endless recitative. She responded to his questions curtly and with evident irritation. When she received the call, it was already "too late," the doctor said, and now Michael heard the echo of a faint Russian accent in the phrase. "The body was in the same position as it is now, sprawled out like a rag, with all the blood, and the legs folded," at the foot of the concrete pillar. She hadn't let anyone touch it, she asserted, no one but she had approached it. She described once more, this time without the note of complaint and condemnation, Nita's hysterical fit, and that she had sent Nita to lie down in "Mr. van Gelden's office."

## *Murder in Jerusalem*

The crowning achievement to a magnificent career, *Murder in Jerusalem* is the final installment in the beloved Michael Ohayon mystery series.

Acclaimed Israeli director Benny Meyuhas's film production of the heartbreaking work "Iddo and Eynam" promises to be a landmark of Israeli film—until his wife and the films' set designer Tirzah Rubin are crushed under a set piece, stalling the production indefinitely. Shimshon Zadik, the head of Israel Television, is among the first at the scene, and the death of this talented and mysterious woman, a colleague of his for many years, sends shockwaves through the film and television community. But more shocking is what comes to light in the investigation—that Tirzah's storybook life wasn't at all what it seemed, and that her death may have been part of a larger network of social and political unrest. The brooding chief superintendent Michael Ohayon has spent his career surrounded by horrific crimes, but nothing has ever disturbed him more than what Tirzah's murder reveals: that the very ideals upon which he was raised, upon which the nation was raised, may have led to unspeakable crimes.

THE KEROSENE HEATER WAS OF NO USE; the room was terribly cold. It was a Jerusalem cold—dense, powerful—of old stone rooms. Schreiber stood rubbing his hands over the soot-covered grid of the heater. "She didn't want to call you people," he said casting a look of reproach at Natasha. "It took me a while to convince her, but in the end I told her she could do whatever she wanted, but there was no way I was getting mixed up with them."

"Who's 'them?' " Michael asked.

"These religious fanatics," Schreiber said. He moved to the half-open door and lit a cigarette there. "It's pretty clear they did this, don't you think? Believe me, I know those people."

The room was very small, most of the space taken up by a single bed in disarray. A few sweaters lay in a pile upon it and at the other side of the room, in a niche in the thick wall, was a clothes hook with several shirts and one skirt hanging from it. There was a pile of books on the floor next to the bed, and perched on a woven-straw stool stood a book in Russian, open-face down. A makeshift kitchen stood facing the doorway; there were water spots and mold on the wall near the electric burner, a single pot and pan hanging there, and a dish rack with three plates, two mugs, a few spoons, two forks, and a knife. Behind a half-open door there was a bathroom: a toilet, a sink, and a faucet with a shower hose.

Michael looked around the room; everything was utilitarian and meager except for a blue vase with a clutch of wilting wild daffodils that stood on the only table in the room, and a long, narrow print in a thin wooden frame hanging over the bed. The print showed a solitary and peculiar tower standing erect in an empty brown field; one side of the tower was brightly lit and the other shaded, the shadow extending from two people, small and displaced, posed in the middle of the foreground. He wondered how it was that in spite of the bright white light on the illuminated side of the tower, the picture exuded the feeling that the light did not have the power to illuminate this world, as though the shadows had overwhelmed it and the blackness in the background was about to flood the entire picture. Four flags blew loftily in the wind from the top of the tower, but even these brought no happiness. The mood of the entire picture was one of regret, of interminable loneliness. Who had painted this picture, he wondered, and why did it disturb him so? Underneath it, in a corner of the bed, folded in between the wall and the simple wooden table on which stood the vase of daffodils and a few plates with the remains of dried-up hummus and pita bread, was Natasha, huddled under a gray army blanket and shaking nonetheless. Michael looked into her clear blue eyes and saw no fear there.

"It's like she doesn't care," Schreiber said, "but at first, from the shock of it, she screamed. After that, nothing. She wanted to clean it up. It took me a long time to convince her to call the police. I didn't let her touch all the blood and filth, I wanted you to see it as it was . . . Anyway, I took pictures of it all," he said, adding in a faint voice. "It was *her* idea."

"What was Natasha's idea?" Michael asked. From outside the apartment they could hear the forensics people arriving, and Balilty's voice a moment later. "Taking pictures?"

"No, taking pictures was my idea," Schreiber said. "Calling you was her idea," he explained, lowering his eyes. "She said that you . . ."

"Schreiber, shut up already," Natasha said. Her voice burst forth from between her narrow hands, which were wrapped around her small face.

"What? What did I say wrong? Didn't you tell me to call him? You said he was the only one worth his salt."

"There's no reason to hurt people's feelings," Natasha mumbled, looking out the half-open door. "There are other people here. Everybody needs a good word."

# *MASTERWORKS OF CRIME FICTION* BY BATYA GUR

## *MURDER IN JERUSALEM*

ISBN 978-0-06-085294-8 (paperback)

The crowning achievement to a magnificent career, this final installment in the Michael Ohayon series is a wonderful parting gift from the incomparable Batya Gur. A stunning tale of a talented and secretive woman's murder, set against the politically charged backdrop of the Israeli media.

## *BETHLEHEM ROAD MURDER*

ISBN 978-0-06-095492-5 (paperback)

The body of a young woman is discovered in the attic of a Bethlehem Road house, in a neighborhood of Jerusalem known for its impenetrability to outsiders. Chief Superintendent Ohayon is called to the scene of the crime, where, beyond the usual horror, an old love and an unfinished romance await him.

"Gur takes infinite care with the exacting studies of the characters who give her stories their extraordinary vitality."
—*New York Times Book Review*

"Gur's outstanding police procedural . . . can hold its own with the best work of P. D. James."
—*Publishers Weekly*

## *LITERARY MURDER*

A Critical Case

ISBN 978-0-06-092548-2 (paperback)

A shocking double murder at Israel's top academic institution brings Superintendent Michael Ohayon to the scene to probe the nature of creativity and unravel the mystery.

## MURDER DUET

A Musical Case

ISBN 978-0-06-093298-5 (paperback)

Features once again the smart, charming, and lonely police officer Michael Ohayon. After his cellist friend's father and brother—who are also well-known musicians—are brutally murdered, Ohayon, a classical music afficionado, sets out to solve the crime. From the opening pages, where the detective plays a compact disc of Brahm's First Symphony, to the newly discovered music for an unknown Vivaldi requiem that provides a rock-solid motive for the crime, lovers of crime novels, as well as music, will thrill to every dulcet note.

## THE SATURDAY MORNING MURDER

A Psychoanalytic Case

ISBN 978-0-06-099508-9 (paperback)

Chief Inspector Michael Ohayon journeys to the Jerusalem Psychoanalytic Institute on a quiet Sabbath morning when Dr. Eva Neidorf, a highly respected senior analyst, is found dead from a gunshot.

"Masterful." —*Publishers Weekly*

## MURDER ON A KIBBUTZ

A Communal Case

ISBN 978-0-06-092654-0 (paperback)

The fourth mystery starring detective Michael Ohayon takes the brooding policeman into an Israeli kibbutz to investigate the murder of the beautiful, headstrong kibbutz secretary.

"Subtly provocative."—*New York Times Book Review*